Redline's Downfall Book 1

INDUCTION

Syntax Takes

Induction

Book 1 of Redline's Downfall

Production copyright FurPlanet Productions © 2024

Published by FurPlanet Productions
Dallas, Texas
www.FurPlanet.com

Print ISBN 978-1-61450-634-8
Electronic ISBN 978-1-61450-635-5

Table of Contents

Foreword

By Karen King 13

Chapter 1

Milestones 17

Chapter 2

Wall Breach 35

Chapter 3

Safety Valve 49

Chapter 4

Dance Practice 67

Chapter 5

Electrochemistry 101

Chapter 6

Resistance 137

Chapter 7

Breakdown 157

Chapter 8

The Old Normal 189

Chapter 9

Separation Anxiety 211

Chapter 10

Downpour 233

Chapter 11

    Overcharge   249

Acknowledgements

Korps Universe Glossary

    Common terms in the Korps Universe   287

About the Author

    Syntax Takes   296

This book contains depictions of: Transfeminine Gender Dysphoria, Misgendering, Deadnaming, Parental Abuse, Religious Trauma, Gaslighting, Queerphobia, Homophobic & Transphobic Slurs, Violence, Electrocution, Blood, Firearm Injuries, Threat of Conversion Therapy, Trauma Flashbacks, and Police Violence.

For the young trans and nonbinary people struggling to live as they want to be.

For the ones forced to go it alone.

For my love.

Foreword

By Karen King

Nearly seven thousand years ago, an event shook the world. An arrival of something ancient: the merging of humanity with the world of the beast, the eruption of superpowers, and the proliferation of the supernatural. In the modern day, this world appears much like our own but for the pantheon of species that occupy it and the extensive presence of superheroes and supervillains alike. While many states have their own super-powered forces, a vast variety of independent actors exist.

Among the most prominent independent supervillain groups is an organization known as the Korps. As far as most are aware, the Korps is an organization dedicated to world domination, led (in theory) by the shadowy Overlord. This sinister being has tried to wrap their vicious claws around the planet, time after time, since the beginning of recorded history.

The truth, of course, is significantly more complex.

Led by some of the world's strongest superpowered beings, the Korps sees itself not as a state-in-waiting, but a governance method — seeking to depose repressive state-based hierarchies to install systems more capable of effectively distributing resources to those in need. It sees state actors — "Heroes," police, paramilitaries — mete punishment out on innocents, yet go unpunished in turn. It knows, —for all the cartoonish pretensions of the supering world — that this is the true evil. It knows, too, that this cannot go unchallenged.

Operating a number of covert front companies and satellite operations for many decades, the Korps has dedicated a great deal of resources to outpacing the world's greatest scientific, engineering and medical minds. Korps medical technology in particular is extremely advanced, allowing its members to essentially build their preferred body from scratch — and permitting this capacity at scale. The Korps has learned well that monocultures become stagnant without personal expression, which it fiercely encourages in its members — a reality at odds with the widespread public perception that they are nothing more than brainwashed drones.

One of the most useful and distinctive tools at the Korps's disposal are Rose-Coloured Glasses, or "RCGs," a high-capacity communications tool, heads-up display and computer-brain interface so powerful they can be used directly as a VR headset. RCGs can function as an assistive device or therapy tool… but the nature of the technology means they have the power to directly access and even alter one's thoughts. Alternately viewed with relief, mistrust, or fear by the supering world, it is known that wherever they are worn, the Korps is not far behind.

Having emerged in the wake of the Second World War, the Korps has gradually spread its influence, eventually emerging fully into the public consciousness in the 1990s. With increased visibility and emphasis on immediate action, however, comes ever more entanglements…

The Korps began as a big pile of superhero and supervillain tropes that I'd built up a love of through various types of media, like the James Bond movies. While I originally just threw it together as an action playset of stock characters, over time, it began to morph into something very different. Using stock pop culture antagonists to take swings at the injustices unfolding around me began to carry more and more emotional weight.

In an era when information became more and more readily available, we were able, at any time of day, to pull out our phones and view some kind of great injustice unfolding, live in front of the world — to see police forces with the budgets and capacities of small militaries crushing peaceful protestors, to watch the deceptions of nations exposed constantly but slip by unpunished, to see the suffering of those in need, on our feeds, 24/7…

It became increasingly clear to me, and to many, that the status quo is not a state of normalcy, but something imposed by force. Equally, to many, the concept of rallying the villains — those who challenged the status quo — and giving us a context in which we can, in some sense, strike back against it all… It struck a chord among those of my generation. In a world where fighting back seems so hard, an entity like the Korps is something compelling.

I am now sitting here writing the foreword for an actual, published work about it, and my mind is reeling. Giving the Korps as a set of narrative tools to the wider community feels like it has uncorked a flood: a need to right wrongs, a need to highlight injustices, a need to tell intimately personal stories, stories of love, and stories of redemption... rushing out onto countless pages, from countless perspectives.

All I have ever wanted to do is to help give people a community, and the tools they need to create, and to build the stories they need. It is an honour and a privilege to introduce this story to you — one of love, one of breaking free, one of deep wounds beginning to heal...

– Karen King

Chapter 1

Milestones

Volta caught herself bouncing her foot again. She had always been bad at waiting; her mind wandered, and her body got restless fast. The red wolf tugged at the front of her test suit, agitated at the material clinging to her neck. The suit clashed with the browns, reds and off-whites of her fur, but it ensured she would be highly visible. The suit was all royal blue, emblazoned with the Texas Protectorate Assembly's logo imposed in yellow over the left pec: Texas' Lone Star, flanked by wings in red, white and blue. She hated how it rubbed against her fur and skin — a little too tight to ignore, but loose enough to slide along her arms, legs, and her chest. Her chest felt the least comfortable, with the cool metal surface of the Dampener in place on a harness right in the middle and the suit brushing against it.

The straps of the harness were kept tight to her chest, a constant reminder of how flat she was. The Dampener made it even worse: a round, shallow-domed device with an entirely metal exterior pressed flush to her body, covering much of her upper chest. It was *always* cold, and it *always* felt like it pulled at the once-shaved skin underneath it. Powered by her body's ambient charge, it wicked away any excess current she pulled in, and could only be shut off remotely.

A leech, just for her. The higher-ups had decided on a mobile solution to keeping her abilities in check, and here it was: her own specialized power-suppressant. She'd resigned herself to just deal with it, like she had everything else. No hero group anywhere near this state had time for a super with dysphoria who complained, and neither did the family. If Bradley Group was going to take notice today, she had to just keep pretending.

But pretending was getting hard in a room like this.

With nothing better to do in the bland blue and white waiting room, the Lone Star Flag painted on the wall behind the receptionist, she sank into her memories.

With perfect clarity she remembered the night she snuck out and got the manor's backup generator running. She could easily siphon power out of it, as natural as drinking water. Her eyes and the inside of her mouth were glowing in a little over a minute — which she, a 14 year old kid obsessed with superheroes, thought was pretty cool. And it *was* cool, until she exploded the manor's east wing. Mom was in tears, Dad was irate, and she was given a backhand and an early plane ticket back to boarding school.

Lightning powers would be cool, even if she wasn't allowed to *use* them. The TPA researchers said she could probably catch a bolt of lightning and just get winded. Hell, she could just as easily *cause* one. The TPA had seen what she could do early on — and they recognized it immediately as an asset against enemies of the state, provided she could control it.

That was why she was here now — another stupid evaluation of her powers, where for a few minutes the Dampener would be switched off. That hadn't happened in more than a month. She even had to sleep with the thing on, and every time she tried to roll over, she felt it pressing into her. Flat. Always *flat*.

Mom made it worse during her last visit, only a day ago. "They made you into a real Adonis! My boy's looking more and more like a proper hero. Oh, I bet you're getting a lot of attention from the ladies on campus. Your father will be so pleased about the progress you've made..." And on and on — interrogating her about her non-existent love life, exercise routine, the whole nine yards. She just had to stand there and smile, show off the abs, biceps, pretend she liked it, pretend to be happy that her mom had the son she wanted, that she loved being...

Not.

Volta had managed to hold it together for her mother's entire visit, but she'd only gotten a few hours of sleep the following night, and that was only going to make this test even harder.

She was finally taken out of her navel-gazing by the sound of the receptionist's footsteps coming nearer to her. "Austin Travers? We're ready for you now — are you all set?"

Volta stood, taking a breath and trying to remember what boys were supposed to sound like. "Yes, ma'am."

"Follow me, please."

The receptionist led her down a tall hallway past the reception desk and pointed to a door labeled 3E. Of course, Volta had been here before; this was the usual field testing chamber for her — the one with a lot more electrical shielding, especially for the observation room with the window peeking in.

As she entered, she took a quick note of today's setup. Three automated turrets made to look like mannequins holding pistols, with canine ears and helix-markings on their chests; they stood at the far end of the chamber, that was normal. The tall battery stack with two metal contacts large enough for Volta to place her palms on was also expected — she'd need the extra juice to do anything impressive.

What was out of the ordinary were the four little quadcopter drones hovering in the air, each mounted with a gun.

"Please state your name, age and training ID, trainee," a bored old voice came over the PA. Volta turned to the observation window and glanced over her audience.

A few nameless assistants and an extra technician stood off to one side, but several recognizable faces were aimed right at her. They were all seated comfortably in a little room with a control panel at the front of it. Standing in front of the panel was a wizened goat: Dr. Brennis Mason, lead superpower researcher at the facility. His assistant, Tammy (a younger, waspish-looking fox) glared imperiously from her seat beside him, her face heavy with makeup. She was tapping her fingers impatiently against her tablet, waiting for a response from Volta. Next, her parents, of course. The pair of red wolves looked like they were planning on visiting the opera later, dressed to the nines: Mom in a gold necklace and earrings designed more for flair than actual style, and Dad in his favorite gaudy suit and cufflinks, which he was adjusting fastidiously even now. Mom looked excited, Dad looked expectant, neither of them waved. Next was…

Volta swallowed. The slightly grey-haired visage of the middle-aged bighorn may not have put anyone else on edge, but no one else was trying to get recruited by the federal government's Hero division. Bradley Group representative, former US colonel and senator Terrence Whitaker sat back with his arms folded, gazing imperiously at the lone occupant of the test chamber. Volta could tell he was sizing her up — that was what he was here for, a talent scout sent to peruse the young, bright-eyed heroes and heroes-in-training across the US. He was here for *her*, to see if she was worth his time. Bradley Group's time. This was her chance.

"A-Austin Travers." *Fuck, stammering already. Slow down, slow down.* "Nineteen, training ID: 110502. What are we here for today, Dr. Mason?"

Dr. Mason glanced over at Tammy while she tapped at her tablet. She glanced back, nodded, and he continued. "We're adding a new spin on a standard routine today, Travers, to show some of your combined skills at work. The drones above you are armed with low-caliber, low-velocity rubber bullets, same as the dummy turrets. All of them will begin tracking and firing at you at the end of the countdown. You are to evade enemy fire with the cover provided…"

Tammy, taking a cue, tapped something else, and a series of tall and short blocks, large enough to stand or crouch behind, rose up out of the floor between Volta and the mannequins. "…And neutralize all targets, drones and dummies both. You will be finished either when incapacitated or when all targets are disabled. Are you ready?"

Volta's eyes scanned warily over the terrain, her long ears twitching involuntarily. The blockers were far enough apart that it would mean making a mad dash between them for cover as the drones repositioned and the dummies took aim. She had done this before with the drones in their own test, and the dummies had started out tracking and firing much more slowly. If this was anything like the last test, she would have to be much quicker on her feet. Not impossible, and with the added charge, even easier. So long as she didn't slow down, didn't hesitate. Just had to focus.

"Yeah, I'm ready."

Now Tammy's bored voice replaced Dr. Mason's over the loudspeaker. "Disengaging the Dampener; charge yourself up. Starting in ten, nine…"

The tugging sensation on Volta's chest vanished, though the Dampener remained strapped to her. Trying not to glance at the observation window again, she approached the battery stack and pressed her hands to the contacts.

"…Eight, seven, six…"

The prickling rush was not new to her, but it was still the most exhilarating thing. For a moment, Volta forgot about her worries, her discomfort, everything nagging at her. Every other thought froze in place. It was as easy as breathing, sucking in the charge just like air. She caught herself smiling a little as she pulled her hands away.

"…Five, four, three…"

Tammy's bored countdown was drowned out for a moment. There was a low hum in the air around her, and the whole room seemed a little brighter, a little clearer. She held up a hand experimentally, watching as arcs of pale blue electricity danced across her right arm, between her fingers. It felt right, *natural*. A kind of power no one else around her knew. She could practically feel the gaze of her audience on her as she stepped forward, determined.

Focus. I can do this. I've got everything I need, right at my fingertips.

"…One, zero." A buzzer sounded, and all four drones, floating only just above the obstacles, turned in sync, training their weapons on Volta.

No problem. She sent pulses throughout her body in time with her heartbeat, tensed, and darted for the nearest barrier. The trained muscles in her legs, bolstered by the current, carried her quickly to the first patch of cover, and just in time; the thudding of rubber bullets followed her close behind — as soon as she flattened herself behind the barrier, several of them slammed into the top. The drones each let out little chirps, letting Volta know they had lost line of sight, and were already spreading out to find her.

She routed current through her arms. She could feel the arcs coming off of her fur — just a prickly sensation, accompanied by an erratic buzzing. She was ready to fire but needed to be closer. Trying to reach too far with a bolt of electricity could mean exhausting her supply too early. Of course, she could get more charge by sucking the drones' batteries dry — but that would mean getting even closer first.

She crouched and moved to the far end of the wall, hazarding a peek — and nearly getting a face full of rubber bullets in response. That one was close enough. She took a breath, feeling her arms heat up as she pumped them full of voltage.

She leaned out of cover again and took careful aim around the corner, raising one hand at the drone currently beeping angrily, notifying the others that it had found the target.

Got you.

She bared her teeth, nostrils flaring, the glow of her eyes casting the drone in a faint blue. With a **CRACK**, a bright blue bolt shot from her clawed hand and struck the drone two meters away. The drone's lights and rotors went dead in an instant and it fell to the floor, its destroyed circuitry smoking and popping. One down, six to go.

Another drone rounded a corner further away, opening fire. Volta dived behind a lower barrier, crouching as the line of bullets tried to catch up, once again showering her in bouncing ammunition. Hopefully that didn't count against her — though *real* bullets probably wouldn't bounce around like that. There was no time to try and siphon anything out of the drone, she just had to keep moving. She could hear another one getting closer, but it couldn't be close enough to hazard another bolt yet.

She crept to the end of her barrier and leapt to the nearest one, and two incessant beeps let her know she was getting even more attention. She glanced at the nearby cover, thankful that for now the dummies were obscured behind several barriers. If she could get to the nearest full-size block, she'd at least feel temporarily safer.

A much louder beep right above her made her jump, and her gaze shot upward. One of the drones had flown right over her current cover, and the gun's little motors were hurriedly training it straight down — at her.

The wolf panicked and shot a hand up. It was only a few feet away; maybe… She reached further, not with her arm, but with her power.

It was always weird, trying to grab a charge from something she wasn't touching, and it was much slower, too. She had the sensation of something extending out of her arm, though nothing was visible. She could imagine her parents murmuring to each other about what she was doing, if something was up. *Focus, focus! Grab it!* The extension finally reached the drone, and she began to pull.

It was a second too late, it had managed to fire three times, directly at her other shoulder. "*Gah!*" she yelled, immediately bending, trying to avoid more shots in the same place, but her other arm remained, and she pulled again, *hard.*

The invisible extension suddenly filled with heat, and another crackling arc jumped from the drone's body to her hand. She'd made a connection, and immediately started pulling further. The closest comparison she'd ever come up with was drinking from an unusually long straw. In another moment, she was flooded with more warmth, more of that amazing clarity. The pain in her shoulder dimmed enough for her to ignore it and grab the drone with her real hand when its rotors petered out.

She held onto it for a moment, making sure its battery was properly dry before throwing it aside, breathing heavily. The feeling of clarity was fading already; the soreness in her right shoulder was coming back in full force.

Fuck. Are they using harder rubber? It's hurting so much more now!

She gripped her shoulder and grit her teeth. Two down, but if she caught any more rounds, she would start losing her ability to focus at all. She peeked over again, hearing the whir of the two remaining drones get louder. They were getting closer, but neither were visible yet.

She broke into a run, pulsing current through her legs again to speed herself up. Volta realized she was starting to breathe a little more heavily — the pulsing meant she was pushing her legs harder than usual. The soreness would set in more and more the less charge she had.

Keep going, don't slow down. Got an audience to impress; try to enjoy it.

She kept running, hearing the drones get further away. At least they were moving slowly — probably a boon from Dr. Mason. She found another tall barrier and flattened herself behind it. She could see the chamber's opposite wall over the tops of the barriers — not far now. If she wasn't careful she'd end up getting pincered; she had to take care of the dummies *now*, while the drones were still lagging behind.

Another pulse, and this time she vaulted over the low cover before her. She could hear the oscillating motors of the dummy turrets now. The last line of barriers formed a tall wall with only two doorways, a kind of bottleneck.

She sidled up to the closer doorway, hazarding another peek. She didn't have long before she was forced to duck back as the turrets rounded and fired. It was enough to see that all three dummies were out in the open — if she went in there, all of them would start shooting at once.

No problem, just pick them off. Lean out and pick them off one by one. Just like every other time, only now if I fuck up I'm never getting — Focus. Focus! I've got this. Right?

More heat in her right arm, more cracking, prickling. She grit her teeth and took aim around the corner. It was far, but once one was down she could… *fuck.* She could do something. *Do something?* That wasn't the kind of imprecise thinking that Bradley Group wanted. Panic was starting to well up in her stomach. She shouldn't have paused to think. Her breathing was getting faster.

Fuck it. Fuck it! Just go, take the shot. What's the problem? Just go, you fucking baby. GO.

She leaned out again, aiming at the nearest one, on the right. It looked even farther than before, but she had to do it. It was just a couple bullets before! If she kept going that was even more impressive. Just a couple bullets. Just a couple of mistakes.

That's too many.

She fired another bolt, realizing a second later she had shouted as she did. The bolt connected, and immediately the dummy that was training on her slackened, smoking and popping like the first drone. She whipped back behind cover, breathing shakily.

Come on, stop panicking. I got it! What's the FUCKING problem? Taking a couple rubber bullets is all it takes to clam up? Is that all?

She slammed her fist against the wall, grinding her teeth. She could feel the reduced amount of charge now — in her panic, she'd pumped too much into that dummy. Getting the other two was going to be even harder now — not even counting the drones, which she could hear getting closer again.

So that's three mistakes so far. How many more 'til you choke and get a face full of polymer?

Volta tried to steady her breathing, her heartbeat thumping in her head. She hadn't even taken another hit, she was getting too into her own head. She just needed a second; maybe she could wait out the drones, let them get close… *then* she could recharge.

She ran again, towards the drones' whirring this time. It only took a few more seconds to round the corner and spot the two of them bearing down on her. More rubber flew by as she hid again, taking another breath. *Wait them out. Don't fuck this up.*

The whirring got louder, closer, their angry beeping further apart from each other — they were splitting up, going to attack from both sides. No problem. If one was coming around one corner, it wouldn't see her if…

She rushed around the left corner, raising both hands and extending her reach again. Rubber bullets hit her right in the torso, right under the Dampener, knocking some of the breath out of her, but the drone couldn't rise out of reach fast enough. This time she grabbed it head on, claws scraping against the thin metal and plastic.

Her lower chest and stomach were burning in protest from taking even a few seconds of direct fire, but she was already refreshing her power supply. The shots petered off a second later, and the rotors stopped. She was still in pain, still breathing raggedly, but she felt fuller, *stronger*, a little more able to focus.

Okay, now the other one, the other one!

Volta whirled around just in time to see the last drone passing over the cover she'd just left, a few feet away again. On impulse, she fired another bolt. More smoking, more popping — it was on the floor in a second, and in her hands a second later. Pulling the charge into herself was like drinking ambrosia, distracting her from the soreness on her chest and shoulder.

Only two left. Not done yet. Keep going, ignore the pain. That's what men do, right? Pity, if only you knew.

She ran back to the bottleneck wall. Five down, two more to fry. She had enough charge, this time — *just* enough. Volta reached out around the corner again and took careful aim. One long bolt, and the left one was out of action. She hid again as the last turret's bullets thudded against the barrier just past it. *No problem.* She waited a few seconds, willing up a huge charge in her hand. If she was done, she could finish in style.

She stepped out from around the corner, and fired a much longer, stronger bolt. There was a much louder *CRACK*, then a burst of smoke and sparks from the dummy. The canine-like facade was charred black, and part of it had caught fire. Perfect. The technicians would probably be upset, but Volta didn't care. Another buzzer cued the end of the exercise, and she let out a breath — right before the Dampener reengaged.

Immediately, her remaining charge disappeared, sucked right out of her and dispersed into the air. The pain from her wounds sharpened suddenly, everything got painfully cold. She let out a ragged gasp, doubling over for a moment and clutching at her chest, shuddering as the wave of nausea and chills washed over her whole body.

"Nicely done, trainee," Dr. Mason lauded, sounding happier now that the procedure was over. "Sorry about the sudden reactivation — academy safety protocols, you know how it is."

"Y-you couldn't have waited 'til I'd gotten some painkillers or, or something?" She straightened up, wincing and holding her chest with her uninjured arm.

"Again: safety protocols, Austin. We'll get you some paracetamol in a moment. Please step into the door to your right; we've got some things to discuss."

Volta walked gingerly through the door indicated and into the observation room. As soon as she was through, she found herself face to face with Terrence Whitaker, his hand outstretched. The bighorn wasn't quite grinning, but she could tell the expression was something approaching positivity. "Mr. Travers, thank you for the show," he spoke smoothly, nodding as Volta took his hand and shook it. He shook back roughly, squeezing her hand tight. "You've got some serious power, son."

"Mr. Travers" was something she was ready to hear, but "son" sank in like hundreds of needles. "You hesitated a couple times but recovered real fast. Impressive! Your powers and skills would be a fantastic addition to Bradley Group."

"Th-thank you, sir!" Volta managed, a relieved smile on her face. She'd impressed him, that was the important part. The nagging in the back of her head could wait. "That's my long term goal, actually: joining Bradley Group. I've always looked up to the heroes under your purview."

Now he grinned. "Well, that's fantastic to hear, son!" More needles. "But, to set your expectations, I'm not at liberty to recruit you while you're still enrolled here."

Volta's heart faltered. "I was under the impression I could transfer to some training facility exclusive to Bradley Group recruits. A-assuming I qualified, I mean."

"Ordinarily that would be the case! But we have policies to uphold with Texas, we can't just poach whoever we like from their hero program. You're to complete your courses here, training and all, and soon as you finish, we'll be the first to knock on your door."

He finished shaking Volta's hand and clapped one shoulder, looking almost like a kind of proud father. "Don't take it the wrong way, son! You're damn good, I can see you've got potential, but the state's got its laws that we can't step on. Don't worry, I'm sure you already know that the TPA's courses are some of the best in the country. You could not *be* in better hands for the remainder of your training."

"I —"

Volta could think of a dozen ways to prove that statement wrong; instructors hired right out of army training bases were the tip of the iceberg. She couldn't complain about any of that to Whitaker — if anything would make her seem like she couldn't handle Bradley Group, complaining about "difficult teachers" would be it.

Just get over yourself, stop being such a wimp, and you'll stop having things to complain about. You can wait until graduation, right, or are you too fragile to get that far?

"…I understand, sir." She tried to pull off a confident smile. "You'll be hearing from me soon as I graduate."

"Good man." Another reassuring clap on the shoulder, and he stepped away. "Now, if you'll excuse me, I'm to let my friends back at Bradley Group know how you did. Best of luck, Travers!"

"Thank you, sir." She couldn't help sounding a little deflated at the end. The "sons" hurt, but she was feeling stupid for not expecting it. It's not like she passed in any way, and if she even *tried* to grow her hair out, she could already imagine what Mom or Dad might do.

Volta walked further into the observation room to be presented with the rest of her little audience. The technicians and aides were already filing out, into the test chamber, to retrieve the destroyed equipment. Dr. Mason was busy looking at something on Tammy's tablet, and her parents were talking with… a woman Volta hadn't noticed before.

She was a slate-colored tabby cat, unusually curvaceous, and taller even than Volta's father, wearing glasses and a lab coat over a work blouse. Her height was increased even further by the (honestly frightening) heels she wore. She had little rectangular glasses on, what looked to be a slight dash of lip gloss, and unusually expressive, distinctive eyes. Was she another aide or technician? Some other examiner? How had she missed her? She looked… *incredibly* hard to miss.

As Volta approached them, the tabby looked over. Her face lit up as she spotted the wolf approaching. "Ah! Just in time." She turned to greet Volta, her voice just as cheery and warm as her expression. "Pardon me, trainee. I was just speaking to your parents about your plans for the future. I'm a student examiner here." Her smile was bright, genuine — almost dazzling. Volta was already overwhelmed.

"She's asking some interesting questions, too," Volta's father came in, turning to regard her sternly. "You're in the big leagues, now, boy. Your mother and I were very impressed — you move just like the heroes on the news. Proud, noble, like a proper American Hero, fulfilling his duty in the field." If it were anyone else, said any other way, Volta might have been heartened.

It was the same with Mom. She came over to squeeze Volta's arms tightly, smiling broadly, her eyes flashing. "Wait 'til Elizabeth hears about this! The whole extended family, too. You're going to be in Bradley Group, so soon now! Serving our country just like we've always hoped."

"Yeah!" Volta straightened her back, trying her best to sound excited. "I can't wait."

"My name is Carmen, by the way," the tabby added, holding a hand out. Volta took it and couldn't help thinking about how different it was from Whitaker's. Gentle, friendly, *anything* but brusque like his had been. "I'm curious, also. Are you thinking at all about your hero name? You'll be done with courses before you know it, it'd be good to have one in mind — so they don't pick one for you."

No one at the academy had bothered to ask that before. Volta couldn't help letting out a little excitement. "I do, actually! I was thinking something like, 'Redline'?"

Mom cleared her throat. "Dear, I thought we agreed you need something nicer-sounding than that! That doesn't sound very heroic at all."

Volta's excitement wilted. Right, that conversation *did* happen. "Well, I thought it sounded cool…" Oops — that wasn't a very proud, broad-shouldered hero kind of thing to say.

Mom pursed her lips, and it was Dad's turn to chime in. "There's more to being a hero than being cool, boy. You've got values and standards to uphold, not to mention the law! You'll be plenty 'cool' once the PR and marketing teams have their turn with you."

Carmen tapped Volta's shoulder lightly. She was still smiling, but it had not turned sour or forced. In fact, the longer Volta looked at it, she almost thought the cat looked… sympathetic? "Well, it seems like a creative basis, if nothing else! I've got to go now, but I'm looking forward to seeing you around campus, trainee!" She stepped past Volta, her striped tail swaying, and said over her shoulder: "You were a real lightshow in there!"

Now, with Carmen gone, came the much firmer admonishment: "Dear, really. I think you need to take this sort of thing more seriously — 'Redline' sounds like, like something out of one of your silly comic books! That isn't the real world."

"Boy, God's given you a fantastic gift." Now it was Dad's turn to put his hands on Volta's shoulders. "You can do… *incredible* things, lightning literally at your fingertips! You're meant to be a guardian angel." Oh, great; Dad's favorite pep-talk, *again*. Volta could have rattled the rest off from memory. "You have an obligation to help the good people of this country, to protect them from the evils both within and without."

"I know, Dad. I don't think a name —"

"You have to be reassuring! *Comforting*, to your fellow Americans. A protector, not a… a *rockstar*. This… *'Redline'* thing is the name of a rockstar! That's not the kind of vanity we can abide. Imagine how the rest of the family would react."

"Why don't you just move on from that, dear," Mom chimed in, shaking her head. "Save the names and alter-egos for when you're taking care of criminals, especially those…" She grimaced, as if willing herself to say a dirty word. "Brainwashing *deviants*."

"I don't think I'll be facing down the Korps any time soon, Mom." Volta remembered a second too late where she was, and who she was speaking to.

Dad cleared his throat, straightening. Mom sighed, looking up at something past Volta's head. "I *really* wish you wouldn't even dignify them with that stupid name," she chastised. "They're terrorists, militant criminals and gangsters. Letting them have that name gives them an authority they don't deserve. You've — ugh, you've *seen* what they wear and what they do. And what they *say!* The news has just been their mouthpiece lately. Really, Austin, you have to be careful."

Volta took a breath, trying to remember how to be patient. "Yes, Mom. I know. I just don't think I'll be pitted against them on my first day."

"You have to treat terrorists *like* terrorists. Don't give them an inch," Dad added, and Mom followed through like this was a practiced routine.

"The TPA's supposed to teach you how to deal with them, and we've already done all we can. Are you sure you're ready for the responsibility?"

And it went *on* like that, for several more minutes. Volta only got it to stop by reassuring them that yes, Austin Travers was taking this *very* seriously, and was ready to be a real hero.

She walked out of the observation room fifteen minutes later, after Dr. Mason had given his own review of her abilities, Tammy glaring imperiously from her seat behind him the whole time. Nothing new, just another patronizing lecture about channeling the proper amount of charge for every target. Not like the goat had any idea what her powers were actually *like*, but he still had criticism and analysis to give. She set her jaw and took it, too. If Austin Travers was going to be in Bradley Group, Austin Travers couldn't be arguing with her examiners.

It was only 11:00 AM, and she already felt ready to fall back into bed. An aide had finally brought her some painkillers, but it would still be a few minutes before they kicked in. She walked down the hall, past the receptionist again, and had managed to get into the outer hall before she leaned against the wall. Her breathing was slow, shaky, and sounded way too close to the beginnings of an ugly sob.

If any other trainees or instructors caught her crying, name-calling would be the least of her problems. She had to tamp it down again, bury it under the tidbit of good news she *had* gotten. Bradley Group was open to her, just, not *yet*. Not until she finished here. Finished her sentence, it felt like; the TPA-run academy might as well have been a prison.

You're ready to be a real hero? Please. Like you even know what that means. You can't even be the man you should be. You can barely make it through a test like that without falling apart. Your parents know you, they know in a real fight they'd walk all over you. This isn't a prison, this is real life, and you still aren't ready for it.

Volta tried to pace her breathing, calm herself down. It was barely working. At the very least, no other classes or training sessions were scheduled for the day, so she might just be able to go back to her room, sink into the funk already setting in over her *again,* and spend an hour online glowering at clothes she couldn't afford and *definitely* couldn't pull off. Not with a body like this. Not with —

"Painkillers still kicking in?"

Volta, startled, looked up to spot the same tabby again, clipboard held to her chest. Carmen was much closer than before, leaning over the wolf with a look of worry.

Now getting a second look, Volta had to acknowledge how… *incredibly* attractive the cat was. A shapely face, strong eyebrows, and very bright, pale-orange eyes. Volta felt her face heat up — which probably didn't help the fact that she probably still looked way too close to shedding tears.

"Uhm, yeah, they're taking a minute." Volta's voice cracked mid-sentence. *Oh, very smooth.* "S-sorry, am I in the way?"

"No, no, that's not —" Carmen held up her hands in a placating gesture, her tail lowering behind her. "There's nothing wrong with taking a moment out here. I don't blame you. The test was already a lot, and then after that…" she clicked her tongue, looking to the side, agitated.

Volta blinked and tried to hide her next sniffle with a cough. "I — what, with my parents?"

"I got acquainted with them after you finished. They seemed like a lot to deal with — and, listen, I couldn't help overhearing some of your talk…"

Volta reflexively tightened, prepared for the worst. "Th-they were that loud, huh?"

"Well!" The tabby grimaced. "They seem like they're really invested in making you a…" she began, clearing her throat, "a 'proper' hero."

"That's one way to put it," Volta sighed, rubbing her face with one hand. "They're just making sure I'm still on-track. We don't see each other as much, now that I'm enrolled here."

"Sounds like a blessing." The tabby's tone was wry. "My parents are like that too. You know, overbearing, uptight and…" She trailed off, not sure how presumptuous she was being.

"Old-fashioned?" Volta offered.

"Yeah, absolutely," Carmen sighed, her long tail flicking behind her. "Pretty grateful to be away from them, all things considered. And," she leaned in to whisper, "for the record, Redline *is* a pretty cool superhero name."

"Oh, well." Volta felt her face heat up again, scrambling to think of what a bashful guy might do. Rubbing the back of her head seemed like a safe bet. "Th-thanks. I gotta admit, I came up with it when I was still a kid."

"No shame in that! You've wanted to be a hero for a while, then?" Carmen's eyes lit up as she asked the question. Had she been waiting to ask this?

"Yeah, I've thought about what being a hero will be like for a long time." Going on eleven years, in fact. "Since I found out about my powers, really."

"And you wanted to join the TPA too, huh?"

"No."

Volta hadn't meant to say that so forcefully. She scrambled to recover, trying to straighten into a parade rest in spite of the protest her bruises gave. "I mean, not at first, but I'm becoming a proper hero of the state here! Learning to do my home and my country proud!"

She had to be enthusiastic. If that "no" were heard by any of the teachers — or, worse, Mr. Olson — she could earn a few days of doing drills to exhaustion. "It's a great honor to be learning how to be a hero in these honored halls," she continued, repeating what the instructors said during drills. "A-and furthermore —"

"Hey! Hey, I get it," Carmen cut her off, she looked startled. "Take it easy, I'm not gonna tell on you for saying that! It was just a question. You don't have to feed me the same lines they feed you. I'm not trying to trick you into saying something." She leaned in and lowered her voice again, that frown of concern returning. "Do you *actually* want to be here?"

Volta took a breath, and in another moment, felt herself starting to crumple back to the nervous slouch she'd had before. "W-well, no, but this is what Mom and Dad wanted. And it's what I have to do. To get ou — to become a licensed hero." She took another breath to pace herself, realizing she was speaking very quickly.

"I wanted to join Bradley Group. Once I finished high school I figured I could, like, apply formally, but if you're from Texas they only take academy graduates." She sighed, lowering her gaze to her chest, glaring at the Dampener underneath her suit. "I just hope I'll actually *get* to the graduation part. It's not exactly easy here."

"I know *exactly* what you mean," Carmen put a hand on her shoulder, and Volta raised her eyes to look at the tabby's compassionate smile. "I was stuck in a place I didn't really want to be, either. It wasn't easy…"

The tabby trailed off, and her eyes went wide. She checked her wristwatch, clicking her tongue in frustration and withdrawing her hand. "Ah, damn. Listen, I've got to get going, but…" She hesitated for a few seconds, trying to find the words. "Do you wanna meet up in the mess hall for lunch? I wanna keep talking about this."

Volta blinked a few more times. She didn't get asked things like this very much. "I'd, uh. I'd… like to?" She furrowed her brow. "This isn't a joke or something, is it?"

Carmen chuckled again. "I already said I'm not trying to trick you!"

"Then why'd you… come talk to me? I-I'm not complaining, it just doesn't happen very often here. Normally it's counselors, or an instructor, or Doctor Mason…"

Carmen smiled — a real, genuine smile. "Well, part of it is the fact that I know what it's like to have a family like that. But mostly it was just, you looked like you could use someone to talk to, and I like to think that's my specialty."

Volta couldn't help but feel heartened. She didn't want to get *too* hopeful, but Carmen looked and sounded as though she actually cared, which was a nice change of pace. Finding someone else at the academy who could understand how *stuck* she felt had been damn near impossible.

Carmen turned, waving over her shoulder as she walked away. "Really gotta go this time. I'll see you in like an hour? Lunch, don't forget!"

"Right!" Volta stammered, smiling nervously. "S-see you then!"

The tabby's tail swayed as if waving at Volta again before she rounded a corner down the hall. Volta took a breath and made for her quarters. She *really* didn't feel like eating in her stuffy training outfit — and especially not if she had someone to talk with.

Someone to talk with!

The realization had taken its time to hit her. This was the first time anyone had really bothered to talk to her about this kind of thing, at all.

Even if it *was* just complaining about strict parents, that was more than she got from the frat boys and jarheads that made up her roommates. She couldn't help but smile again.

It would be enough to just talk in the first place.

CHAPTER 2

WALL BREACH

It was a short walk to the student dorm where Volta stayed — which she was grateful for, given the morning she had. She shut her door behind her and let out a pained sigh through her teeth, kicking her shoes off and lazily yanking off her sweaty test suit. She regarded it for a moment derisively. No tears from the rubber bullets or burns from her powers, so at least she wouldn't have to requisition a new one, just make sure it ran through the wash before her next evaluation. She threw it in the direction of the laundry hamper and trudged over the cheap campus-grade carpeting to her cramped bathroom.

Volta was desperate to shower before lunch, especially if Carmen was going to be there. At the very least, she could avoid smelling like a sweaty dog.

She was staring at herself in the mirror again. The bruising on her chest and shoulder hardly bothered her, but the paracetamol was keeping it from being more than a constant ache. What the drugs *didn't* do was stop her from glaring at her bare torso: sturdy, toned, plenty of definition in her pectoral and abdominal muscles. The only thing in the way was her layer of off-white fur — and the Dampener, ever-present, and miraculously waterproof so she couldn't take it off even in the shower. Always there, to remind her of the chest she was stuck with.

A tired lump started to form in her throat, her breathing getting unsteady. She looked up at her face, wearing a scowl that was trying not to twist into a whimpering pout. "G-get it together," she demanded of herself, her voice threatening to crack.

Not worth just feeling shitty about this any longer. Find a way to get over it.

The shower didn't help her feel much better, and she wound up spending several extra minutes dissociating while she rinsed her fur. Time flew by much more easily if she had nothing to focus on but the water hitting her. The bruises stung far worse when she ran her hands over them, but at least it helped distract her from having to wash underneath the Dampener.

A few minutes of halfhearted soaping up, shampooing short hair, then rinsing off, and she was stepping out of the shower. She avoided glancing at the mirror as she dried off, and her mind wandered instead to Carmen. She'd looked so good in that lab coat, the shoes, the work blouse worn so casually. *Practically a walking fashion model, compared to this.*

She stepped naked over to the small closet where she rifled through several colored tees and a few pairs of jeans — all things that showed off her biceps and nothing else. Fine. Nondescript tee and pants for a college boy going to the cafeteria, that was bearable.

Volta peered back into the bathroom, frowning at her hair again. There wasn't very much to work with. She combed it smooth and spent another few seconds glaring at it. Maybe she could discreetly grow it out a little and her parents wouldn't suspect anything. Lots of college kids got longer hair, right?

Finally, she slumped down in her desk chair and tried to take a few deep breaths. She still had most of an hour left, so she flipped open her laptop. She could at least fill the time by checking Twitter and email.

There was the usual stuff in her email inbox: a reminder about upcoming scheduled tests, another public service announcement to watch for and report any suspected Korps activity on campus, and then finally…

…a request from Doctor Mason to come in tomorrow for some Dampener calibration. Volta's eyes widened; had they finally changed their minds, or was this just going to be part of the new routine? She held her breath and opened it.

> Hello, Austin. I have good news and bad news.
>
> I know you find the Dampener to be highly unpleasant; you have made that quite clear to me. In spite of the ease of controlling how much electric charge you have access to at the beginning of a test, I recognize it is counterproductive both to your training and future examinations. I have just tried to lay these issues out to Administration.

First, the bad news: Chief Tullis and President Richardson remain just as stubborn as ever. They both insist on the continued use of the Dampener for your safety and the safety of your peers and facility staff. It will stay on until further notice.

The good news: I managed to convince them that a complete and constant drain is not necessary and affects your stamina enough to adversely affect your training and test-taking regimen. The Dampener's lower limit is being raised to a maximum of 300 watts. The Dampener will dissipate any wattage higher than that unless disabled for testing or training purposes.

Please come to my lab tomorrow, first chance you get in the morning, and we will reconfigure the Dampener to these new settings. I know this is not an ideal solution, but at the very least it should leave you with a little more "juice" for your ongoing education and Hero Training.

See you tomorrow!

PS: Please disregard the humongous footer. New staff policy is to include the whole spiel, slogan and everything.

— Dr. Brennis Mason, PHD

Head of Research Operations,

TPA FRONTIER HERO ACADEMY
TEXAS PROTECTORATE ASSEMBLY
~The Lone Star's Guardians, To the Very Last.

Volta leaned back in her chair, breathing a sigh of relief. It wasn't much, but it was a start. Even a little bit of leftover charge would give her some breathing room, distract her from the apprehension she felt every time she got drained. Now she had something to look forward to tomorrow; this would hopefully make the training session with her drill instructor less painful.

She logged onto Twitter, glancing boredly over her feed. Nothing special, just more photos from the big party Mom and Dad had thrown to celebrate Dad's purchase of another manufacturing plant. Thankfully Volta hadn't been able to attend — Volta had convinced her parents that not interrupting the examination schedule was, in fact, more important than yet another get-together where a bunch of Southern rich people could titter about extended family drama over champagne. Hell, *anything* was better than having to get dressed in those overpriced suits she'd been fitted for and having to pretend to be the eager heir to the family business.

There were dozens of photos of Mom and Dad hanging around all sorts of high-profile executives and politicians. Volta caught a glimpse of the president of the training facility, Jack Richardson. The middle-aged Dalmatian was smiling broadly, a glass of champagne in one hand, and his other shaking her father's. Of course they'd be treating him nicely. It wasn't like the Dampener was a cheap invention — Dad probably had to convince and re-convince him it was worth it with alcohol and a good party.

That was enough staring at rich middle-aged people. A few more seconds of aimless scrolling and something caught her eye: a series of retweets from a cousin, all of them from a well-known YouTube news personality. It seemed he was ranting about an article reporting the recent arrest of a Texas-local law firm executive.

The Korps has been up to a lot of mudslinging today, and got an upstanding Texas citizen, Charles Quentin, locked up on trumped up bogus charges! He's completely innocent, but don't let the Korps hear you say that, they might try brainwashing you into believing them.
— @TheRealGaryP 11:38, 500 replies, 712 retweets, 1.2k likes

These witch hunts are starting to hurt REAL PEOPLE. Wtf do these freaks know about law malpractice? Do they study law from the same place they get their outfits from?
— @TheRealGaryP 11:40, 200 replies, 500 retweets, 1.1k likes

The rest of the thread was written in a similar tone. Volta could count on all her extended family to supply her with the most aggressive conservative rhetoric and, occasionally, some news mixed in. The comments were predictably anti-Korps, and her cousin had managed to get a substantial amount of attention talking about "showing these pussies the end of his service weapon." Volta started to feel a little sick.

Great thing to read before lunch. Why did you even bother looking?

She went back to her feed, halfheartedly scrolling past a few promoted tweets for joining Bradley Group (#NationOfHeroes) and just as many urging to look out for any Korps Helixes and to report anyone wearing the helix on campus. Why would they need to say that? Of course the Korps weren't allowed here — it wasn't like they would make a habit of showing it off in a place where the campus police often carried firearms of multiple sizes. The most out there piece of fashion Volta had even seen was when Doctor Mason's assistant, Tammy, had come to one examination wearing a very low-cut V-neck.

The folder of porn Volta had password-protected in her documents folder had plenty of outfits that were sure to make the uptight, judgmental fox turn red. She wondered again now, as she had multiple times before, if keeping any images with a pink helix visible (and *porn*, especially) on her college laptop was a good idea, but it wasn't like downloading it in the first place had ever raised any alarms. Now, looking at the warning tweet again, she debated going through and deleting some of the photos with more-visible helixes in them.

After another couple minutes of scrolling through more acid tweeted or retweeted by her family members, Volta finally closed her laptop, her heartbeat thudding in her ears. She felt sickening little chills on her arms and back. It was just further proof that she had to keep quiet, as long as it took to get out from under them. Bradley Group could not accept her any sooner.

She stepped back out of her room and into the hall. She could hear some of her dormmates shouting from one of the other rooms and hurried quickly past their door. She didn't need to deal with any of them right now, and her apprehension about her appearance was rapidly being replaced with hunger.

The cafeteria was thankfully not too packed — lunch was served at 12:00 PM on the dot, and most of the early trainees were expected to scarf down their meals and get straight to their next class. Now that Volta was done with basic training, her schedule wasn't quite so strict, and scheduled test days meant having an afternoon off.

By the time Volta had filled her lunch tray, she noticed Carmen waiting nearby, the cat having replaced her lab coat with a dark jacket cut off at the waist. She still had her glasses. Carmen glanced in her direction and smiled again, inviting her over with a little wave.

Volta approached the tabby and once again became very aware of the fact that Carmen was at least half a foot taller than her. The heels she wore helped, obviously, but this cat would have been imposing if she didn't look so… *friendly*.

"Glad you could make it! Look, there's a quieter table over there," the tabby suggested as she pointed to a table in a far corner of the cafeteria where fewer people were seated. As they walked, Carmen spent more and more time glancing at Volta's chest. "Hmm. Is that Dampener thing still on?"

"Yeah," Volta sighed. "I'm supposed to wear it all the time. It's not like I can take it off, anyway. It's supposed to keep my powers in check while I'm still learning how to use them." Volta took a deeper breath, feeling the thick straps tighten on her shoulders and chest.

"Huh!" Carmen looked like she was trying not to stare. "Is it comfortable?"

Volta shrugged, but the resulting stretch of the straps dug into her skin. "N-no, not really," she muttered quietly.

Finally reaching the lonely table, Carmen sat down and took a sip from her drink, eyeing Volta for a moment before asking, "Why don't you complain? Surely you don't need it on *ALL* the time."

"It's not really my —" Volta looked down at her tray, realizing she hadn't ever told anyone about this before. "It's a stipulation of my enrollment here. My parents recommended restraining my powers to the administrator."

"And he went along with it?"

"Yeah, him and the head of security. They saw my powers and they decided they posed a 'clear danger' to the staff and other students enrolled here." She took a breath, trying to sound resigned, like some of the guy students often did. Picking up her plastic fork and poking at her salad, she continued. "I mean. They're right. They *are* dangerous. Without the Dampener I could do a lot of damage. I used to do a lot. I… uhm. Yeah." She stuffed lettuce into her mouth to shut herself up. It was rapidly becoming evident to her that she had *not* had enough conversations like this to know when to stop talking.

Carmen seemed unfazed. She leaned in, clearly intrigued as she spooned soup into her mouth. When Volta stopped talking, she just smiled. "You were pretty impressive in the examination, honestly. Can you pull electricity from anything?"

Volta felt her face heat up at the compliment. She wasn't used to hearing positive things about her powers — not since high school, and even then, only from one halfway-decent friend. "Uh, pretty much? I've had this on for the entire year I've been here, and I was always discouraged from experimenting too much with my powers." "Discouraged" was putting it mildly. It didn't take long for that particular lesson to stick, bruises and all. "No one's ever really called it 'impressive' before, though."

Carmen looked surprised, but her grin held. "Really? You can do all that and no one's even told you how flashy it looks? That running you did at the start, you had a streak of sparks coming off of you. And all that lightning you shot out — I don't know about you, but *I* think that's pretty cool."

Now Volta could *feel* herself blushing. "I… Well, th-thanks, I guess." She managed a little smile, bashfully poking at her salad.

"Yeah! I mean — I haven't been here very long, but I've really liked what I've seen so far." Carmen took another bite before continuing. "Mm, if you don't mind, I was also curious about what we discussed before."

"Oh, about my parents?"

"Mmhm. If you're comfortable. I was just wondering like…" Carmen pursed her lips, then sighed. "Are they always that stuck-up about this hero stuff?"

The tone was so blunt that Volta couldn't help an awkward chuckle. "Yeah, a little. It's hard to get a word in…"

"*Ugh.* There's so much of that around here. All this bluster and *Patriotism* with a capital P. I get tired of it really quick, just talking to other guys around here."

"Other guys, right…" Volta tried to ignore the return of the chills on her upper arms. "I mean, I do *want* to be a hero, but I always thought it was more important to help people. That's what I liked so much about heroes on the news as a kid."

"Oh, absolutely. Way nicer to hear about people just, trying to help those in need, y'know? Like in old comic books."

Volta's ears perked. "Actually, that was what made me want to become a hero so much." *So much that I'm stuck here.* "I, uh, really liked hero merchandise as a kid, comic books, collectible cards… I had a lot of True North."

"Really!" The tabby's eyes went wide, and her smile widened too. "That's… really sweet, actually. Uh, which True North?"

"Uhhh, I'm blanking on his name," she lied. Of course she knew his name; she knew *every public fact* about True North II she could find. He was her inspiration, the hero she'd dressed up as for every Halloween since age 5, no matter how many kids made fun of her for liking a Canadian hero despite her Texan pedigree. If Carmen got a whiff of how much merchandise was hiding in boxes in her room back home, she'd probably run the other way. "He's the current Minister of Defense up in Canada, uh, Arthur Simonds! Second generation True North! I-I don't like Chris Marcotte as much, he's a bit too much of a…"

"Prick?" Carmen offered. Her expression had gotten very weirdly knowing. "Oaf? Jackass?"

"Something like that, yeah." The red wolf furrowed her brow. "Do you… have something against Chris Marcotte?"

"No, no! He's…" She took a moment, looking for the right word. "Just not a favorite of mine, as far as heroes go. I — oh!" Carmen's ears perked up and she reached into a pocket, pulling out a phone decorated in an orange case. "Ah, family member's texting me, hold on."

"Yeah, sure." She filled the silence by filling her mouth and tried to look at other things in the cafeteria that weren't the eye-catching tabby tapping away at her phone.

After a few more seconds, Carmen snorted derisively. "*Pfah*, of course, more of *this* shit. Sorry, I swear a lot, but look at this."

She showed Volta her phone, tapping play on a video. It began with the American flag catching fire and being replaced by a black flag, marked by the winged helix of the Korps in striking magenta.

"America is under threat of a new kind of terrorist. Not one in the open, but one in the shadows. You can easily spot their members by their choice of salacious attire and the rampant display of this symbol.

Charles Quentin, Chairman of the Texas State law firm Quentin-Goodnow and Associates, is an innocent man. A man who has made a lifetime of defending many upstanding contributors to society but is now behind bars due to a series of accusations regarding fraud, malpractice, and tax evasion. The charges are completely baseless, and serve only to underline how dangerous a hold the Korps has on our nation's media —"

"God, my brother keeps sending me junk like this," Carmen groaned, interrupting Volta reading. "Do people actually think that little of these guys? They're not just *mudslingers*, they're *villains*."

"My parents definitely understand that," Volta snorted. "Which is funny, considering some of my extended family still believes in... a lot of things. Like phrenology."

Carmen put her phone away and winced. "That bad, huh? Let me guess — they spend more time talking about their wardrobes than the actual *crimes*, too?" She asked it as if it were a ridiculous worry — and it *was*, even in Volta's opinion.

"I... don't think they like to look at them long enough to say. They act like the devil himself is gonna show up if they look too much — or even *talk* about them too much." The wolf sighed in frustration. "Any time the name comes up, my mom just shuts the conversation down. I... don't like not being able to talk about them at all, but I kinda get it?" the wolf offered meekly. "They *are* violent criminals, they don't hesitate to do lot of bad things, robberies, knocking down buildings, attacking police and superheroes, but..."

She trailed off, realizing Carmen had been staring at her intently again.

"But?"

"W-well, I was just gonna say. It feels, sometimes, like my parents really just hate them because they're... y'know." Her cheeks flushed as she tried to decide on a word. Queer? Sexual? *Hot?* "...Different."

The tabby smirked. "That can mean a lot of different things, when it comes to the Korps — everything I've seen and heard about them makes them seem... *intense*. But I think I get what you mean." Carmen looked down at her now-empty bowl, her smirk fading. "Your family sounds just like mine. Like, you can't talk about a lot of things you want to, whether or not you agree with them, because it doesn't feel... *safe* to bring them up..." She looked up again, grimacing. "Uh, maybe I'm projecting a little, sorry."

Volta stared for a few seconds. "N-no, that's, uh, actually pretty spot-on." She looked down at her own tray. She'd only had a few bites; she hurriedly took another one to give herself time to think. "...I'm not comfortable talking about a lot of stuff with them. The Korps, my powers, school, church..." She frowned, shifting in her seat uneasily. "They don't know I haven't prayed or been to mass in months."

Carmen got a pained look on her face, as if this reminded her of something really unpleasant. "Yeah, I remember stuff like that. We just don't talk about it anymore. ...Do you have anyone you can talk to? Any friends?"

"N-not really, not since I left..." Grade school? Boarding school? She hadn't spoken with Luke, the only person who ever spent any time around her by *choice*, since they graduated — and even when they *had* spoken, it was all just surface-level comparing notes about the Heroes they liked. When *was* the last time she'd really had anything more than a friendly acquaintance she could discuss capes with? Volta started to feel very self-conscious about how lonely she got. "I usually just keep to myself. I don't like hanging out with most guys around here." She recoiled inward; that was *definitely* oversharing.

"I mean, you don't have to," Carmen said, looking sympathetic. How much repulsion at her own words had Volta let show? "You're not one of the guys. That's not as big a deal as they might have you think."

That hit her like a ton of bricks. *Shit*, it was even more obvious than she thought. She stammered into protest. "Well! I mean. I'm not the biggest fan of sports or bodybuilding; I mostly do the latter for the sake of being a hero, but. I'm definitely still strong, still a Texan, definitely —"

A guy. A GUY. Say you're still a guy, damn it. She's going to know something's wrong. She's going to know what a freak you are. You already said too much. You already messed this up, just like everything else.

Volta realized she had just stopped talking, her mouth hanging open. She shut it belatedly, looking anywhere but the cat in front of her. Her whole body felt too hot, her heart beating against her chest. The Dampener felt tighter than ever.

"Hey," Carmen reached over and put a hand on top of Volta's clenched fist on the table. She spoke in a soft mutter. "Listen, do you wanna talk about this somewhere a little more private? I don't mind."

"I —" Volta finally looked back at the tabby. She had such a worried, alarmed look on her face. It was so disarmingly genuine that Volta took a few seconds to form a response. "Sure, yeah. Please."

If nothing else, the TPA's Frontier Hero Academy had well-cultivated and cared-for campus gardens. The peaceful little walkways with the occasional bench rarely saw foot-traffic. It was far less likely to have someone passing by than the hallways inside any building, especially as the lunch hour ended.

Carmen led Volta over to one such bench and sat down with her. Several seconds of silence passed before the tabby prodded: "You really are alone here, aren't you?"

The red wolf stared straight ahead and nodded, keeping her lips tight. She wasn't sure what was going to come out of her mouth if she opened it again.

"So, you've never talked about anything? Not even the discomfort? What about Dr. Mason, or his assistants?"

Volta thought back to the last time she'd tried complaining about the tightness of the Dampener. It had been the most sheepish little complaint, and that was definitely part of the problem. Tammy had just responded snidely: *"C'mon, don't be such a sissy about it. Suck it up, be a man for once."*

"I don't really… get along with the assistants," she finally said. "I can't talk to anyone here. If I make too much noise, the campus administrator might find out, and then…" *And then he'd tell my parents.*

"I'm not going to talk to the administrator," Carmen said. "You don't have to tell me anything, but, I'm more than willing to lend an ear. I'm really good at that, y'know." She slowly put a hand on Volta's shoulder, and when she turned to look at her, Carmen was smiling. Soft, gentle. The grip on her shoulder was so slight.

"W-why do you care so much?" Volta couldn't help a slight crack in her voice. That was all she could manage to say, hopelessly trying to fight down the lump in her throat again.

"I just…" Carmen's face fell, and for a moment she looked pained. "I don't like seeing people hurting like this. And, honestly, you're very visibly hurting. I want to help, Austin. Do you… do you *want* help?"

Why did hearing *her* say that name sting so badly? Volta had her hands clenched up again, pressing her claws into her palms. The concern in Carmen's voice was overwhelming to hear. Her eyes began to water; her whole body shook.

"Listen, if I'm overstepping, just say so. I —" Carmen withdrew her hand. It felt like part of Volta's flesh went with it.

"No, please…" Volta could do little more than croak. "I don't — Sorry. I don't know how to do this." She tried to manage a little laugh. "Y-you must have a lot more experience than me, talking about… I don't know."

Carmen's worried smile was back, and so was her hand. "You can start now. It's okay, really, Austin, you don't need —"

"*Can you* —" She faltered for a moment, realizing she had almost yelled that. "Can you please, um, not call me that? I don't like that name." *Too much, oh god, too much.* Her entire body stiffened, prepared for the worst. Every millisecond of silence between them felt strained. Like her lungs were being compressed.

Carmen took a breath, but she did not pull away. She did not shout, or laugh, or scowl in revulsion. She just asked, so quiet it was little more than a whisper, "What would you like to be called?"

Don't say it. You know how this will go. You know she'll hate you.

The wolf swallowed, her hands shaking. "Can you… call me Volta?" She grimaced. It sounded so much worse aloud than it did in her head. Her ears were flagged, her back hunched, she was ready for the tabby to scoff. To do… anything other than keep rubbing her shoulder.

"Yeah, I can do that. Volta, you said?" Carmen asked, ever so gently. How did she sound so… patient?

Volta sniffled loudly. "Y-yeah. Please." Her nose had started to run; tears were wetting the fur under her eyes. She felt grotesque next to the tabby. The gorgeous, tall tabby, who was nonetheless here, holding her shoulder. There was a numbness to the rest of her body, except for where Carmen was touching her. It was still just the smallest caress, the occasional little squeeze. "I-I know it sounds stupid. It's —"

"It does *not* sound stupid, not at all." Only now did Carmen's voice become firm. "If you want to be called Volta, I'll call you Volta. No explanation needed."

"I..." Volta had to fight back further tears... and tamp down the voice yelling at her to run. She didn't need it, not now. "Thank you, Carmen."

She beamed. "It's no trouble, Volta. I can tell your family wants certain things for you... from you. But you're allowed to want things for yourself, too. You can be any kind of person you want to be."

"What —" Volta faltered, her throat still tight. She had never felt more scared. Carmen's patient smile was the most terrifying thing she had ever seen, but it still urged her forward. "What if... I didn't want to be, uh, one of the guys?"

Carmen for a moment looked a little damp in the eyes, and then she spoke with another soft laugh in her voice. "Then, Volta, I will help you figure that out." She paused for a moment, going a little still as she thought something over. "Actually, would you like a hug? You... look like you need a hug."

If Volta weren't so fresh off a sob, she might have cared how red in the face that made her. "Y-yeah? Yes? Yes. I'd... yes please."

Carmen smiled again, reached around with both arms, and pulled Volta closer, letting her cheek rest on the wolf's head. For a moment, Volta's little tremors eased up, and her breathing didn't feel so heavy. The fact that someone might see them didn't matter. She just hugged Carmen back and breathed deep.

Carmen made sure the door shut behind her, took a breath, and set her bag down on the desk at the door. Her eyes glanced over the room once, twice. Everything was right where she left it.

The tabby hung her TPA-branded lab coat on a hook opposite the desk and approached her bed. She lifted the far corner of the mattress, retrieving the metal case, just smaller than a shoebox, from underneath it. Emblazoned on the side was a little watch face — a cute little gesture that always got a smile out of her.

She pressed a finger to a button on the side and raised the box to her mouth to whisper into the receiver.

"With opened eyes, found at last, every second is a joy. *Maintenant et pour toujours.*"

There was a click, and the lid released its clasp. Inside was a set of sleek, wide glasses, with earpieces coming off of the arms. They were fitted for Carmen and her feline ears, and had unmistakable, magenta lenses each in their own frame.

She carefully lifted the RCGs out, putting the box down, unfolded the arms and slipped them on. She was greeted by a rotating winged helix gradually coming into focus. A little jingle, a display of the current operating system and release version, and then a momentary pause as they resynchronized with her and established a secure connection.

It took a single thought, as she slipped the earpieces on, to bring up the call dialogue and select a contact. In a few seconds, the call connected and an energetic, androgynous voice sounded through the earpieces.

"Carmen, from Control. RCG Network connection is secure, call's encrypted. There might be a bit of a delay given the distance and physical barriers."

"Confirmed, Control. I am alone and my immediate vicinity is secure, ready to report." The tabby grinned and dropped the official tone. "Hey, Wren, hope you're not too busy."

"Not at all, just got myself some popcorn." His voice became a lot more casual. "Anything interesting? It'd be a nice change of pace."

"Actually, yes," Carmen began, leaning back onto her bed, but keeping an eye on the doorway, just in case. "I found someone. An extremely high potential super — possibly a recruit."

"Oooh!" There was a sound of rustling, then the unmistakable crunch of Wren enjoying their popcorn. "Well don't keep me waiting, hit me with the details!"

CHAPTER 3

SAFETY VALVE

Dr. Mason's office, lab, and workshop occupied the same space in the facility's western building. A few hallways down and Volta would have found the same test chamber she'd performed in for Whitaker a day ago.

This was just a checkup, and the best kind of checkup, too. She couldn't help but smile a little as she stepped through the threshold into the white, beige, and blue lab. Mason's desk was near the far wall, with a wide variety of machines — most of it measuring equipment — strewn between the desk and the doorway. The wizened goat glanced lazily up from his tablet and waved Volta over.

"Right on time, Travers. Sit down and remove your shirt; Tammy will take care of plugging the Dampener in."

She never enjoyed having to show her bare chest for any examination or checkup, but she supposed it wasn't exactly bare right now, and hadn't been for the past year or so. Taking a breath to steady herself, Volta pulled her tee over her head. By the time she'd gotten it off, Tammy was in front of her holding up a connector cable.

Just pretend it's a stethoscope. Breathe. Forget about the thing for as long as you can.

Already she felt her face heating up as the vixen approached her with that same bored condescension she always had. "C'mon, Travers, stop hunching over. Not like I haven't seen your chest before anyway."

Volta straightened her back as much as she could, focusing on the most boring wall in the lab and taking very slow, shallow breaths. Tammy dispassionately stuck the connector in the small port at the center of the Dampener's rounded side and walked back to the monitor she'd been looking at before.

"Like I'd stuck him with a needle..." she muttered just loud enough for Volta's canine ears to pick up. Her stomach felt heavy, and the fur surrounding the Dampener was starting to itch.

"All right, let's see here." Dr. Mason held his tablet further away from him, squinting. "Damn coding team and their UI design... Hold on, Travers, it's been about three weeks since I've had to configure this."

"That's fine," she lied. Every second she had to sit here without a shirt on was increasingly unpleasant. Texas was already hot enough, she didn't need to feel like the room was staring at her. The itching was getting worse, but she didn't even want to touch her chest. This was when the Dampener's presence was impossible to ignore; she could *feel* it siphoning her charge away, every second.

Every breath made her chest feel too tight, every little fidget made the skin under the straps cut. Tammy was glaring at her again. Volta closed her eyes, jaw set.

Stop it. Man up for a second and take a breath. You can't afford to be this pathetic every time. Who knows how long this thing is going to stay on — *another year? Until I get my hero licensing? I'm in this for the long haul either way.*

"There, found it," Mason spoke up, tapping. "Three-oh-oh watts maximum, minimum drain rate. Now just to update — h..." The goat looked up, past Volta to the hall entrance. The distinct even-tempo clack of steel-toe boots came reverberating down the hall, then arrived at the doorway.

"Good, I'm just in time." The gravelly voice of Security Chief Adam Tullis was unforgettable. Volta glanced over one shoulder and up at the immense figure of a muscular, gray-furred Great Dane, dressed in a black, badged uniform with the TPA's colors emblazoned on the shoulders. That metallic blonde military buzzcut looked just the same as ever. He had his permanent glower fixed firmly upon the red wolf huddled in the chair before him.

"Is there something you need, Tullis?" Mason asked, his finger hovering over his tablet, clearly anticipating what the bulky canine was going to say.

"Thank you for asking, Doctor. In fact, I had more questions pertaining to the leniency you're giving this trainee..." He folded his arms, not taking his eyes away from Volta. She didn't dare look away either. Her breath became shallow once again as she tried not to fidget. She just hoped she didn't look too much like a deer in the headlights. "And maybe he can help answer as well."

"Trainee" — *like you don't know me by name. Like you've never shown up at the mansion for some party or TPA event, like Mom and Dad never scolded me for being so scared of you…*

Volta swallowed down more contorted fear and resentment before it reached her face, trying to keep as neutral as she could. It was harder when he stared directly *at* her. All she wanted to do was cower like she was a child all over again.

Dr. Mason continued uncertainly. "Uh, of course, Tullis, what —"

"*Chief.*"

"Chief Tullis," the goat sighed in exasperation. "What do you need?"

"Is this adjustment actually going to improve Travers's performance, or are we just sparing the rod?"

The goat blinked. "I'm… not sure I understand the question."

The Great Dane grinned, clasping his hands behind his back. He stepped past Volta and towards the goat, taking on the air of a general regarding his lowliest troops. "Allow me to state it plainly, Doctor. This whole business with adjusting the Dampener's settings reeks of coddling. You were very eager to stick your neck out for the sake of his, uh, *comfort.*" He glanced over his shoulder at Volta again, sizing her up. "Now, I'm not *officially* in charge of the training programs here, but as you are well aware, I do have a wealth of experience under my belt."

"As you are quick to remind me and President Richardson, Chief Tullis," Mason gave him a very stiff smile, too stiff even for an old goat, "but even as the Golden Gavel —"

"In the *real* world," Tullis continued, speaking loudly and rounding on Volta once more, "there's always fighting to be done. You never know what new threat might rear its head, so heroes can *never* rest — the Korps certainly doesn't." He leaned forward and peered down at Volta. His expression said it all: he wasn't impressed. "The Korps is always plotting, always in the background. Canada's already let them spill over the border and left *us* with the cleanup job. The TPA needs rigor, stamina, and a firm hand. Texas is a battleground for the righteous and the strong, son."

Volta's throat had gone dry, but she had to say something. He clearly expected her to. "That's why I'm here, sir," she croaked, barely keeping herself from stammering.

He smirked, straightening up. "Course you are! You show promise, and you're a Travers — you come from very sturdy stock. Your power's something else, son, but I didn't get anywhere just 'cuz my power was *special*. Nobody went easy on me. It was a fight, and it'll *always* be a fight. America expects nothing less. If this is supposed to improve your performance, it had better improve things tenfold. The standards for your instruction will be increased accordingly. President Richardson agrees with me, that the risks and expenses in the interest of safety…" — he gave the Dampener a hard poke, and Volta had to fight off the urge to flinch —"…need to be justified, Travers. Can you promise me that?"

He stared right at her again. His expression was withering, his smirk completely gone. Volta took a breath, swallowed, and answered in as even a voice as she could. "I can, sir. I will. You won't be disappointed."

"We'll see about that," his smirk came back, and he stepped towards the doorway. "That'll be all. I'll be speaking to your instructors. Thanks for your time, Doctor."

"No, really, it's my pleasure," Dr. Mason replied through another stiff smile; he lost it as soon as Tullis ducked back through the doorway.

He took a deep breath, shaking his head. "Travers, you better appreciate how much I had to argue on your behalf for the sake of easing the Dampener's restrictions. That man doesn't like any kind of compromise, and of course Richardson just does whatever the big lug wants…" He stopped and cleared his throat. "Ah, you didn't hear that last part from me, Travers."

"O-of course, Doctor," Volta muttered, shifting in her seat. "Um, do you still have to —"

"Right, yes, back to it. Hang on, this might feel a little strange as the Dampener resets." The goat tapped his tablet, and there was a single, long beep from the dome on Volta's chest. Then, a second later, Volta felt her fur begin to prickle…

The rush only lasted for a moment, but there was a sudden full-body warmth that was nothing like the heat in her face from earlier. The lights in the lab seemed brighter, and the machinery almost seemed to shimmer.

Just as quickly as it came, it began to fade, but everything still looked a little more clear and crisp. The air felt the tiniest bit easier to breathe, and Volta drew in an easy breath for once. She felt that same electric heat welling in her body in a reservoir that was often empty nowadays. She could almost bring herself to laugh.

The sensation plateaued. The Dampener was doing its job, keeping her at a specific charge. It felt like a collar that was slightly too tight. Not *quite* as suffocating as before, but the pressure was still there.

"Well, it's something," she muttered, flexing her fingers, and letting the charge spread out from her chest, evenly distributing it throughout her body. "Th-thank you, Dr. Mason."

"Just don't make me regret it," the goat sighed, adjusting his collar. "No testing until tomorrow, to help you get used to the feeling. I had to argue for *that* too, but your classes are still on for today."

"Had to convince the 'big lug' to be patient?" Tammy asked, smirking as she walked brusquely over and yanked the cord from the Dampener, barely giving Volta time to react.

"*Please* don't make a habit of repeating that. The man is terrifying enough when he decides he has to make a point. I don't want to see him angry."

Volta pulled her shirt back on, enjoying the feeling of the passive current in the air she breathed. She excused herself and hurried out of the lab, eager to put as much distance between her and wherever Tullis had gone as possible.

She didn't have to wait long to find out what the Great Dane had meant by "increasing the standards" for her instruction. The next period was hand to hand combat, overseen by Mr. Olson — an army discharge with the loudest voice of anyone in the facility. The wiry bear was always intense, but today he spent a lot more time directing his attention on the wolf.

"Travers, widen your stance!" Olson shouted, just as her sparring partner kicked one shin to throw her off balance. "You gotta be willing to get hit in the balls, trainee, don't be a bitch about it."

"Ye-yes sir!" Volta shouted back as she blocked a kick, her cheeks reddening.

"You're a Texas hero, not a divorced mother taking karate classes," he chided. "And you sound like a nine year old, stammering like that."

Volta's face burned as she dodged another blow from her sparring partner; she returned with three rapid jabs that landed against his guarding arms.

Olson immediately spoke up. "Was that a punch, Travers? McGarrett didn't even stiffen up. The fuck have you been doing for exercise? Are you sure that Bradley Group fossil wasn't looking for somebody else? Evans, come switch with Travers, he just wants to play *pattycake*. Show him how to throw a fucking punch."

The taller, burlier lion — Olson's *favorite* student, no less — strode over with only a brief glance in Volta's direction. She couldn't tell if it was dismissive or derisive, she still shrank back out of his view as Olson paired her with someone else. Olson always used Evans to demonstrate proper form — *especially* to demonstrate how Volta was doing things wrong. She had never spoken to him or any of their other classmates before, just because the irritable bear leading the class ensured she never wanted to stick around. Today would be no different, the last thing she wanted to do was get admonished or ridiculed by anybody *else*, if she could help it.

If it wasn't her punches, it was her stance; if not her stance, her reflexes. Nothing she did was right, and Olson rode her that much harder for every other mistake. She left the period like she had left the most recent test: sweaty, exhausted, and wound up, heart thumping in her chest as she became intensely aware of her body.

All the derision from Olson reverberated in Volta's head as she hurried back to her dorm. Could she really do this? She was supposed to be halfway done with her training, but Olson made her feel like she hadn't learned a thing. There was a lump in her throat by the time she'd reached her door.

You can't even handle a drill instructor busting your balls. Tullis knows you're not a real man, and you're definitely not worth the effort — that's why he got Olson to single you out. Probably didn't even need to convince him, you can't even hold the right stance without shaking like a scared little kid.

Her internal dialogue was starting to sound like the bear, too. She immediately stripped and stepped into the shower, water running hot.

She put her head under the stream, trying as hard as she could to stop thinking, to just forget her arms trembling, her heart thumping against the Dampener. If she spent long enough, maybe she could forget herself for a moment. Forget what she looked like, what she had, and what she didn't have. She just had to focus on the water hitting her face.

Half an hour passed, and Volta found herself sitting on her bed, glaring red-eyed at her favorite poster on her wall. There had been a bigger one, initially, with the TPA logo and some generic slogan. She'd replaced it with a poster she'd brought from home, of True North II. Arthur Simonds, her inspiration — the man made her want to become a hero in the first place. The confident smile and twinkle in his eye seemed so bright. He looked proud of himself, happy to be there. Nowadays, Defense Minister Arthur Simonds didn't necessarily look the part anymore — any article with a photo of him always had him looking tired as hell, but that poster was still there, a reminder just for Volta.

Her parents had always complained about her not picking an American hero to idolize. This "Canadian Stuntman," as they put it, didn't even have any superpowers, but that was why she loved him. The only name recognition he had had was that of his father before him, and otherwise he had made a name for himself: helping people all on his own throughout Canada since late adolescence, fighting dozens of villains and even giving the Overlord — the *Overlord* — a run for his money. Two decades of active hero work, being the best he could possibly be, how could she not idolize him?

She remembered vividly the days she spent running around the family home in a True North II costume, repeating catchphrases and quips she'd memorized from the news footage, comics and videos that still circulated. She was still in that costume when her powers surfaced, causing every lightbulb in the foyer to blow out. It had scared her initially, but she was ecstatic when she realized she had superpowers, and so were Mom and Dad. She'd be the first super in the family. Maybe she really could be a hero, she thought — a hero like him.

And now, here you are, second-guessing yourself again. Looking at an old poster of someone who didn't even need any powers to be special. Are you really up to this, or are you just lying to yourself?

She laid back on her bed and stared at the ceiling, willing away the urge to start crying again. She'd been doing that a lot lately; normally she had it under better control, but with the Dampener getting shut off for the test, and now Tullis all but guaranteeing to make all her classes worse... She needed something to take her mind off things. For even a moment, just a simple —

Oh, duh. I just got some charge back.

She raised one hand, and with only a little effort, had gently buzzing blue arcs jumping between her fingers. She turned her hand slowly, watching one travel up between her middle and forefinger — a miniature Jacob's Ladder, just for her.

It wasn't much, but it *was* a reminder of how far she'd come. When she first got enrolled in the TPA, her mother had tearfully recounted to President Richardson the dangers of having an untrained super at home, how much destruction and panic Volta had caused for the family, for any visitors, how she worried it would make her "sweet, simple, Jesus-loving son" into a rabid lowlife. Richardson ate it up.

Of course she'd left out the nights without dinner, how she'd scream and hit you, lock you in the closet with the lights off, and lest we forget Dad's belt...

So, the Dampener had been built, and had been presented to Volta on the first day. Dr. Mason had said it was, ultimately, part of her training regimen. Tried to assure her it would be for the best, in spite of how it felt to go without any charge for extended periods of time. First it was only every other day, then it was two days, three, four, a week, two weeks, until, a year in, she'd only get her charge back for tests and training.

But she'd gotten a little back, today. Enough to entertain herself, like she once had as a kid. The sparks and arcs crawling over her hand gave her a feeling that was warm, almost ticklish. It made it easy to smile, and think back, past the nights without supper, to the days when she'd read through her stack of *True North, True Stories* comic books, and wonder what her super suit might look like as True North's sidekick — or maybe even a hero all by herself.

She'd had so many hero names in mind, that sounded *so cool* to her at that age: *The Frightening Texas Lightning! True North the Fourth! Wonder Thunder!* Eight year old Austin Travers was proud of the rhymes, but eventually, twelve year old Volta wanted something more dignified.

She sat up, and experimentally bared her claws. The blue electricity danced from the sharp tips into her palm, and more still leapt between them. She raised her other hand and lit it up with blue sparks as well. She tried bridging the two, turning her palms towards one another as she willed current into them. Nothing happened, but the Dampener suddenly felt very cold; she was hitting her charge limit. She frowned and brought her palms closer together.

In an instant, a thick bright blue arc connected them, curling and jittering excitedly. The buzz was much louder. *More fun that way.* Volta grinned; it was a lot easier to avoid spiraling when you were your own personal plasma ball.

She breathed out, and eventually pulled her hands apart again. The arc connecting them stretched and broke, and as she let her charge recede back into her body, the blue lightning dancing over her hands dissipated. The second-guessing wasn't gone, but at least she could slow down and think about it rationally. A year ago, she was making lightbulbs explode, blowing holes through walls, blacking out parts of whatever building she was in. If she wasn't violently discharging, she was sucking current up. At the very least, now, she could consistently wield it. Mason and the instructors were career hardasses but even they had to know what they were doing for it to work.

Now if only it didn't mean I had to wear this thing.

She glared down at the Dampener again. The last time she'd gotten it taken off was… at least a month ago, right? She was struggling to remember. Carmen had seemed so interested in it, one of the few people who had, in spite of never seeing it. Volta normally got really self-conscious when people looked at her chest, especially with the Dampener there, but the tabby's fascination didn't bother her as much.

…Why didn't it? Surely it wasn't just because Carmen was so eager to talk to Volta about how she felt. She thought back to when they were walking to their lunch table yesterday. Carmen's bright amber eyes, slits wide in the middling indoor lighting, had been intent on the red wolf's chest. The taller cat peering down at her was already one thing, but…

God, she *was* taller, wasn't she? She was definitely more than six feet, yet somehow Carmen managed to make it look natural, totally normal, if you didn't think about it too hard. It was hardly normal to see a girl like that around here. She was so unusual, so new, so… pretty. Volta's mind jumped, suddenly, to another image of Carmen peering down at her. Not a memory. Those amber eyes had thinned to slits. The way her lips curled upward when she smiled was unforgettable, like a waxing moon.

Tabbies had stripes. Carmen had black ones; they were visible on her arms. Like rungs on a ladder.

You'd need a ladder to climb someone that big. Ha. You don't want to be the one doing the climbing, though, do you?

Volta laid back, suddenly aware of how warm the room was getting. She stared up at the ceiling, taking a deep breath and feeling her heart suddenly beating *much* faster. She could easily steer her thinking elsewhere. She didn't really want to. It had been a while since she'd bothered to get off, what was a little stress relief before lunch?

Carmen certainly had stripes, dark brown on her face and hands, and light brown on her neck. All the way down to her underbelly, probably. The cat's figure was so… pronounced. Her lab coat, shirts, and pants had not hidden that in the slightest. Volta felt her face get hot, as her imaginary Carmen peeled her lab coat off, staring intently at Volta.

Her family may have tried their best to instill an understanding of the sanctity of marriage in Volta, but that had not stopped the wolf from googling a *lot* of things, nor from filling that folder on her laptop. She had plenty of pictures to refer back to when it came to imagining what Carmen looked like.

She could easily picture the tall, curvaceous tabby standing — no, *kneeling* over her. On top of her, a big cat pinning her prey. Those soft hands that had gripped Volta's shoulder caressing her face, claws extended and gently brushing against her cheek. She tried to imagine how it would feel to have Carmen pinning her, holding her there, touching her, petting her, pressing against her…

Volta felt a sudden strain in a *very* familiar location, and the image in her head evaporated. Her erection was pulling at her pants at an uncomfortable angle. She glanced down, and instantly became aware of her body again. Flat-chested as ever, narrow hips, low body fat. Hardly any bulk, but her shape was still decidedly rectangular. Her hard-on was visible through her pants, rigid and starting to ache.

Ugh, you again, standing at the ready when no one asked you to.

Who was she kidding? How would anyone glance even briefly at her like this, and mistake her for anything other than a guy? Just a college boy, fantasizing about a hot girl he'd met. The mood was gone, replaced with disgust.

Volta groaned, and as she sat up again, realized one of her hands had been gripping at the bedsheets. She had *really liked* thinking about that, short-lived as it was, but then her genitalia had to go and… *extend.*

Extend for what? I don't want it, I don't want to use it. I just want Carmen to do… something. Do what?

Now came the guilt. Volta's face was burning, her pants were tented awkwardly, and she couldn't have felt more like a freak. Carmen was *gorgeous,* and witty, and unafraid to speak her mind. She hardly needed a sheepish little pervert who hated the body she'd been stuck with, much less someone who cried as much as Volta had in the single day they'd known each other.

Frustrated, Volta growled and stood back up. In the absence of arousal she was getting hungry anyway, and a quick glance at the clock on her nightstand told her she'd be late. She had *hoped* this lunch with Carmen would be less anxiety-inducing, and ideally wouldn't end with her crying. Now, she was dead certain it was going to be worse.

How the fuck do you talk calmly to someone you just fantasized about being naked, and pinning you to the floor? Oh, easy. You just complain about your awful day to them instead.

"Hold up," the tabby held up her fork, her brow knitted as she finished chewing. "So, President Richardson just, does whatever Tullis asks?"

Volta nodded. "Every time Tullis wants something, he gets it."

"Why should he? I've seen the guy, there's no way he just asks him nicely, but he's just the security chief. Richardson could fire him."

"Tullis was also the Golden Gavel," the wolf explained. "Y'know. Part of the Color Guard, former Bradley Group representative… He knows a lot of people and has a lot of pull." Volta shrugged as she stuck more stew on her fork. "My parents know him… Really well, actually."

"Your parents know a lot of people, too?"

"Yeah, they're probably why I'm here in the first place. They know President Richardson's family. Probably almost every part of TPA leadership, too…" Volta poked roughly at her bowl, her jaw set. "They make sure to get to know everybody with a reputation, especially if…"

"Especially if… *you're* going to be around them?" Carmen finished.

"…Yeah, how did you guess?"

The tabby shrugged. "I got parents like yours, remember? They, uh, might not have so much money, but they have the attitude. They were overprotective of anything that's theirs — that included me. Sound familiar?"

"*Mmn…*" Volta hummed noncommittally, nodding her head side to side. "A little, but do you mean they don't anymore? What wound up stopping them?"

"*Ha*, well, moving out helped a bit, but…" Carmen sat up a little straighter, and took on a proud smirk as she puffed her chest out. "What got them off my back was not taking any more of their shit. One too many arguments, and I decided I was done."

Volta's curiosity was piqued. What might work to get *hers* off her back? "Arguments about… what? Uh. You don't have to answer, if that's prying too much."

"Not at all!" She looked even *more* proud, but lowered her volume, leaning in conspiratorially as she set down her utensils. Her gaze was nonetheless firm, and decisive. Her amber eyes blazed as she spoke. "Simple, straw broke the camel's back; I wanted to keep kissing girls, and Mom hated that. I told her to go get hit by a bus and walked right out."

Volta was frozen, unable to take her gaze off Carmen's. Several seconds passed, where she struggled to find something to say. "J-just like that?"

"Just like that. Been my own woman from that point onward." Carmen leaned back again, flashing a sharp-toothed grin. "I mean it wasn't a *cakewalk*, and I'm still trying to get my brother to pull his head out of his ass, but I wouldn't go back. Not even at gunpoint."

Volta was barely able to focus on Carmen's response. Her brain felt like it had been immersed in molasses — she was stuck on a specific thought.

Kissing girls. Carmen likes to kiss girls. She left her family behind because she liked kissing girls so much. What if you were a girl? A kissable girl, right?

Hey, you haven't said anything for twenty seconds — because you were thinking about the fact that CARMEN LIKES TO KISS GIRLS.

Volta's mouth suddenly felt very dry, as she tried to remember how to speak. "I… I can't imagine talking to my family like that… or leaving them behind completely."

Carmen shrugged. "It took a while getting there, but. I wasn't going to let anyone decide what I did or who I was. I kept the people who supported me, and I dropped the ones who didn't. Best decision I ever made." She picked her fork back up and made a show of twirling it around in her fingers, before stabbing another chunk of stew and popping it in her mouth.

Volta stared, her gaze keen on Carmen's hand as it so casually flipped the fork around — and then on the proud, satisfied look on her face. The tabby's lidded gaze met Volta's, and her smirk came back, showing a thin glint of teeth. She tilted her head up, pointing her fork nonchalantly at Volta. "S'cuze me, but do you always get that red in the face when a girl talks about kissing other girls, Volta?"

The wolf tried to speak. All that came out were disjointed, panicked syllables. "Wha — I ju — th —"

Oh no. Help. What do I do? I need to run away. Surely getting up and running out of the cafeteria is an acceptable response, right? She's still looking at me. She's looking and smiling and — SHE'S SO PRETTY WHAT DO I D —

BZZJT

A sharp crack of electricity suddenly jumped from Volta's hand to her fork, and then struck her dish. Volta jumped back, her hand smacking her waterglass over. Before Volta had time to recover, Carmen reached out and grabbed the glass, allowing only a small splatter over her hand and the table.

Volta was red as a beet and dropped her fork with a clatter. "S-sorry, sorry!"

"It's fine!" Carmen laughed, holding the glass up. "I didn't mean to startle you! It's just a little water, Volta, really."

"I'm *supposed* to have better control over it than that." Volta balled up her fists as she chastised herself, terrified to touch anything else. Her face felt like it was on fire. "I've been at this for a year, god…"

Stop talking. Do you want to constantly sound this pathetic around her?

Carmen was still laughing and held her hands up in a consoling gesture. "It's not a big deal, is it? You only just got the Dampener adjusted after, what, how long?"

Volta hung her head, averting her eyes as her heartbeat began to race. "Not even a week. The last test was *two days ago* and I —" She realized she was raising her voice, and cut herself off, her jaw set.

"Hey, Volta." Carmen was leaning forward again. That same sympathetic look was back on her face. "If anything, *I'm* sorry for pointing that out. I didn't realize you'd *fire off* like that. Don't be so hard on yourself, you just shocked your lunch. It's okay." She hazarded a little grin. "I mean, I thought it was a *little* cold, myself, so maybe it's an improvement."

Volta let out a halfhearted snort and slumped against the back of her chair again. She tried to smile, but she still felt uncomfortably hot. She was still blushing, hard. "Well, it wouldn't take much. The cafeteria's set a really low bar."

Carmen giggled again. The sound was so chime-like and made it a little easier to keep grinning. Even in the midst of her brain still wanting to berate her, Carmen's tirelessly cheery face somehow managed to take her attention away from it, just a little.

They went back to eating for several minutes, which gave Volta's nerves a chance to settle before the cat spoke up again.

"That reminds me, actually. If you don't mind my asking: what does your training usually look like? How much do you think is gonna end up changing?"

"Well, it's supposed to be the usual stuff they put everybody through: hand to hand combat, specialized superpower training, counterintelligence, survival training, some legal stuff, drills…" Volta took another bite, thinking as she chewed. Guaranteed, Tullis would make sure the rest of her training was "up to scratch," as he'd probably put it. She could feel her face falling as she swallowed. "I'm probably gonna be working a lot harder, now."

Carmen was silent for a moment, tapping her fingers on her chin. "Would it help if you had someone to practice with? I mean like, extra sparring lessons, something a little more relaxed?"

"I — Really? You can do that? Do you, u-uh… know how to fight?"

"*Hell yeah*, I do! Just because I've got the lab coat, glasses, and STEM education doesn't mean I haven't earned a few belts. Bet I could be a better teacher than that Olson guy."

Well, that wouldn't necessarily be *hard*, given what she'd measure against. Volta hesitated nonetheless.

"Of course, it's no problem if you're not up for it. If you're getting a full plate I wouldn't impose, anyway." Carmen shrugged and went back to eating.

Sparring with Carmen? She already felt so self-conscious in front of classmates. The cat was so tall, compared to her… Volta took a moment to regard her, in her lab coat, blouse and glasses, quietly enjoying the last of her stew. Was she as athletic as she was tall? Unbidden, Volta's earlier mental image of Carmen suddenly gained several pounds of muscle. Still soft, but firm in all the right places…

She shifted in her seat, squeezing her legs together. She *really* didn't need to be thinking about this right now. Carmen glanced up from her drink, and clearly saw exactly what was on Volta's face. She grinned again, quizzical. "Volta? You feeling okay?"

Shitshitshitshit —

"J-just fine!" Volta squeaked. "Just thinking. About yo-your offer. For extra practice." She bowed her head and stuffed stew into her mouth to make sure she didn't say anything else. Well, at least she hadn't zapped anything, but her heart thumped in her chest nonetheless. It suddenly occurred to the wolf that spending time sparring with Carmen… would entail more time with Carmen.

"Actually, yeah. I'd like to. I could use the practice, uh, so long as you're offering!"

"Great! I happen to know the public gym is pretty empty this time of the week." She shrugged. "S'why I brought it up. They've got sparring mats and everything there."

"Y-yeah! I know them. I can change into exercise wear and be there in, uh, an hour? 1 PM?" Volta hazarded.

"Sounds good to me!" The tabby stood up, her tray clear. "And, hey, don't fret too much about this. I'm not gonna crack the whip — you already got Olson for that, it sounds like."

"No kidding… I, um. I appreciate it." Volta stood as well, wondering if she sounded too sheepish.

"Oh, of course!" Carmen was beaming. "I'm happy to do it. I like helping folks in need, even if it's just sparring. Besides, I talked enough about *me* during lunch. I want to hear about *you* later."

"S-sure, sounds great!" Volta waved as she walked away. There was that blush, again. Carmen was way too good at bringing that out.

The public gym complex and fitness center across campus was a place Volta already knew about — every hero trainee did. She was expected to maintain a level of fitness and muscle mass on par with Marine cadets and had bulked up as much as her wiry frame would allow. She had tried to keep *some* body fat; she didn't need to see her own six pack — the Dampener was bad enough.

Volta had ducked back into her dorm and threw off the usual tee and pants, in exchange for an exercise tank and shorts. She did everything she could to resist looking in the mirror — she didn't need a reminder of how she looked in *boys'* exercise clothes.

Most of the hour was burned away scrolling through Twitter, watching a handful of cooking videos a tweet had referred her to. Until, of course, she stumbled back onto the accounts of relatives. She knew she wasn't going to find anything good, but… her cousin had a way with words, and so did his favorite news source.

> *It's days like these when you really have to wonder what direction this country is going in. First all these new laws about Diversity, now the LGBT agenda attacking US citizens. For the crime of stating their opinion, of course. Guess which group of Inclusivity-First Terrorists is backing them up!*
> — **@TheRealGaryP** *11:00, 623 replies, 809 retweets, 1.5k likes*

That on its own didn't make Volta shiver, though. Not like her cousin's response just below it.

If you ask me, we need to start rounding up anyone threatening free speech, especially people like that. Our kids are in danger. We boys in blue won't stand for it much longer. We need to clean them out before they get any more entrenched!
— @**ThinBlueLupine** *11:05, 111 replies, 65 retweets, 40 likes*

Right, Cousin Jordan *was* in the police; ridiculously proud of it, too. Volta was glad she hadn't seen him at family gatherings for the past year. That branch of the family wasn't nearly so wealthy, but they held the same kind of views as Mom and Dad.

A couple of the responses were pretty critical. One was from someone with a transgender pride flag in their avatar. Her cousin had responded, asking them how close they were to "joining the percentage."

She slammed her laptop shut, fuming. That was her family; that was the person that Mom and Dad had called "brave and selfless" when he'd graduated from the Dallas Police Academy. Cousin Jordan was a stand-up kind of guy. Volta felt sick again.

She got up, turned around, and flopped onto her bed, burying her face in the covers as she took deep, frustrated breaths. She wanted to yell or scream or… something, to calm down. There was no way she could go to spend time with Carmen like this, with her thoughts running away from her again.

And you're still the fuckup. You're the one who almost blew up the house. If they knew about you — about what you think, and what you are… What would they do? You can guess. Have you checked the time?

Volta started, jerking her head out from the sheets and looking at the digital clock on her nightstand: 1:10 PM.

Shit! SHIT —

She leapt out of bed, panic stirring in her belly. She'd left Carmen waiting, just sitting there feeling bad for herself. She bolted down the dorm hallway and tried to ignore the horrible needling goosebumps she was breaking into. Surely the cat would wait for her, right?

"So, he'd need convincing, is what you're saying," Wren remarked. "I'm getting the impression this kid thinks we're just as bad as the media portrays us."

"He knows we're the 'bad guys,' and he's pretty set on becoming a superhero. Like, lifelong dream, stars-in-his-eyes sort of thing. He pretty clearly wants the family off his back — which, having talked to Mom and Dad a little, I can understand why. Plenty of money and scared of seeing too much ankle, you know, like your folks."

"*Ha*, that would explain the kid's skepticism."

"There's another thing," Carmen spoke with more hesitance. "…And this part shouldn't go on file. Yet."

Wren took an extra second to respond as he took another handful of popcorn. "Got it, transcriber's off. Just you, me, and the lady in magenta."

"He wants to go by 'Volta,' and I'm getting some hints that he's struggling with aspects of his identity."

Wren's next swallow was audible. "Uh, is it anything you can poke at without overstepping?"

"Not yet. This wolf is *way* too scared about letting it show. I don't know what stage it's at — if it's at a *stage* at all. Of course I didn't pry too much, but it's clearly hurting him that he can't talk about any of it."

"So, what's the plan moving forward? Obviously, you don't want to push 'em too much, but…"

The tabby looked down at her lap and frowned. Maybe this was veering into a place where she couldn't be impartial. But, she reminded herself, she wasn't doing this kind of thing because she *wanted* to be impartial. This was a recruitment effort — as much as it was analysis and surveillance.

She breathed deep and straightened back up, determined. "I'm going to be someone Volta can talk to — someone to trust. It'll be easy…" she clenched one fist, digging her claws into her palm. "I'll be the one person around him who knows *exactly* what it's like."

CHAPTER 4

DANCE PRACTICE

She sped through the gym complex doors a few minutes later, already panting as her eyes hurriedly scanned the lobby for any sign of the tabby. The lobby was empty, save for a bored desk clerk. They didn't even say anything as Volta ran past them through the doors on the right.

Oh, good. She's still here.

…Oh no. She's still here.

Past the rows of punching bags and ellipticals was the tabby, leaning on one side of a grappling ring and fiddling with something in her hands. She looked up as Volta ran towards her, and her unreadable expression turned bright.

"Hey! Lose track of time or something?"

"Yeah, a bit, sorry…" Volta panted, finally coming to a stop and catching her breath. Then she took a moment to register what Carmen was wearing.

A tight, *tight* exercise top with no sleeves held back what was easily far more of a bosom than Volta had ever seen on *anyone* in the facility. Her breasts took up so much room… How had Volta not noticed? How was she able to *breathe* in a top that tight? They had to have been nearly as large as her head, held firm to her body.

Even in the restraining clothing, they squished a little as Carmen held up her hands and adjusted the straps on a pair of fingerless grappling gloves. She took a moment to flex her arm and hand, testing the tightness of the gloves. Her firm, toned biceps bulged as she did it. Volta couldn't help but stare, at a loss for words.

Athletic but… but huge?? She's HUGE. How. What. Where did those come from? Where did SHE come from?

Then Volta's gaze traveled downward. Had she just not been paying attention before? She had recognized the cat was big and curvaceous, but her hips were bafflingly wide, and her thighs filled out the legs of her exercise shorts to the point of tautness. The muscles there were obvious, too. The muscles *everywhere* were obvious, as was the body fat. She was built like an hourglass-shaped tank, but still looked so soft. *Everything* had to stretch to fit her, but she looked perfectly comfortable.

"Hey, Earth to Volta." Carmen's voice snapped the wolf back to the present, and she looked sheepishly back up at the tabby's face. She grinned and put her gloved hands on her hips. Her wide, *wide* hips.

"I appreciate the admiration, but I didn't bring you here just to sightsee!"

"I —" There had to have been some sort of record for how many times Volta was turning red in a single day. "I-I'm sorry, I shouldn't — I've just never *seen* a girl who —"

"Who's got muscle, and still has *these?*" Carmen gestured emphatically at her chest, making it bounce. How the hell was it *bouncing* in a top that tight? "Don't feel bad, I get *plenty* of stares from people *way* less nice than you."

"I… I still shouldn't be just. Gawking at you. It's really rude and I'm really sor —"

"According to who? Your *parents?* I just said it was okay, who else is gonna care?"

"I-I guess so?" Guilt still gnawed at the wolf. It felt like she'd swallowed a bunch of hot coals.

"Listen, if you were some random dickhead who decided to whistle and catcall, that's one thing. You're being *anything* but a dick right now. In my case, I *want* this body to be admired, it took a lot of work! You're not doing anything creepy; you go ahead and admire me *all you like.*" Carmen's tail swished as she turned towards the mat, her hips swaying a little more than usual.

"Don't worry, I won't tell anyone… But you *do* still have to get on the mat and spar with me."

"Uh, right! Yeah."

Volta hurried over to the bench nearby — where she saw the same shirt Carmen had been wearing earlier, plus her shoes. As she took hers off, she glanced back up at Carmen, who was on the mat doing a series of arm stretches.

Volta took a breath, trying to find something else to say. *Just pretend you weren't ogling her like a dehydrated dog. Thank god you didn't start drooling, too.*

"Hey… Did you have, like, something more specific in mind? For this? And, uh, how much martial arts training do you have, anyway?"

Carmen bent, touching her toes before straightening up and responding. "Well, I did say I wanted to hear more about you, but I guess I *can* brag a little. Let's see… Kenpo, Muay Thai, Aikido, Kajukenbo, Judo, Taekwondo…" She counted them off on her fingers. "Couple more I'm not as well-versed in. Just two black belts, out of all of those."

"Y-you're kidding."

Carmen grinned teasingly, before raising one leg, grasping the underside of her huge thigh with one hand. "You think I got this figure just being a research student?"

"I —" Volta was trying extremely hard to maintain eye contact as she stood back up. She really did not need to start walking funny now — her jockstrap made things uncomfortable already. "W-well, I just —"

"If you don't believe me, I can bring you to my room and show you my belt collection~"

"Nnnno, no no no thank *you that'sfinethanks!*" The wolf averted her gaze as Carmen laughed.

"Sorry, sorry, let's focus. Do you need to stretch at all?"

"I-I think I'm plenty loose! Uh. R-relaxed!"

Carmen snorted. "I'm serious. Take a second, really. Gives me time to finish my routine, too."

"I-if you say so, but, I'm sure I'm okay!" She sounded anything but. A second to *relax?* How was she supposed to relax while Carmen was RIGHT THERE, doing her stretches? The cat leaned forward, bending one knee, stretching her other leg out behind her. The muscles in her legs visibly tensed and bulged as she leaned, then switched legs. The cat let out a high-pitched sigh as she stood up straight again, and then bent over, stretching her back as she spread her legs wide…

I… I want to be like that. She's beautiful. She's powerful. She looks so amazing… How could anyone NOT want what she has? What she IS?

Oh god. Heart's racing again. I'm burning up. Take a fucking second and slow down, you little creep. You're gonna embarrass yourself even worse than you already have if you don't.

She took a deep breath, stretching her arms and gently twisting her back. She needed to focus, or she might say something she'd regret. Carmen was already being so nice to her, after, what, two days? It would be just as well if Volta messed it up now because she couldn't stop staring.

"Okay, yeah, I needed that," Volta sighed. "S-sorry. It's… it's been a long day."

"I'll bet! Don't worry, though, we're gonna keep this short — your earlier class sounds like it was exhausting enough anyway." Carmen pointed in front of her. "Step onto the mat when you're ready. I want you to show me what you've got."

"O-okay…" Volta did as she asked, shifting her weight from foot to foot as she took a position a good six feet from the cat.

All right, do what you just did in class. You've done this for a year.

They faced one another, and Carmen led with a bow. Volta bowed a second later, feeling intensely aware of herself.

Carmen must have picked up on it as she straightened up again. "Take it easy, Volta. Just respectful sparring, no pressure. Go ahead and drop into your stance."

One foot in front, the other in the back and to the side, knees bent. The wolf raised her fists, hoping she looked even remotely like she belonged there. Her claws dug into her palms.

Carmen mirrored her feet, but had only one hand raised, the other was at her side. She bounced on the tips of her feet, feline toes flexing to accommodate the weight. She looked sturdy, but still limber. She looked right at home.

Of course she does. She wasn't kidding about the belts, was she? You're going to try and spar with someone who can… probably kill you with her bare hands. LOOK at her she's RIPPED.

Volta hesitated, fidgeting a little in the middle of her stance. The tabby raised an eyebrow. "You always look this tense when you get on the mat in Olson's class, Volta? Don't forget to breathe — your shoulders are all bunched up."

Volta's ears drooped. "H-he says I get slack easy!"

"Never mind what he says, listen to me. Just breathe out, let your shoulders down. Keep your flexibility."

Volta inhaled and exhaled, feeling her neck suddenly un-knot as she relaxed her shoulders a little. She hadn't realized how hunched she'd been — her head felt *way* easier to turn now.

"Much better already. Mind your legs don't get too tense. Here, watch me." Carmen began to hop in place, switching her leg positions with each other. She looked as light and quick as any boxer.

A boxer with large, bouncy — Oh god no I'm staring again. Focus! Focus.

"Keep an eye on my hips and stomach, here," Carmen spoke as she continued to demonstrate. "I'm keeping them even, my balance is at my core, and my arms aren't out too far, so I can move my legs as much as I like."

"You make it look so easy…"

"I've got four years of this on you, Volta, of course it's easy for me!" Carmen's tone was teasing, but gentle. That smile was just as bright as ever, encouraging the wolf to relax. "Just hop a little. Switch which leg is in front, like I'm doing. Don't worry about getting your feet in the right place every time — what matters more is keeping flexible and agile. Quick on your feet."

Volta did as Carmen told, keeping an eye on her paws as she did so. It was hard not to feel self-conscious — a lot of this was stuff that was covered a *little* at the start of last year. She wasn't so behind that even Carmen was treating her like a newbie, was she? At the very least no one was around to see.

"There you go! You're doing great. Don't forget to keep breathing! Your shoulders are hunched again." Carmen's tone stayed gentle, but she looked more insistent. "Relax! Look, I know you think this might be silly."

"I-I don't think it's silly!"

"Maybe like you're retreading things meant for beginners, then?"

"Well…"

"Maybe they didn't do a good job of teaching it the first time. Maybe you couldn't listen so well, that first time." The cat inhaled slowly, as if to demonstrate. "Deep breaths, it's just us here. I'm not judging you a bit for this."

The wolf's face heated up again, like clockwork. "But you thought I needed to start over," she mumbled.

Oh god, listen to you. Good thing Olson and your classmates AREN'T here. They'd laugh their asses off.

"Volta, this is *not* starting over." Carmen's voice was suddenly firm, startling Volta out of her thoughts. She stood there, frozen by the tabby's stern expression. "I'm helping you review some stuff — maybe stuff you didn't get a chance to learn right the first time." The cat's tone and face softened considerably again. "Listen, Volta, you can't measure yourself *just* by where the school, or Tullis, or even your *parents* want you. Are any of those people here right now?"

"Well, no..." She muttered sheepishly, bowing her head.

"There you go then! It's just you, me, and this nice mat we're standing on. You got a good basis; you just need a little touching up!"

"I-if you say so!"

"I *do*. Now, c'mon. Get into your stance, switch your feet." Carmen started up again, and Volta followed suit. "Good, good. Light on your feet, easy and flexible. Keep your arms up, let's get some space..."

She began to step towards the center of the mat, beckoning the wolf to follow. The entire time she maintained her stance, her legs creeping along without a sound. Her tail lagged a little, keeping a curl near the tip as it held up, out of the way of her legs. Volta tried to follow suit — becoming aware of how much noise her own footsteps made against the mat.

"Eyes on me, right on my face," the tabby reminded, beckoning with her low hand. "All right. I got you warmed up a little, show me what you've got. Try and hit me."

"You sure?"

"Nothing below the belt, just at my center. Throw some punches, try and get around if you can't get through." Carmen held out a hand, beckoning her forward, with the barest hint of a smirk playing on her lips. "C'mon and land a punch — if you can. I'll be responding in kind~"

What are you waiting for, another invitation?

Volta maneuvered forward and aimed three jabs straight ahead. Olson's training had some merit, she knew how to throw a punch without hurting herself — and how to feint, a little bit. Carmen blocked the first two and weaved to the left of the third. Her own fist sped forward, and Volta dodged to the right.

"That's it! That's it," Carmen encouraged as she turned to block, and Volta tried, too late, to sneak a right hook in. "Light on your feet, circle around me. Get out of my cone of vision." Another playful smirk.

Another exchange of jabs, another weave; this time Volta feinted, swapping her leg stance as she began to lean to the right, then ducked to the left, aiming a hook at Carmen's side.

Before she could react, the tabby had mirrored her dodge, and the wolf's fist was batted upward by Carmen's shin, as her leg came up in a kick. She curled it up as Volta tried to recover, and then struck her — much gentler than she was expecting — against her torso. The softness of Carmen's kick was jarring with how fast it had come up, but there was still enough force to shove her stumbling back.

"Good try! You okay?" Carmen asked as she stood straight again. She was smiling, but her eyes were keen on Volta's face. Was she watching for a certain reaction?

"Fine! I'm fine." A little heat on her face was nothing new around this cat, at this point. "Let's keep going."

"That's the spirit! C'mon, show me some kicks. Those legs are long, good for getting them up real high."

Volta felt a stirring of butterflies, even as she dropped back into her stance. She had to force her tail to not start wagging. Her legs weren't anything special, why was Carmen talking about them so... *nice* to hear?

Trying to stay quick, she obliged. Four more jabs to get her blocking, and then Volta aimed a straight kick at Carmen's exposed stomach. Once more, Carmen dodged, but this time straight back. One hand came down, to just lightly knock Volta's foot to the side, forcing her to wobble as she struggled to regain balance.

"*Nice*. I was expecting a high kick when I said that, guess you didn't take the bait~"

"O-oh, sorry!" Volta lowered her guard for a moment.

"Arms up, arms up! No need to apologize, I like you deviating. That's how you beat your opponent, Volts."

The wolf stopped dead in her tracks, eyes wide. "V-Volts?"

"Oh, ah…" Carmen gave a little shrug. "I figured it might be a cute nickname. I can stick with calling you Volta if you'd prefer, though, no pressure! I like it a lot already~"

"I — oh…"

A nickname. A nickname for Volta. She… she likes my name!

"N-no, no I like it!" Volta blurted out, intensely aware of how hot she was getting. Her tail wagged furiously behind her. "I'm… fine with you calling me Volts. You're, uh, the only one who calls me Volta, anyway."

"In that case, *Volts*, get your guard back up — we're not done yet!"

They resumed with surprising ease. Carmen kept encouraging Volta to be aggressive, to initiate, keep up pressure, and use that pressure to get around blocks. The tabby always had a bit of advice to give, but it was never too much at once. One thing at a time, building things up.

In any of the time Volta had ever spent learning under Olson, she had rarely felt confident in her martial arts skills. In just the past 25 minutes, Volta had started to feel far surer of herself on the mat than she ever had before. Carmen took the time to compliment the wolf on every improvement and highlight every success, no matter how minor. She made sure to emphasize how integral every step was to winning a fight — a *real* fight.

Mistakes were addressed, but not dwelled on. Carmen offered viable solutions, explained at a pace that Olson probably would have called "remedial." Every short round was an opportunity to learn something.

Volta let Carmen jab at her, turning to the side to let her straight brush past her face — allowing just enough of an opening for Volta to get a shot in on Carmen's shoulder. The tabby bent, swinging both arms around to deflect the blow — just in time for Volta to aim a controlled kick at Carmen's face. She hadn't been expecting Carmen to swing one hand back and grab her by the ankle.

"Ah-ah!" she tutted, then let her leg go. "You're *way* craftier than you made yourself sound."

Volta shrugged bashfully again. "W-well I did watch a *lot* of superhero shows as a kid! Probably just, remember a lot of moves True North II pulled. He was a *really* good boxer, actually." *Oops, that's a lot of extremely specific information to just KNOW about a specific hero. You're gonna overshare in a second.* "I-I, uh, I mean, so I've been told…"

"I'd been wondering about that…" The tabby's tail swished behind her as she relaxed and waved one hand. "That's enough for now, don't you think? Let's go get hydrated — you didn't get out of telling me more about yourself, hm, Volts?"

"S-sure."

Carmen led her off the mat, and back over to the bench where their things lay. As she slipped her shirt back on, she began to ask. "So, I'm just gonna go out and say it: You *really* like Arthur Simonds, huh?"

"Yeah, I do!" She answered without thinking, breaking into a blush. "I — wha?"

"The second True North! *Canada's Tireless Protector*, you know, while he was active anyway. What draws you to him over, like, any heroes from the US?"

"I… Well…" Volta looked down at her shoes, mulling over her words while she tugged her laces over, under, and through. "I guess it's a lot of things. He started early — *really* early and was basically taken care of by Aurora Squadron after his dad died."

"He wasn't even seventeen yet, right?"

"Yeah, but he never lost his momentum. He was surrounded by superheroes — and he still made such a name for himself. No powers, all gadgets and training… He wasn't *trying* to be the best or the most popular, he always just did his best to help people and get really dangerous villains off the streets. He got famous for trying to do the right thing — I guess I just really like that idea."

"I'm sure it helped that his gadgets and moves were super slick, though."

"Oh my gosh *yes* he was the COOLEST." Volta's heart leapt, and she leaned forward excitedly. She never got to talk about this with anyone. *Anyone.*

"He spent HOURS and hours training every day with the first Aurora crew after his dad's death. Developed his own hand-to-hand style, signature moves… and he always dove in, one hundred percent of the time. It was like he thought he was invincible or just, just didn't *care* about himself, just making sure people were okay. Gave every fight his all and put himself in situations you'd NEVER expect someone without powers to walk away from. Like, the old Fenway skyscraper that collapsed when Doctor Audacious set off his infra-resonator and nearly destroyed most of Vancouver? True North II fought the guy on the top floor *while it was falling over* and not only LIVED but WON. Roundhouse kicked the guy into the floor, and he had *such a cool comeback too.*" She put on her best impression of early career Arthur Simonds's dry Ottawa snark. "'Next time you want to drop a building on me, make sure I'm *under* it first!' And he won — against DOCTOR AUDACIOUS — who until he was incarcerated in nineteen ninety —"

Volta finally took a breath, and realized she'd been prattling on like a kid again. She went pink, folded her ears back and very quietly mumbled, "Uh, yeah, he had a lot of — cool signature moves, or... yeah. Sorry."

"What for?"

"I — well. I didn't mean to babble like that, most people — I mean it's not *that* important, not really, he's..." She was making it worse and worse. Her tail hung limp between her legs. Mom or Dad or anybody at high school would have stopped her or just walked away by now. Instead, Carmen was staring at her and smiling so intently.

"Not *important?* Sounds like it's pretty important to you!"

"I mean, a *little,*" she lied again. Why bother? The cat already knew she was a fragile loser with nothing better to do than memorize four-decade-old True North history.

"No, c'mon, be honest. You love this guy — he and everything he did is why you want to be a hero in the first place, yeah?"

"Y-yeah..."

"Well, that's exactly what I asked for. I wanna know more about *you,* Volts, even if you think it's nerdy or embarrassing. Honestly, I'm impressed you know this much about *any* superhero's history — that's usually just saved for Wikipedia articles. And the accent was *precious.* You're like a one-stop-shop for True North knowledge!"

Volta blushed again but there was no mistaking a compliment. She couldn't help her tail starting to wag again, just a little. She muttered, "Well, the wiki entry isn't *entirely* accurate, but they won't let me edit anymore..."

Carmen began to laugh. "Oh, there's gotta be a story there. C'mon, spill."

For the first time in Volta's life, she spilled without a second thought.

"Sounds like Volta's not used to anyone showing *any* interest," Wren remarked through a mouthful of popcorn. "I know the feeling, but in this case, I can't say Aurora's stooges are my type."

Carmen just snorted. "Be happy they're not a fan of some state or PHL shithead. Volta's got some good taste! Honestly, it's adorable hearing 'em go on about it. Their impression of the minister in his prime was *really* good, not even kidding. They lost the Texas twang altogether, sounded like they walked off a movie set in downtown Toronto. They clearly *adore* Arthur, hero career and all."

"Don't let Audrey hear you think that."

"Pfft, she's not listening this far south."

"She could *try*."

"The point is, Volta's really attached to True North II. Their idea of him in his prime is probably a better dad than the one they got, from what we've seen." The tabby leaned back on her bed, flicking her tail. "I get the feeling they're used to their family just handing them True North comics to keep them quiet."

"Oh, great! Volta can join the shitty parents club. I can teach 'em the secret handshake and everything."

"Wren!"

"What? It's not like both of us don't know exactly what neglectful parents are like."

"Yeah, I guess. I don't mind helping Volta work through some of that — if they'll let me."

"I've heard that tone before," Wren sounded almost wary. "You're really starting to care about this wolf."

"So? They make it easy."

"You also defaulted to using they/them."

"I'm glad you went along with it. It's a feeling I've got, figure it's better to keep it ambiguous until we know for certain. I don't think I can ask about it yet, but soon as I know for sure I'll let you know. Look — you caught me, I'm invested at this point. I hope that's not a problem!"

"I just call 'em as I see 'em! And what I see is my coworker-slash-girlfriend getting *really* into an assignment. All the way in, you might say." She could almost hear the bat sticking their tongue out.

"Oh bite me, you little goblin. I want to be friends with Volta, assignment or not. The more we can do for them, the better."

Another day passed, with Carmen meeting Volta after lunch for another sparring session. They never took too long, but Volta felt like she was getting more and more out of each lesson than anything Olson barked at her. It was another work out on top of everything else, and her muscles protested, but as they walked off the mat again, Volta registered just how relaxed and energized she felt. Carmen took the time to point out where Volta had room to grow, but also how her form and movements were getting more refined, even in small ways. She knew how to throw a punch far better than she had two days ago, and the tabby was convinced Olson would lay off that specific point — even if he did find other things to needle at.

Carmen was checking her phone while Volta pulled her shoes back on. She gave another agitated click of the tongue. "You check your email yet?"

"No?"

"Might want to give it a look. I think the TPA's mad about something."

Volta pulled her own phone — and surreptitiously tried to hide the deep purple-striped phone case she'd decorated it with. It was altogether unremarkable, if androgynous accessory, but now around Carmen it felt like far too garish to overlook.

Still trying to hold her hands over the purple stripe, she opened her email app and immediately saw what Carmen meant. Right at the top of her inbox, the subject "URGENT ANNOUNCEMENT FOR FRONTIER ACADEMY" stuck out. She opened it.

ALL TRAINEES AND PERSONNEL:

THIS IS AN URGENT ANNOUNCEMENT FOR
THE FRONTIER HERO ACADEMY CAMPUS.

Multiple Korps-aligned terrorists have been
sighted throughout the city of Austin in the past week.
Correspondents from Bradley Group and the Canadian
government's Aurora Squadron have notified stateside
superhero organizations that they should expect potentially
increased Korps activity throughout the United States.
This is in the wake of multiple attacks on many different
businesses in Canada and throughout Austin, Dallas, and
other cities throughout Texas. The TPA's counter-Korps
strategy team has concluded that the Korps is bound to be
moving assets and personnel into Texas, as multiple illegal
shipments of military-grade weapons and supplies have
been intercepted.

We would like to remind all residents on campus,
whether trainee or staff, that Augmented Reality Visors
of any variety are strictly prohibited on campus. This
especially applies to Rose Colored Glasses®, a product of the
Thorn® company that our strategists suspect heavy Korps
involvement in. We also must stress that the campus, as
always, operates under a MANDATORY REPORTING
POLICY.

If you see anyone wearing RCGs® distributed by Thorn,
you must immediately notify campus police and inform
them of the wearer's location and appearance.

The Korps's operations and movements are hard to
track and even harder to predict, but the TPA requires the
participation of ALL staff and students in order for us to
prevail against this threat to the state of Texas, as well as
our proud nation. Only when we stand united will we defeat
the anarchist terrorist organization known as the Korps

and thwart their plans to take away our personal freedoms, individual spirit, and property.

As always, be safe, be strong, and be vigilant.

— Paul Richardson,
President of the TPA FRONTIER HERO ACADEMY

— Adam Tullis,
Chief of Campus Police and Security,

TPA FRONTIER HERO ACADEMY
TEXAS PROTECTORATE ASSEMBLY
~The Lone Star's Guardians, To the Very Last.

"The Korps are attacking companies in Austin?" Volta said aloud when she finished reading.

"A few firms, a couple banks, a defense contractor and an investment company, apparently." Carmen remarked, evidently scrolling through current events. "Why specifically Austin city, though?"

"I — well, that's where my family home is."

"Home" was underselling it. One hundred acres, most of which dedicated to timber, connected to a massive house that would make Italian villa owners nod in approval could hardly be described as just a *house*. The last thing Volta wanted to have to acknowledge was how inordinately rich her parents were, though. There was no way to talk about a literal mansion and not sound like she was bragging.

There's also the matter that I was named after the city. The whole city. As a reminder of where my home is, as if I needed it.

"You worried about your parents?"

"I — well, yeah? I guess they would have said something but... they don't really like talking about the Korps much, like we talked about before." That wasn't all that long ago and remembering the rest of that conversation made Volta's chest tighten.

Thankfully, Carmen didn't seem to want to bring it up either. She shrugged, smirking. "I can imagine. Villains knocking down banks would make anybody with enough money to lose uncomfortable."

Volta blinked. "Well… yeah. Wouldn't anyone? A lot of people could lose a lot of money, not to mention the property damage and the civilians and police they could hurt — that they *do* hurt…"

For just a second, Carmen got a very funny look on her face. …Was she trying not to laugh? "Well! I more mean, your parents probably have a lot of vested interests in the area, right? They seemed pretty well-off when I talked to them."

Uh oh, maybe she already knew. Volta's ears folded back. "A fair bit, yeah. They might lose a lot of money, they've invested a lot in local businesses. They're, they're — uh." She blushed. Well, might as well get it over with now. "They're on the executive and financial boards for the TPA, actually."

"Really! Is that why you have the, ah…?" Carmen gestured delicately at the wolf's chest. She nodded.

"Apparently it was really expensive, but it was part of the deal in being enrolled here. They say if I really want to be a hero, it's a worthwhile investment for them."

Did Carmen just wince?

"Oooh no, *hoooly* shit." Wren groaned into his RCGs, his voice muffled. He must have had his head in his hands.

"I know, hold on, I'm not done."

"This wolf's sounding more and more like a sheltered centrist, Carmen. They drank the Kool-Aid and went back for seconds!"

"Hey now, that's not being fair! They've got some learning to do, yes, but Volta is still young, and they're *way* more aware than you're giving them credit for. Let me finish, anyway…"

"Back to that other thing you said, though." The tabby folded her arms, tapping her fingers against her elbow. "About the Korps attacks, I mean."

"What about them?"

"I'm not saying they aren't criminals, but… from the article, it sounds almost like Captain Alamo is the one who actually *hurt* people this time."

"Wait, *Captain Alamo?*" Volta stared at her, ears pinned back. "Did he defect or something?"

Carmen typed something into her phone and scrolled quizzically for a minute. "…No, he's still TPA. Well, he got put on leave, at least." Her eyebrows furrowed. "…for a week. The injuries must not have been that severe, then, or…" She flicked her thumb down the page, then winced. "*Shit*, the pictures are… pretty gruesome. You… don't wanna see those."

"That — well, the news didn't really make a big deal about that," Volta muttered. "I mostly just heard about the injuries, and the Korps taking all the reserves out of the bank. That was a *lot* of money the local community lost."

"Hold on —" Carmen raised a finger. "Not the community — the *company* lost that money. Remember National Bank's not a member of the community of southeast downtown Austin. The company lost a bunch of locally-stored cash and bonds."

Volta stared at her, confused. "Isn't… that the same thing?"

"They lost physical cash and reserves, yes, but bank deposits like that are insured anyway — none of the bank's clientele lost all that much money. And… I mean, I hate to say they *deserve* it, but… it *was* Remember National…"

"But *why*, what's wrong with them?"

"Didn't they get caught by some whistleblower skimming money out of people's accounts or something? And then the whistleblower turned up dead a couple weeks later. I'm not the conspiracy type, but…"

Volta's ears wilted, but her jaw set. "I — *still*, though… heroes have to protect *everybody*, though. No matter what."

Carmen narrowed her eyes, her expression quizzical. "You say that very… *confidently*. That's one of the few times I've heard you confident — about *anything*."

"W-well, yeah." Volta, suddenly aware of how firm — and worse, masculine — she'd just sounded, went back to mumbling. "I care a lot about this. I'm serving my state and my country, and defending our personal freedoms, like the email says. I'm training to *be* one of those heroes. I'll have to fight the Korps and protect civilians from them. It's part of upholding the law."

Carmen leaned in conspiratorially and tapped her chin. "Y'ever wonder what they *do* with all that money, though? It's gotta be for something, the Korps is too organized to be robbing banks just for *fun*."

Volta shrugged, shaking her head. "I don't know. More… villainy stuff? Nobody knows what they do."

"Well, I would think if they're *serious* about the whole… 'commie-anarchist' shtick they've got, you'd think it'd go to, like, community efforts, services run by public organizations, that kind of thing?"

"I… I guess so, yeah?" Volta shrugged again, feeling way out of her depth. "I never really thought about it that much."

"Well! Maybe it's time you started, make sure you understand what you're up against."

Wren snorted in mock-disgust. "'*What you're up against*,' god — you're so *sneaky*, even when you're blunt."

"It's an art~!" Carmen beamed. "I can't lead her right to water without giving myself away, but it's nice to see her gears turning. Anyway, how *are* efforts to redistribute that wealth going?"

"Goin' great! The Taylor Street food bank's walk-in freezer got a badly-needed replacement cooling unit, something the feds have been holding out for years now, *and* the Gravenstein Fund got a hefty donation. Made their treasurer's day. All through the appropriate channels, of course!"

"*Excellent.*" Carmen's smile started to fade. "…Wish I could mention *any* of this to Volta."

"To blow their mind, or to show how not black-and-white the world is?"

"…*Mostly* the latter. They probably wouldn't even believe me if I told them, now. I'm just gonna have to keep leading them to water until they drink it themselves."

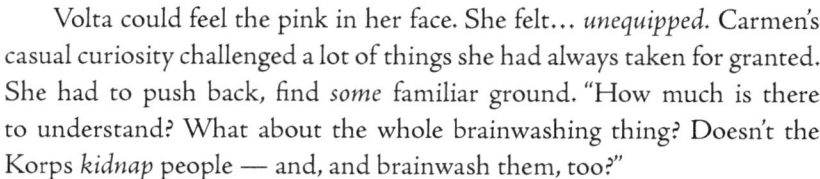

Volta could feel the pink in her face. She felt… *unequipped*. Carmen's casual curiosity challenged a lot of things she had always taken for granted. She had to push back, find *some* familiar ground. "How much is there to understand? What about the whole brainwashing thing? Doesn't the Korps *kidnap* people — and, and brainwash them, too?"

"For a bunch of brainwashed drones, the ones that surface again and come on the news seem pretty snarky — and argumentative, too, sometimes," the cat coolly replied with a nonchalant shrug. "It's probably not *pleasant*, but as a researcher, I don't really think we understand enough about those 'drones' to say yet. *Whatever* the Korps's methods are, they just don't line up with what we know about brainwashing."

"I… wouldn't know much about that…" Volta mumbled. That feeling of being almost naked was hitting her hard now.

"The Korps is a constant presence nowadays, even in the US. You'll have to deal with them a lot once you're a proper superhero — and *especially* after you get pulled into Bradley Group. You should make sure you understand *why* the TPA is so riled up about them, Volta."

She thought she had, but Volta was starting to wonder just how much she could trust what the news said about them. "I… know part of why my parents are, I think. It's not just the money or the lawbreaking, there's something else." Oh god. Was she really going to say this? She hadn't brought it up since that first day they'd talked, it felt *weird* to bring it up in conversation. "The outfits and the whole…" Volta waved a hand, flustered. She knew what she wanted to say but not how. She wasn't sure if she *could* say it. "The… the, uh… The lifestyle. Thing."

Carmen likes kissing giiiirls~ That's a lifestyle now, is it?

"The sex-positive thing?" Carmen asked. "Or, the whole LGBT thing, in general?"

"…Yes?"

Carmen grinned. "I think the word you need is queer."

"Okay, so… the TPA and the media and, well, my *parents* especially don't like them because they're… 'queer,' among other things."

The tabby snorted. "The Korps being so obviously and unabashedly queer certainly doesn't win them any points with people in power, no! Conservative types rarely like people being open about who they are, especially if it's being gay or bisexual or trans..." Volta's skin prickled at that last part. She averted her gaze. "...You mentioned this before, your parent's anger about them seems to stem from them being 'different.'"

"I — Yeah, I did."

"You have *some* experience with how that *anger* can color someone's view and change how they think." Carmen's expression turned sympathetic. "I'll say it outright, Volts: your parents may have other reasons for hating the Korps, but it's *who* and *what* they are, and how proudly they wear that, that pushes it over the edge for them. I may not have talked with them much, but it's easy to see, just from how you talk about it."

She said it so plainly and directly, her gaze never leaving Volta's. How was she so spot-on all the time? Where had this woman come from?

Finally, she managed to form a reply. "You... mentioned your parents being a lot like mine, in that case. I guess they have a lot in common."

"Oh yeah, though, my parents aren't filthy rich."

Volta's eyes went wide with alarm. "S-so you *do* know —"

"I'm a researcher here, Volts, I *do* know how to read a personnel file, and the Travers family are, as you pointed out, helping to fund the TPA. You don't invest in a hero group unless you have *money*, honey."

"...O-oh. Right."

"Now c'mon, we've been resting long enough. Let's go get a little more to eat."

Volta nodded and followed the tabby out of the gym. They didn't have much to say on the way back to the cafeteria, but Volta's mind was rushing.

Mom and Dad won't even talk about that part. The part everyone talks about — about it not being normal, and abhorrent and disgusting. About how they drag people in and brainwash them. They get turned into agents. Beautiful agents, agents who seem so happy about what they've been changed into, so happy that they're eager to serve. They were just dragged in one day, and reshaped.

...Shouldn't I be more afraid of the idea of that happening to me?

"All right, all right, there's hope for the pup yet, I was wrong!"

"Yeah, you were! Even if it means I have to both-sides her into getting it."

"Wanna wash your mouth out with soap after that talk with her, hun~?"

"Bite me. Anyway, Volta's clearly trying their best, here. You were right about them being sheltered — I mean, hell, James Travers is a goddamn *land baron* who donates to megachurches. His kid's probably not got very trustworthy information, and doesn't know how to parse anything other than the far-right news the TV's tuned to at home." Carmen practically had to laugh. "And — actually, that reminds me, we talked about one more thing once we were back in the mess hall."

"Well don't keep me waiting!"

"Found out they're one of those 'socialism is actually fascism' families. The kind that tells their kids that anyone on the political left, even libertarians, are trying to control them."

"Oh my GOD okay I'm starting to really hate Volta's parents."

"You and me both. I sat them down and gave them *The Politics Talk.* They looked like they were firing on all cylinders to wrap their head around this stuff."

"It's to be expected when you're dealing with a kid too sheltered to even *dare* questioning what they were taught. You grow up around shit you start to not smell it."

"I was about to say. You'd know better than me what shitty *rich* parents are like."

"There's a few things I'm hoping our zappy wolf here hasn't had to put up with!"

"Fingers crossed!"

A whole week passed, and Volta was still the most relaxed she had been in, maybe years? At least since high school, thanks to Carmen. Olson still came after her every chance he got; though he did remark upon a few of her improvements, he only seemed to double down on the flaws that persisted. Carmen always listened and helped her where Olson would have just shouted.

It was just as well, since she received a call from Mom a few days later announcing that they would be visiting for the next evaluation, same as the last. She could feel her heart rate spiking again as she relayed this to the tabby when they next met up, who immediately just sat her down to talk it out again. Carmen always being willing to lend an ear made everything seem easier to handle.

Time flew by, bringing the next exam before she knew it. It was in Volta's inbox, and had been on the calendar for several days before, but the sparring sessions with Carmen made days go by so much faster, especially the bad ones.

That didn't stop her from feeling anxious as she found herself sitting outside the testing chamber again, shaking her foot like she had a little over a week ago. Her blue, white, and red TPA-branded test suit clung to her fur and dragged against her Dampener, same as before. The only difference, this time, was that Carmen was sitting next to her.

"You think True North went through stuff like this?" Carmen asked, the end of her tail tapping the bench beside her.

"A little, but his training and evaluation was more personalized. He had teachers who worked *exclusively* with him, and everything. The early Aurora Squadron was all there taking care of him after his dad died. It was a bunch of mentors who knew him since he was a kid, not a *school* like this." The wolf just shrugged. Talking about True North did help take her mind off things, a little. Carmen was good at coaxing it out of her — whether she meant to or not.

"Well yeah, but. I guess he wasn't a super, so the Dampener thing wouldn't have come up."

"No, probably not." Volta shrugged, rolling her shoulders to try and get the Dampener straps to adjust to a more comfortable position, without much success. "Ugh. I suppose it's teaching me to, I *guess,* make the most out of what they give me."

"But you aren't *always* going to just have so limited a charge, right? If you ever face down against, like, a villain in a public place, you're gonna have *tons* of power sources."

…*Oh.* She'd been wearing the Dampener so long she'd managed to forget about that. "…Yeah, I guess, actually. I've been here a while, so I'd… probably need some time to adjust, right?"

"Well yeah, car batteries, powerlines, couldn't you draw even from people's *smartphones* and stuff? You could just drain any of the powered gear your opponents are wearing, too. Just kill their comms battery and juice up, while you were at it."

Volta blinked. "I… hadn't ever thought about it like that." Should she have been? Maybe Carmen had a point. She'd always pulled charge from very obvious things before, whether it was the backup generator at home, or the local power lines in walls… She had a lot of options, options she hadn't seen in at least a year.

All the more reason to get out of here.

"I guess that's only going to become more relevant out in the field properly, not while you have the Dampener on," Carmen remarked. She seemed *uncannily* good at figuring out exactly what the wolf was thinking. Was she giving it away with her expressions or something?

"Austin," the same receptionist from the last test called. "We're ready for you now. Are you all set?"

Volta stood up hastily, taking a deep breath. Carmen stood up with her. "Much as I can be, ma'am!"

"You'll be in testing chamber 3H, today," the receptionist explained, beckoning for Volta to follow. The wolf was able to take one step before she felt Carmen's fingers brush her arm.

She looked back at Carmen holding her hand out, beckoning for Volta to take it. Very tentatively, the wolf put her hand in Carmen's. The cat's larger fingers clasped gently around hers, and she winked. "You got this. Just breathe, Volts, you've got everything you need."

Volta blushed furiously, unable to respond, her tail an excited blur and her ears perked.

She — She's holding my haaAAAND. Her paws are so SOFT and she's stroking the back of my hand with her thummmmmb! HahaaAAAAAAA —

WAIT, wait I'm supposed to be heading in. Shit.

She managed a flustered smile before she pulled her hand back and turned to follow the receptionist, who now looked a little impatient.

The wolf rolled her shoulders and calmed her still-wagging tail as she walked towards the door to chamber 3H. What would it be this time? More drones? Another, bigger maze? Maybe Olson would be on the other side, ready to tell her off some more.

There was the power access pedestal, and to the far left, the observation window. Dr. Mason, Tammy, same as ever. Mom and Dad in their Sunday best once again, and Carmen seated not far away. She was smiling brightly and gave a little wave with the same hand she'd taken Volta's in earlier. Seated behind her, arms folded, was…

Chief Tullis. His cold gaze met Volta's. The Great Dane didn't smile or frown, he just *stared*. She had to look away, feeling his eyes pry into her. She felt practically naked. Ever since childhood he'd made her feel uncomfortably *small* just by looking at her, now the effect was doubled by her parents sitting and looking on expectantly next to him.

Dr. Mason's voice came up over the intercom, taking Volta through the same routine. Name, age, training ID. "We're trying something very new, today, Travers." The Goat's tired eyes scanned the control panel for the test chamber one more time. "At *Chief* Tullis's insistence, we're putting you through a slightly more advanced course than we had initially planned…" Panels began to shift, walls sprung up, forming several enclosed rooms. "*Originally*, this course was going to be used to encourage you to find new ways to use your powers, after several more basic evaluations in areas we have yet to cover, measuring stamina, heat tolerance and magnetic field measurements… All of the ways we'd gauge whether this test would be *safe*, but…" Dr Mason glanced at the broad-shouldered dog behind him, who continued to glare at Volta. "Chief Tullis has *persuaded* us that you may show greater improvement if made to improvise."

The wolf swallowed. The *last* evaluation was a combination of a lot of things she'd already dealt with. What did "new" mean?

She got her answer very quickly; she heard a door slam open and multiple armored figures filed into the testing chamber, dispersing into the high-walled obstacle course. A chill crept up her spine as she realized what they were there for.

"No drones or turrets today, Travers. These test aides are all trained security staff. A few of them are armed with nonlethal ammunition, the rest are experts in hand-to-hand combat, several of them armed with nonlethal weapons. Your goal is to neutralize all combatants, same as before."

Aides? *Aides?* These were police, a lot of them ex-military. She hadn't ever had to actively attack people before, not outside of Olson's classes. That was almost always one-on-one. Just how many steps was Tullis having them skip?

How is this helping? How is this ensuring I show improvement? You're just setting me up to fail, right as I finally get some breathing room. Maybe he knows I'll mess up under the slightest bit of pressure, so he just decided to save everybody time…

Volta tried to take a breath, feeling the nervous knots in her stomach and chest. Her heart was already pounding against the Dampener. There was *no way* she'd come out of this in one piece, much less actually pass. In a barely contained panic, she frantically looked to Carmen in the observation seats again.

Help. Help me out of here. I don't know what I'm gonna do…

The tabby was leaning forward in her seat, and their eyes met. Carmen was nodding, ever so slightly, with one hand balled up in a fist on her lap. She was confident, eyes bright and intense. With that gaze, she was repeating what she had said before.

Just breathe, Volts, you've got everything you need.

Volta stared back into those amber eyes, inhaling and exhaling slowly. Her heart was still racing, but looking at Carmen's face, remembering what she said, helped slow it a little. She just had to keep calm, not get in her own head. Just remember what Carmen had said and remember she could handle this.

"We'll be shutting the Dampener off in just a moment, Travers. Use the charge panel, like usual," Dr. Mason intoned. "Let us know as soon as you're prepared to start."

Volta breathed deep, closing her eyes for a moment, and tried to etch Carmen's gentle, reassuring face into her memory. "…Ready."

The Dampener shut off. Her chest loosened considerably as she put her hands on the metal contacts again and urged the current through her body. Carmen's words rang throughout her, and she felt the whole world brighten. She could do this. This was just another obstacle.

It wasn't much higher than before — evidently, they didn't want her to permanently wound any of the security team, but still enough to hurt, and stun. When Tammy's countdown hit 5, she heard the cocking of handguns from behind the sterile white walls.

They're all suited up and fixing for a fight. Well, so am I.

"…two, one." A buzzer sounded, and Volta began to move. The footsteps of the security team echoed through the modular chambers, and one immediately showed up on her right. She ran for cover as they trained their pistol on her.

Currents coursed through her legs, blue arcs trailing after her as she powered herself to the wall. Gunshots followed not long after — just as loud as the drones, but without the hum of the rotors to go along with it, just cold bootsteps. Hard rubber pellets, larger than what the drones had fired, embedded themselves in the wall opposite. Volta steadied herself, urging her electric warmth into one balled up fist. Every precious watt had to count, and she *had* to make sure she didn't overdo it, now more than ever. Just enough to knock them down, no more.

She whipped out around the barrier and took aim. Her armored target was trying to close the distance, gun coming up to meet her gaze. She bared her teeth, lightning jumping over her arm, and pushed.

A thin blue bolt struck the guard with that familiar CRACK. Louder still than the gunfire — but all the more pleasing to Volta. The aide's arms curled inward as they let out a yelp, their muscles convulsing and sending the gun flying out of their hands. Volta closed the distance, focusing on her opponent's less-armored legs. She went low, sweeping one leg out just like Carmen had taught her, and swung her foot into the stunned guard's ankles. He hit the floor with a pained grunt but stayed down. A chime sounded.

One down, how many to go?

More footsteps behind her. She ran in the direction the guard had come from and turned another corner. Two more guards were coming down the far end of the passage. The first with a baton, the second with another handgun. The gun came up as the first guard ran at her. Volta's muscles tensed, and blue current crackled around her clawed fingers.

I can do this.

The baton-guard was on her in another second. He swung right for her head — she went left, and struck at his elbow. Just enough voltage went into his arm to make it jerk upward. His grip was tight on his weapon, though, and in spite of the impulsive grunt he let out, he immediately took another swing. Another dodge, as Volta tried to keep him between her and the gunman — who was looking for a clear shot, several feet away.

Breathe. Breathe! You have to hit him where it hurts.

He was wide open as he raised his baton a third time. She gave him a straight, right in the upper chest, accompanied by a sharp electric *POP* as she jolted him again. He stumbled back, making a guttural noise.

Oh no, that didn't sound right. Did I punch him too hard?

Her stance softened, eyes going wide for a second.

The guard recovered abruptly and jabbed his baton forward, knocking against the side of Volta's face. She reared back, failing to stifle a gasp of pain.

*Fuck. **Fuck, fuck fuCK FUCK.** He was faking and I fell for it. Ow. OW.*

Your entire face hurts now, and it's because you hesitated. Imagine if he had a knife. The Korps won't just be using batons.

The wolf growled, filling her right fist with charge as she yanked herself back into stance, and went for a gut punch. She could feel the firm body armor come up hard against her knuckles, but it winded him, and the shock got him on the floor. His baton twitched out of his hand.

Another chime.

Which means I have no cover.

The gunman was steadying his aim — right at her chest, this time.

She bared her teeth again, raised her hand, and threw the current forward. The bolt hit him in the face; he bleated and crumpled, gun clattering to the floor. Volta's heart was racing, her breath catching in her throat as her cheek continued to throb. She couldn't mess up like that again. These guards were here to test her; she wasn't going to make it easy. Chime number three.

How's that for a punch, Olson?

As the guards twitched and whimpered, footsteps filtered back in from the surrounding corridors. That was three, how many more were there? Were even more coming? Was —

Volta ran for the far side of the passage and rounded another corner. She needed time to get her bearings. She still had plenty of charge left and was trying to use even less than usual to avoid *really* hurting them. On top of that, the more she used, the more she'd have to rely on her hand-to-hand skills, all while the pain of the hits she took grew worse and worse. How was she going to do this? What if she messed up again? How would Tullis react? How would her parents, or... or Carmen?

Breathe, Volts. You have everything you need.

Thinking of Carmen immediately brought those words back to the forefront of her head. The tabby, staring at her intently. Not expectant, not judgmental, just... hopeful. Encouraging. Completely confident.

...In me.

Volta's breathing steadied, heartbeat slowing. She put a hand to the growing bruise on her face. He hadn't hit her eye, just her cheek and jaw. It would be sore for a few days, but she could walk that off. If Carmen smiled at her like she did throughout their sparring sessions, Volta could walk anything off. She turned around, shaking her hands out, arcs crackling off of them.

Two more came into view, both with batons. They came at her at once, and she met them in stride, feinting to the right, baiting out a swing from one of them. It was easy to duck and aim another electric jab to their stomach. Their knees buckled and their companion swung their baton at Volta's outstretched arm.

Volta bent out of the way and kicked, current buzzing into the guard's thigh. His baton hand swung wide as his muscles convulsed. She drew back and punched again; down he went. Two more.

...And that was definitely more than two pairs of boots running at her from her left.

Volta leapt back as gunshots rang out, and hard rubber pellets sped past where she had been standing. The drones always took an extra second to start firing, while the guards bearing down on her were firing on sight. *How much does Tullis just want to see me get hurt?*

Another deep breath, welling up the charge in her hands. The crackling buzz of electricity reverberated across the fake walls. Volta had gotten this far; she could finish this. She wasn't going to fail in front of Tullis, she was going to show Carmen just what she could do.

The footsteps came closer, and three baton-wielding guards came around the corner. Two ran at her at once; the third hung back. She ducked low, trying to get underneath them again. The first saw her coming, knocked her hand away while the second took a swing at her side. She swung her arm just in time, the baton slamming into her forearm. She blew air out through her teeth. It hurt like hell, but it gave her an opening. She grabbed at the second guard's sleeve and swung her hand wildly at the first again, firing a pulse through both palms.

Two loud, energized pops; she could feel number 2 convulse in her grip, and his knees buckled a second later. The chime sounded again. Number 1 was still on his feet, but stumbling back again, and 3 was coming to join in.

Light on your feet, ready to move…

They swung; she veered to the left, just as Carmen had taught her, and kicked low. Blue arcs crackled off her leg as she knocked 3's shin out from under him.

He groaned and began to fall, right as 1 jabbed his baton forward. Volta jerked her head to the side — just in time. Her cheekbone still throbbed; she wasn't keen to take another one to the face.

Breathing's fast, even less charge than before. Play it safe, just knock him down.

She grabbed his wrist and twisted, forcing him to bend over with her. She shoved, slamming him against the wall opposite, helmet knocking against the hard metal. He went limp in her grasp, and she let him fall.

Two more chimes. That made six, right? Or, seven? How many —

More footsteps suddenly came to a halt. She whipped her head around, just as the gunshot made her ears fold back.

Red hot pain blossomed out from her left side as the wind was knocked out of her. She slumped against the wall with a strained gasp, clutching at the wound. The "rubber" round struck her in the ribcage, just left of the Dampener. She could already feel the welt forming under her testing suit, displacing her fur. Tears blurred her vision into an excruciating smear.

None of the rounds the drones and turrets had used felt like this. These were much bigger, and *much* harder. Her lungs burned, and the left side of her hurt more than anything she could remember. Her mouth was held open in a paralyzed scream with no air.

HELP ME HELP ME **HELP ME HELP ME —**

This is what it's really like. They're not pulling any punches, what were you expecting?

She tried to focus, straighten up. It was hard to inhale, almost harder to *see*. She could barely make out two more guards, aiming their guns at her. They almost seemed so slow.

It hurts so much.

I can't stop now. I'm so close! I JUST got some freedom back, Carmen's right over there, watching me. I can't…

…Breathe, Volts. Just breathe.

Her side burned and stung as she inhaled, but she had to get air in. She grit her teeth, bared them in a pained snarl as she straightened. The "aides" tensed; one of them kept their weapon raised, the other muttered something. They were going to shoot her again.

No, you're not.

Moving current through her body felt sluggish. What was running going to do? She couldn't hope to get close enough. Not with a run, not with a sprint.

*What about a **jump?***

She couldn't afford another hit. She couldn't *take* another hit. She wouldn't have to. Blue lightning illuminated the walls around her. Heat spread through her chest, up through her shoulders, arms, and face, then her torso, and legs. It was all she had left, but she wasn't going to let it go to waste.

She had to move faster. She had to close the distance, and she had to hit them both hard. Volta couldn't think about dealing with any more, she just had to get rid of these two. That would be enough.

A low, crackling hum filled her ears, made her fur bristle. Lightning ran up and down her arms and legs, up her entire body. She took a step, wound up with one leg under her. The guards raised their guns again. The wolf's glowing blue eyes were reflected in their visors, as was her mouth, spread wide in a fierce snarl.

The walls melted away. The pain in her torso evaporated. Her whole body went hot, and she jumped.

The guards, the floor, the entire world stretched, and then compressed around her. She flew, no — *bolted* forward through the air.

In a blur of bright sky-blue lightning, Volta crashed into the guards, knocking them down and landing just past them.

She stumbled to her feet as the testing chamber melted back into view. She was gasping, tears were drying on her face, and the ends of her testing suit's sleeves were singed. She was exhausted. Her left torso was throbbing again, charge completely gone, but the last two chimes were followed by a buzzer.

She was finished. She grinned through her gasps for air, as the walls sunk back into the now-scorched floor.

"The — That was… new!" Did Dr. Mason mean to sound impressed? "Come through, Travers, we'll get you set up with painkillers and have the medics look you over."

Still holding a hand over her welt, she shuffled into the observation room. Tullis was waiting for her, peering down at her with an unreadable expression.

"All right, Travers, you impressed me," he grunted. "You put two of my best men in the infirmary with that last trick. I don't get to see a lot of supers develop their powers that quick, anymore."

*I wasn't trying to impress **you**…*

"I guess adjusting the Dampener did some good, Chief Tullis," she said with a halfhearted smile, still trying to catch her breath.

"Sure. Glad to see you finally taking some of my advice, Travers. Keep it up." He shrugged and stepped away. "Though maybe don't get shot next time, son. The Korps uses live rounds, not like my boys in there."

"F-first on my to-do list, sir…" Volta sighed, trying to stretch and wincing as the throbbing kicked up again.

"Austin!"

Mom's voice came next. She was clutching at her purse as she strutted towards him, arm in arm with Dad. She actually looked genuinely worried, her eyes going down to Volta's torso where she was still holding the bullet welt. Right alongside her were two nameless medics who immediately ushered Volta over to the bench in the back of the chamber. As they checked her over, Mom signed the cross.

"What was that — what was that last thing you did? Where did you get hit? Is anything broken?" she demanded of the medics, as they put their hands not-too-gently on Volta's chest.

Trying to think of anything else but those hands, Volta gave a non-committal shake of the head. "I don't think*gh* — *ow*. I don't think so. It just… hurts." *A lot.*

"My goodness, Austin, you got hit with real police riot gear, and you're still standing. You must be making progress!"

"Some *real* progress, then." Was Dad grinning, for once? Something approaching that, at least. "You're becoming an actual superhero, thanks to Tullis's help."

The slightest glimmer of dad being proud felt like seeing sunlight for the first time. Volta bowed her head to try and hide a very small smile.

"Tull — I mean, he talked to some of my instructors but…"

"He explained it all to us while we watched. Your training's finally hitting its stride." The gray-tipped wolf took a breath, seeming satisfied for once. "My boy's finally coming into his own. All you needed was a real challenge for once!"

The wolf had to blink, rapidly, willing tears away. She couldn't start crying *now* — But that was a mistake. In the tears' place, trembling indignation churned in her belly.

That was a "real challenge"? That was a curveball. I had to improvise! I almost took a plastic shell to the face and he's acting like it's finally the schooling I needed. Does he think they should be using a belt, too? Is getting hurt the only way I can ever make you proud of me…?

One of the medics holding out a pain pill for her to swallow pulled her out of her stewing, and she took it — just in time to register all six and a half feet of tabby rushing towards her, her smile bright as the sun.

"He's clear. Nothing beyond a mild fracture. He'll just be sore for several days." The medic announced boredly, beckoning for Volta to stand up. She was about to mutter a thanks when Carmen brushed past Dad and grabbed her.

"Volts! *Volts!* That was *awesome!*" Carmen cheered, shaking Volta giddily by the shoulders.

"I-I guess!" Volta said, weakly. Mom and Dad were bewildered, looking from her to Carmen.

"No guessing about it! You *killed* it out there, and that last thing — that, like, electrified jump you did!? That was so fu —"

She glanced for an instant over at Volta's parents.

"— fantastic!"

"Y-you're the same cat from before, aren't you?" Mom spoke up first, clearly at a loss.

Finally, Carmen let go of Volta and turned to look down at the older wolf. She was still grinning broadly. "Sure am! Carmen Rayne, if you've forgotten. I'm a friend of Volts's — that's a nickname I have for 'em."

"*Volts?*" Mom snorted. "That's so… *silly*. You're a friend of Austin's? He never mentioned you."

"We only recently started talking!" Volta protested.

Carmen just chuckled, completely nonchalant. "Yeah, I've been talking with Volts for a week or so now. I'm really interested in seeing 'em grow! Anyway, I've got something I need to check up on real quick." She pulled out her phone and patted Volta gently on the shoulder. "I'll leave y'all to it, come find me after!"

"O-okay!" Volta grinned after her. The painkillers definitely hadn't kicked in yet, but even her gentle touch made the pain in her side recede.

"Austin," Mom piped up again, eyeing the cat up and down as she departed. "Is there… something between you two?"

Volta blanched. "Wh — *No!* No, Carmen's just a friend of mine."

"A *friend* with nicknames for you, who grabs you like that…" The wiry wolf snorted. "Please, Austin, I may be getting old but I'm not out of touch. Your mother *knows* what this looks like."

"I *promise* you're reading too much into it," Volta urged, checking behind her to make sure Carmen couldn't hear. Oh god, she had heard part of their talk last time, had she heard any of that?

Dad was still raising an eyebrow. He almost looked impressed. "I have to say, boy, you've never been one to seek the girls out, but she's not bad. She's… *taller*, bigger, but she's mighty attractive. You've got every opportunity, boy, if you can get anywhere with her."

I wish. Way to rub it in my face. "It's *really* not like that, Dad, I swear."

Mom pursed her lips. "Mmn, she's a cat, though. And an aggressively *common* breed, too. Austin, it's fine if it's just a fling, but you *know* how important it is for us to continue the family."

"It's not a fling — it's not *anything!*" Volta felt a pit start to yawn open in her stomach. "We are *Just. Friends.* I — I haven't forgotten how important it is to have an heir."

"Our enterprise is four generations old," Dad insisted, straightening up with pride. "Nothing but purebred red wolves in my family. Son, you've got to keep an eye out for the *right* one."

Mom nodded enthusiastically. "The survival of our family depends on it!"

Maybe our family isn't the only thing at stake here, did you ever consider that?

God, you still sound like a whiny little teenager in your own head. Good thing you learned to keep these thoughts to yourself. Not like anyone else would care, anyway.

"I know, I know. I'm… not planning on starting *anything*, unless it's with another wolf," Volta conceded, feeling herself deflate a little.

Another wolf. *Please.* There was no question of affection or intimacy, Mom and Dad just wanted grandkids — ideally pureblooded *red wolf* grandkids that could take the business over. Where was she supposed to find another red wolf girl? It wasn't like she had seen more than maybe two or three she *wasn't* related to before. And that wasn't getting into that the idea of using her genitalia "as intended" just… made her feel *sick*.

She had already tried explaining some of how she felt to her parents before. They wouldn't hear any of it. Mom got disgusted, Dad got angry. She didn't need that again. She had to prove she was still listening, still with the program, even if it was impossible, at this point.

What red wolf girl would even settle for a scared, nerdy freak like me, anyway? The last one Mom and Dad dug up wished she was dead instead of being stuck with me. Ran away and everything, and everyone just blamed me for not doing a better job of romancing her. They were right.

Eventually, Volta escaped the conversation and quickly hurried to the nearest exit out of the testing building. There was Carmen, waiting on one of the outside benches. She immediately jumped up and ran towards Volta again.

"Okay, *okay*, Volta, your parents are a bummer and all but *holy shit Volta I've never seen anything like that.*" The cat didn't waste a second in grabbing the wolf again and pulling her into a firm, giddy hug. Fireworks went off in Volta's head as the tabby's chest and body unabashedly pressed against hers.

Oh my god oh my god she's — ow owOWOW —

"Okay, *ok* — *OKAY that's enough hugging!*" Volta yelped, trying to wriggle out of the cat's grip.

"Sorry! Sorry, just… *Wow* that was incredible." Carmen pulled away, beaming. "Volts, you didn't pull your punches at all, you were amazing in there. And that thing at the end! We have to come up with a *name* for that! I didn't know you could, I guess, *zap-jump* like that!"

"I didn't either!" The wolf had to laugh, noticing a moment later that she was vigorously wagging her tail.

D… Do I start wagging my tail anytime Carmen compliments me? HOW LONG HAVE I BEEN WAGGING — *Oh no.*

"C-can we figure out a better name than zap-jump, though?"

"Definitely, we need to workshop names for every move you'll ever have. How about over lunch?"

"O-oh! Sure, yes!" She'd completely forgotten about food up until now, and now her stomach was feeling *especially* empty.

"Good! You've earned a treat anyway, c'mon."

Carmen turned and beckoned for Volta to follow. Blush be damned, her tail began to wag again.

Chapter 5

Electrochemistry

"…Carmen? You usually don't check in for another hour and a half. Don't you and Volta normally do lunch pretty soon?"

"Volta's showering and getting a change of clothes — I don't have super long before lunch but *holy shit* Wren I have *got* to show you something."

"Today's test? It wasn't bad, was it?"

"No, it was good! *Really* good, well, considering the circumstances. Volta nailed it, even impressed Deputy Dipshit, but…"

"But?"

"*Wellll*, so, the good news first: Volta was *fucking amazing*. They figured out how to do something *new*, mid-mission. Wren it was fucking *cool*. They covered their entire body in LIGHTNING and jumped a fifteen foot gap in a second. Here, ROSE can pipe you a clip from memory." Carmen summoned up the sight of Volta, immersed in blue energy, dashing forward faster than she could follow. Her RCGs immediately responded, and copied it over to Wren's side, clean and crisp, albeit with a much more significant delay.

There was a pause, as Wren took in the network-shared memory. "… Holy shit."

"Right? *Right!?* That's some hardcore shit! I didn't even think Volta could do something like *that!*"

"Okay, okay, that's *cool as hell* but where's the problem?"

"Weeell, even ignoring the rest of the exam — which was *way too much* to just spring on Volta. Deputy Dipshit wanted her to fail, or wanted her to suffer at least. Maybe to 'toughen her up,' maybe just to prove a point, I don't know."

"Another tally in the Tullis Sucks column, yeah, but ignoring all that?"

"*Afterward*, I overheard some of Volta's talk with their parents."

"Not a good start."

"It was pretty bad. A lot of guilt-tripping about Volta *'finally'* showing improvement. And then some shit about finding a red wolf girl, *specifically* to reproduce with."

"I'm gonna guess not out of a desire to help with conservation?"

"Nope, they just want an heir."

Wren made a disgusted noise. "Okay I really don't like where this is going."

"I cheered Volts up afterward, but that first look on their face walking out of the observation room… They looked *terrified.* Like they were waiting for someone to hit them, or scream, or… I'm not sure what Volta was expecting, but guaranteed it involved their parents."

Carmen tapped the frame of her bed with one claw as she spoke. She had tried to prepare for the silence she knew would follow her saying this, but even now it made her wince.

Wren's breathing was audible, and slow. "…Carmen."

"To be clear, I'm not jumping to conclusions, Wren. Volta's clearly not ready to talk about it yet."

"Carmen, I've heard this before. I've *lived* it. You know what this kind of thing comes from."

She sighed. "Yeah, I do."

"Based on everything we *do* know about the Travers family, I'm gonna go ahead and believe it. Dad was a *big fan* of their business model."

"So, I guess, the question becomes… 'How do I help train someone who worries I might start beating them if they make a mistake?'"

"Well to be fair, you're training Volta in hand-to-hand stuff. Hitting them is kinda part of the deal."

Carmen snorted. "And here I thought you'd be *less* flippant about this."

"Being a child of abusive parents didn't make me less of a snarky bitch, but it *did* make me funnier!"

"I guess I just need to keep being careful — coax them out of their shell, bit by bit. The more time I spend with Volts, the more I'm sure they've been aching to talk about a *lot* of things, not just their heroes. I think they just aren't sure where to start."

Wren sounded thoughtful. "You mentioned having a lot in common, a few days ago. Does that include the gender thing?"

Carmen had to take a second to mull over her response. "Maybe, maybe not. They've said a few things that have made me wonder. I'm not gonna push for anything until we can sit down and *really* talk about it, though. That's *not* a subject I'm gonna force. That's all up to Volta."

"Got it. Hey, Carmen…"

"Yeah, time's up." The cat shooed away the wiggling clock that her RCGs were flashing in the upper-right of her lenses. She sighed as she stood up and pulled on a more casual jacket. "Same check-in time later, bat?"

"Same as ever! Love you, be safe, scheme to castrate Tullis and all that."

"Love you too~ Carmen out." The call closed, and ROSE helpfully reminded her of the fastest route to the cafeteria. Right before she pulled the magenta glasses off, she paused, an idea dawning on her.

Hey Rosie — suppose I wanted to knock on Volta's door and walk them to lunch?

[One floor down, third hall from the left. You're either gonna frighten the poor thing or make their day, y'know!]

Aiming for the latter. Thanks as always~

Volta had just come out of the bathroom, hair and fur still mildly damp, and pulled on unremarkable jeans. She winced at the welt on her side where the bullet had hit her. It didn't look that ugly *yet*. She was more surprised to hear she hadn't broken a rib, the pain made her wonder if those medics' assessment could be trusted.

The Dampener straps are gonna rub up against it if you're not careful. Will need a lot more pain pills than last time. Tammy's gonna call me a pussy again…

Yeah, well, she'd be right.

Three gentle knocks came from the door, shaking the TPA Peacekeeper Taskforce poster on the back of it. Volta got to her feet with a start. Nobody came to see her unless it was her parents. Panicked, she suddenly looked around the room, yanking her bed covers into place, adjusting the cross on the wall from being askew, and then remembered her open laptop.

Her laptop, open to the folder of porn she really should have deleted by now. The Korps porn. Rife with massive dragons and curvaceous grey wolves, maned wolves, many different athletic cats…

Heart thumping in her ears, Volta slammed her laptop shut, much louder than she meant to.

Shit! There's no way Mom didn't hear —

"Hey, Volts?" Carmen's smooth voice came through the thin wooden door. "It's me, if you were wondering. I figured we could walk to lunch after your shower."

Sh — She's here! Outside my room! Not my parents, just, Carmen!
…Shit!

Very unsteadily, Volta approached her door, one trembling hand reaching for the doorknob. "J-just a second! …Uh." She glanced downward, realizing suddenly she still wasn't wearing a shirt. Mortified, she ran back to her dresser and yanked out the first tee she could grab.

Back at the door, she yanked it open and put on her best calm smile. She was still way too surprised for it to land properly.

"C-Carmen! I wasn't, um, expecting you to come find my room."

"Yeah, I figured we could walk to lunch together!" Carmen shrugged, her grin faltering in surprise when her eyes traveled down from Volta's face. "Oooh. Is that an *actual* vintage True North shirt?"

Goosebumps forming, Volta glanced down at the tee she had hastily pulled out. It was an extremely mid-80's design, with the titular grey wolf in a halftone silhouette and an abstract set of shapes made to represent the Canadian maple leaf behind him. Cost her a lot of money to get one in good enough condition to wear. She swallowed.

"Y-yes it is!" she began, smiling the least confident smile. "I just — I just figured I'd go casual. U-unless it's really — uhm. I can go change again, if —"

"Easy, *easy!* Slow down, Volts," Carmen grinned. "You're good. It's a good shirt, retro as hell."

The wolf blushed. "Uh, you can come in, if you want…?" *Ohhhh no, no no no why did I say that. I've never had a girl in my room before. Another girl. Shit. Fuck.*

The cat took a step forward, glancing through the room. Her eyes quickly landed on the TPA posters on the wall, and she clicked her tongue in agitation. "Ah, this shit. I had to take down *six* of these posters in my room."

"The staff has to put them in every room, I think. I, uh, only changed out a *couple* with my own…"

As she trailed off, the wolf realized with a sense of dawning horror what was about to happen.

"Wait, is —" Carmen's eyes went very wide as she rounded on the other major poster. She smiled, bemused. "That's not a True North… pin-up, is it?"

Volta went red, hurriedly standing between her and the poster on the wall. It didn't do much — Carmen was a whole head taller and could see over her easily. The poster of True North had him fully clothed, but True North II's classic outfit defined the chest and abs *very well*, to say nothing of his forearms. That dazzling smile was inspiring… in all sorts of ways.

"O-of course not! They wouldn't make a *pin-up* of True North! He's a hero, not a… Korps Agent, or something."

Carmen's smile became wry, eyes narrowing as she peeked over the wolf's head. "And how would *you* know that the Korps puts out pin-ups with their agents on them?"

"I-I mean, I *assume*, I have no idea if the Korps does that!" Volta laughed awkwardly, shrugging her shoulders unconvincingly and taking an intense interest in the ceiling. "B-but that's not a pin-up! It's a collectible *full-body profile diagram!* It's nothing like a — Cuz he's not scantily clad, it's promotional and he's —"

"Relax, Volts, *relax.*" Carmen laughed, putting a hand on the wolf's shoulder. "You don't hafta justify your poster to me! I get it. He's your big inspiration… *and* he's hot."

Volta tried to mumble something, but all that came out was a sheepish chuff. She looked everywhere but Carmen, fidgeting, ears flagged as she tried. "I — I *guess*, yeah he's — He's very… Hey can we go to lunch now?"

"Sure! Thought you'd never ask~"

Volta had never been more grateful to step into the dormitory hallway, a nervous smile stuck on her face as she closed her door.

"…I know it's really dorky."

"Not a bit." Carmen was still grinning.

"Then why are you smiling so much?"

"Because, Volts…" Carmen leaned in, tilting her head down to stare at Volta intently. Those amber eyes fixed on Volta's blue ones, as her smile widened. "It's not dorky, it's *cute.*"

Aaaaaa? Aaa. AAAA. Waaaaahaaat does she mean by that — ooohh no. Oh no I'm staring. Am I smiling? SHOULD I be smiling…? She thinks I'm cute. I'm… CUTE? Can I be cute…?

Trying to force herself out of her thoughts, Volta's best attempt at modest chuckling turned into more flustered stammering as she rubbed the back of her head.

Carmen began to walk, beckoning the wolf with a flick of her tail. Volta fell in next to the cat, eyes glued to her. She *had* to just be ignoring the few seconds of non-words from the wolf, out of mercy. The cat continued; "Honestly, it's interesting! And at this point, I'm curious: How did your thing for True North even start?"

"H-he's always been my favorite. Since I was six, someone uh… someone gave me some of his old comics. I guess I started with those, and then I saw the TV shows and the old movies he advised on. Well, he didn't advise on *all* of them… a few were made where he just signed off without consulting and it *really shows.* The Caper of Colonel Clue was so unrealistic, it made him out to be a totally different person, not at all like he was in the interviews. That's where I — uhm. I'm talking too much, aren't I?"

"Did you hear me interrupt you?" Carmen was still grinning, tail perked up, ears pointing towards the wolf. "You can finish, but I did have something to ask…"

"Y-yeah?"

"The, uh, 'zap-jump'?" Carmen took on an almost conspiratorial tone. "We need to figure out a cool name for that."

"O-oh! Yeah, right." Heroes usually named some of their signature moves, or otherwise risked leaving their fans to come up with one for them. "I mean, Zap's… appropriate, but I've never thought it sounded really *cool.*"

Carmen shrugged apologetically. "Yeeeaah, it just occurred to me in the moment. Bet you've thought a *lot* about cool words for lightning, though, right?"

The red wolf perked up, tail a blur. She couldn't help it: *This* was something she had an answer ready for. "Oh yeah, tons. They aren't *all* good but there's a lot of good, like, snappy words. Like charge, maybe, or — or better yet, *bolt*."

"And 'volt,' too?" Carmen prompted with a wry grin.

"W-well, yeah, but, since I'm already kind of… *using* that one for something else…"

"I get you! Bolt's a good start. Bolt Jump? Bolt-Leap?"

"Nnnno, leap's worse. It's not a leap it's like — it was like I suddenly *shot* forward."

"Bolt Shot, maybe?"

"Maaaaybe."

"Bolt Sprint?"

"No, that's about as bad as 'leap,' do you — I mean you don't *have* to come up with names *for* me…"

"I don't, but I was brainstorming them already on the way over. I've got a few more for you, if you like?"

"Uh, sure!"

They talked throughout arriving in the cafeteria and getting in line for their food, where Carmen kept floating names, and managed to convince Volta to share a few herself. In the midst of their brainstorming, however, someone caught Volta's eye.

A tall, muscular lion, eyes locked on her, was walking towards the buffet line — towards *Volta*. It took a moment to realize it was Evans, Volta's classmate and Olson's favorite student, less recognizable out of his exercise gear and instead sporting a TPA star-branded tee and jeans. The two of them had basically never spoken before, in or out of class; why was he suddenly coming over *now*?

Volta stiffened nervously. Carmen noticed and snapped alert.

"Hm? Volts, what's — ?" The tabby turned her head to the approaching lion, who halted at her gaze. "Is that someone you know?"

Volta cleared her throat, glancing apprehensively between him and Carmen. "That's… one of my classmates from Olson's classes."

"Are you two friends?"

"…No."

"Huh! Maybe he wants to come say hi?" Carmen tilted her head with curiosity and raised a hand to wave the lion over. Instead of coming closer, he backed away, turned around, and went and sat down at a table among other classmates Volta hadn't bothered to commit to memory.

Volta blinked in confusion. Was Evans… *afraid* of Carmen? Was he trying to talk to Volta in private? …Did he have some bone to *pick* with Volta? What could she have done? Why would Carmen being nearby stop him?

"It… really looked like he wanted to talk to me, for a second," Volta muttered, eyes lingering on the table Evans now sat with.

"Weird!" Carmen declared, shrugging with one shoulder. "If he really wants to talk, he can come find you some other time. Maybe he's shy around girls as tall as he is. A weakness *you* don't seem to have, do you, Volts~?"

Volta blushed and shook her head, scrambling for more familiar ground. "Y-you make it easy to *not* be so shy, uh, usually… *Uhm*, w-what were we talking about, before?"

"Electro-jump?"

"Yes! Yes, okay, *no*, I don't like using *jump* at all, it sounds clunky…"

By the time they were setting their trays down on another secluded table, Volta hit on the idea she really liked, and she was chatting a little more confidently. A little.

"Okay — okay I *know* I said I liked the idea of calling it electro-something, but… I think we were more on track with 'bolt' for the first word."

"Bolt's a good mainstay, but what are you thinking about?"

"…Bolt — um. Promise you won't laugh."

"I haven't so far!"

"Bolt Dash?"

"Oooh, I like it. Nice and simple, not too long. *Look out for Redline's devastating Bolt Dash — the fight'll be over in the blink of an eye!*"

Volta had to stamp down on the urge to giggle. "You almost make it sound like it's from a wrestling match!"

"Or one of the old True North cartoons?" the tabby grinned.

The wolf's eyes sparkled. "Yeah exactly! I mean, sorta, not too —"

"Hey Volts?"

"…Yeah?"

"You hunched up your shoulders again. Breathe, take a second to eat!"

"Well *now* you're starting to sound like my old nanny."

That's weird. That's a weird fucking thing to say, no she doesn't. She obviously doesn't!

"Wow, you *are* rich," Carmen laughed while Volta squirmed. *Mom and Dad are rich; I didn't have anything to do with that.* "So, you had a live-in babysitter — was Mom too busy?"

"Yeah Mom, uh, wasn't around much, before I was eight."

Not like she was around a lot MORE often after they sent Thalia away, anyway. That... means I haven't seen her in more than ten years...

No, nope, not thinking about that, I'm sitting here in the cafeteria and I'm talking to Carmen and I'm not gonna be so fucking weird, I'm gonna be as normal and not-weird as possible and I haven't said anything in half a minute oh god I need to SAY something —

"She and Dad were always focusing on their work."

"So they... really didn't make much time for you either, huh?" Carmen smiled sadly.

"N-no, I guess they didn't." Volta resisted the urge to squirm more, looked at the table and put a forkful of pasta in her mouth — and immediately started coughing when she swallowed.

Carmen started to stand up. "Oh, shit, are you choking?"

"N-no, no, I just — *ugh* they used too much pepper in this..." Volta wheezed, reaching for her water glass. "I'm not — I can*not* handle spicy food."

The cat blinked. "Really? Mine's fine. Hang on, you mind if I try..."

"N-no, go ahead!"

Carmen quickly reached over, stuck a bunch of saucy noodles on her fork and gulped them clean off. Anticipation died from her face in seconds.

"...Volta, these aren't spicy at all. They... just used regular old pepper."

"I swear it was *really strong* though!"

"Volts do you... *know* what spicy food is like? This is nothing, this is just pepper and garlic and oregano."

"I — Well, we... we usually don't *have* a lot of spicy food back home."

Carmen stared at her, a mix of horror and bemusement dawning on her face. "Volta, we live in Texas. Please tell me you've had *something* actually spicy. Fried chicken?"

"...No? Why would I? It's so flavorless."

Carmen snorted. "Oh my god, you're serious."

Volta became indignant. "What? Mom and Dad may not have been around a lot, but they gave me a refined taste in cooking."

"Oh *really,*" Carmen leaned in, a sardonic smile growing on her face. "Please, illuminate me on your *refined palate,* Volts."

"Oh no, no don't tell me."

"Yep. Yeeep, yep, *yep,* they're one of those upper class families —"

Wren sounded like he was in pain. "Carmen please I can't take this."

"Let me finish — they're one of those super-rich, old English-style families that thinks *paprika* makes food inedible. Volta's never eaten anything actually spicy in their *life.*"

"This is in no way worse than the abuse but this is just adding insult to injury."

"Do you want to hurt a little more?"

"Oh, please."

"They think pot roast is supposed to be dry; that's how their dad insists it gets cooked."

"I'm gonna hit their dad. Please tell me they've eaten any shellfish."

"Nope."

"Anything fried?"

"Too 'low-class.'"

"Oh my god, Volta's never had french fries. No wonder they're depressed."

Carmen had to stifle a laugh. "Wren!"

"Am I *wrong?*"

"No, but you're sidetracking again."

"Next you'll tell me they don't like tomatoes on pizza."

"Bold of you to assume they've ever eaten pizza."

The sound of Wren hitting his desk was unmistakable. "What the *FUCK.*"

"Suffer with me."

"*WE HAVE TO FEED VOLTA PIZZA.*"

"We'll get there! One thing at a time. I have to ask, though…" Carmen's tone turned more serious. "This Evans guy — he's *just* a student, right?"

"Yep. I dug up as much as I could about him; he's *just* a student, he doesn't show up in any other database aside from records of his graduation from high school a year and a half ago. He enrolled at the same time Volta did, comes from a very small town near Waco. Apparently he got in on scholarship. Pyrokinetic, too. Damn." Wren whistled. "Real sturdy looking guy, easy on the eyes… shame he's apparently scared of you, Carm."

The tabby's tone remained serious. "But he's not a plainclothes cop, or a TPA plant sniffing around for 'deviancy' in the student body."

"Nope, just a regular Hero-in-training. Poor guy, he's too cute for that stupid little hat the TPA's gonna put him in."

"Fine, okay." Carmen exhaled, letting go of tension she'd been carrying since she sat down. "So whatever he wants it's not *my* problem, though it might be Volta's."

"His intentions could be noble! Who knows — maybe he wants her to try pizza!"

Carmen finally snorted, smiling again. "One thing at a time…"

"So, the range of meals are really narrow at home, huh?"

"I guess, yeah?" Volta huffed. "I mean I just… never spent a lot of time thinking about what kind of food I ate. I only had the one choice of meal anyway, and it's proper manners to eat what you're served." She abruptly stopped trying to pick out the pepper she could see and stuffed noodles into her mouth, resigning herself to her fate.

Carmen made a face, then shook her head. "Let's change the subject a little. I had another question: Do your parents normally come to every examination you do?"

"Sometimes? They've been showing up more often lately," Volta snorted. "Maybe they miss me, I don't know."

Maybe the mansion's finally a little lonely with only the two of them and the staff in it.

"They seem very insistent on reminding you about their expectations, based on what you've told me."

"Mom and Dad *did* spend a lot of money on the Dampener… and they want the best for me! Is there something wrong with that?"

"Well! There's a difference between wanting the best for you and wanting what *they* think is best. That's a difference my mom didn't get." Carmen mirrored Volta's earlier shrug. "S'why I left home when I did, I guess."

Kissing girls and leaving home is a bit easier when you're this incredible, though. When you're that attractive and confident and strong… Volta felt a pang of envy. Carmen knew *exactly* who she wanted to be — who could ever stop her?

The wolf squirmed; she had to ask. "I know we already talked about it but I just… can't imagine just *leaving* my family behind. Where would I go? Where did *you* go?"

"To be fair, I wasn't completely on my own; I had my grandmother! She taught me what unconditional love *really* meant." Carmen waved her hand emphatically. "With Mom it was *always* something going wrong with me, but with Gramma C she just… always took the time to listen and understand me. She chewed me out a few times, definitely, but she respected me enough to let me make my own choices — and support me no matter what I did."

"You make it sound so easy."

"Nothing about it was easy for me, but I guess it helped having Grandma there. She made a big difference. Do you… have anyone like that? Someone you could trust implicitly?"

Volta had to stop and think. Of course, no one in her family would help her with what she needed. Mom and Dad were emblematic of the entire extended family's beliefs — they were just the richest and most influential. Carmen was probably right about what they *really* wanted for her.

There had never been anyone else in her life she felt close enough to trusting, either, not since her parents fired the au pair who had looked after her since she was two.

That was just a nanny, though. Of course, you trusted Thalia. Mom wasn't there half as much as she was, who else would you have connected with? That doesn't mean anything.

*You're **not** thinking about this right now.*

In fact, the only person Volta could think of that might help her without asking for anything in return was the tabby sitting across from her, spooling noodles around her fork and popping them in her mouth. Her ears flagged.

"Not really, I guess. …But your grandma sounds really nice."

"She's the best." Carmen beamed. "She's practically my new mom at this point, and she taught me everything I needed to stand on my own two feet. Helped me practice my French too!"

"You know *French?*"

"Mmhm! Grandma's from France — she helped me figure out German and Spanish, too. I'm working on Cantonese right now, actually!" She bragged in such a matter of fact way, it was hard to even call it bragging.

Volta felt almost as intimidated as when Carmen was flexing in front of her. "A-are you serious? When did you find the time to learn all those!?"

"Languages just come naturally to me, I guess! Here, I'll show you." Carmen grinned wide and leaned in, locking eyes with the wolf. "*Je t'aime bien*, Volta."

"…What's that mean?"

She snickered. "I like you, of course!"

"O-*oh*. Uh… Really? You're not messing with me, are you?"

"Of course I like you~ That's the literal translation, word for word."

"W-well, I — je tem byen too!"

Oh god no. Why did I say that, that sounded awful, that was the worst thing I've ever done. I wish I could just burst into flames right now and — Oh, she's — she's laughing! She's laughing, that's good, right?

Carmen's almost singsong giggles evaporated the sudden panic in Volta like water boiling out of a pot. "Your accent needs work but yeah, you got it!"

"I wouldn't mind learning another language at some point…" Volta muttered. "Mom and Dad always said I shouldn't have to learn anything but English."

"Hey, maybe I can have you meet Gramma C sometime! She'd love to help you learn one if you wanted to try."

"M-maybe!"

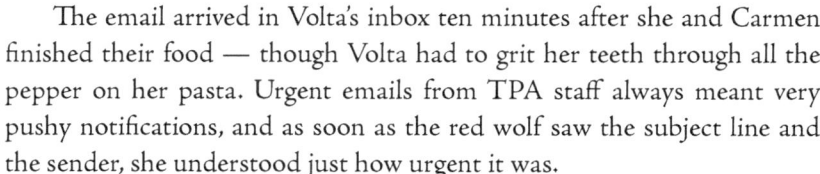

The email arrived in Volta's inbox ten minutes after she and Carmen finished their food — though Volta had to grit her teeth through all the pepper on her pasta. Urgent emails from TPA staff always meant very pushy notifications, and as soon as the red wolf saw the subject line and the sender, she understood just how urgent it was.

URGENT: Meet with Security Chief Tullis in his office in 20 minutes. Don't be late.

Carmen, reading over her shoulder, put a hand on her arm. "It can't be that bad. You said he seemed impressed at the exam; maybe he wants to congratulate you?"

"Maybe he wants to give me another inspiring speech," Volta groused. "Not like I need one."

"Just relax! Take slow breaths, and don't let him get under your skin. You're the one with a life ahead of you — he's just a washed up superhero, yeah?"

A really big, really angry washed up superhero who can turn his body into super dense metal. One who kept scaring me to tears when I was little because he thought it was funny. One who used to get drunk when he came to parties Mom and Dad threw, and yell at me for not being a fan of his hero career. One who kept calling me a spineless fag when I wouldn't look him in the eyes…

…Sure, no big deal! Just walk in and ask him how the weather is, like that's **easy,** *like I haven't hated being in arm's reach of him since I was six.*

"You already know what I'm gonna say, Volta," Carmen spoke in hushed tones, leaning in close to make sure the wolf could hear. "You got this. It's not like he can *do* anything to you, especially given who your parents are."

"I don't just want to hide behind my parents, though…"

"I know you're not into pulling rank, but, if not that, find some way to stand up to him a little. He's got boundaries he *has* to follow." Carmen patted her on the back. "I'll be waiting for you after, maybe we can go for another walk, or chill in one of our rooms. I mean, if you'd like!"

"Y-yeah…"

She felt even less confident walking up to the tall door in the brick-and-concrete admin building. Volta stared up at the door's signage: ADAM

TULLIS, engraved in a plaque above the TPA's insignia. Mustering all the bravery Carmen had instilled in her, she knocked. There was a pause before she heard the Great Dane's gruff voice on the other side:

"Door's open."

She turned the knob and swung the door open, figuring a quick entrance would set a better tone than nervously peeking through the slightest opening.

The security chief sat in a large, comfortable-looking chair behind a wide, light mahogany desk, his large fingers clasped on top of it as he stared intently at the wolf. The security chief's room was decorated with shelves of paperwork and files on either side, with the wall behind him almost entirely covered with newspaper cutouts, magazine covers, a decorative gavel painted gold, and the Great Dane's old hero outfit, all in bright and reflective golden yellow, with blue and white accents. It looked like he hadn't outgrown it at all — especially since it took up most of the wall behind him.

Tullis calmly gestured to the small swivel chair on Volta's side of the desk, vastly dwarfed by the one he sat in, his large frame filling it.

"Sit yourself down. Travers. I'd like to talk some things over."

Without a word, Volta did as she was told, scooting as close as she was comfortable to the mahogany desk. She noticed a set of collectable models on little pedestals to one side, in amongst paperwork and pens and a desktop. The largest was a very detailed model of, who else, the Golden Gavel, in his prime from fifteen years ago, brandishing a hammer with an arm entirely composed of brassy gold metal.

I know I have a lot of True North merch, but at least it's not my OWN merch…

"So, Travers…" The security chief leaned forward, resting his head on his clasped hands. "You're kind of a fish out of water here, aren't you?"

"I — Yeah, I guess so?" She tried to speak in a lower voice than usual. She *hated* how it sounded but surely it was important to at least *act* a little more sure of herself in a way Tullis would expect a young man to. "I'm not sure what you mean, Chief Tullis."

"Not every student here is the son of the richest man south of Dallas," he explained. "Nor do they have gifts like you do, or the…" He gestured at her chest. "*Investment* in training and safety that you do."

"No, sir..." Volta muttered, resisting the urge to shift in her seat.

"But a lot of my men have kept an eye on you, Travers," the Great Dane continued, "and I myself have watched you over the past year, when I get the chance. You don't like to draw attention to yourself, you're always the first one out of a room — and the only time I've seen you move faster than when you're leaving is when you're running tests, or in hand-to-hand training."

"I... guess I'm not into showing off too much, sir!" That was mostly the truth. She wasn't a hero yet, she was just a student. Besides, every time she imagined too many people looking at her for what she was, she felt like garbage — but Tullis didn't need to know that. "I don't expect to be drawing attention until I become a hero proper, sir. I want to earn it."

Tullis's slate blue eyes narrowed a little, and his chair creaked as he leaned back. He glanced up at some of the framed newspaper clippings behind him. "Travers, you remind me of a lot of younger heroes I knew, back in the day. Eager to make a big splash, *earn* your place on the headlines with everybody else. I was always doing my best to be humble, but the 7 O'clock News always had other ideas." Tullis smirked. "Bet you didn't know how famous I *got*, despite my best efforts."

"No, sir," Volta lied. The Golden Gavel had a reputation for showboating, ensuring the camera always got his good side and that he nearly *always* had a chance to say a few words for whatever breaking article would be written entirely about him. Volta may have been a True North fan through and through but picking through hero history from the 1980s to the 2000s for her favorite meant trawling through a lot of unrelated trivia. The Golden Gavel was Texas-born and proud of it, and it was impossible to go to any hero history site throughout the state without him showing up.

"Well, Travers, if you care about making it as a hero in Texas, or with *Bradley Group* as I know you're keen on..." He leaned forward a little, eyes glinting. "Then you need to learn some lessons none of the other staff here will teach you."

He trailed off, obviously wanting her to ask. A lot like Dad did, actually. She took a breath and obliged. "Lessons about what, Chief Tullis?"

"About the *politics* in play, boy, and about serving the spirit of the law."

"I'm... not sure what you mean, sir."

The Great Dane reached behind him, taking one of the framed newspapers off the wall. "This here headliner, from 1992. 'Golden Gavel Breaks The Mold!'" He held it out to the wolf. In the middle of the front page was a color photo of a much younger Tullis in his Super-suit, flexing for the camera. Both of his normally pale-furred arms were instead turned to gleaming gold-colored metal. There was a collapsed building behind him, and some of the rubble was stuck to one of his fists.

"That was about three years after my debut, but this is when the news *really* started followin' me," he said, with a kind of pride. "My first terrorist bust — bunch of anarchist types were holed up in that building behind me. They had guns, and bomb-making plans. See, everyone *knew* they had enough explosives to level a building, but the police were draggin' their feet. I walked in, knocked a support or two down, and had the boys in blue drag the perps out of the rubble," he chuckled; it was clearly a fond memory. "Honestly, if all they wanted to do was pick up the trash, they should'a turned in their badges and drove garbage trucks instead." He grinned at the wolf, clearly proud of this joke. She offered a grin and a nod back.

Probably best to be stoic anyway, since the joke sucked.

He pulled the newspaper back and hung it back on the wall. "But the point is, afterward, the police chief and my commander were spittin' fire at me. Due-process this, probable cause that. It was all bluster for the cameras — they found *more* than enough fertilizer in that rubble for all the probable cause they needed. Certain *publications…*" he put extra emphasis on the word, looking exasperated, "…put a spin on the whole thing — 'Out of control deputy!' 'Renegade super!' Buncha ungrateful wimps, you ask me. Same guys who put flowers in their hair, combed their beards then put on *frilly dresses* before they marched in the streets holdin' hands and singin' for peace and equal rights for the reds, and then the queers. Same shit, now they just had a job."

Volta squirmed in her seat, not daring to take her eyes off of Tullis's face, in spite of how much she wanted to look anywhere else. The extra mocking inflection he put on "dresses" made her stomach turn. She didn't know if she was more angry or scared.

"*Anyway…*" He fixed Volta with a much more serious look. "These people are *everywhere* now. Every other news station's a liberal one. They care more about *feelings* than they do about the law — and public safety.

Sometimes you gotta bend the rules, do the things everyone else's too scared to do. You gotta be the man in the room and be ready when all the sissies start to whine about it."

"I-I'll keep that in mind, sir…" the red wolf said sheepishly.

Tullis shook his head. "That ain't good enough, boy. You're gonna be facing the emasculation of our politics. The Korps is a threat to all our ideals, and their vision of the future is a world I never want to see. We're under attack, Travers; you gotta be ready to *fight*."

"I'm… doing the best I can, sir!" Volta tried to puff her chest out and sit up a little straighter. Maybe this would be over sooner if she kept nodding to everything he said.

"Yeah? You have been spending a lot more time in the gym complex, lately." He sniffed, his eyes fixed on hers again.

Volta blinked. Where was this going? "I — Yeah, I guess I have. I've been doing a lot more sparring work, lately. What about it?"

He shrugged. "I'm chief of security, so I get access to all the camera feeds on campus. Your extra sessions with Miss Rayne caught my attention…"

"Is… is there something wrong with sparring with Carmen?" Volta asked, nervous.

"Ain't nothing wrong with getting your practice in, shows commitment! But uh, *well*. Miss Rayne's an awful interesting cat. Mr. and Mrs. Travers were *very* concerned about the time you're spending with her."

W… Why? Do they REALLY think she's that much of a threat to them getting grandkids? Isn't it enough that I have no appeal aside from the money?

Tullis continued. "She's an eyecatcher, though she's awfully tall for a girl. Got an… interesting physique. She can *fight*, way better than you'd expect for a research assistant."

"Yeah, she uh… said that it was something she spent a lot of time on when she was younger."

"*Really* now." Tullis clasped his hands again, leaning forward to rest his chin on them. "Did she explain anything *else* to you, Travers? Why's a… sweet young lady need to learn to fight like *that*?" He said it with a smirk, almost sarcastic.

"Well, I never bothered to ask *too* much…" Volta muttered. "I figured self defense was pretty important for anyone."

"If a girl isn't gonna find a man and stay home, she might as well be prepared for the worst, I guess." Tullis shrugged; Volta had to redouble her effort to keep her face neutral. "But it seems to me like she's got a lot to teach you. Is she a better teacher than Olson, Travers?"

"I… don't know how to answer that, sir."

"Is she *nicer?*"

"W-well, yes, sir."

"Prettier to look at, at least? Or do you wish her face was more like her body? You like masculine girls, Travers?"

Volta stared at him, trying to figure out what he expected to hear. The Great Dane's expression had gone from the more relaxed look he had had talking about the good old days to a much harder, colder look. Like the one he'd fixed her with in Doctor Mason's lab.

"Masculine's… not the word I'd use to describe Carmen, sir."

"Yeah? *I* would. But hey, looks like she's helping you, and I suppose that's the most important thing, even if she's not what your folks *want* you to be sweet on." He sneered.

First her parents, now Tullis. That was it, Volta had to speak up — if not for herself, then for Carmen.

Mustering all her courage, she straightened up again and spoke as clearly as she could. "It… ain't like that. She's been a good… friend, for the last couple weeks, sir. She knows her stuff, she knows how to teach, and she's been pushing me to try harder every time. I'm glad to have her around and I'm stronger for it. …Sir."

Tullis's gaze turned icy. Was he looking for some other response? Something else? A show of weakness? She refused to show it, much as she felt like hanging her tail and cowering. She sat as straight as she could, shoulders squared as she stared back at him.

His more casual smile returned. "You're not the typical rich kid, Travers. Ain't all that cheeky, ain't full of yourself, don't want unearned fame… and the first thing that really gets you to straighten your back is standing up for a girl. You almost sound like you mean it."

The wolf's ears pointed forward in agitation. She was fighting to keep from just scowling at him. "I *do* mean it, sir."

"Sure." He waved a hand. "That'll be all, Travers. Keep up the good work — better not keep that girl waiting, if she's so special."

Volta was out of the door in record time. She wanted to hit something. Where did the old man get off, needling her like that? Did he *enjoy* trying to get under her skin, or was he just trying to flex?

Wait.

Was that an interrogation?

It started to click when she got back to her room. She began pacing in front of her bed. Her breathing had gotten heavier on the way. She felt herself getting warmer as gears turned in her head.

*That was an interrogation — a "polite" one so I wouldn't put my guard up. He wanted me scared and uncomfortable. Why was he so interested about what I know about Carmen? What did Mom and Dad tell him? Of course, they start to pry as soon as I start to seem even mildly happy. Of COURSE something must be wrong. I'm doing so well, so they have to stick their hands in everything to check! Like they always do, every time I'm improving. For one week, for one MINUTE, why can't they just **leave me alone!?***

Heat welled up in her chest, spread through her shoulders and arms. Buzzing energy collected in her right hand as she balled it in a fist. She punched the wall, and a loud electric *CRACK* reverberated around her small room.

She pulled her hand away from the displaced TPA poster, now sporting an electrical burn right in the center.

…Oops.

She folded her ears back as her Dampener went cold against her skin. That was the most property damage she'd dealt in a few years. She was still panting, anger dispelling and replaced with embarrassment. If it was that easy for Tullis to get under her skin, how was she going to handle any more "talks" he wanted to have?

Her phone buzzing pulled her out of her thoughts. She breathed a sigh of relief, seeing Carmen's message pop up.

'Hope it goes ok with Tullis, when ur done tho if you wanna talk about it I'm open all afternoon!'

She quickly tapped out a reply, a smile already back on her face.

'Sure, I definitely have a lot to talk about this time.'

Wren blew out a breath. "Sooo, do you think you need to be careful? Batten down the hatches?"

"Not yet. If I change my routine at *all* then someone will notice. I have to act like Volta's perfectly innocent friend who's never even gotten a speeding ticket," Carmen snarked. "I have to seem harmless, so it seems as weird as possible for Deputy Dipshit to be looking into me."

"On behalf of Volta's parents, too. They *really* care about getting a grandkid, never mind what Volta wants, or who they're actually into."

"Well, let's not get ahead of ourselves. Volta's *interested*, but she's not pushed for anything."

"Would you expect a sheltered pup like them to try to initiate *anything*?" Wren snorted. "C'mon, Carmen. They probably do have the hots for you, but they aren't gonna say it."

"Well, maybe I can get them to say it in *other* ways," she mused.

"The way you say that almost frightens me. You're gonna work your magic on Volta — like you haven't been *already*."

"I'll just turn up the heat a bit, find out for sure. Who knows! Maybe I'll make a few other things click for Volta while I'm at it."

Two days passed, and Volta and Carmen had another sparring session. Her wounds from the exam still hurt, but she was bearing with it as best she could, and had even managed to *almost* surprise Carmen a few times. Carmen was enthusiastic, and it was getting contagious.

"That was fuckin' *great*, Volts!" Carmen cheered, loud enough to ring off the gymnasium walls. "You're already doing so much so well, I hope you can see that!"

"I-I guess I'm starting to!" Volta wagged her tail bashfully while she shifted her footing on the mat. She was flustered, but unable to keep from grinning with bashful pride. "Well, I *know* you're going easy on me."

"Who, me?" Carmen pointed at herself, taking on a wide-eyed, exaggeratedly naive look. "I would *never*!"

"You were just talking last week about how you had *two* black belts!"

The cat dropped the naive look, grinning from ear to ear. "Okay, okay, but how am I supposed to teach you if I'm just showing off what *I* can do? The priority here is helping *you* improve, Volts, and I'd say you're damn well improving!"

Volta smirked, putting her hands up again. "Humor me, then. I wanna see what you'd do if you *weren't* teaching me."

Oh boy. You're asking for it. You are absolutely asking for it. Why not? We're having fun, might as well take the chance to ruin it.

"You sure? Like, really sure?" Carmen quirked an eyebrow, her eyes narrowed. "I'm willing, but I don't think you'll like it."

"C'mon, I wanna know how they teach researchers to fight!"

"*Pfah*, I didn't learn *any* of this at the TPA, but if you insist…" She dropped into a wider stance, her body perpendicular to Volta. One hand was kept low, the other hand up… and beckoning the wolf closer. "Go on and throw a punch, Volts, if you're so sure~"

Volta obliged. She moved forward and threw a straight — right at Carmen's wide-open side.

The glint in Carmen's eyes was the only warning she got. The tabby swung one leg forward and kicked the wolf's advancing foot out from under her. Her high hand grabbed Volta's suddenly slackening fist and pulled. Volta was yanked forward, her legs flailing as Carmen pulled her clean off the floor, and into her arms.

Before she knew what direction she was facing, Volta felt Carmen's other hand on her back, firm, but gentle in supporting her as the room swirled around.

Wait —

Carmen held her close, practically horizontal, only a foot off the floor. The tabby's hands caressed her back, as her bright amber eyes stared, like two spotlights, into Volta's startled blues. Their faces were inches apart, close enough for Volta to feel Carmen's steady, rhythmic breathing — and become intensely, *vividly* aware of her own panicked hyperventilating.

Carmen just smirked. "Gotcha~"

Volta's mind went into overdrive.

She's so close. Close enough I could — I… What would I do? Help. HELP. SHE'S RIGHT THERE, SHE'S GORGEOUS AND SHE'S HOLDING ME! SHE'S PRESSING AGAINST ME AND SHE'S SO

CLOSE — HOW IS SHE THIS PERFECT? WHAT DO I DO. DO I DO ANYTHING?? I don't want this to stop...

It was then that Volta registered a pressure on her chest, and glanced down, She was met with a sight that made her suck in a breath. Carmen's bosom, in its tight exercise top, was squishing right up against Volta's chest — and the Dampener.

And that just made it more confusing. A sudden influx of excitement, embarrassment, fear, anger, and complete... bafflement.

She looked back up into Carmen's face. The cat's smirk was replaced with a worried frown. Almost as quick, she straightened up, helping Volta back on her feet.

"You good, Volts?"

"Totally...!" Her voice cracked, nice and sharp. She shut her mouth quickly, looking anywhere that wasn't Carmen.

"Sorry, that wasn't overstepping, was it?"

"I-I mean, no..." Volta muttered, almost too quiet for Carmen to hear. She couldn't help the extremely nervous smile on her blushing face. "Th-thanks for, uhm. Thanks for showing me."

"You bet, Volts." Carmen winked. "I don't mind giving you *lots* of demonstrations~"

What does she mean by that? W-what else COULD she mean? Oh no. Uh oh. I don't — I don't know what to do. Help. Say something SAY SOMETHING.

No words came, she just stared, red as a tomato. She wasn't going to have a repeat of zapping her lunch, if she could help it. Carmen just started to laugh that same, perfect, songlike laugh.

"No doubt about it, Volta's crushing."

"That's the least surprising thing you could have told me. You put all the moves on them, what do you *expect* will happen?"

"I admit it, I'm seducing the innocent young pup into a life of sin and debauchery!" Carmen put on her most dramatic noir lilt. "Take me away, judge, or I'll just do it again, I'm *insatiable~*"

"Aw, you're not gonna break the wolf's heart, are you?"

"*Hell* no. They're sweet and passionate and clearly have been *dying* for someone in their life who really cares." It was easy to care for someone struggling so hard to prove their worth, to be fair. Carmen could relate. "But I don't mind taking that further, if they don't. Our end goal is getting Volta *out* of here, remember?"

"Damn, Carmen. If I didn't know any better, I'd say you were probably into Volts yourself."

"I don't mind admitting that. They're adorable!"

"And they're strong yet needy, just the way you like."

"That is simplifying it *a lot* and you know it."

"I know you, Carmen! You go for the high-potential ones, but *specifically* the affection-starved ones."

"Yes, I *go* for the ones I can dote on, the ones who need a friend and need company, maybe sometimes a *leash* too. Having a lot of expectations put on your shoulders makes you lonely, stressed out, and hungry for comfort and direction. Sound familiar, Wren?"

"...Oh. Oh, you can be *such* a bitch —"

"Of course it's more than that, don't worry." Carmen's voice went low and smoky, crooning. "But these long assignments do leave me very pent-up. I'm not gonna force Volts into anything they aren't into. If they don't lean that way, I'm happy to wait until *you're* around to help me get some relief~"

The bat let out an excited little squeak. "Don't threaten me with a good time!"

"It's not a threat, honey, it's a *promise*."

Volta winced, sucking in a breath as she tried to stretch. The searing pain from her bruises had been creeping up on her for two days straight now. She knew she'd been straining it even more with these extra sparring sessions, but she'd managed to bear with it even in front of Carmen. At least until today.

The tabby, already in her exercise gear with her arms and abs on full display, put one hand on her hip, head cocked to the side with concern. "… Volts, you're still sore, aren't you?"

"Y… I mean a little." Volta mumbled, taking her hand away from her side.

The cat stepped closer. "Lemme have a look."

"Uh…" Volta straightened, her body going warm. "I don't think that's — Carmen it's *not* a big —"

"Let me have a look!" she insisted, eyebrows furrowed over wide, keen eyes. "If you're still really hurting then it could be something serious. You can just pull up the side of your shirt."

Volta scooted back on the bench, tail drooped over the other side as she held up her arms. "Y-you *really* don't need to! It's fi —"

"Volta!"

She froze, staring up at the cat. Along with her voice, Carmen's expression went hard and commanding. Irrefutable. Her pupils thinned as she glared expectantly down at the shorter wolf.

For a moment, Volta forgot the embarrassment. She was frozen, but her heart was pounding. She felt hot all over but didn't dare move or break eye contact from Carmen's controlling gaze.

"Pull up your shirt."

She did what she was told.

"*Thank* you…" Carmen bent down and leaned in close to peer at the bruising on Volta's side. The autumn reds and browns of the wolf's fur did little to hide the wide purple welt. Nor, Volta worried, would it help to hide how hard she was blushing. As the cat looked, she struggled to control herself, but the stony expression in those amber eyes had left her almost paralyzed, capable of little more than a quiver.

"…Shit, Volts, we should take a few days off from sparring." Carmen, ever so gently, put a hand on the wolf. Volta froze, face burning as she felt the cat's pawed fingers beside the wound, almost touching her stomach and not her chest. "I'm sorry I didn't check sooner, you need a break."

"R-right! Yeah!" she squeaked. "I just figured I should —"

"I know you don't like admitting you need a breather, but everyone needs one, especially if they're, y'know, shot with rubber bullets."

"I —" Volta was trying to ignore the delicate press of the cat's hand against her. Her thumb was rubbing against one rib, just under the Dampener's lower strap. It almost felt like she was threatening to pet the wolf's belly. "I don't want to lose any momentum. I'm making so much progress…"

Carmen sighed as she straightened up, giving Volta the gentlest little stroke on her front, taking care to avoid the bruising or the Dampener. It sent a very different kind of jolt up Volta's spine, an almost giddy flutter, based in a very basic, obviously *canine* response. The cat smiled sympathetically, the hardness from before gone. "You don't make progress without taking breaks too, Volts. C'mon, let's walk a little instead, you up for that?"

Volta looked up at Carmen's much wider, kinder eyes. There was barely a trace of that commanding demeanor, but the memory of it was still making her shiver. Her tail wanted to wag *extra* hard when Carmen beckoned for her to follow.

Even after they entered the campus gardens, Volta still had her mind on Carmen's voice. That, and getting swept off her feet the day before. She had barely *slept* the night before, going over it again and again in her head.

"H-hey… Carmen?"

"Yeah, Volts? Is… something wrong?"

Volta blinked, scrambling to find the words. "I… uhm. I'm fine. I was just, y'know. Thinking about the, well…"

"About what?"

"Your, well, your voice, when you said my name…"

"When I snapped at you?" Carmen grimaced apologetically. "Sorry, I get like that when I'm worried about someone."

Volta bowed her head. "When you're worried, and they aren't, uhm. Acting very smart?"

Carmen gave her a reassuring grin. "C'mon Volts. You're trying to push yourself, you just have to be careful how you do that."

"I know that, but I was also wondering about when you swept me off — when you grabbed me, a day ago. On the mat I mean."

"*Ah.*" The tabby smiled wider, paused, then frowned. "Wait, shit, that *was* overstepping, wasn't it?"

"No! Nooo, no, no, no. I... You don't need to — I mean I don't want to just assume that it's okay —"

"Volta, if I didn't want to know, I wouldn't ask. Be honest, what's up? What was on your mind?"

She felt like a little kid, trying to explain why Mom's favorite vase was broken, or why the lights were all blown out, or why she'd been staring so longingly at women's clothing sections, or, "I — This is dumb. I shouldn't just assume you mean anything..." Volta rubbed the back of her head, finding the most interesting plant off the walkway to stare at. *Oh GOD why did I say that that's worse.*

Carmen started. "Assume...? Volta, this isn't dumb. You're interested, I get it, I don't mind that at all."

But you want to kiss girls. I can't be that, even if you say you don't mind...

Volta bowed her head. "I — Well that's not —" It felt like she'd been stabbed in the stomach, just to even get close to saying it. "I mean I — I *am*. A lot." Her whole body felt hot and sticky in such an uncomfortable way. "But that's not *all* I was — There's something else. It's stupid anyway, it's not something I should bother you with..."

"No! Hold on." Carmen moved forward, reaching toward her. Volta recoiled impulsively, eyes going wide with fear. "I — Volts, you can tell me. You don't *have* to dismiss it, and you clearly need to talk about it. That's what got us talking in the first place, yeah?"

"You make it sound so easy — just like everything else." She curled her hands into tight fists, pressing her claws into her palms. "No one's *ever* talked with me about this before."

"You want to sit down first, maybe? You look like you're gonna fall over."

"...Fine."

They found a secluded bench and Volta slumped onto it instantly, staring straight ahead into the only barely native flora. She couldn't decide if she was terrified, or bitter, or about to start crying again in front of Carmen. Beautiful, *perfect* Carmen. The cat sat down beside her, and cautiously put a hand on Volta's shoulder.

"I know what I said, but, ultimately, you don't *have* to talk about it if you don't want to."

"It's not that I don't want to," she grumbled, trying to will away the scared lump in her throat. "It's — I don't know. It's hard to even talk about it."

"Do you not know… *how* to talk about it, maybe?" Carmen hazarded, inching closer to her on the bench. Volta only nodded.

"Does it have to do with what you mentioned that first day we talked, on the bench nearby?"

"Yeah, a little."

God, she felt like she was back in middle school or something, being talked down to by a teacher. Carmen clearly meant well, but she must have not been able to help that tone she took on.

Meanwhile, Carmen was frowning at her with concern. "Does it have something to do with what you asked me?"

"I don't remember what I asked you," she lied. Of course she did, but she didn't want to have to say it again.

Carmen got the hint. "'What if I don't want to be one of the guys?' Those were your exact words. I said I would help you figure that out, and that hasn't changed."

Volta felt a chill go down her spine. This wasn't what was supposed to happen. Carmen hadn't ever mentioned that first day on the bench since then. She hadn't talked about what they said, or the hug… she'd just, started calling her — *him* —"Volta."

But she hadn't ever used *him* in Volta's presence since then. Volta went still, the possibilities pouring over her like hot water. Carmen wasn't spit balling, no… Carmen *had* to have guessed.

If she guessed, then you've done a worse job hiding this than you thought. There's only one kind of "help" they offer around here. You know what that is. It's what Mom and Dad almost sent you to, five years ago. You're in danger.

"Why would — *How* could you help me?" she asked, starting to bristle a little.

"I mean, we can talk about what you actually *want* to be — what you want to do with yourself, especially after you leave training behind." Carmen's calm, collected look was so disarming. How was she so calm? What did she know? What had she pieced together? What was Volta giving away?

"I — I want to be a hero, that's it. I just want to be a hero like True North, you know that." *Shit.* Her tone was getting way too harsh. She had to reign herself in, she couldn't let —

"Volta, you know that's not what I mean." Carmen sighed, looking… Worried. Sad. "That's not the whole of what you want. Look, I don't know what you're thinking right now…"

I'm panicking, that's what. I'm losing it.

"… But I know you're holding something back. You looked like this around your parents, last time they were here. You looked like this around — well, *everybody*. You're scared and you're alone — I know exactly how that loneliness feels."

"How would you?" Volta snapped, finally. "You wouldn't — you wouldn't know what it's like. You can't."

"And why not?"

"I — You're interesting to talk to. You're smart, you're strong, a *badass*, and you're fun and funny and you're — you're *beautiful*." Volta had to take a breath, and it suddenly hit her that she was simultaneously hot in the face and trying to force a lump back down her throat. "You're so many *amazing* things and you're still hanging around — around someone like me. I don't have any of that."

"I, uh, appreciate the compliments, I think…" Carmen said with a bemused grin. "But what do you mean?"

You can't know. You wouldn't still be here if you knew. Maybe I should just tell you and get it over with.

"I mean I'm —" She swallowed again. The lump wasn't going away. "I'm not smart. I'm not funny or interesting. I don't — I don't know how to be fun, all I know is superhero trivia, and I'm definitely not…" *Don't finish that sentence. That's too much. You know how she'll respond. Just like Mom and Dad did.*

"That's not being fair to yourself at all, Volts."

"I don't have to… to be fair. I h-have to be *honest*, about what I *am* and what… w-what I'm *not*." Volta's voice cracked. Her hands were at her sides, gripping the bench. She couldn't help it. Tears were already blurring her vision again. The straps and the cold metal of the Dampener ached.

"I'm not — I'm never gonna be…"

"Beautiful?" Carmen finished. Volta couldn't respond. She lowered her head, staring through angry, terrified tears at the floor. She barely registered the cat putting a hand on her arm, trying to get her to look at her. Finally, sniffling, taking shaky breaths, she glanced back up at Carmen.

She was smiling so gently and sweetly, and her eyes were glistening. "But you want to be, don't you?"

Volta couldn't piece together any words. She just let out a little sob, ignoring the voice telling her how childish it was to cry right now. Even that voice vanished into white noise. Slowly, she nodded.

"…You don't want to be 'one of the guys,' or… a *guy* at all, do you?"

Volta shook her head, trembling.

Carmen leaned in and scooted closer on the bench, just like she had that first day. Her hand cautiously went over to the wolf's other shoulder, rubbing it gently as she cried.

"…Would you say, Volta… that you *aren't* a guy? You don't consider yourself one?"

"I g —" She hiccoughed, unable to stop weeping. "I guess so, yeah…" she croaked.

"You want to be beautiful, like me, yeah?"

"Y-yeah. I know I…" She sniffled again. "I know I — *can't* be. I can't, really be —"

"Be beautiful? Or, a girl?"

"I — Yes. B-both. I can't be either. I'm —"

"You're wrong, Volts," Carmen said firmly. "You're *absolutely* wrong. You can be a girl."

Once more, Volta lost the ability to speak. She just swallowed, sniffing and hiccupping.

Carmen stared intensely at her, amber eyes blazing. "I'll say it again. You *can be* a girl. And, in fact, you can be beautiful, too. You can be *everything* you just listed. I know you must be used to not thinking that being a pretty girl is even an *option*, but it is."

"W-wha…" Volta had to take several more breaths to gather herself enough to speak. The croak of her emotion-laden, but still masculine voice felt so raw in her throat. "But — but it couldn't… They — How could — how could you say that? Like, like you just *know* it?"

"Because I do." In spite of the tears in her eyes, Carmen had never looked so sure of anything before. "You're already a girl, Volta. Because you know, for certain, that you aren't a boy, right?"

"Y-yes?"

"But does the thought of being called a girl, of me saying, 'Volta is pretty, *she* is beautiful,' does that make you happy?"

I — She — you? Wh — ?

She drew in a deep breath, trying to understand the flood of feelings that had just struck her. Words were gone again. She just nodded and sniffled.

"Then there you go. You're a girl, Volta. Hell, the *first day we met*, you wanted me to call you Volta. Not the name your parents gave you, but the one *you picked*. Who you are is up to you, and nobody else."

"But —" Volta tried to steady herself, in spite of the ongoing tears and snot and — *god*, it just hit her. She was full-on crying in front of her crush. "But my parents —"

"Whatever they told you, about what you were *allowed* to be? Is bullshit." There was that intense gaze again. The tabby gripped her shoulder, just a little, and her grasp made breathing just a little easier. "Your parents don't know a damn thing about who you are, or who you want to be. On some level you must know that, you're… trying so hard to get out from under them."

"…Yeah, I… guess I am."

"You're trying to be the real you. I can see it — I could see it right off the bat. The very first conversation we had. You had a name you wanted, and your parents immediately started telling you off. …You've had similar conversations with them, a few years back, haven't you?"

She was dead-on. How did she know? How could she possibly have known? "Y-yes but… Is that, is that really the real me?"

"You get to make that choice, Volts. That's not up to anyone else."

"But I can't be —"

Carmen gripped her tighter. "Yes you *can*, Volta. I'll keep saying it until you believe me. I know it for sure."

"But h-how can you *be* so sure?" Volta asked in a whimper.

"Because I'm like you, Volta." Carmen said, her smile returning in full. Her eyes shone through fresh tears. "I'm, well, you know the word, right? I'm trans too."

…What?

She's lying, she has to be.

The shock stopped the tears in their tracks. Volta blinked at her, completely nonplussed.

"…Y-you want to be a guy?"

Carmen immediately burst into laughter, gripping Volta tighter. "No, definitely not, Volts! I never did. I'm a *trans woman.* I'm just like you."

She had to stop and stare all over again. That didn't make any *sense.*

"You're — but… but you're tall and feminine and *gorgeous* and —"

Carmen let out a laugh. "Yeah, I am. And it took some effort, but a lot less than you might think. I was assigned male at birth, and on my nineteenth birthday, I transitioned fully. The clothes, the mentality, the body… everything. I did it, and I can *guarantee* you can do it too. You need to be the real you — that's all you need."

Volta stared for several seconds, trying to remember how to breathe. The woman she'd been crushing on, the one she'd envied, *lusted* after, was… just like her.

And she looked like that; strong and pretty and smart and perfect.

…Could I look perfect?

Did she dare even consider it? It had seemed impossible for years, but here Carmen was. Nothing about her gave it away. Yet she *knew* the cat was telling the truth. The look on her face was completely new. Happy, firm, and determined — to make it clear to Volta that this was the full truth.

Oh god… I think I love her. I'm… a girl, and I love another girl. …Mom and Dad won't be happy about this.

"You'll never guess what happened today, Wren."

"…Volta's trans?"

"Bingo. She/her, from this point on."

"*Ha!* I called it! I mean, I know we shouldn't try and speculate but *all the signs were there,* and it already *made sense* to use —"

"No time to celebrate yet. She's still stuck here, in conservative Texas, in an *extra* conservative superhero academy."

"Right, right. Volta's trans, can't be out around here, so: *now* what?"

"Volta's been trying to get away from her family ever since she enrolled under the Teepa — *because* she wants a chance at transitioning. There's no way she can do that as long as she's here."

"So, we're… well wait, what does this change?"

"This is a recruitment assignment, right?" Carmen's tail flicked with intent. "I'm recruiting her, but I'm moving my timetable forward."

"Wait, wait, why? Shouldn't we be gentle with her?"

"I don't know if we have the time. Volta's not emotionally stable here, and I can only do so much. She's had to lie to *everyone* around her for years and it's eating at her more and more every day."

"I know the feeling, but…"

"The longer she goes on, the greater the chance of her parents finding out. If that happens, Volta's situation is going to get a lot worse. Her folks aren't the type to disown her like yours did. They'd want to fix their 'mistake.'"

"…Shit."

"That's putting it mildly. I can't help her if they detain her and take her to… fuck, I don't want to imagine. We have to break her out, one way or the other, this month."

"Woah, woah, *woah.* Can Volta handle that? Can *you* handle that? You've never done any gradual recruitment in — It's not a slow burn if it's in the next three weeks, Carmen. If she's as unstable as you say, this could really hurt her."

"What choice do we have?" Carmen asked. "She's still stuck under her parents' thumb. If they find out she's trans, being unstable isn't gonna matter. She won't be allowed to complete her training, and Bradley Group won't bat an eyelid when her parents ship her off somewhere even worse than the TPA."

"Obviously she's in trouble," Wren retorted, "I know what might happen if she's left on her own, but we don't have the resources to mount an assault on a TPA base. Not this quickly. We're too far south, it'd take months, maybe longer just to get everything ready, and that would *still* mean an open attack on a State Hero Facility. We can't walk that back."

"I know, I know." Carmen rubbed her face with her hands, pushing her custom RCGs into her eyes a little. Think. *Think.* "We can't mount an open assault, maybe this month is too short, but… but I could, maybe —"

"No. Carmen? No! Listen to how desperate you're getting. It would be suicide if it was just you! This isn't Bradley Group, it's *Texas*. The TPA is *vicious* when it comes to us. I know how much she means to you, but we have to take the time to think this thr —"

"Stop. *Stop.*" Carmen snapped, and Wren went quiet. "I *know* we do. That's what I'm trying to do. Fuck. Wren, she needs to get *out*. She needs us. *Me.* We may not *have* time to think this through, something could crack any day now. I can't…" Her voice wavered, then cracked. She felt a lump forming in her throat as she glared down at her lap, hands balled up into fists. "I can't leave her like this."

Wren's voice became much more cautious. "I… I'm sorry, Carmen. I didn't mean to —"

Carmen pulled the glasses off her face and wiped at her eyes. She took several deep, shaky breaths. She had to calm down; none of this panic welling up in her would help. She slid the magenta glasses back on, and ROSE immediately took the hint.

She felt a nudge, a sudden *insistence*…

It was not numbness that came over her; it was clarity, right in the moment when she needed it.

This panic didn't need to be here. It was messing everything up, so it had to be packed up and moved to the side. The pain would be dealt with when there was time, and that was okay. Better, even. Waiting to cry without the pressure, without the pain. There would be time to manage it, but later. Not now, now there had to be…

Focus. There it was, easy and direct.

Her heart rate had slowed back down; her breathing steadied. The tears stopped, though she felt the lump in her throat remain. She couldn't panic now. This was too important — Volta was too important. She had to try, she *would* try.

"K —" Carmen took another breath. "Karen, are you listening?"

There was a beat, where the only audible thing through her RCG earpieces was Wren's anxious breathing. Then, She spoke.

"Aren't I always?" Karen's voice was wry and calm. "This channel was getting heated. Sounds like you're stuck."

"That's, yes…" Carmen took a breath, pacing herself. "It's about that potential recruit I've been talking about; Volta."

"I've been listening, yes. Extremely strong electrokinetic, and in the closet far later than she should be. The two of you are still getting along fine, I thought?"

"Yes, more than fine. *Great*, in some ways, but today just showed how desperate she could get. She's scared, she's miserable, and if things don't go well… I can't take that chance. I want to pull her out, extract her from the facility and bring her in."

"Mmmn, but as Wren already told you, RIV cannot support an open attack on a Texas Protectorate installation. Not to mention how it would turn our occasional spats with the western state governments into open armed conflict. Golden Coast would have a fit. …So, we need a delicate touch, as I'm *sure* you're thinking."

"I know, I know, just…" Carmen fumbled with her own hands, squeezing them nervously together. It was getting a little easier to talk; Karen's voice was almost always so calm, so soothing to her. "She's really, really stuck. The same kind of stuck I was — that a lot of us were."

"You don't need to remind me," the dragoness intoned. "I don't forget."

"I think ultimately, she would be happy to join us, and moreover I think — I think I'm obligated. To try? To do… to do something. Please, I can't just leave her like this."

"I understand what you want, Carmen, but short of a full operation, that would mean just using you."

"So just use me!" Carmen spoke rapidly, trying to not break down again. "I don't want to move too quickly. If it's too abrupt, it'd scare her. Volta trusts me, but she doesn't really trust the Korps yet — she hardly knows anything the news hasn't spun. I think… if I can keep building her confidence and get her to learn more about us — the *real* us — I might be able to get her to break out with me. All we'd need at that point is an extraction chopper, and we could handle the rest ourselves."

"Can she do that? She's young and has very little actual combat experience. Based on everything you've seen, she's scared of the same powers she so badly wants to use."

Carmen tightened her hands into fists in her lap. "I *know* she can do it. She's already grown a lot, and I can keep helping her like the Korps helped me."

"Hmmm." There was another beat as Karen went silent. Carmen held her breath. "Very well. If you believe you can get her out, I will trust your judgment. But take every measure to ensure your safety, Carmen. As much as you do not want to lose her, I do not want to lose one of ours either."

"Thank you, Karen."

"Thank me *after* you get out. Be safe."

Chapter 6

Resistance

The walk back to the dorms went by like a blur for the red wolf. She didn't remember passing anyone to or from it, but she did remember doing something that *could* have been described as smiling.

Volta's room felt a little warmer when she returned to it. Everything felt warmer, looked a little brighter. Even the beige and white walls of the student dorms seemed colorful for a change. A lot was still on her mind, but she didn't feel as bogged down by her own thoughts. For the first time in a long while, Volta was happy to just take the time to think.

Carmen had been overjoyed to discuss more with her — about how many trans people she knew who had been in situations like Volta's, who didn't think they could ever be their true selves, and were surprised, wonderfully, to find just how much of a difference even small changes made. Clothing, makeup, hormones… things Volta had heard about in abstract and been too afraid to ever look into. Now she almost wanted to open her laptop and start clothes shopping immediately.

But instead she was sitting down on her bed, not so much staring at the opposite wall as staring into space as the facts washed over her once again.

Carmen was a trans woman, and she looked *flawless*. By her own description, there was barely a trace of the figure or demeanor she had in her pre-transition body, and Volta's options could and probably *would* be just as various and just as effective.

And Carmen wanted to help. Carmen wanted to help *her*. She'd called her a girl, as if it wasn't a big deal. It shouldn't be, but it *was*. Hearing the words from the tabby's mouth made Volta's heart flutter and her stomach fill with giddy butterflies. She wanted to wag her tail, run in circles, scream, maybe cry again. It was just a conversation, but it was the *first* conversation.

Carmen knew near everything — more than her parents — and was still there for her.

And, and! She likes to kiss girls. I'm already a girl. Maybe I could be a kissable girl, too. Maybe? One day?

Volta took a deep breath, then blew it out in a loud sigh. Her voice, upper masculine in range, was already making her have second thoughts. She hadn't thought to ask Carmen how she'd sounded before. Was that even okay to ask? Carmen's voice was feminine, and she usually went low in a very warm way — but still in a softer, *decidedly* non-manly way. Her voice was that of a girl's, in all the ways Volta understood that to mean.

Where had she even *started?* Were there lessons? Did people actually teach other people how to sound like women? …Or, for that matter, men? And how did *that* work? And how long —

Volta shook her head in frustration, standing up from her bed. It wouldn't help to try and stew in it alone. She would have texted Carmen, but Mom already knew the password to Volta's phone, and casually checked it any time she visited her in her room. Besides, she could always ask Carmen later over lunch or before sparring.

Instead, the red wolf sat at her little desk and flipped open her laptop. Carmen had suggested something that sounded a *little* silly, but she still wanted to try it. She had tried looking at completed outfits before, but those always left her feeling empty. They were all lofty, impossible goals, for people who had actual decent, curvy bodies to work with. Carmen had suggested a middle point, looking for short term goals. Women's clothes were not something she understood the finer details of *at all*, but Carmen had told her to look for something simple: girls' shirts.

They all had names Volta had heard most often in clothing commercials: V-necks, scoop necks, on tees and crop tops that showed a *lot* more midsection than Volta had ever even fathomed being visible. Every one was modeled by women in a relatively narrow range of body types. One husky in a square-neck with a whole tuft of fluffy neck fur caught her eye.

The wolf leaned in, eyes wide with a fascination that was altogether new. She brought a hand up to her own neck, where the two layers of fluffy fur every wolf had was particularly thick, from the top of her neck to right below her collarbone. It wasn't anything so pronounced as the example in the image — Volta had never been allowed to let her fur grow nearly that long. Mom and Dad said it was unsanitary and unsightly… but the husky was *rocking* it — as much as a clothes model on a Google shopping tab search could rock anything.

Volta closed her eyes, trying to imagine that amount of fluff on herself. How would it feel to be that… bushy? A lot warmer, certainly. She hadn't seen a lot of red wolf girls that grew their fur out super thick. Texas was too hot to have that year-round, and brushing out winter coats was *already* a chore.

…But what if she could end up looking like *that?* That was a chore she could learn to enjoy, with those results. Her own color pattern was wholly different, with the ruddy orange and autumn browns framing a lot of creamy off-white spots on her face, neck and belly. And yet… it was easier than she thought to imagine fur like that, a shirt like that, framing a chest that wasn't… *massive* like Carmen's, based on the model, but enough to show off.

As Volta tried to breathe deep, the Dampener straps dug in.

Carmen once again insisted on taking a break from sparring when they were at lunch the next day; "It's as good an excuse as any to talk more about, y'know, the T-R-A-N-S thing." Volta couldn't argue with that, and she was having a hard time pretending she wasn't excited to pick up where they'd left off the day previous.

The red wolf glanced around at the rest of the cafeteria. It was crowded that day, but once again Carmen had led her over to a more secluded table. No one was near enough to overhear a quiet conversation. Even so…

"I-is it okay to talk about it here? Around all these other people?"

"As long as you're comfortable doing it! We can be discrete. If you wanna move this to someplace less bustling, though, I don't mind."

"We can stay here, uh, while we're eating, I guess." She poked at the roasted meat on her plate. "I… actually had some more questions. I don't know if they're… *okay* to ask?" Volta swayed a little in her seat, every so often glancing up to make sure no one was walking their way.

Carmen smiled. "If you're worried about offending me, don't be! I know you're asking in good faith. You gotta start somewhere, right?"

"Th-that's it, actually. How… *did* you start with your voice? It doesn't sound at all like… well, a man's. Like mine does."

"Yeah, that took a little more doing," Carmen sighed. "I'd already been *trying* to practice going higher and more, y'know, *traditionally feminine* in my inflection, for whatever that was worth. Gramma C got me in touch with a few connections, though, and what I couldn't manage with voice training, they helped me with voice box massaging."

"Th-that's a thing?"

"Oh yeah. There's a lot of little processes and surgeries they don't talk about. Some of it is *cutting edge stuff*, too." Carmen leaned in, taking on a mischievous tone. "Some of it's not technically *legal* yet. Didn't stop me, though."

"That can't have been cheap…" Volta mumbled, feeling discouraged. How would she pay for that kind of thing if she wasn't going to rely on her parents' dime? Was there any way Bradley Group would cover that kind of procedure?

"Oh god no, most places would make you pay hand over fist for all of the work I got done…" The wolf's heart sank, and her ears folded down. Carmen immediately took notice. "…But Grandma helped out by putting me on her insurance! I paid for the rest myself, in installments." She shrugged emphatically, making an extra effort to make her chest bounce a little. "I'd say it was worth every penny, though."

Volta swallowed. "I — Yeah I'd… say you got your money's worth!"

The tabby giggled. "Take it easy, Volts — like I said before, you're allowed to look!" Carmen paused, looking thoughtful. "What if I told you I *wanted* you to? Would that help?"

The wolf went pink in the cheeks. "Uh — I mean… Th — maybe?"

"You *did say* you were interested, right?" Her smile widened. "Otherwise, you could consider this an in-depth product demonstration~"

Volta squeaked, putting her chin on one palm and finding great interest in the wall to her left.

"Aw, c'mon, Volts. Don't be shy, they're just boobs."

"S'not polite to just stare at a girl's chest!" the wolf stammered. "I j —"

There was a loud thump, and all the silverware on their table shook.

"Hey, Volts, look at me."

There was a hint of that commanding voice again. Volta turned her gaze back only to see the cat's *considerable* bust, barely contained by her work blouse, resting on her end of the dining table. It felt like there was a siren ringing in Volta's head as she stared, red as a beet.

They're so big. They're SO BIG, SHE SHOOK THE TABLE. SHE THUMPED THE TABLE WITH HER — How did I EVER not notice them she's **so big** *—*

Volta shook her head as Carmen straightened up again. She was laughing like before, smiling at her. "Sorry, Volts, I can't help it. You're *really* cute when you blush like that. You get so bright red through all that fur! Just over lil' ol' me, huh~?"

"Y —"

I'M CUTE WHEN I BLUSH?

"I — h-ha, thanks, I g-guess…?"

SHE LIKES IT WHEN I BLUSH FOR HER WHAT DO I **DO** *WITH THAT INFORMATION I'm gonna fall over. Did I stop breathing?*

The wolf remembered how to inhale a moment later. Carmen was laughing even harder now, making her shoulders — and, *un*fortunately, her chest bounce too. "Oh my *god* Volts, you are way too easy to tease."

"T — Well to be fair I've… never had much experience being teased by a girl before. N-not like that, I mean."

"*Never?* What, not even in high school?"

"I didn't exactly try to leave an impression there, either."

"You must have had friends, though, right?"

"A few. Uh, none I still really talk to anymore."

"Not the kind you'd trust with…" Carmen gestured at herself, then the wolf.

"…Yeah. I already don't know what my parents would do if they found out."

"So why trust anybody else, right?" The cat grinned knowingly, and she nodded. "You're not alone there. I don't think I've talked to my mom in five years."

"You… you can't have *no* friends, though, right?" the wolf hazarded. "You… seem a lot more social than, well… me."

"Transitioning helped a lot with that, but, yeah. I've got a nice little bunch of friends — there's a few I'd love to introduce you to! I think you'd get along great."

"R-right, uh, do they… *know* about you being…?"

"Sure do. I met a few of them at the clinic I went to, and a few more after the fact. A lot of them were there for me when my actual family had abandoned me. I'd trust them with my life."

Volta felt a pang of envy. "They, uh, sound really nice."

"Hey, I know the rules are a little strict on coming and going from the campus, but maybe someday I can introduce you! Honestly, I can't think of a better crowd to be openly *yourself* around."

There was no getting around the feeling of covetous desire that welled up in her at that. Volta smiled weakly. "I'll… hope it happens before I graduate! The sooner the better."

Carmen beamed, holding up her water glass in a mock toast. "The sooner the better. And, on that note, did you try the thing I suggested?"

"O-oh! Yeah I did!" She perked up right away, tail wagging a little. "I just went for shirts, and there were… a *lot* of them, but…"

"Buuuut?" Carmen leaned in.

"There was this, uhm, square-neck cut? On a fluffy husky girl. It looked really, well —" She went red again. "I mean it looked *really* nice."

"Oooh," the tabby purred. "Go on, go on. What did you like about it? Did it look like it'd work on a fluffy wolf?"

Her blush deepened, but she was determined to stay more excited than embarrassed. "Yeah, a little, I think! It went so well with her fur, which was a lot like mine, and…"

"Carmen… I want to talk," Wren began cautiously.

"About our, uh, last call?"

"It's been hard to stop thinking about it, even with the anxiety adjustment on. I haven't heard you that upset in a long time. You really do care for Volta, and I can see that. I didn't mean to try and talk you out of…"

"I know you didn't, Wren, I lost my temper and that's my fault. I'm sorry I shouted at you."

"Thank you. Will… you be okay?"

"I'm better now. ROSE helped a bit, but the best thing for it was sleep. I'm not used to getting so mad I start shouting, ha. Haven't done that since I still lived with my family."

There was a pause. Wren recognized the direction the conversation was going and diverted. "Ideally, y'know, we save the shouting for better circumstances, yeah? Like, y'know, celebrating you bringing Volta in safe, us all going to karaoke, stuff like that?"

Carmen laughed. "It's on the list. We just need to be careful. I know I made a big deal about acting quick, but I need to make sure not to rush Volta *too* much."

"Give her *some* credit, she's taken to you being trans pretty fast!"

"That's different, that's something we have in common. She *still* doesn't see the Korps as anything other than criminals with a soft side and a queer positive bent. Emphasis on the criminal part."

"Well, if you can't change her mind while keeping your cover intact, maybe just focus on continuing to build trust with her? It's been, what, around three weeks now?"

"Just about. She's still so giddy about clothes. *Terrified* of makeup, thinks it'll make her look silly. God the way her face lights up, though, when she starts talking about the square-neck she found…" Carmen chuckled. "It's nice seeing her that unabashedly happy, for a change."

"Your voice changed in the middle of that. You sounded pretty damn happy yourself."

"Yeah! Yeah, I am. Being around Volta, being *there* for this… normally anxious little ball of feelings, getting her to relax a little, even for a *moment*, just…" She sighed. "I'm really starting to like her, Wren."

"You sound *so* gay right now," the bat replied dryly.

"Wren, I'm going to come back from this mission and wring every last ounce of sass from your tiny little bat body."

"Promise~?"

"God — YES I'm gay for her, Wren. I'm an easy mark for a girl who's been needing a break. I like being her break, letting her feel comfortable for once. She deserves it."

"You deserve a break too, Carm. You know how much you tilt, *especially* for jobs like this."

"Not until I get her out of here. I'll rest when Volta's free."

Another week passed, with more lunches and walks across campus spent talking about outfits, makeup, hair… Volta was learning more new terms every day, and Carmen was quite happy to provide as many explanations and re-explanations as she needed. The wolf couldn't remember a time when she had been happier.

Until, of course, the Friday Carmen asked something out of the blue.

"So, you're obviously not *straight*, Volts."

Volta choked on her soup. "Gu-uh?!" she replied, descending into a coughing fit and reaching for her water glass. After a few gulps, she looked up at the cat and replied with a gasping "S-sorry?"

Grinning at her from ear to ear, the cat began circling the rim of her own glass with one finger. "Well! You're a trans girl, clearly interested in another trans girl. There's nothing straight about that, so: I'm curious! Who are you attracted to? Who else *excites* you?"

Can't I just say "you" and be done with it?

Volta opened her mouth, closed it, and found another interesting patch of wall to look at while she tried to put together a reply. "I… guess I don't know. I like girls, uhm, I g-guess there's no denying that…"

"Uh huh?" Carmen prompted, leaning in a little.

"B-but that doesn't mean I'm not interested in guys, too…!" Volta trailed off near the end, eyes glancing around the cafeteria to make sure they weren't being overheard. "I — well. There's a couple… uh… I guess men who I think look… nice. I don't know what about them I like, I just—"

"Can't put your finger on it, but you *know* it's something you enjoy, right?" Carmen interrupted, the big tabby smiling playfully.

"Yeah, that…"

"Unlike girls, who you *know* exactly what you like about." The cat shifted her shoulders, raising and lowering a heavy bust that was barely held back by a V-neck.

Volta hurriedly gulped down a mouthful of soup. "Yeah — I mean, sort of? L-like I know what you're — it's not *just* that. I swear it's not just that —"

"I know, I know, I'm teasing, Volts. Sorry~ Besides, I already had figured out you liked masculine types plenty. One look at that True North pin-up in your room told me *that~*"

"I-it's not a pin-up!" Volta protested weakly, speaking in an indignant, if flustered hush. "It's a *full-body* —"

"A full-body profile diagram, I didn't forget! But I didn't hear you *denying* you were into True North."

Volta sat there wondering if she might catch on fire, and very cautiously put down her soup spoon when it began to spark. "I — Yeah a little, okay? He's hot. You called him hot before — so that's — that's why I'm using — Like I'm *interested* but I wouldn't want to make it weird —"

"I get it, I get it~" Carmen chuckled. "But there are a few different words for that, even if you don't know yet."

"…Bisexual? I guess Bi-curious. Kinda, well — I haven't really… It's not like I —"

"Not had very much chance to experiment, huh?"

Volta shook her head, smiling nervously.

"I'll… just stick with bi-curious I guess."

"Works for me! It's not like you *have* to know right now. Maybe when you transition you can revisit this, think it over again."

When I transition — that's funny.

"Yeah, maybe I will. I've got a lot of other hurdles to get over first…"

"Not the least of which," a familiar gruff voice interjected, "being getting *back* to your training regimen, Travers."

Volta knew who it was before she even swiveled her head to look up, *up* at the dour look on Tullis's face. It was a good thing her shirt hid her hackles raising in apprehension as the Great Dane looked from her to the tabby sitting opposite.

"I hope I'm not interrupting," he continued callously, "but, Travers, things have been easy on you for the last few days. Your new sparring partner, ah — Miss Rayne, was it?"

Carmen smiled sweetly up at Tullis, showing off both her upper and lower rows of sharp feline teeth. "Why, Chief Tullis, you know about our little extra lessons?"

"I *am* the head of security; if something new happens on CCTV, I know about it damn quick." He glanced back at Volta, his gaze almost… *disappointed.* "I'd expected after our little chat, Travers, that you'd be full steam ahead on completing your training here as fast as possible. What's stopping you?"

"I — Well —" Volta was completely unprepared. Especially in front of Carmen, what could she say? *Every second of silence or stammering is just going to make me look worse…* "W-well, you see, Chief Tullis, w-we figured it would be a good idea to, um…"

Tullis raised an eyebrow. "*We?*"

"Yes, we!" Carmen chimed in now, still bearing that sweet, almost simpering smile. The end of her tail twitched and swayed. She leaned forward again, pressing her shirt against the edge of the table, which made her whole bosom tighten up — impossible to miss. "I looked Volts — that's, ah, my nickname for my friend over there, I looked 'em over after the last exam, and *we* decided it would be best if we held off for a few days. Just a few, Chief, to be clear. I figure we can get back to our extra sparring sessions today, in fact."

"That's mighty considerate," Tullis remarked sardonically. "But I'd like *Travers* over there to explain it, not his, uh, 'friend.'" Tullis said the word with a grin; the concept of Volta having friends — much less one of them being a girl — seemed to amuse him.

Carmen chuckled, nodding apologetically to Volta. "Oh, *pardon* me — please, Volts, you can finish explaining, right?"

She turned her smile on Volta, but in that moment, it became much less of that too-wide baring of teeth. It was more natural, much *warmer.* It took until now for Volta to realize just how icy the look in Carmen's eyes had gotten, and how much her expression thawed as soon as she was beaming with encouragement — though maybe a little too much expectation — at the wolf.

Me!? I can barely get a sentence out around this guy, much less you!

"R-right! Well, uh, sir, the only part she left out is that it was… kind of spur of the moment. I'm still keeping up my exercise regimen, and I'm doing all I can to — to not slack off during sparring instruction with Olson."

"Really." He leaned toward her, broad shoulders square with hers — emphasizing his size advantage. She knew dominant canine posturing when she saw it. Fighting the urge to shrink away, she continued.

"R-really! I'm just as determined as I was when — when I left your office before. S-Sir. Carmen's been nothing but helpful."

The warmth of the tabby's smile carried her through every word she said and made it just a little bit easier to meet Tullis's eyes as he skeptically furrowed his brow once more. The wolf took a deep breath, trying to keep her shoulders even.

"You said something to that effect before, Travers. It's the one time you sound sure of anything, in all the time I've known you. *Hm.* Whatever you two talk about in the gym, it seems to be working."

"I studied plenty in physical education and mentorship, Chief Tullis," Carmen said with pride, tail curled up neatly behind her and ears pointed forward. "I figure the *least* I can do for Volts over here being so friendly is teach 'em some of what I know!" She really looked like she was giving Tullis her full attention. That wide smile was back, as was the hard gleam in her eyes; Volta wasn't sure if Tullis picked up on it.

"Keep up the good work then, Travers. Don't stick with that nickname, though. Heroes need better branding than that." The Great Dane finally heaved a sigh, glancing around for a moment before about-facing toward the cafeteria's buffet. "And keep that lady company, if she's so special — but *remember* what your family needs, son."

Volta deflated a little. "Y-yes, sir. Haven't forgotten…" She trailed off as the Great Dane moved beyond earshot. She glanced back at Carmen, who with pursed lips was stirring her drink with a finger.

"God *damn*, Volts, you weren't kidding," Carmen remarked, glancing up at the wolf. "The man has an axe to grind with, well, *everybody*. You really had to deal with him staring you down all on your own like that?"

"He's really good at getting people to talk. Or… just getting *me* to talk." Volta grumbled. "Which is surprising since he… spent so long talking about *himself*…"

Carmen rolled her eyes in sympathy. "Yeeeaah, I know the type. I know we talked about it before, but if you don't mind going back to it, well. Did you… say anything you *regret* mentioning in that, ah, *'chat'* he sprung on you?"

How would I know? He didn't seem to like ANYTHING I say. He's just like Mom and Dad.

"M-maybe?" was all Volta could stammer out. "I wouldn't know, I've never been interrogated before…"

"This might sound weird but, how *much* did he think I was like, a threat, or something?"

"A-a little?" She smiled awkwardly. "I-I mean it was just, talking about how you were helping me. He… he um, talked about your…" Volta clammed up again, trying not to glance down at the tabby's tightly-contained chest.

A corner of the cat's mouth curled up. "How *friendly* and *well-equipped* I was, I'm guessing. And my fighting skills, I remember you saying as much."

"Y-yeah."

"Hmm. Do you think he told everything you talked about to your parents?"

"Probably," Volta sighed. "I don't think they want me getting, um… getting involved with you." *Ohhhh no you can't stop talking there, SAY SOMETHING ELSE.* "I mean, like, a-as if that'd ever happen!"

The tabby's smirk only got wider. "Hey now, don't count your chickens, Volta. Who cares what your parents think? Is having a red wolf grandkid that important?"

"P-pretty important! But, but it's… they're just concerned about keeping the family line going."

"The *family line?* What, are they worried about 'pollution' or something?"

Is it just "worry" when I'm supposed to have an arranged marriage?

Volta laughed nervously, looking away from Carmen's face. "Well — well…! I-I think they're overreacting, it's — it's not anything they need to worry about. I'm supposed to find a red wolf girl, eventually… and start a family with her. It's what my parents want and it's not that big —"

Carmen brought a hand down on the table with a smack, her expression going hard. "Volta, honestly, *fuck* what your parents want."

Volta froze, eyes wide as she finally looked up at Carmen's intense stare. The sudden slam of her palm against the table was… a little too familiar of a noise. Her ears pinned back, and she kept silent while the tabby continued.

"You need to look out for *yourself* here, Volts. Maybe a little proactiveness wouldn't hurt — and if that means telling your parents to fuck off and not looking back, maybe that's exactly what you should do."

Are you kidding? That's exactly what I shouldn't do!

"I — I don't know about talking to them like *that*." Volta folded her arms, anxiety quivering up her spine at the mere thought. She could hardly remember the last time she'd tried raising her voice at either Mom or Dad. "No backtalk" had always been the rule, and she *did* remember, vividly, all the nights with fresh marks and no food that drilled it in.

Carmen shrugged, almost callous. "It's what I did! Of course it wasn't easy, and my mom reacted just how you'd expect. Getting out from under my mom was *hard*, but it was a lot better than just putting up with her trying to control me."

But I'm not you. I could never be like you.

"I guess…" Volta mumbled. "I'm not used to being that assertive, like you are. That's not — that's not *me*."

Carmen frowned, leaning in and lowering her voice. "Volta, be honest. How much of what you let your parents see is really *you* anyway?"

Volta had no answer for that. She felt heat wash over her face in frustration. Something about Carmen's tone, how she leaned forward, how she looked at Volta with so much worry and pity, was getting a little patronizing.

"You *have* to stand up for yourself sometime, Volts," Carmen continued. "Not me or anybody else. *Especially* if you're gonna transition. I know better than anyone how important this is."

"I believe that you do…" Volta grumbled.

"So, believe it for *yourself*, Volta!" Carmen almost sounded desperate, nearly… *angry*? Angry at her, or angry on her behalf? Volta wasn't sure she could tell the difference. "You *have* to do this. It's the only way out of this situation you're in. It may not be *you* right now but, well, *maybe* you need to stop being *you* for a minute and try being somebody with a little more *backbone*."

Volta froze. That *stung*. She stared, stunned, at the cat. For the first time in all the time that the wolf had spent with her, saw hesitation in her eyes — and then, regret.

…So she CAN see how pathetic I am. She just wasn't saying it.

The din of the cafeteria around them poured over Volta abruptly as they both remained silent. She was once again very aware of the Dampener, her heartbeat thumping gently up against the conductive metal surface.

"…I can't do it the same way you did, Carmen." It took all of her willpower to keep from stammering. She kept her blue eyes locked with the tabby's amber ones, almost too scared to look away. She wanted to shut her eyes and scream. "I'm not just like you. I don't — I don't *have* that same… *something* that you do."

Carmen kept quiet. Did she not actually have a response this time? She stared back, unblinking, her mouth still tight. Her striped tail, visible behind her, flicked at the tip from side to side, like the ticking of a clock. Those thin pupils of hers almost felt like knives, sliding past Volta's fur coat and through her skin.

Steadying herself with a deep breath, Volta proceeded. "You want me to stand up to my mom and dad. I… I don't know *how* yet. H-how am I supposed to? They've been there all my life. They're — they're my parents! They *know* me. How am I just supposed to ignore that?"

"It's not like they've really done much good with the whole '*knowing you*' part…" Carmen began softly — but there was a hard edge to her voice that hadn't been there before. She was upset, the most upset Volta had ever seen her.

"I — I guess not." Even that almost hurt to say out loud. She knew it was true, and that didn't make it any easier. Maybe for Carmen it didn't matter — or it stopped mattering. "… But they're still my parents. I'm here because of them. I still have to — I still have to listen to them."

Carmen looked intensely angry for a moment. Her hands, which normally looked so soft, bore their long, sharp feline claws, threatening to leave scratch marks on the table. The tabby stiffened her tail, shut her eyes, inhaled, then exhaled and opened them again. Her whole expression softened. The anger and tension was gone, replaced with a worn out, sullen look.

"…Yeah, you do. As long as you're stuck here they have control over you like this, don't they?"

Thanks for the reminder…

Volta nodded in resignation.

She took another breath, and screwed her eyes shut while she did it. "Shit. I got way too angry. I'm sorry I slammed the table like that. I'm sorry I said you didn't have any backbone, Volta. Really, that was a shitty thing to say. I'm sorry about this whole… *thing* that you're stuck in. None of it's fair, and it's not your fault that it isn't."

She didn't get very many apologies. For a moment Volta had to let the words process before she could even piece together a response. "It's okay. I know you want to help."

"Me helping should never come before your comfort, though," Carmen said ruefully. "I should have remembered how uncomfortable this all is when it comes to your parents. You get to decide what you want to do, Volts — that's, well, that's my whole point, hah." Carmen grimaced.

"W-well, thank you, Carmen. Thank you for — for wanting to help me so bad that you called me spineless." She blurted it out suddenly, face heating up for a completely different reason.

Oh god did that sound as bad to her as it did to me? Fuck, shit.

Carmen laughed, and in spite of how her demeanor had changed, her laugh stayed the same: just as sweet and singsong and comforting. "Haaah, fuck. Well, Volta, if you ever need me to kick you into shape, uh, be sure to ask first. It's up to you how much I help."

"O-okay!"

"Wren, I'm going to say some words you *love* hearing, and I'm going to ask very politely that you not lord them over me like you have before."

"My curiosity is piqued, go ahead."

"I fucked up."

"OOOH — *Oh*. Oh shit. Oh no hun tell me what happened."

"I did the exact thing I said I shouldn't do. I tried to rush her, and I went too far." Carmen flared her nostrils and closed her eyes, steeling herself with a deep inhale. "You know that thing I did when we were first getting to know each other better?"

She could tell Wren was smiling as he spoke. "The thing where you were a condescending bitch who thought you were the smartest person in the room, and that you had the magic solution to everyone's problems?"

She let her breath out all at once, her eyes shut tight. "*Yes, Wren, that thing.*"

"So, you just threw some of that at Volta, didn't you."

"Yeah, I did."

"Is she okay?"

"Actually, yeah. To be honest she took it *way* better than I was expecting. I was worried I'd shut her down but she's… a lot stronger than she gives herself credit for. She's still so scared of so many things, me included, but she still stood her ground. I just hate that I… *made* her have to."

"Earth to Carmen," Wren intoned, suddenly much more serious. "Think about what you just said real hard for a second. She's not *strong*, honey, she's traumatized."

Carmen, stock still, blew out her breath like she'd just got the wind knocked out of her. "Fuck, I just did it again, didn't I?"

"Yep! Sounds like you should spend some extra time making sure Volta is *really* okay."

"Yeah, actually. Maybe I should also set aside some time for me and ROSE to talk about some things."

"Sure! Maybe ROSE, maybe one of the base therapists? I know Nurse O recently branched into offering sessions for people away on missions."

"There's an idea." Carmen put her face in her hands, rubbing at her eyes under the lenses of her glasses. "Fuck, I should say sorry again. Here I was calling her strong when she was… *probably* just trying to mitigate how angry she thought I was getting."

"Carmen, if she thought you were getting angry, you were probably getting angry."

"…Yeah. Good point. Hah, shit, I *do* need to call somebody, this place is getting to me."

"Hey, Carm, nobody's perfect. Not even you!" Wren chimed in, albeit gently. "Much as the old you liked thinking you were, and as much as Volta may *want* to think you're perfect, you're still going to stumble."

"Yeah, yeeeaah I know."

"Don't you worry, I'll be right here to tell you how much of a dipshit move that was after."

"*Pfah.* God, I miss you. Volta needs me to be perfect, and I know I can't *be* perfect, but I want to be as close as I can for her. She deserves nothing less."

"Wee woo wee woo!" Wren wailed dramatically. "The gay detector's off the *CHARTS* now. We're officially in triple-gay territory."

"Oh shush, you. I still feel bad about the whole thing, but keeping Volta happy will help. It's a lot more important than me wallowing, anyway."

"That's the spirit! Go get her, tiger, she's all yours~"

"Not *yet*, Wren, not yet…"

Volta knew exactly how Olson's class was going to go the moment she walked into his sparring room. He immediately took her to task. He paired her up with the largest classmate she had — one she recognized glumly. "You've been slacking off, Travers; I can tell," the lean bear chided. "You're with Evans today so you get a proper warmup."

The thick-maned lion stood five inches over Volta and had a physique that came closer to rivaling Carmen's bulk. Right, Evans was Olson's favorite student — probably because he was the biggest, and even if he pulled his punches he still hit *hard*. He wasn't exactly mean, but he didn't take much time to be friendly either.

It didn't help that he was a pyrokinetic, in *perfect* control of his powers, and on track to go to work for the TPA — a sure thing for him that he didn't have to qualify like she did with Bradley Group's representative. Volta was at least comforted by the fact that the lion wouldn't graduate any sooner than she would.

But that didn't stop Evans from making her feel completely outmatched. Nothing scared her more than a masculine type that clearly *belonged* in their masculinity in ways Volta never could. The lion nodded down at her and held up his right hand — the typical respectful gesture Olson wanted.

They tapped knuckles and dropped into their respective stances. Volta kept low, prioritizing a guard over a more aggressive stance. Evans responded in kind, one fist already pulling back for a strike. Volta tried not to look too worried.

At least Carmen isn't watching right now…

They had managed to exchange only a few blows before Olson turned from the rest of the students to the two of them. Or, rather, just her.

"Travers! The hell are you doing, waiting for permission?" he snapped. "TPA heroes are *active*. If you can't get aggressive —"

Okay, fine.

Volta blocked another jab, and immediately threw one back, smacking Evans's hand as he brought it up to block — almost too slow.

"Oh come *on* Travers, you're not playing pattycake," the bear laughed coldly. "If you're gonna hit him, *mean* it or just keep being Evans's punching bag."

Her face felt hot already. She didn't dare look away from the lion as they circled one another, and the lion tensed up again. He threw another punch; Volta swerved to one side and connected a heavy left hook with the lion's shoulder — maybe the third time she had ever gotten a body hit in on Evans. He looked surprised for a second. Very, very briefly, Volta grinned up at him.

"Not a bad beginner's jab…" Olson sniffed. "But you're still too passive, Travers. Evans, if he waits too much, go for the parts he's *not* protecting."

"Yes sir," the lion muttered, tightening his fists threateningly at Volta.

Uh oh.

Volta lowered her fists a little and hurried to throw another punch — only to have it deflected almost completely by Evans's own guard. He swung one leg wide, aiming a roundhouse kick at Volta's side. She jumped to the side, bringing her elbow down on his foot. Just like Carmen taught her.

Olson made some kind of approving noise as Evans had to regain his balance.

"Travers, do you plan to look so proud of yourself *every* time you actually hit someone?"

Volta blanched. "I-I didn't —"

"And you're stuttering *again*, in *my* class," Olson barked. "You're not a scared little puppy, Travers, *grow up* and grow some balls. TPA men are supposed to show their *tenacity*, and all I'm seeing from you is why you still haven't found a girl, Travers."

She wasn't ready for that. In spite of every other insult hurled at her, she froze for just long enough for the lion to follow through on the bear's instructions and hit her straight on with a jab. His fist smacked right into the Dampener, forcing it into her chest and knocking the wind out of her.

The wolf stumbled back, gasping for air. Her face burned as she grimaced in embarrassment. Finally Evans stepped back, lowering his fists and walking towards her. Olson jumped at the chance. The bear leaned over Volta as she caught her breath, speaking in a ridiculing growl. "What, Travers, now you can't even take a punch? You can't just put your tail between your legs and mope like a little girl." Volta looked up at him, trying not to scowl too hard. Olson just sneered. "You've been here for a year and a half. *Act* like it or I'm holding you back a semester."

The idea gave her chills all over. She straightened up slowly and stiffly, mumbling another "y-yessir" in response.

"Attaboy. Evans, don't let up. Travers needs to learn what being a *man* is all about. You don't get girls by cowering like one."

Volta swallowed and put her fists up again, trying not to hang her tail as the burly lion opposite her cracked his knuckles.

Chapter 7

Breakdown

It was her worst class to date. Olson's constant heckling led to more mistakes — which only gave him more ammo whenever he passed by her and Evans. The entire time, the lion just stared at her getting chewed out. Was he enjoying it, or did he just not care enough to speak up? Volta didn't know if she cared too much about the answer.

As soon as the clock struck 2, Volta hurried off Olson's training mat and spent a good ten minutes in her bedroom trying to recuperate. It was only Carmen's text reminding her about their next meetup that got her off of her bed — and into the shower, finally. She didn't like being late, but at this point it was better than not seeing Carmen at all after a day like today.

One more embarrassing check under her shirt later, Carmen finally deemed Volta fit enough for a little extra practical training — but not before prying out of her how Olson's class went. She checked and double-checked that the wolf wouldn't mind another workout after enduring so many hits from Evans, and even then, Volta could tell that she was being a lot more gentle.

Carmen had her work on deflecting hits the same way she did; knocking jabs and kicks downward with her arms. She was clearly holding back with everything she threw at the wolf, focusing more on reaction time and form than enduring an impact.

Volta was almost a little sad when Carmen ushered her off the mat. At this point she was starting to actually feel confident, maybe not in taking Carmen down, but at least in holding her own and not getting thrown to the mat — which had happened a few times already. Still, it was far more concrete than Olson could ever manage by shouting about her mistakes.

She hadn't even been worried, until she caught Carmen looking at her with concern while she rested her legs. "You're not still thinking about what Olson said, are you?"

"I'm… well I'm *trying* not to," Volta admitted weakly. "He's the first one to point it out since —"

Since Mom and Dad did four years ago.

The tall tabby bowed her head, arms folded as she mulled that response over. "Hey, Volts, you… *know* that stuff doesn't *really* matter, right?"

"What do you mean?"

"Like, being a virgin, actually knowing how to, like, 'get with the girls,' and impressing the other guys. You're already fine with the last part — or you say you want to be, but… none of that *matters*, right?" Carmen leaned forward a little, trying to meet Volta's eyes.

"I — Well, I try not to think about it."

"Any luck with that? Any *more* than trying not to think about what Olson said?"

Volta hung her head and folded her ears. "N… No."

"Mmmn, I was worried about that."

"I-I know it *shouldn't* matter, I just — I just don't want everyone seeing me trying to be a hero and just seeing… seeing weakness."

Carmen shook her head. "None of those things have anything to do with being *strong*, Volts. It's about standing up for yourself, sure, but that doesn't mean hooking up with a lot of girls or being 'manly enough.' That's just being a shitty person, most of the time."

Volta snorted. "…Maybe that's why I don't like my cousin Jordan so much."

Carmen got a knowing, bitter look on her face. "Lemme guess: Is he training to be a superhero too?"

"No, he's a police officer. He joined the force in Dallas two years ago."

"Ah," Carmen said simply, tapping her chin. "Guessing he's not all that friendly, considering the whole cop part."

"I — I mean, just because he's a cop doesn't mean he's rude," Volta protested.

Carmen deadpanned and leaned toward her again. "But he *is*, isn't he?"

"I — yeah. He constantly acts like he's got something to prove. Every time I see him at family gatherings, he — he just struts around like *he's* the one with superpowers." Volta's jaw tightened as she spoke. She felt her hackles raise a little. Cousin Jordan always put her on edge already — really spending time *thinking* about him was making her *mad*.

"He — he always brings a new girlfriend every time, and he always treats them so bad and laughs about it with his friends like — like it's just a *game* to him. He drinks so much, he shoves his badge in my face, he makes jokes about — about queer people. Gay people, mostly, but sometimes about…" Volta blew out the rest of her breath. She was starting to feel hot all over, fur bristling. An electric hum rang in the back of her head.

"About trans people?"

Volta dug her hands into the bench, claws digging into the wood. She felt the hints of a snarl on her lips. "Yeah. About — He talks about arresting… he calls them 'neckbeards wearing dresses.' His parents and his friends laugh, and my parents think it's *so funny*, they think he's great, they think he's the kind of person I should be. Like I need to be like him to be successful, to be *worth* any —"

"*Volta*," Carmen interrupted, loudly. "Volta, you don't need to keep going."

"They always tell me how proud they are to have an officer like him in the family," Volta muttered, a little quieter. "They call him a real hero. Like he's actually helping people, when all he ever seems to do is —"

Carmen finally raised her voice proper. "Volta, *stop*."

Volta finally looked back up at her, expecting the same domineering expression from before. She was taken aback by the sadness in her face. The humming noise faded away, and Volta realized just how tensed up on the bench she had become.

"Please, at least take a second." Carmen bent down in front of her and very gently put a hand on Volta's shoulder. "I get it. You *really* don't need to put yourself through it like that."

"S — Sorry…" Volta lowered her gaze again, a far more embarrassed heat pouring over her face.

"You don't have to apologize, Volts, it's *infuriating* when parents talk like that." Carmen sighed and sat down beside her on the bench once again. "I get how you feel. My mom said a lot of similar things to me for *years*."

"I just…" Volta took another breath, relaxing her fists. "I don't understand why they compare me to him so much, and everyone else they approve of. Is…" She trailed off, her face screwing up with a rueful scowl. "Is it because Cousin Jordan is just… so confident? So full of himself? Is he just *better* than me? What's wrong with me that I look at that and I just feel so... angry?"

"He's *not* better than you for that," Carmen reassured, hand on Volta's shoulder. "That's not at all why they do it, that's a promise."

"Then why?"

"Because you're not the perfect child for them, Volts. It's the same thing we talked about from before. They want you to fit their mold, fit all their expectations and ambitions. All the things they try to push on you are things *they* want. They expect *so much* of you and they're seeing some of what they want from you in Jordan. Just because they want you to be a certain way doesn't mean you have to be, or even *should* be."

"Why not? What's the difference? They're — They're supposed to want what's best for me, aren't they?"

"What they want is what *they* think is best. It doesn't necessarily have anything to do with your feelings or, honestly, your well-being. Every time I've seen you do anything they *slightly* disagree with, they have to make sure you feel guilty, make you less sure of yourself. Surely, you've noticed *that* at least."

Volta thought back to the day they first met, with Mom and Dad chastising her out on her hero name, for not taking the Korps seriously. She had felt like a child, standing there in front of them, reassuring them despite the doubts and worry their words instilled in her.

"...I-I guess so. But..."

"Remember when you told me about their feelings towards the Korps and LGBT people? You noticed that they don't bother making a distinction," Carmen observed. "That's just one more part of it. If you were trans, Volts, you'd be part of that group to them, and on some level I think they're worried you *might* be. They want to make it clear to you how *evil* all that is. They want you to constantly think about what they'll do if you express that part of yourself, if you dare veer off the one path they've picked for you in any way."

As Volta stared at the ground in front of her, a heap of memories began to bubble up all at once.

In most of them, she was still a child; in a scant few, a preteen. Most had Mom or Dad standing over her, sometimes shouting, sometimes dictating from the Bible, sometimes holding her by the jaw to make sure she didn't keep lowering her head.

Sometimes it was the belt.

But one stuck out: when she was 14, finally more gangly than chubby, and starting to get bushier facial hair that she hated. One Sunday afternoon, she made the mistake of admitting to her parents that she didn't want to live through puberty if it meant turning into a man.

The rest of the memory was one that she had re-lived in her sleep for weeks, months, *years* afterward, along with too many others. They all ended with her locked in her room, kneeling at her bed, praying like Mom instructed, begging a wall with a cross for mercy and forgiveness. Volta's chest felt tight, and her head throbbed from the returning hum, louder than before. What did forgiveness even mean? Mom and Dad never showed any unless Volta went to bed with sore arms and a bruised back.

God never bothered to reply; the cross just hung there over her bed, as mute as the wall it was nailed to.

"…Shit. Volta, are you okay?"

Carmen's worried voice pulled the red wolf back to the present. Volta wasn't sure when her vision had gotten blurry, but she hurried to wipe her eyes and look at Carmen directly. The tabby looked really worried now. She extended a hand slowly, and very, very cautiously, Volta pressed her shoulder against it until the cat was gently stroking her back. The touch warmed her and helped her steady her breathing.

"We're dwelling too long on this. I'm sorry, let's change the subject."

"Y-yeah," the red wolf sniffed. "Yeah, okay, I just. If… if I never hear another word about Cousin Jordan, I'll be happy."

"I feel you there, when it comes to *any* cop role model," Carmen said with a shiver. "*Eugh.* Point is, I get it."

Volta's mind was racing, trying to change the subject. It wasn't exactly a *different* topic, but… "Do you not like cops?"

"*Hell* no, I fuckin' hate em." Carmen hunched up her own shoulders, as if the mere thought disgusted her. "The problems you got with your cousin? Yeah, I don't blame you. I'm never comfortable around cops. I see assholes in uniform do terrible shit all the time."

"Really?"

"Oh *yeah*. Every policeman I've ever met treats anyone who doesn't look like them and act how they want to like shit — and even then, that doesn't always help."

"I…" Volta started. "I know the news talks about a few cases of police brutality before, but —"

"What, the news your parents let you watch?" Carmen gave her a doubtful look. "I'm sorry, Volts, I'll try and put this gently. There's no way you ever saw an honest news report on police brutality as long as you lived with your family. Your parents want you to be like your asshat of a cousin, and they gave *him* a badge and a gun."

"But he's just one guy, right? It's not like *every* cop is just like him, are they?"

Carmen guffawed. "Wow. Wooo*wowoww*. Okay, I explained what your family *thinks* communism means, versus what it actually means, you remember that right?"

"Yeah," Volta's brows furrowed. "…Wait, is this the same kind of situation?"

The cat straightened up again and gave her an exaggerated nod. "Uh, yeah. *Yeah*. You don't know the half of it…"

"Volta's parents would really benefit from some time spent buried alive in a landfill," Wren declared. "It'd build character. They'd learn a few things about the world, I think."

"You won't hear me complaining," Carmen muttered. "They've fucked this wolf up so much that she *knows* she's been abused — and still isn't sure whether she deserved it or not."

Wren let out a defeated sigh. "Okay, okay, all that information is logged. ROSE, please just help me feel a little better."

Can do!

The bat took several slow, steady breaths as the RCGs on his face worked their magic. After a few seconds, he piped up again, sounding much more relaxed. "All right, let's move on to a lighter subject, sorta."

"And what would that be?"

"Volta thinking there are good cops."

"Oh *god* yeah, I nearly choked listening to her talk about it. This is right up there with her experience with food."

"I know both of these things are because of her godawful family, but, ohhhh my god, Carmen, you know what she pulled on you."

"What?" Carmen asked with a grin, already knowing the answer.

"A FEW BAD APPLES!" Wren howled.

"RIGHT?"

"JUST A FEW BAD APPLES, YEAH VOLTA HOLY SHIT. THAT'S ALL. S'NO PROBLEM."

"To be fair, she admitted afterward that she had barely ever interacted with cops before her cousin joined up."

"That doesn't change the fact that *you got 'bad apples'ed by Volta*, holy fucking hell Carmen. And they say *we're* the ones who brainwash people, fuck's sake."

"We *do* use mind control, Wren."

"Yeah but at least we don't pretend we're not doing it!"

"We all gotta start somewhere!" Carmen sighed.

"Yeah, but her cousin's Twitter handle is @*Thinbluelupine*, that's so fucking on the nose. Do you think she even gets it?"

"She definitely gets it. Don't be too hard on her, Wren, *you* started as a rich kid too."

"Yeah, my parents propagandized me just as much and I *still* didn't like cops."

"You were ahead of the curve, then. She's still getting into the groove of this kind of thinking."

"So, how's she feeling about the fact that all her life she's aspired to be like the guy who's barely removed from being a federal-level supercop with more money and professional martial arts training? And! — And, that the only thing that ever stopped True North II from being a shithead was that he *wanted* to be nicer than his dad?"

"I don't think it's hit her yet, I was gonna wait until *after* I brought her in."

"…So, when *is* that gonna happen, anyway?"

"Soon enough! We're getting closer."

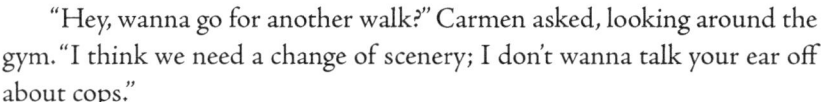

"Hey, wanna go for another walk?" Carmen asked, looking around the gym. "I think we need a change of scenery; I don't wanna talk your ear off about cops."

Volta perked up. That was way easier to do than follow along on what Carmen had to say about police — in spite of how much of it fell neatly in line with the anxiety Volta already had around her cousin.

They took another walk through the campus gardens and took some time to talk about far more relaxing things. They talked about Volta's steady improvement with her form and discipline, a bit more True North television trivia that Carmen *insisted* the flustered wolf finish explaining, a few more outfit ideas… By the time they found a bench to rest at, Volta's tail was up high, wagging happily. As much as the tabby knew how to bring up a lot of uncomfortable topics, she also knew how to get the wolf to relax and, in spite of everything, enjoy herself.

And that was when Carmen, tapping her chin, decided to ambush her. "…Hey, Volts, have you ever kissed anyone before?"

The wolf hunched up where she sat on the gym bench. "Oh *no*, no, no. H-ha, I didn't ever know that many people who felt that way about me."

Smooth, real smooth.

"But have *you* wanted to, with someone, before?"

She bowed her head, brow furrowed. She didn't like what that question reminded her of. *Yes*, she had absolutely wanted to kiss multiple people before. One of them had been 'betrothed' to her by another red wolf family her parents were close with.

Austin Travers was hopeful, if nothing else, that it would be painless, but *Jennalee Moran* wanted nothing to do with the arrangement, and made sure everyone knew it. Volta wasn't under any delusions, she knew her fellow red wolf wanted nothing to do with her, but *still* Jennalee took the time to try and confide in her, like two prisoners with the same sentence, chained together.

Jennalee was *fierce*. She spoke her mind, she pushed back against everything her parents made her do. She took as little shit as she could manage, and Volta couldn't help but admire that. Jennalee was everything she wished she could be, and though she ensured Volta knew that their marriage would end up a hollow one, the closeted wolf couldn't help herself. She *did* like Jennalee, and kept hoping, despite their situation, that she might change her mind.

Of course she didn't. Why would she? I was the wimp she was trapped with. No girl wants a limp-dicked pussy for a husband. She ran away, because that was better than being stuck with me.

"W-well, uh," Volta coughed. She had been silent several seconds too long. *Again.* "I mean — yeah, I have, but only one… one or two people when I was in high school. A-and, y'know, um…"

Volta looked up at Carmen guiltily, who couldn't help but giggle. "Thanks for your honesty, Volts."

The wolf lowered her head a little more, staring at the floor. "Y-yeah, I haven't really um, had the chance…"

"Sorry, I don't mean to sound like that's some kinda *requirement*. Lots of people don't have their first kiss for a while! I know quite a few personally!"

"Really? But you're so…" She trailed off, embarrassed by Carmen's knowing grin.

Carmen chuckled, nudging Volta with her shoulder. "I mean I took my time with it, I didn't exactly want to be close to anybody before I transitioned. You gotta remember just how much we've got in common, Volts. S'totally normal to not have kissed anybody yet." The cat paused, clearly contemplating something. "That said…"

"What?"

The cat sat down next to her again and curled her tail around the bench. "Well, I don't wanna make you uncomfortable, but I have a question."

The wolf blinked. "Uh, go ahead?"

"Well, would you like to kiss me? I know you're interested in me, like it's hardly a *secret*."

Volta's stomach jumped, and she almost squealed out of flustered shock. "A-are you — Are you *serious?* Wait — but —"

Is this good? She's just… OFFERING, just like that. She has to be telling a joke. Maybe I'm on camera again.

Carmen glanced to the side, tip of her tail swishing behind her. "I get it if you're not, like, okay with doing it now, given how things are."

The red wolf went wide-eyed, blushing as naive, overexcited thoughts filled her head. She immediately knew her answer, and was *terrified* to give it. "I... uhm."

"Again, I don't wanna make you uncomfortable. You're already dealing with a lot, when it comes to all this, but if you'd like...."

"...No, I... I would like to."

Carmen perked her ears. "You sure?"

The wolf's face burned. This definitely wasn't real, she must still be dreaming. Carmen's smile was so comforting, as she started to inch closer.

"Y... Yeah. I would. I — as long as you're offering!"

The tabby hummed, clearly pleased. "Well, in that case, let me take the lead..."

The cat leaned in close, until the wolf could feel her breathing. She started to lean away and had to stop herself. Still red as a beet, she held firm, let the bigger tabby catch up with her. Carmen had a hand on the wolf's arm and was rubbing it gently. Her height meant Volta had to tilt her head back just a little to line up.

Even now, the cat was whispering instructions in that same soft, caring voice. "Just open your mouth a tiny bit. You've seen it in the movies, right? Very gentle, just purse your lips a little, and..."

Their lips touched. Carmen held her breath, and Volta followed suit. The cat pressed a little until their noses brushed up against each other, ever-so-gently. The cat's bright amber eyes were lidded as she stared at Volta. She couldn't look away; she didn't *want* to look away. The panic in her head was struck silent.

It was almost over too fast. Volta let herself be led along; she closed her eyes, heart racing. Her face felt like it was on fire, and for a fleeting moment she forgot where she was. She forgot about the Dampener, about her chest, her body. For a brief, beautiful moment, it didn't matter. Carmen was kissing *her*. *She* was kissing Carmen, the woman of her dreams.

It was too much.

She pulled away, her eyes darting away. The cat's startled expression quickly turned to one of worry.

"I'm sorry, I didn't mean to... Was that too long? Too much too fast? Should I..."

Volta shut her eyes as reality creeped back in, trying not to let it overwhelm her. It would have been nice if they could go one day together without her ending up in tears. "N-no, it —"

Her voice was cracking.

"It's n-nothing you did. None of this…" Her hands balled up into fists as she glared tearily down at herself. "None of it works. For just a second, for a *second*, I could… I almost forgot how, how…" She wiped at her own eyes, trying to take a steady breath, only to have it quiver and shake. "*Damn it.*"

Carmen very tentatively leaned against her, wrapping a hand around and gently rubbing her other arm. "It's okay. You don't need to feel bad about getting mad about it… I got mad too."

Her breathing gradually evened out; her heart stopped racing. She still felt like garbage, but she could think, and she could wipe the tears away.

"S-sorry. I'm crying too much lately."

Carmen gripped her more tightly. "No such thing, Volts. You're never going to bother me by letting your feelings out."

How much do you really mean that? No one's that patient.

Volta sniffled. "All I do is cry on your shoulder and you still smile at me like that…"

"I really, honestly don't mind, Volts. This is what I *want* to do. I want to be here for you, let you breathe a little bit. You need it, I enjoy providing it for you. Do I need any more reason than that?"

Volta tried to chuckle, and it came out as a hiccup. This wasn't how things were supposed to go, and she still didn't want this to stop. Carmen smiling, gently stroking her back… Without the tabby's soft, pawed hands on her body, she felt like she would fall to pieces. Carmen held her together.

There was a moment of silence, before Carmen silently began to wrap her arms around the wolf. Their eyes met again, and she just asked simply: "Hug?"

The wolf nodded, and they embraced again. The wolf relaxed her head into the larger cat's shoulder, breathing a shaky sigh.

"…For what it's worth, for a first kiss that was pretty good. Not too wet, not too long." Carmen remarked.

"I interrupted it with my crying, though…"

"If you'll believe it, not the worst thing to interrupt a kiss, for me. You're a natural."

"H-ha, thanks," Volta muttered, smiling.

She gradually got more control of herself as they hugged, until she was able to pace herself through a full sentence. "It's... does it ever get easier? Does this ever go away? How did you ignore... *everything* that comes up, until you..." She squirmed uncomfortably. "Y'know..."

"Until I transitioned?" Carmen rubbed her back with one hand, almost clinging to her with the other. "Well, I didn't just suppress everything. Grandma helped a lot, but ultimately, I was just... counting the days. Crossed them off on the calendar. Having a goal I was working towards did wonders — made every bad day go by faster. That's what I want to do for you, Volts, if you'll let me."

"You make it sound so easy." Volta tried not to sound too jealous. "I've had a goal in my head since I was eleven, and I still don't know how long it'll take..."

Carmen went silent for a moment, and Volta could tell she was thinking over her words. "Maybe... maybe it'll be sooner than you think. It's not easy, the wait is never easy, but I'll be here for you every day, until the time comes."

"Th-thank you," Volta whimpered. The cat squeezed her once more.

"So, it sounds like things are going well — tears included?"

"No thanks to Tullis or her parents, but we're handling it."

"That's to be expected. So, what's next?"

"It's the part I'm... *really* not looking forward to."

"I got a pretty good guess what that is."

"I have to tell her."

"Yeeep. Your turn to come out, I guess. You think she's ready to take it?"

"The sooner the better, at this point. I've already gotten her to start thinking about the situation with the Korps more critically. There's not really much else to do except just… *tell* her the truth." Carmen breathed in, feeling tense. "…Shit, it was a lot easier with you."

"Yeah, well, I had advance warning. There's not much you can do to warn Volta, is there?"

"Nope! I'll just… be direct and make it obvious and hope for the best." "And expect the worst?"

"Obviously. I *am* a professional!"

"And you don't like admitting to hiding things, at all, it makes you anxious."

"Yeah! It does! I'm kind of stalling now!"

Wren's snarky tone turned soft. "Carmen, you got this. You've been trained for this. Volta trusts you."

"I know, I'm just…" She sighed. "I'll deal with it. No more stalling, I'm telling her today. I'll give her my spare pair of RCGs, make it obvious this is about helping her."

"Fingers crossed she lets you put them on!"

"Fingers crossed she puts them on *herself*, Wren."

Volta had feared that talking about the kiss was just going to end awkwardly. Not just afraid, she was *terrified*. She almost didn't show up in time, but Carmen urging her into her seat and encouraging her to talk about it was the best surprise she could have hoped for.

"We didn't *really* discuss it too much after the fact, huh?" Carmen began.

"I, uh, guess not!" The wolf smiled awkwardly, then grimaced. "…It wasn't *too* bad, was it?"

"Not even a little," Carmen beamed at her. "It was clearly your *first* kiss, but you were gentle and careful — that's way more important than nailing down things like passion or *firmness*."

"Y-you have to be firm with a kiss?"

"If you're the one initiating, it sure helps." Carmen stirred her glass of water with one finger. "You can't be a wet blanket about it, *both* you and whoever you're kissing need to offer *some* pushback. Not out of any like, macho bullshit, it just *feels* better that way."

"Y-you sound like you have a lot of experience…" Volta muttered.

"That's not a problem, is it~?" Carmen batted her eyelashes. She took her stirring finger out of her drink, and with casual poise that stirred up the butterflies in Volta's stomach again, she slipped it into her mouth to suck it dry.

"No! No, no, no, not at all!" Volta stammered, heating up a little. "I just — that's so… weird, to me. I-I mean, I don't *know* anyone else who's done a lot of kissing on a lot of other people. …Not that I've, um, really *talked* about it with anyone, much."

"I guessed as much," Carmen winked. "Don't worry, everyone's gotta start somewhere — and as far as starting kisses go, hey, at least you weren't too wet or *too* pushy."

"Th-thanks, I guess!" Volta shrugged and began to eat.

Carmen dug in as well, then, after a minute, looked back up at her thoughtfully. She pursed her lips, mulling a question over for a moment, before she asked, "Hey Volts, you wanna come to my room?"

Volta almost choked on her steak; her eyes went wide and her ears flat. A thousand thoughts, half of them already making her face redden, began rushing through her mind. "Y — Uh, uhm, well — Well what, what for?" she asked, screaming internally at her own stuttering.

"Just for a little more casual hanging out!" Carmen shrugged. "You've been going at it pretty hard lately, I figure you could use a break."

Her… room! Just, just to hang out. What does that even ENTAIL? I can't just talk about True North the whole time that'd be BORING, I need to —

"Hey, if you don't want to, that's all right," Carmen reassured, "but I figured I'd offer. I, uh, kind of have something I wanna show you."

Volta blinked at her, trying to think of what that could mean. "You mean your belt collection?"

Carmen laughed, tossing her fork onto her plate. "*Well,* I did make that offer! But, no, it's something else, it's something I think you'll like."

Now her curiosity was piqued. "Uhm, sure! I don't mind. I… could use a break from sparring, I think…"

"Great! Soon as we're done, I'll take you."

The rest of their lunch conversation went on with a lot less talking as they finally took the time to finish their stew. They cleared their trays, and Carmen motioned for Volta to follow with her tail.

O-oh. Do that again please? God, I feel like such a creep but —

Her own tail wagged behind her as they walked together. She was starting to get a little antsy. "So, so what *did* you wanna show me?"

"You'll see! It's a surprise."

The cat sounded a little… anxious, all of a sudden.

What could Carmen want to show her that she *didn't* want to say now? Especially something that would make her nervous — that *never* happened. Volta couldn't help but feel twice as uneasy as she usually did as a result.

They reached her dorm room quickly — Carmen knew a few shortcuts — and the cat opened the door, motioning for her to enter first.

"After you!" she said with a flourish.

Volta stepped cautiously through the threshold, taking in the layout — not unlike her own, but much more of a square than a narrow rectangle, with a bigger desk, papers strewn over it, and a slightly larger bed. Several of the walls were decorated in TPA posters — the same ones in Volta's room. There was a whole open space in the middle, with a rug with a Texas Lone Star pattern. And then, on the wall next to the bed, there was a shelf — with a large case mounted on it. Ten different martial arts belts rested behind the glass, neatly folded, each a different color with a label underneath.

"Well?" Carmen shut the door behind her, hanging her lab coat on a hook beside the door. "Not too scary, right?"

Volta swallowed, staring at the numerous black belts among several blues and browns. "W-well at least I know you weren't kidding, now! No wonder you're so good at training…"

"You do something a lot, you're *damn* good at it," Carmen said almost nonchalantly. "The TPA doesn't really expect hand-to-hand stuff at this level, but it certainly wouldn't *hurt* anyone looking to square up against supervillains."

"Like the Korps?" Volta offered.

"Yeah! Exactly like the Korps." Carmen's response came quickly, and her tone was suddenly curt. She took a breath and gestured around her.

"So! Girl's room. Not that spectacular, either, huh? For the record I didn't pick the rug out — or the TPA posters."

"I could figure that part out!" the wolf laughed. "This is the first time I've… *ever* been in a girl's room."

"Don't you mean *another* girl's room?" Carmen grinned at her, and Volta blushed brightly. That little question on its own made her feel lighter on her feet.

"I — I guess so, yeah!"

"There we go." Carmen took another breath and closed her eyes for a moment. "Okay, Volts, so, I said I had something else to show you."

"Yeah, you did!"

"I don't wanna overwhelm you, maybe you should sit…" Carmen gestured to the chair at her desk. "Unless you're okay with standing?"

"U-uh, sure?" Volta blinked, smiling awkwardly to try and hide the sudden rush of possibilities that ran through her head.

"It's pretty serious. Like, if I'm being honest, I'm kinda nervous about this — how you'll… *react*." Carmen's shoulders were tense, and she was wringing her hands. She was looking down at Volta's chest, rather than her face. "You sure you don't wanna sit down?"

"No, no, I think I'm okay!" Volta reassured her with a confident smile, while her mind raced with possibilities.

Oh my god. Is she going to — She wouldn't say she's in love with me, would she? No, it was just a kiss, that's wishful thinking. …But what if she did? I could finally say the same thing. …But what if she says the opposite — asks to never see me again? Do I even know how to respond to that? …It'd make sense, I know I'm a pain. No, focus, don't dwell, just, let her talk and —

She abruptly snapped back to Carmen's room. Carmen was holding what looked like a long… flashlight? It had a long, tube-like lightbulb, with the handle connecting either side of it. Carmen looked… nervous. Really nervous. She inhaled deeply, and let her shoulders rise with her breath.

"Okay. I've been waiting to show you this for a long time, Volts. Can you promise to keep a secret?"

"O-of course! What kind of question is that?" Volta laughed. "We already know we're both trans, right, we're the only people for miles who, well, *know*."

Carmen sighed, straightened up, and aimed the elongated not-flashlight at her stomach. She flicked a switch on the side, and the tube-shaped bulb began to glow a soft purple.

Volta thought she might have been ready, but as the tattoo gradually began to fade in, marking the fur over her lower midsection, she went from nervously excited to numb.

It was a winged helix, all in black on Carmen's stomach. The tattoo spanned across her navel, framed by her lower waist. It was *huge*; Volta stared, mouth open and tail limp. Carmen held up the little purple light again and shone it over the tattoo from one wing to the other. Before Volta's eyes, it faded, completely, until her midriff was seemingly bare again. Nothing but striped, brown fur.

It felt like time had stopped moving again as a hard, prickling chill crept up Volta's back. Carmen smiled at her, but the smile looked… *off*. Awkward. Tense.

"I wanted to tell you, weeks ago. That first day. Really. I had to be sure I could trust you." She held her hands up, giving them a little shake. "Ah, surpriiiise?"

Volta opened her mouth, but it took several seconds more for her to speak. "Trust me… about this?"

Carmen let her hands down again, her smile faltering. "Yeah. I'm an agent of the Korps. I wanted to tell you over that first lunch we had, but I had to wait. I had to make sure that you'd know me, and believe me, and trust me."

Volta's heart still thumped in her chest, but now it felt… strangely hollow. She felt even colder standing there with a stiff slouch, her arms loose at her sides. She felt like such a child in her posture, but she couldn't make herself move. She looked up at Carmen's face again as she spoke.

"You wanted me to know I could tell you anything. You wanted me to… to believe that I was safe around you."

"That's right."

"Why?"

"Because I'm with the *Korps*, Volta. I hope I don't need to spell it out, after the conversations we've had." Carmen's expression turned wry. "We're in the middle of a Teepa Academy — it needs to be on the downlow so I can work."

Volta felt like her body was turning to stone. "Work on — on what? On TPA intel? …On *me?*"

Carmen's face lost any trace of humor, replaced with bewilderment as she lowered her tail suddenly. "No, Volta. You're not — you're not a *project*, you're my friend." The look in her eyes was unrecognizable.

"I looked like someone who needed someone to talk to. That's what you said before." Volta muttered, still staring, unable to look anywhere else.

Someone to talk to? *Please.* What kind of pathetic excuse was that? How hadn't she realized it before? Of *course*, Carmen didn't just want to be nice. A Korps agent would want to *seem* nice. To be helpful, to be trustworthy. That was what they *did*. That was exactly what she was warned about. Carmen was just using her — just like Tullis. Just like her family.

And she'd *fallen* for it.

"You said it was your specialty — talking to people." The chills twisted and grew uncomfortably warm. "You… *you said* you needed me to trust you. Why? Were you just using me? Were you trying to… to brainwash me? What else haven't you told me?"

"No, no — Volta? Hold on. I was *never* trying to trick you into anything." Carmen held up her hands placatingly, taking a step towards her.

But that's exactly what you would expect a Korps agent to say. To trick you. Make you think you can trust them. Her. It's the kind of thing YOU would fall for.

Volta took a step back. "You got me to talk to you so easily. You got me to come out to you. Were you lying? About…" Her face was starting to heat up; she clenched her fists. "Were you lying about being like me?"

Carmen's face twisted in confusion and alarm. She got louder, and much more firm. "*No*, absolutely not, Volta. I would *never* lie about that. No one in the Korps would. That's —"

Volta stood her ground, her face frozen in indignation. "How am I supposed to believe you? You're only *now* admitting you're in the Korps. You *hid that* from me, because you *knew* I wouldn't trust you anymore. You even said — you *even said* the Korps was dangerous, you said everything you had to if it meant I trusted you no matter what. *You didn't want me to know you were exploiting my weaknesses to get close to me.*"

Carmen was starting to look desperate, almost hurt. "That's not what I was doing at all, Volta. You have to understand, I can't just *walk up* to someone and tell them I'm in the Korps. What would you have done, had me arrested?"

Volta's face twisted with anger. Her whole body had gotten flush with burning heat. She'd let Carmen in. Told her about *everything*. Her worries, her fears, the name she wanted, and why… She had told Carmen that name the same day they met. She had let her guard down so *easily*.

*Of course you did, because you're pathetic. You fell for it because you're easy to manipulate, you're overly sensitive, you're **flawed**, and she could see it. She saw you as an especially easy mark. She's just using you, just like, mom and dad, just like you should have known the entire time.*

Always managing to find new ways to mess things up, aren't you?

Carmen was taking several steps closer, her hands outstretched, almost pleading. Her face looked so… *confusing*. Was that sadness? Worry? …Pity? Derision?

"Volta, please, listen to me," the tabby begged.

"What, so you can… can butter me up more!?" Volta spat. She took another step back and fell into a panicked fighting stance, claws bared to either side. The heat was overwhelming; it spread down to her hands, blue electricity arcing from her palms to her fingers. "I'm *done* listening."

Carmen looked down at Volta's sparking hands, her expression turning to a mix of disappointment… and wariness. "Volta, come on. You don't really want to do this. You know how our sparring matches go."

Volta bared her teeth. "You think I can't take you, is that it? I wasn't using my powers on you before."

"You still have the Dampener on," Carmen reminded, pointing at her chest. "Volta, really, think about this for a second."

"I *have* been! I've been thinking about everything I've told you — everything I *trusted you with!*" The clicking and sparking on her right hand became a violent, harsh crackle as electricity raced up and down her arm. "No *wonder* you wanted me to spar with you. You wanted to see how useful I was. You just want to turn me into one of your puppets!" She threw herself forward, aiming a right hook at Carmen's face.

The tabby ducked backwards to Volta's right, eyes wide, still holding her hands up. Volta's punch whiffed where Carmen's head had been, blue lightning trailing after her arm in a jagged streak.

Carmen's voice rose. "Volta, calm down, you *know* that's not true. I saw someone who needed help. I saw someone *like me*."

"You mean someone you could use!" Volta followed through with a running left swing, bright arcs flaring in the space between them as she swiped at Carmen's winding form. "That's why you're here, isn't it?" she barked. "For recruiting? To get all the wannabe heroes while they're young and impressionable? To get them to think you *care?*" Her voice was going hoarse from emotion, eyes blurring with tears. She couldn't slow down now. She threw another punch; Carmen weaved around it again. She just wanted to land a hit, get Carmen to feel even an ounce of the pain she was feeling.

"Volta, you *need* to calm down and listen. Please, give me a chance to explain!" Carmen reached out, supplicant. "I *do* care about you, I —"

Volta didn't slow down. She threw a kick, and Carmen dodged — but too narrowly. An arc reached out and struck her arm, making her jump back even further as she cried out in surprise and pain.

"F-fuck *me!*" Carmen spat, clutching her forearm and flexing her fingers, trying to make sure they all still worked.

Volta felt a surge of vindictive pleasure and maintained her stance. "Never let your guard down — that's what you told me," she snarled. "I'm *not* gonna let you fool me again."

Carmen looked back up at her, resolute, and straightened. "Okay, fine." She dropped into a high, narrow stance, one hand raised in front of her face, the other lower, angled out, almost like a dare for Volta to come closer. "You wanna dance? Let's dance, Volts."

Volta obliged. She launched herself forward, extra current pumping through her legs and doubling their speed as she aimed another kick. Carmen effortlessly sidestepped again, circling around towards the bed. Before Volta could even see her hand coming, a sharp jab struck her in the waist, sending her stumbling as she sucked in a breath.

Carmen straightened again, now both hands raised. Her expression turned sardonic, but her eyes blazed. "Going to have to try harder than that."

Fine. Volta's entire body felt overwhelmingly hot, seething with anger and as much electric current as she could muster. She was trying to snarl still but couldn't tell if it was working any more. She certainly wasn't winning this. She never had, even when Carmen was going easy on her. She always wound up on the floor.

And this time you'll be alone afterward. There's no reason for her to stay, now that her cover's blown. You'll be alone again.

The Dampener felt ice-cold against her heated skin, her heart thumping so loud she could barely hear the buzzing and cracking of lightning firing off from her body.

Volta rushed forward again, bright blue arcs of electricity crackling around her, jumping to the ceiling, the walls, the furniture. The charge in her muscles magnified every movement, and she sped towards Carmen, who was patiently waiting there, in front of her bed.

Too patient.

Volta had one second, scowling through angry tears and a haze of buzzing and crackling sparks, to see Carmen's eyes darken. The whites turned black as tar, and the bright amber of her irises instantly bled out into a rich, deep purple. The entire room grew dark, even the blue glow of Volta's lightning beginning to shift, as all the colors were overtaken by deep, murky violet.

Why hadn't she reached Carmen yet? That lightning arc erupting from her hand should have struck *something*, but it was crawling outward like molasses. Volta strained to turn and look at it, painfully slow. Everything was slow — except Carmen.

Those purple eyes seemed brighter than everything else as she approached Volta, completely untouched by the lightning around her. The air around felt heavy, the world so much darker except for those wide, fierce, unblinking eyes.

And then Carmen punched her in the jaw.

Volta's head reared back, paws stumbling as the force of the hit threw her entire upper body backward. All the lightning crackling through the air dissipated in a second. As Volta dazedly tried to take her stance up again, she realized Carmen had closed the distance. The tabby grabbed her, flipped her around, and hoisted her up by the arms.

"W-wha —"

Volta couldn't even get a word out before the tabby had her in a full nelson, lifting her clean off her feet.

"Let me go!" Volta snapped, trying to kick back at her. "Let me go *now!*"

"Calm! Calm." Carmen muttered in Volta's ear, tightening her grip a little. "Please, just… calm down, so you can listen."

"*You're not gonna fool me again!*" Volta shouted, straining her arms uselessly against Carmen's. She was forced to confront again how much bigger they were, how much bigger *all* of Carmen was than her.

"I'm not letting you go, until you *cool it*," Carmen said more forcefully, but she lowered down enough for Volta's feet to touch the floor again. "I'm not going anywhere. I'm not tricking you. You *need* to believe me, Volta."

"*Let me GO you BITCH!*" Volta screamed so hard her voice cracked. Tears were still falling down her face. "Fuck you! F-FUCK YOU! *You're JUST like Mom and Dad! I'm not your puppet! I'm NOT! I'm not…*"

Her yells were getting weaker as the lump in her throat finally caught up with her.

Carmen held her tighter, still holding her arms back, but now the cat pressed her face against her, her soft cheek held firm against the back of Volta's head. She held her firmly to her entire body, as much of an embrace as she could manage while still restraining her.

Volta couldn't see through her tears anymore. Her face was contorted in an angry sob. She was managing to be even more pathetic. *Useless.* Even less the man her parents wanted her to be, that she knew she could never be. Her fists balled up once more. She let out another strangled yell, managed to fire off another branching bolt of lightning, and felt the last of her charge drain away.

The anger that had shot through her body felt like it was bleeding out of her. She felt nauseous and wounded. She couldn't stop crying; she bowed her head and slumped back against Carmen's grasp, gasping and weeping.

Carmen pulled Volta down to the floor, clinging to her still. She let her lean against the cat's larger body. The tabby was whispering in her ear as she moved her arms around her in a gentle hug. The Dampener's straps dug into her again, the ice-cold metal surface making it that much harder to stop the outpouring of emotion.

"I do care about you, Volta. I cared about you *so, so much*, ever since the day we met, even more when I learned just how much we share." She squeezed the weeping wolf gently, taking a deep, unsteady breath. "I'm not going *anywhere*, and I'm not going to brainwash you. I just want to help you out of here. The *only* time I haven't told you the full truth was about the Korps. Everything else was the truth." The tabby squeezed her again. *"Everything."*

"I-I can't..." Volta whimpered, her voice broken and hoarse. "I don't know w-what I'm gonna d-do... I *hate* it here. I hate m-my family. I *h-hate me...* If you left, I — I d-don't kno-ow what — P-please, *please do-on't leave...*"

She broke down again as Carmen leaned into her. "You couldn't get rid of me if you tried, Volta, I promise. You're getting out of here, and I'll be with you the entire time."

Carmen's eyes burned, tears ran down her face. She didn't let go, but she did begin to gently and slowly sway from side to side, rocking Volta gently on the floor. There was no noise in the room save for the wolf's uncontrolled sobbing.

She lost track of time easily. Carmen may have spent an hour sitting there with her, reassuring her, holding her. Volta still felt a little sick, her nose streaming and eyes red.

At some point, she managed to get a hold of herself enough for Carmen to coax her towards the bed, the cat sitting beside her as she reached for a box of tissues.

Eventually, she managed to find her voice again, stuffed up as it was. "S-sorry for trying to hit you. And — uh. Sh-shocking you." How much current had gone through Carmen's hand in that swing?

"Believe me, Volts, I can handle that. It just caught me off guard. Which, hey, honestly?" Carmen grinned, bumping shoulders with her. "Nice job, you almost hit me straight on!"

"Yeah..." Volta trailed off for a moment, before it suddenly clicked. "Wait, y-you're a super too!"

Carmen blinked at her for a moment, then burst out laughing, and for the first time the wolf registered tears on the cat's face — just before she wiped them away. "Hell yeah, I am! It's my little secret~ Aside from the trans thing, and the Korps Covert Operative thing." She considered a moment, thoughtfully tapping her chin. "I suppose I *am* kind of an overachiever."

"Hold on, so you have — what *do* you have? What the hell did you do?"

Carmen smirked. "Slowed down time, Volts~ You got to experience it point-blank. Cool, huh?"

She said it as if she hadn't just socked Volta in the mouth.

Super smart, super hot, and superpowers she knows how to use. Of course she's got it all, everything I wish I had.

Who am I kidding? She's everything I want, and I tried to electrocute her because I got scared. Great. Fuck.

Volta could feel her face burning with shame and looked away, snatching another tissue from the box the cat had handed her. Carmen's smirk faded into concern. "How's your jaw doing, by the way?"

It had slipped her mind, but as soon as the cat reminded her, she felt the pang of soreness. "Fine, I guess. Never felt you hit me that hard before though."

"I had to get you off balance, Volts, sorry. I won't make a habit out of punching you unless you *really* need it," she winked.

"R-right…"

"Volta, listen, long as I'm being honest…" Carmen put an arm on Volta's shoulder, squeezing it gently. "I d*id* have another reason for wanting to get to know you. I saw how much you were hurting. I saw all the shit you had to deal with, from all sides, and how it was just hurting you more, and I… I saw someone I could relate to."

She shifted her weight and folded her arms, and her chest rose in a deep breath that she let back out in an anxious huff. "I've already told you about my family, Volts. They're awful. Complete dogshit, and I'm glad I cut them out of my life. But I had my grandmother. She helped me figure a ton of this stuff out. You didn't have anybody. You were trapped, completely alone, convinced you weren't worth anything. The Korps disagrees with you."

Volta looked away again, sniffling.

"Volts, c'mon, look at me."

"I don't see what the Korps would want with me," Volta mumbled wetly. "I'm not worth the effort."

"You're wrong, Volts. Dead wrong. The Korps is *made* for girls like you."

"W-what do you mean?"

"Think about it — you're trans, you're stuck with a shitty Christian family, and you have superpowers — superpowers that, despite what you keep telling yourself, are fucking *amazing*. The Korps is meant to set people like us free. Why else do you think your family calls us the devil's servants?"

"It would explain a lot. It…" Volta sniffled again, her expression turning very sober. "Actually, maybe I should have suspected when you made me start wondering how much violence was really the Korps's fault."

Carmen snickered and squeezed her again. "I tried dropping a *couple* hints, here and there, but — did you hear what I said? The Korps wants you, and…" She bit her lip, eyes flitting about as she looked for the right words. After a moment, she looked back at Volta, her eyes shining. "And… I want you, too."

"I —" Volta stared back at her, eyes going wide. Her body was heating up again, but not from anger. She became *intensely* aware of how close Carmen was, just like they were when she gave her that first kiss. "W-what?"

Carmen held onto her, as if she were afraid Volta might fall to pieces. Her look only became more intense. "I mean it. I want you, Volta. I — well, screw subtlety — I love you, Volts."

The wolf couldn't move. She couldn't do anything but continue staring into those bright amber eyes. The woman she'd dreamt about for a month was smiling at her in a way she never had before. She didn't know what to do; nothing had prepared her for this. None of her fantasies, or dreams, or desperate wishes focused on *this* part.

"I… I love you too!" Volta blurted. There was a pause. Was she supposed to be embarrassed? She wanted to smile, or laugh, or maybe start crying again. She wasn't sure *what* her face was doing, or any part of her. She was terrified, overjoyed, and…

Then Carmen leaned in and kissed her. The wolf was frozen for a second, then pressed in as well. The room around them became dim and distant. This wasn't like the first kiss, it wasn't a reminder of everything wrong with her. Carmen was kissing *her*, because she loved her. The wolf could forget about everything else, for at least a few moments, as the world became quiet and still. She and the tabby were the only ones in it.

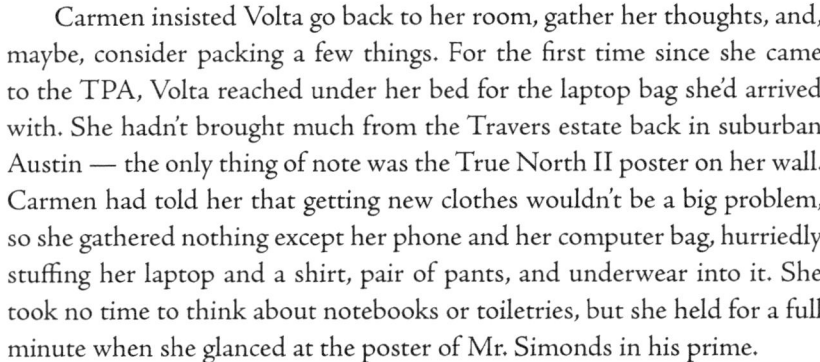

Carmen insisted Volta go back to her room, gather her thoughts, and, maybe, consider packing a few things. For the first time since she came to the TPA, Volta reached under her bed for the laptop bag she'd arrived with. She hadn't brought much from the Travers estate back in suburban Austin — the only thing of note was the True North II poster on her wall. Carmen had told her that getting new clothes wouldn't be a big problem, so she gathered nothing except her phone and her computer bag, hurriedly stuffing her laptop and a shirt, pair of pants, and underwear into it. She took no time to think about notebooks or toiletries, but she held for a full minute when she glanced at the poster of Mr. Simonds in his prime.

That confident smirk, those well-defined pecs, and the unfading glimmer in True North II's eye still stirred the same childlike giddiness in her as ever. That poster had been facing every bed Volta had slept in since she was 15. Plushies weren't for *guys*, but a poster of a personal hero? Sure, that passed Mom and Dad's smell test.

That was the one major piece of memorabilia she had brought from back home. The rest of it was either put up in her room in the Travers' mansion or organized neatly into boxes in the closet and under her bed. A very stubborn, and admittedly very childish pull kept her from just tearing her eyes away. For a moment, she entertained the idea of taking it with her.

To be fair, she was going to join a gang of anarchist supervillains that had come down *from Canada*, so maybe walking into the evil lair touting a poster of a local old adversary of theirs was a little disrespectful.

This might be the last time I see this poster. I saved up my allowance for a year to afford it… What if I —

…No, okay, I am not risking folding that up in my laptop bag. I'd rather leave it here than risk creasing it.

The pang of yearning didn't go away as she turned towards the door, but she was at least ready. Ready to leave the TPA facility, leave Olson, Tullis, Mom and Dad, maybe forever. *Maybe.* The thought thrilled and terrified her in equal measure, just as much as it had when Carmen had made her offer.

"We'll meet up in the campus gardens outside, and then we'll make for the western campus exit," the tabby had explained. "We're coming up on a shift change, so that will be our best chance to draw minimal attention. I'll be calling in a stealth chopper to pick us up, about a 20-minute walk into the woods near here. It won't be easy, especially since I'm betting that the Dampener has some kind of tracking device…"

"Y-you think so?" Volta had blanched upon hearing that. She had gripped at the ice-cold metal dome with a newfound paranoia.

"Your parents are the controlling type, Volts, and they *paid* for that thing. I'd be more surprised if it didn't." Carmen had placed a hand on her shoulder to reassure her. "Don't worry, though. It shouldn't be hard to get it off of you once we have some privacy. At that point we can just huck it into a dumpster and give you some breathing room.

"B-but, without the Dampener, my powers will be back completely."

"Yeah! That's, sorta the point?"

"I… don't know how well I'll be able to control them." Volta had hung her head in embarrassment. "The only times it was ever shut off was when I was in an insulated room with only a little charge. I… before I came here, I got… *really* close to seriously hurting people. What happens if —"

"Volta. *Volta,*" Carmen had cut her off. "Don't worry about controlling your powers. I have a plan for that, and I can *promise* you it's a way better solution than just turning them off with the Dampener. Just come back to me in the garden with anything you can carry; I'll handle the rest."

She was still so curious what Carmen had in mind as she shut the door to her dormitory and hurried down the hall to the nearest exit. She made her way into the gardens, dismissing the reminder from her phone about her next class with Olson as she fast walked, trying to look as innocent and not-like-a-runaway as possible.

Now out in the open, more anxiety began to sink in. Even amongst the greenery in the campus gardens she had to feel apprehensive. So many things could still go wrong, but Carmen assured her that she would be there to keep her safe, and that together, they could get out of this place without a hitch.

As the bench Carmen sat at came into view, Volta prayed to no one in particular that Carmen would be right.

The tabby waved to her brightly, and Volta's tail broke into a flurry of wags from sheer excitement and nerves. She hurried over to the bench and took in the cat's change of clothes. Her blouse and lab coat combo was gone, replaced with a deep violet jacket and an unusually thick-looking tank top. Was that… body armor? She didn't have much time to think about it as Carmen motioned for her to sit down.

"Got everything you want?" Carmen asked, scooting closer to the wolf until their hips were pressing together. A giddy jolt went up Volta's spine.

"E-everything I could carry! Like you said!" she replied.

"Good! Now, for the hard part." Carmen dropped into a hushed tone, leaning in closer and beckoning for Volta to do the same. "We're going to sneak out of here as much as possible, but in case things go loud — just in case — we need to be ready. Which is where my plan for your powers comes in…"

"Y-yeah?" Volta's heart raced. Had Carmen found a way to control the Dampener? Was she going to take it off right now? She kept her ears pricked, at full attention.

"Well, we need to get this over with fast…" Carmen glanced around, making sure no one was nearby. "You need to be able to control your powers, Volta, and as soon as we get the Dampener off, we need you as close to your A game as possible."

Volta's excited grin faltered. "B-but how —"

"I'm getting to that, just…" Carmen reached under her lab coat. "Hear me out, Volts. You'll have to trust me on this, and I'm not going to force you to wear them, but I *promise*," Carmen paused as she pulled out a pair of —

Volta's heart stopped. A single, curved, magenta shape, with arms to either side meant to hold it to the face. She knew exactly what it was before Carmen said it.

"If you put these RCGs on," she continued, "you will have a *much* easier time controlling your powers, and it'll be *you* who decides how much charge you get." Carmen's smile was bright and giddy too — she had definitely been wanting to do this for a *while*. "Not the Teepa, not your parents, *you*."

"I —" Volta stammered, trying to figure out how to feel about this. "Th-those are, those are the same things that brainwash people, aren't they?"

"Not without a *lot* of extra settings turned on," Carmen explained, holding the pair in her hand as though it were carefully crafted jewelry. "With the basic stuff, just the things you need to control your powers — well, you'll see. Think of them like training wheels — there to keep you upright. Hell of a lot nicer than rationed out charges and cops with batons and hazard pay, right?"

Volta swallowed, a little reassured, but still…

"…Will it hurt?"

"Not at all," Carmen grinned slyly. "I know the stories on the news say otherwise but, well, we already talked about how much you should believe those."

"O-okay," Volta breathed in, then out. Her hands shook as she raised one. The tabby's amber eyes were wide with anticipation, as Volta began to reach for the goggles. "Okay, okay okay okay, I —"

"*FREEZE!*"

Volta's hand stopped, yanked back as if burned, as both she and Carmen whipped their heads around to see three security officers encircling the bench, guns leveled at Carmen.

The wolf's body began to prickle with adrenaline and fear. She turned her head again, terrified, to see Carmen looking back at her. There was no hiding the disarmed shock on her face.

"C-Carmen…?" Volta muttered as the tabby stood back up and shoved the RCGs back in her jacket in one fluid motion.

"I said *freeze!*" the guard shouted again. Several hammers clicked back. The cat's expression was icy cold as she whirled around to face them — and then put up her hands.

No…

"I'm putting my hands up. I surrender," Carmen spoke loudly and clearly as she stepped away from the bench. Her eyes did not meet Volta's.

Two of the guards circled around her, and another rounded on Volta, weapon lowering. "Austin Travers, please come with me to the station. Chief Tullis wants to talk with you about this Korps spy."

Volta looked between him and Carmen, heartbeat racing. "I — Carmen —"

"Get on your knees," one of the guards ordered the tabby, pointing his handgun right at her face. "*Now.* Hands behind your head."

Slowly, deliberately, the cat followed his orders, eyes not leaving the guard in front of her as she bent one knee, and then the other.

"Mr. Travers, you *need* to come with me," the other guard ordered. He held out an expectant hand to Volta. "We need to get you away from this woman, *now*. She's a serious danger to you."

"Not like she's making much of a fuss now," the guard standing behind Carmen snorted, as he raised a pair of handcuffs and clasped one side to one of the tabby's wrists. "All bark and no bite, huh —"

Carmen pulled her cuffed hand down, faster than Volta had ever seen, yanking the guard with her as he tried to keep a grip on the other side of the cuffs. The other guard raised his weapon again, shouting, right as Carmen's eyes flashed that same deep purple from before.

The other guard grabbed Volta by the arm and was pulling her out of the bench when Carmen knocked the wind out of the guard in front of her with an elbow. The one with the cuffs yelped as her hand snapped around his wrist, and with little effort she *threw* him onto the footpath, slamming him down and kicking up dust as she straightened up and *tore* the handcuffs off with both hands.

"Jesus Christ —" the third guard started, but he had no time. In a blink of an eye, the tabby leapt at him, and she kicked it out of his hand before he'd even turned his gun at her. Another kick sent him down, and a third to his side got a strangled gasp of pain out of him, making him curl up.

"C'mon," Carmen ordered, and Volta snapped alert. The cat took her hand and began to run. Volta struggled to keep up with the cat as she rushed off of the footpath with her and into the trees and underbrush.

"Carmen, Carmen wait —"

"I've been exposed," the cat responded. "We don't have any time, Volta, we have to go *now* or we're — *Shit!*" She skidded to a halt, taking hold of Volta in both hands and shoving her back. As the wolf stumbled away, the crunch of a tree coming down made her realize what Carmen had seen.

A huge, muscular fist with a metallic gold sheen flew at her from between the trees. The cat's eyes flashed purple again, and she dodged away from Volta. The immense form of Adam Tullis, one whole arm a deep, reflective golden yellow, came crashing down between them, swinging wide. As the hulking form of the Great Dane landed, she brought an elbow down on his back — and Volta heard a metal *clunk* as Carmen's arm bounced harmlessly off of him. The tabby recoiled, gritting her teeth from the sudden pain.

As Tullis straightened up, Volta could see he was smiling wide, eyes fixated with a seething hatred on the cat in front of him.

"Lookie here — caught myself a *kitty* cat," he growled, his voice dripping with a vicious excitement as he raised two gleaming golden fists. "You got claws in those paws? Gonna make this *fun* for me, kitty?"

Carmen, finally, turned her gaze on Volta as she took a step back. Now she looked afraid, but not for herself.

"Volta, *run*."

No, no, we were so close —

The wolf stumbled backward, terrified, as Tullis swung at Carmen. For someone so big, he was *shockingly* fast. Carmen's eyes were glowing purple — *clearly* she was using her powers — and even then she was only barely weaving and ducking out of the way of those huge gold-plated hands.

Tullis bellowed with laughter. "This all you got? Everyone's pissin' their pants over you people, and this is *all you queer freaks got?*"

Carmen didn't reply — she *danced* around the huge dog with all her focus. She only diverted it for an instant to shout over her shoulder: "Run, dammit!"

Now Volta's legs began to work. She turned and ran directly into one of the guards from before. He grabbed hold of her arms, and then wrapped his arms around her chest.

"W-wait, wait — !" Volta gasped. She looked, desperately, at Carmen again. She weaved out of the way of another punch, and had countered — not with a jab, but with a shove. She grabbed the Great Dane around the waist and dug her feet in. He grunted as he started to tip over to one side, one leg pushing out to give him balance while his metallic arms wrapped around Carmen.

"Stop struggling, Austin!" the guard snapped, putting the wolf in a full nelson as two new guards rushed forward to try and grab hold of the cat. The guard began to drag Volta away. The little charge she had wouldn't come. She tried, and in her panic all that came out was a ruffling of her fur.

"Fuck, help me with this rich kid —" Two more guards were on her in seconds, grabbing her shirt and arms and pulling her towards the police station.

Please, please, don't take me away from her…

"It's okay! It's okay!" Carmen shouted as she writhed in Tullis's grip, twisting and wrenching her way down, out from under the Great Dane's gold-clad arms. She went for another throw, and finally got some leverage as Volta was tugged past a collection of trees and the two of them were obscured by the greenery. The wolf's ears were ringing, her heart pounding in her chest. She felt cold, the Dampener chilling her from the chest outward.

Carmen's voice already sounded so distant, but her words could not have been clearer:

"Don't struggle! You'll be okay! I'll come find you, I *promise!*"

Chapter 8

The Old Normal

Carmen slammed the side door shut behind her, then slumped onto the seat opposite. The helicopter's drone pilot started lifting off as soon as she sat down. Carmen's heart pounded as she fumbled for her other jacket pocket, pulling out her own square-lensed RCGs and slipping them on. The adrenaline from wrenching herself out of Tullis's grip and running the fastest she ever had was already dying down. She needed relief, and ROSE immediately provided. The pain, the apprehension, the panic that had been welling up in her died down. She was still aware of them; she didn't want them gone, but she needed time.

She tried as hard as she could to relax, leaning back into the cushioned helicopter seat in an otherwise empty passenger cabin. No one had seen the chopper lift off — the optic cloak and low-noise rotors were doing their job. Carmen knew as she stared at the side door window that Wren was keeping an eye on her through her RCGs just as much as ROSE was.

The ride was brief, but every second felt longer than the last. Even with the emotional dampening, she couldn't help but think. Every dragging instant of this flight took her further and further away from Volta. It felt like something was slowly being torn from her body as the distance grew. ROSE offered to help pass the time; she graciously accepted. She breathed, blinking slowly. One, two, three, four, five…

By the sixth blink, they were touched down on RIV's western landing pad, obscured by tree cover. The lift engaged, and she watched the greenery disappear as the landing pad lowered into Hangar 03. The door opposite her slid open, and Carmen stood up. Wren was waiting for her by the exit to the tram platform, fidgeting with a bunch of magnetic rings in his hands. His eyes fixed on Carmen's the moment the chopper door slid open, and the cat stepped out.

The short Honduran White Bat approached her cautiously, eyes wide with concern. "Carmen?" Wren asked. "Carmen, talk to me."

Carmen's composure cracked as she looked down at her partner. Her voice was barely more than a croak. "She's still there, Wren."

"C'mon," Wren took her hand and led her into the exit hall. "We can talk about it later when we're home. You need a minute."

They walked up to the platform, where a train car was already waiting, doors open.

Thanks, ROSE.

[No need to thank me. Let me know when you want full feeling back.]

They rode in silence but kept close together. The bat held her hand the entire time, rubbing a thumb over the back of her palm. They didn't say anything — they knew well enough that she wasn't ready to talk.

They arrived at RIV's long-term stay apartments in just a few minutes. ROSE was still making sure those minutes passed quickly. The tabby again walked robotically to her front door, and it slid open for her and Wren.

She pulled off her roughed-up jacket, throwing it on the side table beside the front door.

"Do you want to sit down?" Wren asked cautiously.

"Not yet," Carmen answered quietly, closing her eyes and taking a deep breath. "I need to vent, please."

Wren, immediately understanding, took a step back.

Okay, ROSE, now.

[I'll bring it back slowly.]

She curled her fingers into trembling fists as emotion began to wash over her again. She clenched her teeth, letting out a shrill snarl as she screwed her eyes shut. There was no going around it. There was no running, now. She was here, without Volta, because she had failed.

Carmen lowered her head and screamed.

"Fuck, *fuck*, FUCK!" She beat a fist into the side table, denting the metal siding in the shape of her knuckles. She took several breaths, let out another angry, incoherent shout, and tried to stand up straight again. She couldn't bear to look at Wren, at anything — how could she? Somewhere, she'd made a mistake so colossal that she had led them right to her and Volta. *Volta.*

She just screwed her eyes shut and tried to fight back tears. "She's alone again. I'd finally gotten her to believe that someone cared. That *I* cared. And then I *LEFT* her there like she — like she was *so scared I would*, and —"

Carmen lost her voice and hid her face in her hands as an uncontrolled sob shook her.

Cautiously, Wren reached for her, as high as his diminutive height would let him, to caress her arm. He knew there was nothing he could say that would help, and just slowly reached for a hug. She fell to her knees and leaned against him, taking shaky, sob-laden breaths, still covering her face.

The bat gently wrapped their arms around her, and the two clung to each other.

"She ran away from me. I don't know where she went."

The badger officer leaned in over the desk, clasping his hands together on the table. "Was she trying to give something to you? Has she ever said anything, *anything*, about the Korps or our internal network prior to today?"

Volta took a breath, trying to look as calm as possible. "No."

"Bullshit," Tullis growled. The Great Dane glared daggers at her, eyes lit with anger. "You've been seen talking with this girl, every day, for a month. She had RCGs in her hands when we grabbed her — at least three guards saw them."

"She never said anything about the Korps!" Volta repeated, her mouth feeling dry as the lie left her lips. How long could she keep this up? The interrogator was intense enough, but Tullis was *livid*. It was only a matter of time before he registered the agitation and fear wafting off of her. She had to think of something.

"Listen, Austin. I get it." The badger raised his hands, trying to appease her; apparently he was going to be the good cop. "She was a nice girl. Damn fine to look at, too. You wanna protect her, but you gotta get it through your head, Austin. She doesn't care about you. The Korps *uses* your weaknesses against you, takes advantage of vulnerabilities, until you're willing to *lie* for them."

"I'm not lying!"

"If you think hiding anything about her or your relationship will help you here, Travers, you're wrong," the badger continued, jabbing a finger at her. "She's already abandoned you. The best thing you can do is tell us everything you know, starting *right now*."

Volta swallowed. "I already did. She never mentioned the Korps." She met Tullis's gaze. Never mind the badger. If she didn't convince *him*, it wouldn't matter. "And she never tried to —"

Tullis slammed his fist into the desk with a loud bang, startling Volta into silence. He leaned forward, daring the wolf to look away. "Don't try to bullshit me, Travers. Your accomplishments won't save you — especially since they very recently and *conveniently* started racking up right around the time that bitch started hanging around you."

"H-how do you think that looks, now?" the badger tried to chime in. "Plenty of students and staff can testify to seeing you together. You were *inseparable*, by all accounts. Even if she didn't give you anything you *know* about, you could have very easily fallen under some kind of Korps brainwashing. Something to make you an ideal servant, to tear you down."

Volta clenched her fists. "The only thing she *gave* me was sparring sessions and advice for staying levelheaded. We… we ate lunch together. Is that what tearing down looks like?"

Tullis stuck a finger in her face. "Watch your tone, boy; remember who you're speaking to. You don't get to be defensive about your girlfriend when your girlfriend turns out to be an anarchist terrorist *whore*." His mouth twisted up in a sneer. "Unless you're about to spout pro-Korps rhetoric like you've been programmed to by your new masters, hm?"

Volta scowled back up at the Great Dane's disgusted expression. Anger heated up her face; she could feel some of that heat traveling down her arms. She was scared, she was alone… but she wasn't going to just let Tullis mouth off. "The Korps may be villains, but at least they're *doing* things. And you — you couldn't even catch her, she — she got away from you!"

Tullis grabbed Volta around her snout, digging his clawed fingers into her jaw. His other hand grabbed her shirt, and with little effort she was hoisted clean off her feet, out of the interrogation chair, and shoved against the wall behind her. Tullis's face was inches from hers, snarling, eyes wide with a kind of anger she had only ever seen from her parents.

"You listen to me, you little shit," he spat, "I don't give a *fuck* who you're related to. I don't give a fuck what your powers are, what 'promise' you show. You're nobody, here. You're *nothing*. You don't get to back sass *me*. I'm the Golden Gavel. I was putting degenerates in the *ground* while your nanny was giving you formula. You're just a rich college boy who got pussy whipped by some Korps *slut*. No one's gonna stop me from showing you *exactly* how little you and your feelings on the Korps matter. Am I understood?"

"U-understood," Volta stammered, staring back into his eyes. She was barely aware of anything that wasn't Tullis's crushing grip, but she could tell she was trembling. He finally let the wolf fall to the floor. Her whole body felt uncomfortably hot, there was a buzz in her ears. Her eyes were wet already.

"God damn, Travers, get a fucking grip," Tullis barked. "Get off the floor and go back to your dormitory. We'll find you if we need anything else, and we're keeping an eye on any outgoing network traffic now. Do *not* call your parents."

"Yes, sir…"

Volta stood up, legs and arms numb. The badger held the door open for her and she ducked out of the interrogation room, head down and eyes not meeting theirs.

As soon as she was outside the police station, she began to run, and didn't stop until she reached her room. She locked the door, slumped down against it, and let out a whimper that had been building for the last hour. Her vision went blurry, and she hid her face in her hands as she cried.

She barely managed to sleep — she kept expecting someone to barge in. It was several hours since she'd stopped crying, too exhausted and starting to feel sick from it. She had barely tried to get clean in the shower, just stood in the stream and wavered as she tried to stop thinking and overthinking.

Any minute now, certainly, her parents would come back, or Tullis, or *someone* would break down the door, declaring her brainwashed, and drag her away. She only managed to get to sleep by staring at her phone, scrolling through her Twitter feed until she fell unconscious.

She rarely remembered her dreams in much detail, but she knew when she was jolted awake by her phone alarm going off two inches from her face that they had *all* been about Carmen. Her arms holding her tight, how she refused to let go, no matter what…

The red wolf sat up again and took a shaky breath. She could already feel the lump in her throat, but she didn't want to start crying again. She shook her head, growling desperately as she tried to think about anything else.

So, it's back to the original plan. Carmen's not coming back, so you're just stuck here until Mom and Dad think of something else to do to you. And who says they'll ever let you leave? Not like you would be able to escape on your own, anyway. You were too much of a pussy to move last time, what's changed?

But she *had* to be coming back. She'd *promised*. Volta's jaw tightened as she forced the lump in her throat back down. She had to hold onto that, for as many days as it took until she could force herself to stop feeling again. Either Carmen would return, or…

Her phone buzzed again, knocking her out of her dread for just a moment with a sudden surge of hope. She lunged for it, turned the screen to her face, tail thumping behind her as —

Oh. Of course not.

Not Carmen; just an email notification from Dr. Mason. It was time for another routine checkup on the Dampener.

She'd managed to ignore it this long, too stuck thinking about Carmen and *everything* else. Now the Dampener's cold contact surface and the slightly-too-tight harness were back at the forefront. She was suddenly aware of the *itch* it gave her on one side of her chest. No use trying to put it off; if it could distract her from all this, maybe it would be worth all the usual discomfort — and the derision from Tammy.

And that's when she remembered what Carmen had said, right before everything had gone wrong. It made her stop dead in her tracks and look back down at the convex curve of the Dampener, strapped to her chest. That creeping *itch* of paranoia came back, making her raise her hackles little by little as she stared.

Yeah, no use putting it off. Now I have to know.

"Travers, you're early! That's a surprise." The aging head of research squinted at Volta with his pale blue eyes.

Tammy glanced over her tablet from where she sat with her legs crossed, looking Volta over with vague disdain. "Didn't have anything better to do?"

"I just… want to get this over with," she muttered, not meeting Dr. Mason's gaze. "And I had… I had a question. Some questions, actually."

"I can try and answer." The goat motioned to the usual seat next to the diagnostic equipment from the last time the wolf had visited. "Just sit down and we can begin."

Ordinarily this whole process would have made Volta's skin crawl, as it had every time in the past, but she had already spent the last sixteen hours dwelling on everything Carmen had said or struggling to fall asleep. For once, Volta was far too preoccupied to focus on anything that wasn't that same worry, that same doubt, that Carmen had instilled in her.

It wasn't like she didn't already not trust her family; she had tried to hide as much as she could. Now, she had to know how much they had circumvented that.

The snooty fox finally approached and glanced her up and down. "Damn, Travers, you look worse than usual. Losing sleep thinking about that Korps slut now?"

Tammy's usual derision wasn't much easier to deal with, but at least Volta could respond in a coherent sentence this time.

"Just nerves, finding out she was an… *agent*, and everything. It's, uh… a lot to think about."

"You always have nerves, that's your baseline. Feel like you should be getting used to it by now, don't you think?" Tammy sniffed as she plugged the cable into the Dampener's sole opening once again and glanced at the machine's readout. "Looking normal as ever: biometrics are good, charge siphoning is all green, usage log reporting… huh." The tall blonde fox squinted at the screen, then over at Volta, hunched in her seat.

The wolf blinked back at her. This hadn't happened before.

"Doc, come look at this."

The old goat dragged his hooves over to the display, adjusting his glasses. He raised his eyebrows and then furrowed them in worry, turning to Volta.

"Austin, about yesterday…"

Volta stiffened, ears pricking up in alarm.

"The usage log is showing a sudden discharge. Several, actually, from yesterday afternoon. Around an hour before…"

The red wolf blanched, eyes wide in realization. *Shit*, she hadn't been expecting this at all.

"…before, uh, the Korps spy's escape." He looked a little lost, unsure what to do with this information. Unlike Tullis or his badger lackey, Dr. Mason was clearly no interrogator. Tammy, meanwhile, was glaring accusingly at Volta, as if she expected to force some teary-eyed confession out of the wolf purely with her gaze. Volta squirmed under the fox's piercing look, feeling indignant.

What do you want from me? I didn't DO anything! I just got angry at Carmen when I found out she was in the Korps, started to swing at her, tried to electrocute her, and…

And I can't tell them I knew Carmen was in the Korps. That would mean they'd KNOW I was lying about everything else. And then…

"I was practicing with my powers, in my room." It was a very bad lie, but Dr. Mason didn't seem to like having to ask these questions in the first place. Maybe she could work with that.

"Just *practice?*" Tammy scoffed.

"At full tilt, just, in your *room?*" Dr. Mason asked, clearly baffled. "The Dampener's charge usage log doesn't show a gradual increase, it shows an *instant* peak, *several* in fact."

…*Fuck.* She gave a weak shrug. If Dr. Mason dug any further into this it would be *obvious* that she wasn't just "practicing," and if Tullis came at her again, now with the knowledge that she *had* lied already, how much harder would he go?

"You didn't break anything, did you? If you did, Austin, I *do* have to notify President Richardson and Tullis."

"*No!* Uh, n-nothing was broken, I just… wanted to get out as much as I could. To, um, d-destress."

Tammy rolled her eyes, tail flicking behind her. "Yeah, you have a *lot* to worry about, rich boy. Were you worried another Korps agent was gonna try and seduce you?"

Volta squirmed in her seat. The vixen rarely deigned to even speak to her more than she had to; what was different about today? She was *especially* biting now. "I — I didn't know any better about her, if that's what you're wondering."

The blonde fox deadpanned. "Oh, of *course*."

Dr. Mason stared at Volta through his glasses, working his jaw as if he were trying to *chew* what she was saying. She didn't need to be a people-reader like Carmen to know he didn't really believe her.

Nevertheless, he straightened up and shrugged as he turned away. "If you say so, Travers. Long as you're not doing property damage, or, say, electrocuting someone… you can, uh, 'relieve stress' how you please. Not my department."

Volta swallowed, nodding and trying not to look at the still scowling Tammy. She *clearly* didn't believe her at all, but she wasn't going to press on that.

"I, uh, had a question though…" Volta started up again, making the goat turn back to look at her. "I… Someone mentioned something to me, a few days ago. …Tullis, I think." Long as she was lying, why not go all in? "Is… am I being tracked, with this?" She pointed at the Dampener.

Dr. Mason stared at her again, looking between her and the device on her chest. He took a breath as he visibly decided whether or not to answer. "Well, no reason *not* to tell you. Yes, there's a GPS locator built into the Dampener; we could, potentially, pinpoint your location on the campus down to the building you're in. Your parents suggested it, actually."

So, Carmen was right. *Again.* Volta hunched forward in her seat, looking down at the Dampener as anxious goosebumps ran up her arms. Mom and Dad wanted a close eye on her, as usual. She thought them asking Tullis to pry at her was bad, but at least *he* told her outright.

Can't believe I'm giving an "at least" to him of all people…

Another, far more frightening thought entered her head, one that put a chill down her spine. "There's — there aren't any microphones or — or cameras on this thing, are there?"

"Not a one," Dr. Mason sniffed, looking far more disgruntled now. "In fact, your parents suggested we put one of those in, too. For what it's worth, Austin, I *really* don't have the time or the desire to be reviewing 24/7 footage of a rich kid with nosy parents. Ah, don't tell anyone I said that either, please."

"Won't tell a soul…" Volta sighed, the rush of relief bringing her nerves back down a little. So, she got *some* privacy, at least — but not for lack of trying on her parents' part. "Those were all the questions I had. Uh, thanks for being honest, Doctor."

He shrugged as he nibbled the end of his pen. "I don't get paid nearly enough to lie to you, Travers, and it's not like anyone said I *couldn't* answer a question, just that I probably *shouldn't* mention it. Anyway, if that's everything, Travers, we can finish up here. Go ahead and unplug him, Tammy. Uh, Tammy…?"

The fox stalked towards Volta, still staring down at her on the chair. Volta straightened back up, almost leaning back to get further away from her as she looked down at the wolf with a disgusted expression. "You really don't have *any* backbone, do you?" she snapped. "Is that all you have to say for yourself, you just didn't *know* better?"

"Tammy, this isn't necessary," Dr. Mason chimed in from the side, barely raising his voice.

"I —"

Volta had no idea how to answer that. This was the most the fox had talked to her directly in a long time.

"You barely spent a month with her and you're all pussy whipped. You're such a limp dick most of the time anyway, it must have been easy. How'd you never guess what she was? Were you just *too distracted* by her *assets* and her smile? Some hero in training *you* are."

That last part left a *sting* in Volta's chest. The wolf felt her face heating up; she looked away again. "It wasn't like that, she just… I thought she was my friend, okay? W-why do you care?"

Tammy just snorted. "A *friend*, huh? Just a friend? You think people didn't see you around campus? She really had you going, huh? What, did you think she'd take you to second base, too?"

"Stop it…" Volta mumbled, trying to turn away.

She sneered, turning her nose up as she went on. "And tabby girls aren't supposed to *look* like that. She had a pretty face, but no girl should have muscles like a *man*. You wouldn't catch me alone in the locker room with that freak of nature, but I guess some wimp like you has to get his rocks off somehow, right? Is that why you never figured it out?"

A surge of anger made Volta finally look back at the fox, who was still sneering, just *waiting* for a reaction. The wolf's ears rang, her clothes *itched*.

"*Breathe, Volta.*" Carmen's voice echoed in her head. She swallowed, inhaling slowly and deeply.

"Why do *you* care so much?" she asked again, managing to keep the stammer to a minimum.

"Because guys like you piss me off," Tammy spat. "Heroes are supposed to be *strong* and *confident*. *You* look like you're gonna piss yourself anytime I touch you. You let a Korps agent butter you up for a whole month, and you didn't do *anything* to stop him. You put everyone here in danger, you put *real women* in danger by letting a roided up freak walk all over you. Why do you think you'd be a good superhero? Who's gonna get saved by a coward?"

"Tammy, that's *enough*." Dr. Mason interjected — way later than he should have.

Volta had no reply. She ducked away from Tammy's glower as the fox finally pulled the cord from the Dampener. The lump in her throat was back; she could already feel her eyes getting wet.

You can't argue with her. You know she's right about you. You ARE a coward. Why are you even here?

The red wolf tugged her shirt back on, stood up, and made for the door. She didn't look back, even as Dr. Mason began to feebly admonish his subordinate.

"Tammy, *really*, that was out of line."

"Someone had to tell him to his face, Doc. I'm not sitting here and letting some lovestruck puppy put us all in danger and *not* speaking my mind."

It was routine at this point. Go back to her room, feel sorry for herself, wait until next period, next mealtime, next… everything else.

The rest of the day came and went with Volta feeling, if anything, worse. Another sleepless night left her groggy and already in no shape to leave her room for anything.

An urgent ping from her phone grabbed her attention. She had a new demand from the security office to report directly to Chief Tullis's office in two hours. The wolf stared at the message for several seconds, trying to wrap her head around what it would mean, having to talk to Tullis directly again. She shivered at the idea — but *now* she was fully awake.

He'll see I'm not handling it, he'll know exactly why right away. I'm already falling apart, it's obvious to everybody… how much longer before they put me in an even smaller box?

Two hours meant she had time to go eat breakfast and psych herself up for it, at least. She was too awake now to try lying back down; she would just have to deal with feeling like shit until she could get a nap in after her meeting with Tullis — assuming she wasn't being locked up, or worse.

Normally, breakfast in the cafeteria wasn't anything to look forward to; for Volta, she did it to stop being hungry. After days and days of spending every lunch with Carmen, however, eating in the cafeteria completely alone again felt *wrong*. Her seclusion even from the other trainees and staff filling the cafeteria pressed in on her from all sides, just as the Dampener *pulled* relentlessly at her innards. Carmen being gone made the already icy draw of the device *ache* so much worse. Today was no different.

She ate in silence, staring at an empty seat across from her, trying to distract herself by actually trying to enjoy the eggs in the breakfast sandwich. It almost helped — eggs were always a favorite no matter what shape they came in.

But she knew this wasn't going to work forever. A week? A month? How many more months until she graduated, anyway? How many more days of dealing with Olson, Tammy, Tullis, and her parents looming over her? How many more days would she be stuck here?

Carmen said she would come and find me, she promised…

And how long are you gonna wait before you stop believing that? She already hid being in the Korps from you — why would she bother coming back? What are promises to a Korps spy?

But… she never lied about anything else. I believe her! I don't care what Tammy, or anyone says, she was real. She had to be…

"Hey, Travers."

A barely familiar voice jarred Volta out of her thoughts. She looked up, *up* at the square shoulders and slightly wild mane of —

"O-oh, uh — hi, Evans!" She offered a small wave at the lion. *Fuck, that was way too dainty.* She scrambled to put her brain into a more social gear; the sudden surprise of a classmate actually talking to her *outside* of a class helped some. "Uh, d'you… need something?"

It was then that she noticed the meal tray in his hands, right as he pointed to the seat opposite hers. "Actually, uh, you mind if I sit with you?"

Oh god he's gonna sit here. Oh fuck, oh no, I'll have to KEEP a conversation going. Carmen would know how to do this, she could handle something like this easy —

"S-sure yeah, okay!" she blurted out before she had the time to reconsider. She felt her face warming up; panicked, she dove into her sandwich.

The imposing lion sat down with his tray, brow furrowed in thought. Thankfully, he seemed as hesitant to speak up as she did. He stirred the hot cereal in his bowl around for a moment before he finally spoke up again.

"Hey, for the record, you fight pretty good for someone your size."

"Oh. Uh, thanks!" That meant a lot, coming from the guy who'd knocked her around pretty thoroughly the last time they were sparring partners.

"Olson's a serious hardass. I don't know why he goes after *you* so much, though," he mused before he took a bite of his cereal. "Is it just cuz you're a rich kid?"

"H-ha, it's… a mystery to me," Volta shrugged feebly. "I just try to keep my head down."

"Yeah, you seem like you've, uh, gotten good at that," the lion sniffed, looking like he wanted to ask something else. A *lot* of something elses, but he seemed to reconsider. "You, uh, really aren't what I thought you'd be like, Travers, when I heard who your parents were."

"Really?"

"I don't know, you're not, like, *hoity-toity*, not talking down to me or nothing."

Now it was Evans's turn to shrug. "You just seem nervous — like you don't wanna piss anybody off."

"Well, sure, I guess!" Volta answered, smiling nervously. "I, uhm, try to just stay out of folks' way. Well, I guess, except for yours, Evans, uh, during sparring…"

The big lion frowned, and his eyebrows knit together again. "Y'know, uh, last names only never quite felt right to me. Call me Otis."

"Austin!" She managed to not shrivel up at saying it, but she still felt like she'd just put something way too bitter in her mouth.

"I knew yours, actually, hah," Otis grinned awkwardly.

Volta blinked. "Uh, is… is that good?"

"I mean, your family *is* pretty famous, dude. You're a rich kid. Your parents basically *own* the TPA — or close enough." He grinned again, a big, almost doofy one, with all those huge lion teeth. "I mean, *most* people here have heard of you. Especially after yesterday, like —"

He cut himself off suddenly, registering having said something he shouldn't have. "Uh, sorry — I don't wanna push but… I gotta admit I'm really curious. What happened, with that Korps spy and everything?"

Volta's ears folded back and she shifted in her seat. Okay, so he wanted to talk about Carmen.

At least it's not an interrogation.

…I think.

"I — Well, she was undercover here. She, well, I *thought* she wanted to be friends, but…"

"Okay, Austin, hold up." Otis started laughing. "I know she was a spy and everything but y'all were *clearly* more than just friends."

"I… W-was it that obvious?" Volta asked, flustered. *What a stupid question. If Tammy and Tullis could tell, maybe the whole academy could. Fuck.*

"I saw you walking with her every day around campus, and, y'know! People talk…" He rubbed the back of his head. "Lot of us noticed you two sitting together. Couple of my friends were jealous, too. Said a girl like that could only be after —" Otis laughed awkwardly. Was *he* blushing now, too? "Well, I — yeah. It was nothin' nice."

Volta managed a tired smile. "I… can imagine what they said, yeah. I know what I look like."

"Nah, dude, it ain't like that, they're full of shit," Otis went on, looking indignant. "Look, I know I don't let up in Olson's classes, but… the fact that you're able to keep getting up even when Olson's yelling at you means a lot more than anything else those guys might say. Honestly, listen, I figured… Olson would see me going easier on you, but maybe I should —"

"N-no, no, that's fine," Volta interrupted. "You *really* don't have to do that. It's… not gonna change how Olson talks to me." *Especially now that Carmen's gone. Tullis will make him go even harder — not like he needs much encouragement…*

"You sure? I don't mind, I used to do backyard wrestling, I know how to fake some hits."

"I-I appreciate it, but I don't need that!" Volta protested. "I… don't mind it, I guess. Olson's never gonna let up on me, but, you shouldn't — Don't let up on me, either. I ain't a coward, and… I'm glad you're, uh, taking me seriously, at least. …If that makes sense, at all." She grimaced; did that sound as cheesy to him as it did to her?

"Huh? I mean, yeah. Especially after that tabby girl came, you got a lot faster, more confident. You were harder to knock back, actually, and you got *way* more aggressive. I could tell you were always going for it, even if Olson acted like you weren't." He raised his eyebrows, gesturing emphatically with his spoon in hand. "Whatever that spy was doing was *good* for you, I guess."

Volta replied with a nervous laugh, glancing to the side. "Y-yeah, I guess she did help a little."

Otis grinned. "Well, all right, Austin. I ain't gonna pull my punches, long as you don't pull yours."

She managed a grin back. "I… can live with that."

They talked a little longer while they both finished their trays. They chatted about the class schedules, whether Chief Tullis always walked with a stick up his ass or just while on the clock, and Volta had to cut herself off from detailing how True North II could *absolutely* beat the notorious Pyrokinetic, Cerberus, in a fight.

Otis stood up first, looking pensive. It made him look odd, like he wasn't used to really mulling over something that he was about to say. "Man, you really aren't what I expected you to be."

Volta blinked; that could be taken a lot of different ways. "W-what do you mean?"

"Well, I said before, you're not full of yourself like most rich dudes are; you're not a prick, either. And you're not a pussy, you're just... I dunno, quiet most of the time. I don't see why people have a problem with that."

"Well, thanks, I guess." Volta squirmed. She wasn't quite sure how to follow that up. "I'm... not exactly *trying* to, uh, defy any expectations. I'm just... trying to get through my classes and graduate."

"I hear that. Uh..." A few more seconds of mulling. "I... Look, dude, I know this is weird, but... are you angry at her? Uh, Carmen, I mean."

Volta stared wide-eyed up at him, her mind racing ahead. This wasn't a trick, was it? Did Tullis put him up to this, or was he just genuinely curious?

You couldn't tell that Carmen was hiding things from you; do you think you'd even be able to tell if this guy was, too?

Besides, you know the answer already. Of course you're upset. She promised you a better life, she disappeared, and you're still here just waiting for the walls to close in on you.

If he was here on Tullis's behalf, there was no answer she could give that wouldn't make her look suspicious. If he wasn't, well...

"...Yeah, a little," she admitted. "I thought she was — I thought we were close. I thought she understood me, that she *liked* me..." *What if she does, what if she's trying to get back here right now?* "But it — none of it matters, now. I guess. Carmen got caught, now she's gone."

Otis's brow furrowed and he responded with a short, thoughtful "huh." His jaw worked from side to side, like he was rolling her response around in his mouth to see how it tasted. "All right, I'll see you in Olson's class tomorrow, Austin. You take care, now."

"Yeah, same to you!" Volta waved a little as the lion turned away, and then slumped against the back of her seat. She glared at her empty lunch tray, turning her fork over in her hand. It still felt like so many needles at her insides every time someone used "Austin" for her, and it was *worse* when she had to say it herself. In spite of that, however, Otis was... a lot nicer, when he didn't have to throw punches.

No wonder he's a prodigy. He's on track to get out of here, soon as possible, because he deserves it. He can turn the rest of himself off, just focus on doing what he's told. It would all be so much easier if you could do that, but you can't. You've tried, and it just makes you feel worse.

Volta shook her head and took out her phone to check the time. 11:40. Shit, how long had she and Otis been talking? Tullis would be expecting her in twenty minutes.

She stood up, cleared her tray, and made for her bedroom again. Maybe it would be easier to psyche herself up if she tried to dread the impending meeting from her own bed.

It wound up not helping much. She lay on her sheets and stared at the ceiling, the walls, the True North II poster on the wall, and had to force down more tears as she recalled the rush and excitement from just two days ago when she'd considered taking that poster with her. The lack of decent sleep was starting to catch up with her. Carmen's voice was so easy to imagine, and with it came everything else. The warmth on the cat's face whenever she smiled at Volta, the softness of her padded fingers, caressing the red wolf's face…

Volta sat up again, taking a deep breath and stifling a whimper. She tried to turn it into a growl, then a *snarl*. She gnashed her teeth, gripped the sides of her bed with her clawed fingers. Her lupine lips curled up as she tried. Maybe it would be easier to try getting mad and *bitter* rather than just… being stuck feeling powerless and sad.

Several more minutes, and she finally got herself back on her feet and out into the hallway in the direction of the security building.

They hadn't spoken since the interrogation, now three long days ago. Would he be just as angry? *More* angry, now that he'd had more time to poke holes in her story?

No sense just standing here and wringing your hands over it. Get going, don't be a coward.

By the time she reached Tullis's office, she had managed to keep her eyes dry. If she could manage to keep an even temper in front of the big grey Great Dane, maybe he would be easier to handle.

She knocked on the door, and his gruff voice replied right after, just as before. "Door's open, Travers."

She opened it slowly, just in time for the broad-shouldered dog to swivel around in his chair. He didn't look angry at all. Now, he was… grinning? Smirking? Something between the two.

"Right on time," he nodded. "Take a seat, Travers. This won't take long."

The red wolf timidly stepped forward and very carefully took a seat, never taking her eyes off the Great Dane grinning at her. He leaned in, peering at her face. She leaned back into her chair, resisting the urge to grip at the sides with her claws.

"Y'know, Travers, I think I need to clear a few things up," the ex-hero began. He shook his shoulders as he spoke, eyes downcast at the desk in front of him. "I think you and I got off on the wrong foot somewhere."

He went quiet, his expression… expectant. Volta got the hint — she had to *ask*: "Uh, what do you mean, sir?"

"I'm talking about in the interrogation room, and every time we've spoken. Well," the dog snorted, "you think I got it out for you, that I'm waiting for you to fuck up. You keep thinking I'm your enemy, and that's gotten us in, well…" He gestured at the surrounding walls. "In a tight spot, with *Miss Rayne* or whatever her real name is."

The only "tight spot" I can see from here is the one I'm in right now…

"I, I guess so…" Volta muttered, shifting in her seat and starting to fidget with her hands.

"Let me make it absolutely clear for you, Travers: we're on the same side." Tullis regarded one of the small Golden Gavel article snippets that was still off to one end on his desk. "And you and me? We're the ones with *initiative*. I know how much time that cat whore spent with you, but you were always tenacious enough to try and cut it here in the TPA…"

Volta nodded, shifting her weight a little. "Well, s-sure, but… I know that Carm — that the Korps Spy was… too much for me."

Her body flashed back to Carmen's soft, gentle caress, as if she were still holding her now, as if their fight had been mere moments ago.

Tullis gave a very forced-sounding chuckle. "No shit, Travers. If you're tellin' the truth that you really had no idea, pffh, no wonder your family wanted me to intervene. We still gotta shape you up, son; sharpen your instincts."

Volta squirmed again, grimacing. Right, she'd almost managed to forget that particular detail. Had he brought her here to double down on that? Her nostrils flared as she took a deep breath, inhaling the decidedly *alien* smell of what had to be Tullis's cologne, and all the old newspaper hanging behind him…

He put his hands together, fingers clasped as he stared at her intently. "I ain't the bad guy here, Travers. You understand that, right? Now, I'm sure that pretty kitty tried to get you all mixed up, made you think she was your only friend here…"

"Sh — She didn't, sir…" Volta mumbled.

"Well, you might not *think* so, but…" The Great Dane tapped the side of his head, winking at her. "That might be exactly what she *wants* you to think, Travers. You gotta really, *really* put your mind to it. The Korps ain't no slouch when it comes to mind games. I watched them just get better and better at it for my whole career, and every time we squared off, they'd found some *new* way to get everyone all twisted up with the facts. So, believe me when I say, that cat did *something* to you, Travers…" His smile came back but did not extend to his eyes. "And you need to tell me what."

So, it was another interrogation. It had to be. Volta stared back at him, her lips tight as she tried to not shrink back into the cushioned seat.

"Travers, I'll be frank…" Tullis pushed himself back from his desk and stood up to his full height. He clasped his hands behind his back, and began to pace around to Volta's side, taking long, *heavy* strides. "Being a superhero's never gonna be easy. You'll deal with the Korps, with other terrorists, with loner types who get ambitious… and that's not to mention the *press.*"

He was behind her now. She knew what he was doing — he wasn't being at all subtle. The wolf didn't turn her head to follow him; she just sat there, glaring at his desk while he went on.

"There's a lot of roadblocks, and those roadblocks will pile onto each other if you don't play the game exactly right. Me, I got enough mud slung at me by the liberal media 'til Bradley didn't *want* me on active duty any more. So, I quit, hung up my cape and, well, wound up here, back in my home state, working at the place that helped me turn into a real man. *But,* guys like us learn something important in this line of work…" He put a heavy hand on Volta's shoulder, fingers squeezing enough to get her to look up at his grin. "If you wanna get rid of roadblocks, you gotta know who to get in good with. You gotta make friends, and you gotta find out ways to make powerful people keep their promises. Be smart, gamble *just* a little and you can make some very loyal friends, Travers. You understand what I'm getting at?"

The wolf nodded, cautiously. Of course she understood; it wasn't like Tullis *needed* to be subtle with the bribe talk — she'd seen Mom and Dad dole out plenty.

"Course it helps if you, uh, have an *in* or two…" He grinned wider. "I bet you know all about that. Your mom 'n' pop got you in here, after all…"

He finished circling around her and came back to lean against the front of his desk, arms folded as he stared Volta down. "So, here's my proposal, Travers. I can get you that *in*. Any steps you wanna skip? Consider them skipped. Don't take me for some washed up background act; I know guys all the way up. The state government, the western state heroes, hell, Bradley Group? You wanna get there one day, right?"

Oh. Okay, this part she hadn't seen coming. Volta's eyes went wide; there was a strange sensation, like gravity lightened up for a few moments. If Tullis was telling the truth, then…

"Hah, I see that spark in your eyes. You don't have to like me, Travers, but I have resources you very *badly* want. You cooperate with me, not only do you get off scot-free, I'll clear the road for you. Bradley Group's cert rules are just there to discourage the ones who don't want to push forward. The ones with real ambition, the real *heroes*, they don't care about the rules. Think you're up for that, Travers?"

Volta swallowed, averting her eyes again while her mind raced. What Tullis was promising was… everything she could have wanted, before she met Carmen. Freedom from her family, from having to adhere to anything she'd been stuck to for the last twenty years.

You know it's not that easy. It never is. If it was, you could have run away years ago.

Tullis was waiting patiently now, picking his teeth with one dull claw while he waited. She knew what he wanted her to ask. She swallowed again, wetting her lips with her tongue. "So, what's the catch?"

"You cut the bullshit. You tell me everything you know about this 'Carmen' bitch, and you help me find her again. The Korps have hidden nests everywhere and they like to do things close to home. You and me, we could find the one I *know* has to be nearby. It might take a while, but a freshly licensed Bradley Hero like you would have nothing but time…"

His smile vanished, and his voice shifted down into a low, dangerous rasp. "We'll find your girlfriend, and then you'll help me put her down."

Volta blanched, her skin crawling as his words sank in. Everything, well, *almost* everything she wanted, hers for the taking. At the price of…

Tullis straightened up again, his faux-smile returning. "You do that, and I'll call in every favor I have from those buttoned up goody-two-shoes. You'll be home-free. We got a deal, Travers?"

You'd be free, only so long as you promise to kill the one person who ever cared about you. The one person who knew the real you and loved you still.

Volta didn't have to deliberate long. "N-no. No, we don't."

Tullis's smile faltered, but he didn't look surprised like she had expected. "That's your final answer?"

"Y —" *Breathe, Volta.* "Yeah. I'm not going to help you… *hunt* her down. Sir." She grew bolder the longer she spoke. Tullis just kept glaring down at her, his fake grin gone once more. He didn't look angry, just disappointed.

She kept going. "If I see her again, I'll… it'll be fair and square. I'll face her down, like I will every Korps agent. I'm gonna do it the same way True North did; I'm not gonna take shortcuts."

This time, Tullis's grin was real, and *cruel.* "That cripple you love so much had every shortcut possible, don't kid yourself. He was the son of Canada's *only* competent hero, he was *surrounded* by talent, of *course* he was gonna turn out capable. Well, as capable as some unpowered sore loser like him could ever be."

Volta bristled, scowling up at the Great Dane. "He… he wasn't a *killer*, though. He wasn't…"

"He was a coward, who couldn't take any responsibility," Tullis growled.

"Arthur Simonds is a *hero!*" Volta snapped, finally, standing up. Her whole body was warming up now, a low thrumming filling her ears. "He never lost his principles, he had personal *rules!* He kept getting up and kept fighting until he couldn't any more, and he wasn't *ever* going to let *anyone* push him to be something he *wasn't.*" There was a beat of silence between them. Now Tullis *did* seem surprised; his brows were raised and he kept quiet long enough for Volta to add on a hasty "sir."

His eyebrows came back down, and the rest of his face followed, tilting into a scowl. "Okay, Travers. You want to take the high road all the time? I won't stop you. Don't worry, I won't *have* to put any more roadblocks in your way, they'll fall on you all on their own. …But uh, don't expect Olson's class today to get any easier."

"Th-that's fine," Volta faltered. "I'll deal with it. I'm… I'm *not* a coward."

"Heh, if you say so, Travers. By the way, we should wrap this up…" He glanced at the clock. "You ought to get going, actually."

"Wha —" She glanced at the clock on Tullis's wall. Fifteen minutes to one. Olson's usual class time wasn't for another hour and a half. "For what?"

"Oh, damn, I meant to tell you," Tullis sighed. "Must have slipped my mind. We let your parents know about Miss Rayne's sudden, uh, *change of heart*. They should be at the Admin Building to speak with the Academy President… right about *now*, actually."

All of the gathering warmth in Volta's torso evaporated. The ringing in her ears stayed, as an involuntary tremble shook her body. "They're… h-here?"

"And they'll be expecting you, too, Travers." Tullis bent down, his nose inches from hers. "Told 'em myself you'd be there. They wanna have a word with you, when they're done with Richardson."

"But — But I —"

"Better hurry, pup. Don't waste your time yipping at me about some softie Canuck."

Heart pounding, ears ringing, Volta turned and ran.

Chapter 9

Separation Anxiety

The red wolf shifted in her chair, trying to make herself as small as possible between her parents in the campus president's office. Dad sat to her right, bouncing one leg, clearly fuming as President Richardson cautiously explained the events — clearly as Tullis had reported. The Dalmatian wiped sweat from his brow; he clearly knew full well who was actually in charge of this place.

Mom hadn't let go of Volta's left arm since she had entered the Admin Building. Her thin fingers with their long, painted claws squeezed her tightly, but Volta didn't dare say anything. She stared ahead at the cowering Dalmatian's lapel pin — a little TPA star — while her mother did the same.

"I assure you," Jack Richardson continued, a nervous smile plastered on his face. "We are doing everything we can to secure the premises. We are in full lockdown — no one in, no one out, and we'll stay that way for the next week at minimum."

"*Minimum?*" Mr. James Travers snapped, standing up from his chair. "You just caught a spy on your own campus and you're going for the minimum? What kind of sorry excuse for security do you people *have* around here!?" Volta winced at her father's raised voice, ears pinning back. At least this was one time he wasn't yelling *at* her. "First I hear that one of their *agents* is snooping around, next you tell me she was the same girl my *son* was associating with?"

"You have to understand, Mr. Travers," the weedy Dalmatian simpered as he held up both hands, as if trying to placate a raging bull. Volta couldn't blame him. "We have to maintain regular operation, and I promise that Security Chief Tullis is taking this *very* seriously."

"We already made ourselves perfectly clear with him," her mom chimed in, speaking in clipped tones. "We wanted Adam to keep an eye on that girl, check up on her. Our son spent so much time with her — why did Adam not intervene sooner!?"

"Chief Tullis talked it over with me!" Richardson pleaded. "He was very clear that intervening any sooner would be a mistake. He said —"

"I wanted to be sure."

The Great Dane's gruff voice made Volta's stomach drop. Her parents whipped their heads around to look at the looming dog walking into the office. Volta didn't move, heart pounding in her ears. Had he just meandered after her? He looked... *proud* of himself.

Dad broke the silence first. "You — But — all right, *fine*. What about securing this place *properly*? A week is too little time. She could come back."

"It's one thing to be secure," Tullis began in a grandiose tone of voice, walking slowly around to Volta's right, to address her dad. "No one gets in or out, you're safe, but it's a *very different* thing to be just insecure enough that you leave an opening. A small one. Then you'll know which crack the pests will crawl in through."

Mom, Dad, even *Richardson* looked confused, but Tullis seemed glad to explain. "We stay in lockdown for a week, then we open up again. Business as usual. *Then* we can expect them to make their move. This is the *Korps* we're talking about, James; they're tenacious, like roaches. You let them come back, they will. They'll all run in, and we'll lock the door behind them. It'll be like fish in a barrel."

"So, our..." Dad began quietly, clearing his throat. Volta looked cautiously up at the Great Dane, who grinned back at her. "You want to use him as bait?"

"Don't you worry. I'll keep our puppy safe, James," he growled, sneering down his nose at her. She flagged her ears again and averted her eyes. "Not like he can do that himself, anyway. Isn't that right, Austin? Olson ain't happy with you, but I guess he'll have to get in line."

Volta swallowed and felt her mother's fingers dig harder into her arm. She didn't dare look at her.

"G'on, James. Walk your pup back to his room, since he needs the help," Tullis continued, clearly enjoying himself.

The older red wolf blinked, clearly a little disarmed. "Adam, are you *sure* about this?"

"The Korps aren't getting anywhere near your kid. If they try..." He raised up a dark furred fist. Instantly, the fur went *solid* as his entire lower arm turned to a hard, golden-yellow metal, with a quiet, resonating ring. "I'll put them down myself. You have my word on that."

Icy fear gripped Volta. If Carmen did come back, she'd have to face him again — and she had just barely gotten away unscathed, if Tullis was to be believed.

...And that was *if* Carmen came back. Volta had been trying not to think about the fact that she was gone, but there was no ignoring it. Carmen had promised she wouldn't leave her, and yet...

"Get up, Austin." Mom pulled her out of her thoughts and stood her up, pushing her toward the door. Dad followed after, walking at Volta's other side as they departed the building.

It wasn't exactly the first time she'd been almost frog marched around by Mom. How fitting, now, to be pressed between her parents again, feeling like a little kid who had just caused another outage at school. She knew what was coming, but she tried desperately not to think too hard about it. The mere memory of previous punishments was already making her body itch with dread.

"You better have a good explanation, young man," Mom hissed at her. "We told you, we *told* you again and again, that you're supposed to find another red wolf. A *red. Wolf. Austin.* You have an obligation to continue the family line, and when that... *woman* showed up, we were patient with you! We gave you a chance to shut things down with her. So, what do you do?"

"I'm sorry, Mom," Volta mumbled numbly.

"You just keep on going, like it's the most normal thing in the world!" she continued. "Your father and I were always patient with you when it came to finding a girl. You've ruined everything *else* we could line up, and now you're just rubbing it in our faces."

"I'm sorry," the younger wolf tried again. Either her mother hadn't heard, or she didn't care.

They arrived at the dormitories, and then to Volta's door. Dad took out his personal keycard, and the door clicked open.

"Get *inside, now.*" Mom shoved Volta into her room, finally releasing her arm. Volta stumbled as she turned around, the place where Mom's claws had dug in throbbing uncomfortably. The door slammed shut behind her, and she turned slowly to face her parents again.

It was a different bedroom this time, but the feeling was just the same as it was at home. The apprehension, the remembered marks and stings and screaming, were all bubbling up again. The only thing that was missing was the cross on the wall.

"Of course I suspected, as soon as I saw her. So tall, and the aggressive look in her eyes when she looked at us…!" Mrs. Travers groaned. "Of *course* she was one of them. No woman should ever be that tall or that athletic, it's not *right* for a girl to look that mannish."

"Knowing them, she probably wasn't *really* a woman at all," Mr. Travers chimed in. A cold spike shot through Volta's chest at the words, but she didn't dare show it on her face. Her father looked around Volta's small room. The older wolf growled in distaste as his eyes passed over the True North poster on the wall.

"I can't bear to think about that. Austin, think about what she could have done to you! Who's to say she didn't *already*? Have the doctors checked you over?"

Volta raised her hands weakly, ears folding back. "She didn't do *anything* to me, Mom."

And you thought Richardson looked cowardly. At least he still looked like an adult; you're doing the same things you've done since you were seven to try and placate them, and you know they won't work.

"Are you sure? How would *you* know what she did, Austin?" Mom accused. "You knew her for weeks — *weeks* — and you had no idea. I *knew* we should have been more worried about her."

"She didn't!" Volta protested. "All she did was get to know me, she never asked me for anything. I already told all this to the police — Tullis interrogated me himself."

"Watch your tone, Austin. And yes, Chief Tullis told us about the interrogation," the older wolf narrowed her eyes, raising a finger. "How *dare* you raise your voice to him, to an officer of the law — the *Golden Gavel*, no less, a family friend! I thought we raised you better than that, and instead you're giving him backtalk about those… those *freaks*. She was so *close* to us, too." She shivered with disgust.

Now it was Dad's turn, as his wife finally took a breath. He stepped forward, fixing her with the withering gaze Volta knew very well. "She had you wrapped around her finger. Do you have any idea, boy, *any idea* what she might have done to you?"

Volta felt hot all over. Her jaw clenched, she tried to keep her voice level. "No, Dad. Can you tell me?"

The older wolf narrowed his eyes, humorless. "I don't want to get into the details in front of your mother, young man, but I'll lay it out for you since it seems to be escaping you. Every week there is a new story about some poor sucker getting seduced by them, kidnapped, or taken willingly — there's no way to *tell* with these people. They target anyone weak-willed enough to listen." He pointed up at the poster of True North on the wall. "And you know what happened to *him*. He walks with a cane now, Austin; he got off easy. If you can't be converted to their agenda, they will *hurt* you so much worse than a broken leg. That tabby could have done things to you *so much worse* than what you hear in the news. That's *real life*, Austin, and it's the realest part of that woman, or whatever she calls herself."

*You mean she could hurt me like **you** hurt me?*

Volta couldn't take it anymore. Her claws dug into her palms as she tightened her trembling fists. She took no time to think, she just spoke. "She *is* a woman, Dad, and her name is *Carmen*."

James Travers raised a hand; Volta's tail twitched downward in a suppressed flinch. "*Austin Henry Travers*, you watch yourself. My son is *not* going to talk back to me like that. We raised you better."

You barely raised me at all until I started breaking things; then you were all over me.

Volta's nostrils flared, but she kept silent, even as bitter anger, hot and stinging like bile, simmered in the pit of her stomach. Her ears were ringing; it was getting hard to *think*.

"How can you say she didn't do anything when you're acting so strangely, Austin?" Mom stepped forward, holding a hand out to Volta. She took a step back and averted her eyes. "You've *never* been like this, not around us."

Never let me get that far before you grabbed the belt, you mean. Do you even remember? Do you know that I remember?

Heart thumping in her chest, Volta took in a shaky breath. "I'm *fine*, Mom. I've been fine. I was *fine* the entire time Carmen was here. She didn't hurt me, she didn't control me…" *She* did *trick me, though.* "All she did was help me with my training and talked to me. We were friends, that's all."

"*Friends?*" Mom spat the word out, disbelieving. "With a terrorist spy?"

"I — I *thought* we were," she hastily added. "…But then she showed me what she was, and then she got caught. I told Chief Tullis the same thing."

"She got *caught* holding one of those mind-control goggles!" her mother snapped. "She was *that close* to getting it on you — do you care at all how often that thought has *haunted* me since that day, Austin? You could have been brainwashed in seconds. You wouldn't even be *you* anymore, you'd just be a *drone* for them to control!"

That jogged her memory. Carmen had said something, weeks ago, a few days before she had gone.

"*How much of what you let your parents see is really you, anyway?*"

Volta remembered the harsh look on her face, the sudden steeliness in her amber eyes. Behind that harshness had been a genuine concern for Volta — Carmen wanted her to be *safe*. If her mother shared that same concern, she was doing a good job of hiding it.

"Austin, I keep getting the feeling you aren't *really* thinking about the danger you were in," Mom continued. "Carmen — if that's even her real name — was able to get close to you, to trick you into trusting her. Do you even know if she was really a *she*, Austin?"

She had been here plenty of times before. Standing there, too afraid to move or even shuffle while Mom let out her frustration. Years ago, she had realized that not talking and not moving minimized the chances of Mom getting the belt out. Now, even standing an inch over her mother, she kept rigidly still, not breaking eye contact with her again.

"You know about them, you know what they *like*. Attention-seeking, godless scum who desecrate their bodies and plot to convert everyone into thinking like they do, and you thought one of them was your *friend?*"

"I thought —"

"You know what I think, Austin? I think you let yourself get distracted with her, you *wanted* that freak to control you. Your father and I have tried our best to keep you on the right path, in spite of everything you did over the years to make it so much harder for us."

She couldn't take it. She screwed her eyes shut; the ringing in her ears was getting worse, the heat all over her body made her skin crawl.

"You can't even look at me anymore. That just *proves* me right. You were thinking about the same *evil* things as before. You haven't learned anything, have you? Look at me, Austin. I said *look at me.*"

She didn't open her eyes. Fists quaking, she fought the impulse to hide her face behind her hands as she felt the tears well up. The Dampener's cold surface ached against her hot, prickling skin. The low ring in her ears became a hum.

"Even now, even *now* you're throwing it in our faces, letting yourself get so close to one of them. Are you even thinking about any of this? Are you even *considering* that you might have almost gotten pulled away from us by one of those disgusting *trannies?*"

"Stop…" Volta whimpered. Her voice sounded alien even to her.

"*Excuse me?*" Now the real, affronted anger was coming through Mom's tone. Volta didn't need to open her eyes to see the vindictive snarl on her mother's lips.

She wasn't going to cower to it again. "Mom, p-*please* stop," she said firmly.

"You look at your mother when you talk to her," Dad growled dangerously. "Don't hide; you're a grown man."

"You don't treat your mother like this," Mom hissed. "Look at me, Austin, *or else.*"

Volta felt Mom's grip on her arm. Her mother yanked her forward, and she knew the open hand was coming.

She swung her arm out, twisting it out of the older wolf's grip. Her heart was thudding so loud she almost didn't hear herself scream.

"DON'T TOUCH ME!"

Now she opened her eyes, and her streaming tears could not hide the electric blue glow that shone over her parents, shocked into silence. Arcs of lightning crackled up and down her arms, radiating off her shoulders. The lights on the ceiling flickered as she inhaled and felt the Dampener's chill against her too-flat chest.

"*Don't touch me again,*" Volta snarled, feeling her hackles rise behind her. Her ears were folded backward, and she bared her teeth, nostrils flared. "I'm not — I won't *let* you."

Mom was frozen, eyes wide like saucers as Dad spoke — hesitantly, for once. "You're — You're still not in control of it, are you? Son — Austin, think about what you're doing. You're threatening —"

"*Stop. Calling me. Son.*" Volta hissed, blue arcs crawling up the walls to either side of her as they shot off her body. "I don't care. I don't *care what you think. I'm SICK of hearing you say it over and over. I'm sick of hearing 'son,' and 'boy,' and 'Austin'* — "

"You're not talking sense," Mom protested, maybe even *pleading* a little. "Calm down, Austin, before you —"

"Shut up, shut *up*, **STOP CALLING ME THAT!**" Volta barked. For once, Mom listened.

They kept stock still, standing close together, eyes wide. Mom was affronted, Dad was stunned, *both* of them were, clearly, afraid.

Finally.

The electric blue glow dimmed as the crackling sparks died down. She hadn't lost much charge, but finally with her parents silent, she could take a moment to think — and as soon as she did, she thought of Carmen again. Carmen, reminding her to breathe, telling her she could handle it, reassuring her that she'd be okay. The arcs crawling over her arms dissipated completely, and she was left standing there, shoulders rising and falling with every breath, heart still racing.

"*I'm not letting you yell at me again,*" Volta growled. "*Get out.*"

They stood there, continuing to stare.

"*Get OUT!*" She shouted again, and this time they obeyed. Her father swiftly yanked the door open, and ushered her mother out behind him as he looked back at her.

"You — you're not thinking of doing anything dangerous, are you?"

Volta faced him, took a breath, and answered. "No, Dad. I'm going to my next class. I'm going to graduate, and then I'm getting *away* from *you.*"

Before he could reply, she slammed the door in his face, sank into her bed, and started crying again. She let herself fall face first into her pillow to hide the noise, even from herself. She could hear their muffled talking from the dormitory hallway, then their footsteps. They faded gradually, and she was left alone again, in the same cage her parents had shoved her into.

And Carmen was still gone.

In spite of wanting to just stay in her room, curled up in her bed and trying to pretend the rest of the world didn't exist, Volta still made sure she wasn't late to Olson's class this time. If she could do *anything* to lighten the load, after everything else…

"Right on time, Travers," the lean bear grunted. "Come on, onto the mat. You're with Evans again today."

Fuck; no getting out of that this time. As she kicked her shoes off and hurried onto the practice mat, she tried to consider the silver lining. Maybe getting pummeled by Otis would at least take her mind off… everything *else*.

The lion waited there, in the same sparring gear as her. Thin gloves, shorts, even his T-shirt this time around was thin. *Very* thin. Wow, that was a lot of arm and chest muscles to just have on display. Volta swallowed, willing herself to make eye contact instead.

Otis smiled at her, raising a hand. "Not gonna hold back on me now, right?"

"Long as you don't, either," she half-smiled back.

Of course, we said we'd do that before I had to talk to Tullis, before I… blew up at my parents. What have I gotten myself into?

Olson blew his whistle as the two of them put up their fists. "I want all you kids to focus on reaction time today. Feinting and deflecting, people. Punish your opponent for misreading you, hit 'em hard and hit 'em fast."

Otis was taking the bear's instructions to heart, it seemed. He immediately stepped to Volta's right, aiming a jab at her head. She ducked, and saw his other hand swing out in a hook to catch her. Her arm was ready; she knocked his fist away, aimed low and connected a punch right into that chest, *hard*, just like Carmen had taught her.

Carmen taught you so much, but she didn't teach you how to handle Tullis, or Mom, or Dad. It was so easy for her — she just left home one day and didn't look back.

Otis fell back a step, not letting out more than a grunt. As always, though, he was tenacious. He immediately swung again, continuing to circle around her, forcing her to turn with him.

You're not going to be able to do this forever. It's only going to get harder. You think Tullis WON'T make things harder for you, just because? He won't let up until you do what he wants.

The next jab knocked straight against her shoulder, and the pain brought her back. This was *supposed* to be distracting, but it wasn't working. The lion took a step forward, winding up. That *had* to be a feint. Volta stepped to his right, narrowly avoiding the uppercut from his off-hand. At least Otis was very good about telegraphing things.

She went in just as he got his hands back up, delivering three blows against his guarding arms.

How long, do you think, before your parents come down on you for that little stunt you pulled, though?

He got her with his next swing; she weaved just in time, and his fist glanced off her side. She went for his face, next, to get his guard up…

Mom never loses a fight. You think your fists and your powers will help you? All they'd have to do is tell Dr. Mason to turn the Dampener all the way back up again. You'd be back where you started, and just as miserable. Because you know, this time, no help is —

WHAM.

Otis's fist hit the bottom of the Dampener, slamming the metal right into Volta's solar plexus.

"Ghk — !" The air left her lungs. She fell, gasping, to one knee. The tender spot of nerves right under her ribcage felt like it was on fire. The nausea rolled over her and kept her staring at the floor, terrified something might come up. She couldn't get air in fast enough.

Otis stopped dead in his tracks. He started to bend down over her, casting a shadow. "Oh shit, *shit*. Uh, Austin? You okay?"

"Walk it off, Travers, it was just a chest blow!" And there was Olson, stepping closer. "Don't be a pussy about it, stand up!"

Volta trembled, a wave of embarrassment welling up in her belly and still-stinging chest. The more time she took to breathe, the more aware she was of the sudden lack of noise from the surrounding pairs. A fair number had stopped to watch, watch *her* struggle with a single hit.

What surprised her was suddenly hearing Otis's voice, interjecting. "Sir, c'mon, give him a break."

"I'll decide when he needs a break, Evans. You keep going, and Travers — straighten up already!" the bear snapped.

"Sir, I'm serious, I think he might be hurt!" Otis protested. "Austin, are you all right? Say something."

"I-I'm — I'm *fine!*" Volta's voice cracked as she said it.

Perfect. As if this couldn't get any worse, you're sounding like a preteen again, in front of everyone. Are you going to start crying now, too, just to hammer home how much you can't handle any of this?

Volta swallowed and tried to blink away the water in her eyes. She managed to get back on both feet, and now stayed bent over, hands on her knees as the nausea persisted. She looked up to see Olson's unforgiving glower, and Otis's frown of concern.

"See? He's fine, Evans, he's just acting up." Olson stepped closer to Volta, pointing a finger. "You disrupt the class with a kicked puppy show like that again, Travers, and you're not gonna like what happens next."

She kept her head low, avoiding eye contact. "Y-yes, sir."

"Right. Keep going, you two. Don't make me come over here again."

Otis frowned, working his jaw from side to side in frustration. "This isn't right, sir, I'm not gonna just keep beating on him."

Olson's next words came through clenched teeth. "You do as I say, Evans, or I'll hold you back for another semester."

"Do whatever the hell you want to me," Otis replied, just as heated. "I'm not hitting him again."

Olson ignored him and rounded on Volta. He bent down, hissing into her ear. "Travers, stop being a pussy and straighten the fuck *up.*"

The nausea wasn't going away. Her ears were ringing again, heart pounding in her chest.

The bear leaned in, putting a hand on Volta's shoulder. "You listen to me, Travers. If you keep going like this, I'm holding you back for another year. Tullis told me all about your 'girlfriend,' and your little training sessions." She looked up at him, heat welling up in her chest as the humming got louder. Her face twisted up in a grimace, her vision blurring with more tears.

"Are you seriously going to start crying right in front of me?" Olson growled, looking disgusted. "You're standing here, slowing *everything down* and crying like a little kid with bruised knees. Evans doesn't even need to hit you — *I'll* fucking give you something to cry about, Travers. We need heroes, not *cowards*."

She balled up her hands into fists, nostrils flaring as she kept blinking. There were too many coming for her to just blink them away, now. She could barely see straight, couldn't see *anything* save for the brown bear sneering in her face, snarling under his breath.

"You come into my class and you half-ass everything. You pout and whine like a little girl every time someone punches back. Were you expecting Hero work to be easy?" He prodded her chest, just to the side of her Dampener. "Is life getting too hard for you? Not getting the silver spoon treatment you're used to back home? Take a good look around, Travers. No one else is just standing around and crying like a little bitch. You gonna go running to your friend in drag again, too? Too bad he's not around anymore — maybe then you'd finally be good for something: being someone else's bitch."

"I'm —" She tried to speak; it came out as little more than a wet croak. "I'm n-not a —"

"*You don't fucking talk back to me you entitled little shit!*" he hissed, grabbing the front of her shirt and shaking her. "You suck it up, *you put your fists up*, or you get ready for another *year* here. Be a *man* for once in your *goddamn life*. Am I clear?"

Don't touch me.

Her fists shook at her sides. There was murmuring around them, rapidly getting drowned out as the inner *hum* overwhelmed the noise. Olson was still holding her, *shaking* her now, with both hands.

"You even listening to me, Travers? Don't you fucking space out on me. I've put up with you sulking around in my class for a year, I don't mind knocking the rest of that out of you *right here and now.*"

Don't TOUCH me.

Volta's shoulders rose and fell as she took deep, unsteady breaths. The dull ring was unbearable; the heat made her head hurt.

The cross on the wall looked as cold as ever. The feeling of her short, young claws against her locked bedroom door was fresh in her head. She was nauseous from the crying, but still so *hungry*.

Mom was raising her hand again, screaming at her to repeat the scripture.

She could hear the familiar *clink* of Dad's belt as he held it high, promising her it was for her own good.

"Travers, *answer me!*" Olson barked in her face.

It happened in an instant. Her vision was still blurry with tears, but she could see her knuckles impacting Olson's jaw, could see the painfully bright blue sparks radiating off her arm and hand and *into* the bear's face. For just a moment, he looked surprised.

The bear's head flew back as her charged punch carried through. The rest of his body came after, hands slipping free from her shirt. Olson fell to the ground with a dull *whump*, a stifled yelp, and an electric **crackle.** He lay there, eyes wide as he convulsed and grunted. He tried to get a breath in as the charge shook his whole body three times, four, five, six, until finally he went slack.

The red wolf stared down at him, gasping and whimpering, tears streaking down her face. Her teeth bared in a confused, overwhelmed snarl. For several seconds, she couldn't take her eyes off the unconscious bear in front of her, his stunned form drooling on the mat.

What finally shook her out of it was the ringing in her ears dying down just enough to register the stunned silence of the entire gym surrounding her. All of the students stared at her, at a loss for what to do.

Until one ran for the emergency phone on the wall.

Volta's eyes finally found Otis, standing closest to her, completely nonplussed. *He* was frightened. "Uhhh, Austin…?"

The longer they stood there, the more noise kept filtering in. People were muttering, and then clamoring around them. Most of the students were backing away from her as if she might hurt them, too. Volta raised her hands, staring with dull awareness as blue arcs leapt off her arms and legs and into the floor and air around her.

The lion was the only one who didn't move. Was he too scared too, or was he trying to calm her down? "I… I think you're in trouble."

Volta still couldn't speak. She nodded slowly, wavering in place as the bolts around her died down, little by little, until she was just standing there, looking as useless as she felt. There was a clattering of boots, at least five pairs, from somewhere behind the wolf. She couldn't move, rooted in place, sniffling and blinking. She wanted to speak but words weren't coming. *Nothing* was coming. She had no idea what to do.

"There he is, don't startle him," a voice muttered from behind her.

Tullis's voice came next. "We're past that now," he said. "Take him down. Activate the failsafe."

There was a click, and the already cold chill of the Dampener became *icy*. Volta went rigid, sucking in a ragged breath as all her charge dissipated in under a second. She didn't have the energy to double over anymore, much less turn around.

"Wait —" Otis started, holding his hands up. "Please, don't. He's not — You don't have to —"

She heard someone approach behind her and felt a sudden pressure against the side of her neck. Ice-cold numbness spilled into her, and immediately her vision smeared, going dark as she fell forward. Someone caught her, holding her up as she felt the rest of her body go slack. The last thing she heard was Otis's pleading and Tullis telling someone to pick Olson up and get him to the medical wing.

"Okay, okay, so you're going back now and that's fine!" Wren almost yelled, having to run to keep up with Carmen's long legs in RIV's west-facing main hall. "Just that, well, it's been four days and there's *no way* they're out of lockdown, Carmen! Are you sure about this?"

"I'm not making her wait any longer," the tabby replied curtly, turning abruptly out of the corridor, through a sliding door, and into the armory.

As she had requested, a full array of mission supplies rested on one countertop, being inspected one last time by one of the armorer's assistants. As she approached, the crow straightened up, tipping their RCGs up in greeting. "All accounted for, Agent Rayne."

Carmen nodded, glancing over the assortment of knives, the mission-standard first aid, the lockpicks, the signal jammer, the sidearm…

"…And my suit?"

"Hanging in the changing room."

"Carmen, hold on…" The Honduran White Bat ran in front of the tabby, holding up both hands.

Carmen raised an eyebrow. "You better not be expecting to stop me, Wren."

"I'm not, I just…" His hands dropped to his sides, and he sighed. "I know we've been planning this every *hour* we've been awake, but I'm…"

He trailed off, his eyes wide and glossy. Tears welled rapidly, and Carmen's eyes went wide as the usually unshakeable bat put his hands on his shoulders and his powers triggered. A sudden protrusion on his right shoulder stuck up past the wide collar of his shirt, between his fingers, followed quickly by another, like solid stones trapped beneath his skin and flesh.

Wren gripped harder around the jutting lumps as he winced in pain, trying to force himself to calm back down as he stared tearily up at her.

"I want to save her too, Carm — but I need *you*, too…"

Carmen stiffened, heart sinking. The Honduran bat's mass-altering powers never manifested unbidden like this unless he was far more anxious than he let on. Carmen allowed herself a moment's self-chastising for not thinking about checking on him sooner.

"I get you're worried," the tabby said as she squatted down, cupped Wren's face in her hands and planted a gentle kiss on his leaf-shaped nose. "Look, we'll be touching off when it's already dark, 8:30 PM. There's gonna be pretty heavy rain, so I'm going in with cloud cover. No one will see me coming until I'm too close for it to matter."

The bat gave a weak, strained chuckle. "Well, it's pretty easy for me to see you coming, most of the time…"

She made a face and kissed him again, lightly patting the side of his cheek as the hard protrusions receded, leaving his shoulder unblemished. "*All right,* I guess I walked into that one. Keep up that mood when you're watching me break in, and we'll be golden."

A familiar clicking of heels behind them made Carmen straighten up again. "Oh, don't stand at attention on account of me." The silver dragon waved her hands dismissively as she entered. "Are you all ready, Agent?"

"Getting there!" Carmen replied, gesturing to the changing room door. "Man, it's weird, I haven't put on my infiltrator gear in… shit, it's been over a year."

"We've made sure to keep it properly sized for you," Karen grinned. "Cosetta's portion sizes aren't about to outpace our tailors."

"It's mostly just gone to her hips! I thought *everyone* could see," Wren remarked, earning himself another bap on the shoulder.

The dragon tittered and winked at the tabby. "Nevertheless! It will fit you like a glove."

"Thank you," Carmen smiled, then paused. "Wait, you could have let me know about this through my RCGs — did you just want to see me off personally?"

"Actually, I'm coming with you," Karen explained, putting her hands out to either side, as if presenting herself as a gift. "Assuming all goes well, I want to see her *personally*. I'll be in the chopper, circling us around until you're clear of the campus, and ready to call in support if things need a *little* helping along."

"I appreciate the on-site support, Karen. And! I guess I better go test your claim…"

The tabby strode over to the changing room door and disappeared through it.

"And between you and me," Karen bent to whisper into the bat's big ear, "the hips were *easy* to see, and we've accommodated their growth accordingly."

"Oh *phew*." Wren wiped nonexistent sweat from his brow. "For a second there, I thought her suit might be a little *too* tight."

"Ha, no danger of that," Karen remarked with a grin, as the changing room door slid open again and Carmen stepped back out.

From her ankles to her neck, she was decked out in a skin-tight suit with a hexagonal pattern. The whole suit, glossy grey — save for the deep purple helix that went from her chest to her underbelly.

The tabby wore slate colored, reinforced boots over her digitigrade feet, covering everything save for her claws. Her sleeves ended at her wrists, and she was just adjusting a pair of seamless half-finger gloves with hard studs on the knuckles. Both boots were latched onto the hem of the infiltrator suit's legs, and despite them clearly being metal, Carmen's light footsteps barely made a sound. Segmented armor plates on her shoulders, arms, waist, hips, and legs bore a consistent serial number and a scrawling of words, both of which were written in the Korps's signature cipher.

As she stepped closer, Wren leaned forward to read the writing on one knee. "'*With opened eyes, found at last, every second is a joy.*' Damn, Carm, even your sneaking suit waxes poetic."

"I know infiltrators who use subtlety, and they're cowards," Carmen deadpanned at the bat, grinning more with her eyes than her mouth. The tabby raised one arm, flexing it and watching the synthetic fibers of the suit stretch noiselessly over her muscles. "You weren't kidding. It's as perfect as fit as the first time."

"If you like, after this, we can see about dispatching you to shorter, *quieter* missions again," Karen offered. "You always were a perfect fit for them."

"I'll think about it," Carmen replied, stretching her back out before she slipped on her more angular, face-conforming RCGs. "Ooh, a new interface suite. You've been busy!" Her suit began to shimmer. The shine of the material faded, rendering the whole outfit a non-reflective matte black.

"If you're going to break into a semi-military state facility, go in style, I say," the dragon smirked.

Wren whistled as the cat sauntered over to the equipment table again, reaching for the holster and belt covered in packs. "Damn, though, Carm. That look suits you, if you'll forgive the pun. I know *why* you stopped, but there's other infiltration work you could do — even if it's just an excuse to wear this getup more often!"

"I *could*, but I would miss the dance."

"The what?"

"The *dance*." Carmen turned as she slid one knife into its sheath on her shoulder, another snugly onto her calf. "You know. What I did with Volta, what I *love* to do. Talk, learn, take people apart, help put them back together again, better than before. I don't get to do that when I'm just, y'know…" She drew a finger across her throat.

"Standing offer, same as always!" Karen shrugged. "No pressure. I'm considering this a one-night-only revival unless you say otherwise."

"Honestly, after dealing with Teepa bullshit for more than a fucking *month*, I might just need a break." Carmen wore a joyless grin, and for a moment, she let them see how exhausted she felt as her shoulders slacked. Only for a moment, though. "After I get Volta back, I'll see about tackling everything else."

"I would expect nothing less," Karen beamed.

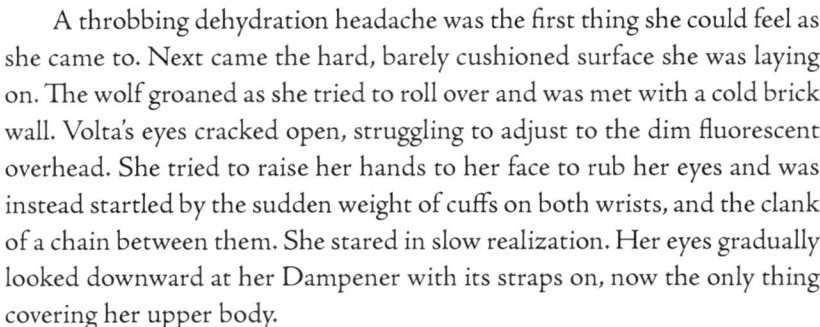

A throbbing dehydration headache was the first thing she could feel as she came to. Next came the hard, barely cushioned surface she was laying on. The wolf groaned as she tried to roll over and was met with a cold brick wall. Volta's eyes cracked open, struggling to adjust to the dim fluorescent overhead. She tried to raise her hands to her face to rub her eyes and was instead startled by the sudden weight of cuffs on both wrists, and the clank of a chain between them. She stared in slow realization. Her eyes gradually looked downward at her Dampener with its straps on, now the only thing covering her upper body.

So, it finally happened. Just like you knew it would.

Volta sat up slowly from the cot, eyes still adjusting as she took in her surroundings. The jail cell walls were all tan-painted brick, save for the hard concrete floor and the dark blue metal door. There were only two windows: a small one on the door, and an even smaller square near the top of the wall opposite that let in chilly, ozone-smelling air and the sound of falling rain.

They wouldn't even let you keep a shirt. That way they could keep an eye on the Dampener. It's not going to turn back off again, ever.

Volta stared up at the fluorescent, feeling chills travel up her sides. There was a tightness in her chest, even without considering the device strapped to it. She wanted to cry, to scream, to claw at the door, yet couldn't even find the energy to stand up.

Her ears perked at a loud click from the door. It swung open, and Volta's stomach pitted as her mother stepped through the threshold.

"*Austin. Henry. Travers,*" Mom growled, staring down at her as she stepped in. Volta's eyes went wide, but she kept quiet. She knew what was coming even before her mother stepped closer, grabbed her by the chin and forced her to look her in the eyes.

She raised her hand, and Volta shut her eyes. The open-handed slap stung at her cheek and jaw, and right when the sharp, tingling ache seemed to subside, her hand came down again. "You are a *disgrace* to this family. You ungrateful, selfish, humiliating, arrogant boy…" Another slap. More stinging. Over, and over, punctuating every word.

"*You. Will. Learn. Respect,*" she snapped, finally pausing as she shook out her hand. One whole side of Volta's face burned. She stared at the wall, eyes getting wet again. So much for not having the energy to cry...

"Your father and I thought you had learned to honor us and our wishes. We were wrong, *again!* Do you have *any* idea how humiliating it is, to be shouted at by our OWN SON, and then learn that he's gotten himself arrested... for assaulting a *teacher!*"

"All this is a damn mercy, boy..." There was Dad, approaching her from the door. "Three scheduled meals, and still a place to sleep. *Tch.* I thought Adam was supposed to understand *discipline.*"

"And after what you've done, *hah*. You are *lucky* we aren't at home, Austin." Mom gripped her face again, squeezing her fingers against the same sore, throbbing spot. "I have tried, again and *again*, to be a good mother. Do you have any idea how many nights I have prayed? Prayed for *you*, that you would finally see His light. I prayed that you would change, that you would see that you *had* to change, to fit in the Lord's plan — *our* plan! You've never even considered changing. You're still the selfish, horribly behaved little brat you have been for years, Austin, only *now* you're finally facing the consequences."

She finally let go, and Volta winced, bringing a shaky hand up to her face. Even lightly touching it stung, now. She finally met her mother's infuriated gaze, her whole body trembling. "I'm... I'm sorry m —"

"It is *far* too late for apologies," she spat. "I can't believe your apologies anymore. If you were sorry, you'd have stopped years ago. Do you even realize what you've done? You put Mister Olson in the hospital. The *hospital*, Austin. Now, how do we know that spying whore didn't *brainwash* you?"

"But, sh-she d —"

"Enough of your lying," she cut her off. "I'm not hearing another word of it. You don't even know how much you've hurt *us* in all this..." She took a deep breath, looking away as though overcome with emotion.

"Boy, there's no telling *what* that cat did to you." Dad stepped forward, glaring down his nose at her. "But you best *hope* that this... *tantrum* of yours was just your programming coming to the surface. There's only one way to know, now."

"Wait," Volta stammered, eyes going wide. He couldn't mean... "Wait, I don't need —"

"Be *quiet* when I am *speaking*, Austin," Dad growled, and Volta snapped her mouth shut, eyes locked on his glower. "That's just perfect proof. You're completely undisciplined now, you're just as wild as you were in that classroom. It's everything we were always afraid of; you're aggressive, you're disobedient, and now *violent...* all because of this girl. Consider yourself lucky, Austin. The TPA has their own procedure for this kind of brainwashing."

No, no no, no no no no no —

The wolf froze, staring in disbelief up at her father's scowl. Tears had already been welling in her eyes from Mom's hand; now, they started to fall.

"No, no, please — I —"

"Hellen and I already signed off on it." Dad spoke in a clear, measured tone, teeth gritted. "The TPA has some extremely effective deconditioning programs, and they're led by a personal friend. Her anti-Korps-Brainwashing techniques are unparalleled."

"D-Dad..." Volta held up her cuffed, shaking hands, drawing in a shaky breath. "I-I'm sorry, Dad, I kn-know I m-messed up... Y-you don't — you don't have to do this."

"Yes, we *do*," Mom sighed, wiping her hands together as if trying to clean them of some unpleasant substance. "They follow the same therapy techniques we've talked about in the past. They'll deprogram you, then recondition you as best they can. Adam *personally* assured me this would work."

No, no no, NO NO NO —

"M-Mom...!" Volta croaked. It was the same threat they had made six years ago...

Only now, they were following through on it.

"W-wait, Mom, *p-please just wait* — I don't need... I-I swear I'm not..."

"I want my son back, and the longer I look at you, I..." The older wolf's face twisted up. "I am not sure who I'm looking at, anymore. You've been *corrupted*, Austin. I'll pray that the therapy works as quickly as possible."

No, no, please, don't leave me...

Volta's heart was thudding in her ears. It was getting hard to get a deep enough breath in. Her chest tightened as she was wracked with a full-on sob. "Mom, no, no, I... I can't — you *c-can't*..." She reached for her, pleading. "I — I won't do anything, I won't — Mom, p-*please*... I promise,

I-I'll do whatever you say. I-I can p-prove I'm not — I'll do b-better, y-you don't have to l-leave, M-Momma! I c-can still…"

Hellen Travers backed away, not a trace of sadness or regret in her face. "I can't trust anything you say anymore, Austin. No one can. When you finally start to change, after the therapy, maybe you can finally stop disappointing us. You should be *happy*, Austin. They're going to help you."

They're going to break me. I'm going to die here…

"There's no point crying over it now, Austin, *if* those are even real tears anymore." James Travers shook his head in disappointment. "Be a man — *for once* — and accept it. You'll start first thing tomorrow morning. *We*, meanwhile, have to prepare a press statement explaining why our son attacked one of his teachers unprovoked…" He turned toward the door. "Come on, Hellen, we're wasting our time."

"D-don't leave…!" Volta whimpered, stumbling to her feet, trying to reach after them. "P-please, *Da* — Dad, Mom, please…"

Mom took another step back, quickly, eyes on Volta's hands. The revulsion and fear in her eyes were unmistakable.

Volta took another trembling step, but they were already hurrying out of the cell, the guard silently moving to keep her from following. The iron door slammed shut again and she fell against it. She began to beg, and then she began to *scream*, her claws scraping at the door.

"*Mom, Dad, I* — M-Mom, MOMMA, PLEASE, I'm s-sorry! Please come ba-ack-k, I-I'm SORRY! Please D-D — Daddy, d-don't go, p-ple-e-eaase… M-Momma, Dad-dy, I-I'm s-sorry… Ple-ease, p-please come b-back…"

Her wails reverberated around her, met only with silence, devolving into incoherence as she got more desperate. She scratched until her claws went blunt, pleaded until her throat went hoarse, and only then did she huddle up against the cold metal door. Sniveling, gasping and coughing uncontrollably, she clutched the sides of her throbbing head and wept.

Over time, a damp chill from the outside window slowly crept over her. She shook, unable to stop sobbing. Feebly, she crawled over to the cot and curled up on it.

She clutched at herself and tried to remember what it felt like to have Carmen hold her tight.

Chapter 10

Downpour

Just as the weather computers had forecasted, the rain clouds had thickened after sunset. Little flashes of lightning illuminated the clouds in the distance, but nowhere near the chopper passing through the thinner strati. The pilot — the same drone from Carmen's flight — employed some of the Korps's more involved aeronautics and a whole array of cameras, so actually *seeing* from the pilot's seat was altogether unnecessary.

The deep thrum of the stealth chopper's engine overhead would never reach the ground, the rhythmic chop of the propeller drowned in the rainfall and thunder. The pilot aimed the radar jammers downward as they approached the vicinity of the TPA's walled-off training facility. The rain clouds made it hard to see anything but gray, but Carmen still peered out the window on her side of the cabin, tapping one boot rhythmically against the floor.

"Nervous?" Karen asked, sitting opposite the cat, legs crossed.

The tabby nodded, tearing her eyes off the window. No point in trying to lie to the boss. "They're still following lockdown protocols; no one's left the facility save for a certain pair of VIPs, and there'll be active patrols throughout the campus. Wren tried to get into their intranet again, and apparently, they changed a *lot* of passwords, and plugged a lot of leaks —"

"*I'm working on a solution to that right now!*" Wren's voice came through her RCGs, and Karen sighed, shaking her head.

"Remember your strength and drive, Carmen. I wouldn't be letting you do this if I wasn't completely confident in your ability."

The cat shrugged a little. "I'm more worried about how Volta's going to handle it."

"If you're there by her side, no amount of armed guards is going to stop you two."

Carmen bowed her head in humble acknowledgement. "Before I track her down, though, I have a quick detour — maybe a couple."

Karen leaned forward, eyes alight with curiosity as if she somehow *hadn't* been listening in to her and Wren's planning at every stage. "*Do* tell."

"First, I look for the Dampener's schematics, make sure I can just pull the thing off," Carmen began, starting to count off her fingers on one hand. "Second, I figure out where Volta is. *Third*, ideally after I find her… we kick Tullis's ass, *hard*."

"Sounds like a plan to me!" Karen laughed. "Sorry for the interruption. Go ahead and start psyching yourself up, in case things get ugly."

"Karen, *please*…" Carmen straightened up, puffing her *considerable* chest out, nose held high. "I've been psyching myself up for this for most of a week. I'm ready as I'll ever be."

"And don't you forget it."

They began their descent. The stealth chopper's engines started to quiet until they were hovering over a rocky crop to the east side of campus. Not all of it was walled off, but clearly someone had decided a chain-link fence was just not *manly* enough.

"Time for the main event!" Carmen rose, the snug webbing of her harness, weighed down by an array of knives and one solitary sidearm, jostling against her figure as she crossed the cabin. "Wish me luck."

Karen slid open the door for her, and as Carmen stepped out, the dragon squeezed her shoulder. "Dressed like that, what's a girl like you need with luck?"

The tabby afforded her a strained grin, then hopped out onto the grass. The stealth chopper revved back up, lifting off and away as the tabby climbed the small hill between her and the east gate.

Carmen adjusted her footing in the dark grass and soil below her, creeping slowly back down the opposite side of the hill. The concrete walls flanking the eastern gate of the TPA facility stood tall before her. A well-lit security booth to the right of the gate served as the only checkpoint. As the gentle sprinkle of rain pattered down on her head and shoulders, she crouched low and approached the booth, eyes on the pair of security guards sitting inside, boredly watching TV.

Easy pickings.

The cat's eyes flashed a dark shade of purple. A deep violet haze filled the air around her as she leapt toward the booth. She was at the door in a second; she yanked it open, and the guards both jumped up from their chairs… or *started* to. They moved sluggishly, surprise plastered on their faces.

Carmen casually walked up to them, grabbed both heads, and *shoved*, smashing one against the top of the flatscreen itself and the other into the desk. The haze disappeared, and they crumpled to the floor; either made a sound.

Ruining a downed guard's weapons and equipment was still second nature to her. It was only a few moments before, satisfied, the tabby plucked a keycard from the front of the further guard's jacket and straightened up again. She slid it through the card reader on the wall of the booth and flicked her tail in satisfaction as a smaller door on the large metal gate swung open.

One guard shifted, letting out a pained moan as he started to come back around. Carmen produced a small hypodermic injector from one of the packs on her belt, pressed it to the stirring guard's neck, and watched him slump back into unconsciousness as she injected the other. She shut the booth door as she walked back out and slipped through the gate door as noiseless as she arrived.

Hang in there, Volts. I'm keeping my promise.

First things first: Dampener schematics. She hadn't been to Dr. Mason's lab before, but that's what the preplanning with her handler had been for, anyway.

"You're gonna like this," Wren chimed in, right on time. "Got a whole layout of the place pulled up. What I don't notice, ROSE will. We went over this before, but just to make sure: You want the wide building labeled 'Research,' to the right of where you are now. Red bricks, big windows."

There it was, just to her right. She kept low, boots sinking into the slightly muddy grass as she crept toward her target. All of the patrolling guards wore dark blue rain ponchos, and several still took refuge from the drizzling under the overhangs of each building, their flashlights either off or held askew. The only *real* concern was the number of them with automatic rifles hanging from their shoulders. *Way* too many to risk being seen from a distance.

Welcome to Texas! Here's your assault weapon.

She hurried along the outer wall, eyes aglow and fixed firmly on the prize. Hushed paw pads cut through greenery, skipping over the paved walkways and making use of the trees and bushes she had become *very* familiar with on her walks with Volta.

"Hardly even need my help," Wren muttered. "You probably know this place forwards and backwards."

"*I didn't go inside every building,*" Carmen replied wordlessly, her RCGs transmitting her thoughts, rather than her voice. "*So, tell me: Mason's lab. Floor and room number?*"

"Second floor, room 303."

"*See? Never hurts to have a spare bat on the line. Especially one as helpful and encouraging as you.*"

"*Aww,* now you're just buttering me up. Don't lose your focus!"

"*I am focusing,*" Carmen replied smugly, coming to a stop between the research building and what was — judging by the sign out front — the admin building. "*I'm here on the north-facing side. Any fire exits I can use?*"

"West side, opposite you. You'll have to jimmy a window lock… and the ladder's about twelve feet off the ground."

The tabby held herself flat to the wall, keeping her silhouette obscured as she circled around the building. There was the fire escape ladder, mounted to one window.

"*And here I thought this might be hard.*"

Carmen scanned the garden pathways for any more guards. Just one stood around fifty feet away, not looking in her direction, his face silhouetted by the soft glow of a cigarette. She took a few steps back, and with a running start, leapt at the wall, kicked off it, and snagged the bottom rung of the ladder with one hand, pulling herself the rest of the way up.

"Can't keep a cat from high places, huh?"

"*Don't sound so surprised! Grandma's cooking isn't **that** heavy.*"

"I didn't say anything~"

The old window latch didn't even need a key. *Pitiful.* She leaned against the sliding pane, delivered a sharp *smack* with her palm to the frame, and it popped open with little more than a rattle that the smoking guard *clearly* didn't hear.

Carmen clambered inside, stepping into the outer hallway, and took a moment to shake herself off. Thank fuck the outside of the suit was completely hydrophobic… but her head wasn't. As she squeezed at the wettest part of her hair, she took a moment to glance around the hallway, then paused.

"*The lights are all still on.*"

"Someone burning the candle, maybe?"

"*Maybe.*"

Claws bared, Carmen crept through the hallway, eyes scanning the room numbers over each door.

303 had a set of double doors, one of which was propped open. The sound of whirring computer fans came from within.

Carmen slowly poked her head around the corner to see a blonde fox tapping away at a computer on a cart, headphones around her ears. pop-country music blared from them at a volume the cat would have considered deafening.

"*Someone burning the candle, all right — I recognize this girl. This is the snippy bitch who works with Dr. Mason!*"

"Have you talked before?"

"*If you call getting a lot of disgusted looks from across the room 'talking,' sure. I overheard her calling Volta a crybaby soy boy once, during one of her tests.*"

"Mmn, don't like that. What's your plan, then?"

"*I think I'm going to scare the shit out of her.*"

"Oh, I like this plan."

Carmen slowly rose to her full height as she crept closer. She yanked the headphones off and threw them aside, an arm wrapping around the fox's neck. Tammy yelped, hands coming up to claw uselessly at Carmen as the larger feline yanked her out of her chair and up onto her feet. Restraining Volta had been a little difficult; this girl was *easy*.

"*Hello,* Tammy," Carmen purred into her ear as she extended her claws against the fox's neck. "Remember me?"

"Y-you're — *How* — !?"

"Scream for help and I put you in intensive care." Her claws dug into the fur of the fox's thin neck. "But really, go ahead and try. I'd *love* to have an excuse."

"O-oh god, oh my god," Tammy whimpered, trembling. "You're going to feel me up, aren't you?! I always knew you were — *ghk!*" Carmen cut her off with a tight clamp around the fox's throat. Tammy went completely still.

"Pipe down and listen, okay? I don't give a shit about *you*, I want *info*." The fox kept quiet this time, clearly too scared to dare say anything else. "Your boss designed the Dampener, right?"

Tammy nodded slowly. Apparently, this was not what she had been expecting.

"So, the schematics, all the design notes — you still have them, don't you?"

"Y-yes…?"

"You don't sound super sure…" Carmen cooed, dragging the sharp tips of her claws along the fox's jawline. "Why, Tammy; are you *nervous* about something~?"

"Wait, *wait!*" the fox stammered. "I know where they are, I swear!"

"Save me some time. Point them out to me, please."

The fox raised a shaking finger toward a shelf on the other side of Dr. Mason's desk.

"The big blue binder, on the third shelf…!" Tammy explained, wriggling uselessly in the cat's rigid grip. "Please, please don't hurt me. I'll do anything you want!"

Carmen purred. "Take a nap, then."

"Wha —"

In the blink of an eye, the tabby had her in a stranglehold. The fox kicked and gasped as Carmen not-so-gently squeezed her carotids, lowering her to the floor.

"Shhh, shh. Don't worry, Tammy, I'll leave everything *right* where I found it…"

A few more seconds of feeble struggling and the fox was out like a light; Carmen let her slump onto the floor. She produced the sleep hypo again, pressed the applicator to the fox's bare neck, and squeezed the trigger. Tammy didn't so much as flinch, and she probably wouldn't be doing much of anything for the next couple of hours.

"*Can't be too careful; don't want her sounding the alarm.*"

"At least, not 'til you get Volta out of her cage. Because you're *probably* gonna have to go loud at that point."

"Believe me, I'm looking forward to it."

She made no effort to not kick the fox as she stepped over her and towards the bookshelf she had pointed out. There was the slender three-ring binder, blue, with the label on the side reading: *SUPERPOWER SUPPRESSION DEVICE 10-B.*

She slipped the binder out and opened it on Mason's desk.

FOR RELEASE ONLY TO TPA COMMAND BRANCH AND R&D DIVISIONS:

10-B.XS.09 - SGEFA: Experimental suppressor, Superconductive Generalized Electrodynamic Field Attenuator, or "Dampener."

The tabby turned to the table of contents, running a finger down the list. Thankfully, *"anti-removal countermeasures"* was its own section, further into the document.

She flipped through the pages, glancing at the various diagrams and descriptions as she went. Multiple hard-coded failsafe switches (to be given to security staff) would turn the Dampener on full-blast with the click of a button. The details of the precise inner workings went from easily parsed to soaring over her head very quickly, especially when it came to the part that actually dispersed charge back into the open air and *kept* it out, but she didn't need to know that much anyway.

"Seems like this old goat had a lot of ideas for modifications or upgrades... and going large-scale with the technology."

"You think they might have done that already?"

"Probably not. This thing was built for Volta in the first place, on her parents' dime, only a year ago. Seems like, if anything, what Volta had strapped to her was still a prototype."

"The thing they forced Volta to wear 24/7 wasn't even *finished?* I guess I shouldn't be surprised, but..."

"Okay, here's the important part: I was right about the GPS tracking, and all there is to keep Volta from taking it off is a silent alarm system. It sends out a signal to Teepa security staff if the Dampener gets removed, and that's it."

"Oooh, okay, so, not a problem for us." Wren laughed with relief. "…Out of curiosity, what was *going* to be in it?"

Carmen's expression hardened, her whole body going cold as she read through the rest of the section. "There's plans for a shaped charge embedded in a later version, to detonate on a remote trigger."

"…Are you serious?"

Carmen spoke under her breath, one hand clenching at the side of the binder. "They wanted to *kill* Volta if they couldn't control her. Her parents signed off on everything in here. They… *had* to know about this. There's no way they didn't."

Wren took a slow, deep breath. "…Okay, okay. Her parents being… *shit* was nothing we didn't already know, Carmen. You need to focus."

"I know, I know, but…" Carmen stared at the diagram of the charge. The disarmingly straightforward illustration showed how it was intended to punch straight through its wearer's chest. She let out an infuriated hiss and slammed the binder shut. She paced around in front of the desk, having to work to *not* growl with every word. "The Dampener uses the campus-wide network for precise positioning information. We're in the network again, right?"

"Yeah," Wren replied quickly. "We were in the minute you walked inside."

"The locator's access code is ATSD0311." Carmen made for the door, striding to the same window she'd entered through. "Find her, *now*."

"Working on it…"

When she returned to the courtyard, lurking in the shadow of the lab building, she found that the one guard had finished his smoke break and was wandering around again. The tabby's eyes trailed him, baring her teeth in the dark. One hand stayed clamped around the knife holstered on her shoulder, her whole body tense as she watched him approach the building. Her mind was still stuck on the shaped charge, and Mason's signature approving it for future implementation. Her jaw tightened with rapidly boiling rage.

*You helped design that thing, old man. You had the plans printed and signed them. Mom and Dad Travers are probably overjoyed at having a new way to have final say on her life, but **you** gave them that. You're no better than Tullis, or her parents. Greedy, petty, cowardly **dreck**, all of you. You'll just destroy whatever you can't use, tear down anyone who doesn't fit your mold. None of you see the beauty in her that I can. You can't see her potential, the way she could **shine** if she had the chance. All you see is another tool...*

[Carmen, do you want help? You need to keep your focus right now.]

...Yes, ROSE, make this easier.

She inhaled, exhaled, felt the building tension freeze, and then slowly... Release.

She sat there, hidden in the fire escape as the world around her melted away. Her muscles unclenched, her breathing evened out, her heart rate slowed back down. That evenness would remain, as even as she needed to be, and she could save the anger for later.

Inhale, exhale. The rest of the world —

— Faded back in. She kept her eyes trained on the guard as he walked nearer, glancing to his left and right... but not above him. She grinned as she watched him turn around again, oblivious.

Thanks, ROSE.

[Of course.]

The tabby straightened up again, hopped over the same handrail she'd climbed up, and landed in the shadows she'd approached in.

Wren spoke up again. "Carmen, you're not gonna like this."

She closed her eyes again, steadying herself. *"Just tell me where she is, Wren."*

"She's... been in the security building for the past several hours."

Inhale, exhale. *"So, she's being held there."*

"The schematics show they have secured holding cells in there. ...Do you think they figured her out?"

"Maybe I should have asked Tammy before I choked her out." Carmen wore a rueful smile. *"Doesn't matter — she's in the security building, that's where I'm going."*

The rain fell harder, now. The soil wasn't mud yet, but Carmen took extra care to bring her feet down quietly as she crept between paved walkways, on gravel in between trees, as she made her way across the campus once again.

"*Floor, Wren?*"

"Ground, the holding area in the back of the building, two big hallways… No idea which one she'd be in. Ironically, precision locating isn't *that* precise."

"*I can work with that.*"

The tabby came up to a large oak, pressing herself up against the bark and carefully peeking out, surveying the entrance to the security building. It was practically a police station from northern Austin City: all angles, but way fewer windows, a *much* higher fire escape, and, of course, several cameras covering the front door. Carmen almost snorted. Well, it was a good try.

"*Anything else I should know?*"

"They've got a security checkpoint right after the front door, so, unless you want to go in guns blazing…"

"*Fire escape again, right.*"

She stepped back, ears perked, as a pair of guards approached the entrance, each from opposite directions.

"Hey Gary. Still nothing. How long's the chief gonna make us wander around at night like this?"

"Lockdown's only for a week, Mike. And knowing the chief, he's probably gonna make us go for a few extra days, just in case they try anything. Might as well keep our eyes peeled, right?"

"Oh yeah, when I actually get to see a lady with a rack like the ones that spy had, I'll make *sure* I'm lookin' hard enough."

"Pretty sure that's how they hypnotize folks," Gary laughed. "Don't look too hard, you might fall in!"

"Okay, okay, let's get outta this damn rain already."

The guard turned at the door, waving to the camera and stepping inside.

Two more potential problems in the building already — no sense waiting around for more. Carmen wasted no time in ducking away from the front door camera's cone of vision, creeping through a patch of low light and making her way to the far side of the security building.

Another leap, another kick, and she was climbing over the handrail and eyeing the lock on the window. This one looked brand new and needed a key. Carmen sighed and pulled her set of lockpicks out.

"Bet you wish you had me there now," Wren snarked.

Carmen huffed as she slid a pick in, and the lever next to it. "*I can do this just fine, thank you! I don't need the cheat code.*"

Click.

"Oooh, am I the 'cheat code' now? Wonder if any of the other handlers still get this kinda guff from *their* partners."

"*They've probably heard worse. …Is this really the best time to bring them up?*"

"We're in the middle of a one-night revival of your last line of work and you don't want to bring up old work friends? I can picture exactly what Gabi or Wight would say if you took too long to get through a lock this tiny."

"*Shush, you know better than anyone that I'm* **quite** *good at making big things fit in tight places, don't spoil my focus now.*"

"Right, sorry."

Click!

She turned her lever and the lock along with it. The window popped open a little, and she pulled it up the rest of the way.

"*See? Easy as pie.*"

"That's what she s —"

"*Focus!*"

Climbing through (and out of the rain again), Carmen took stock. The building was well-lit on the inside; the tile floor and plastered-over walls were already good at muffling her footsteps. Holding was on the first floor — the stairs had a sign pointing to them down the hall. She wiped her slightly muddied boots on the office carpeting as she walked, gently, and kept an ear out. Voices were coming from down the stairs; apparently, the pair she'd watched enter were still talking.

"I dunno, man, that girl was *really* big…" Gary sounded concerned.

"Right?" The one called Mike replied, as if in awe. "Like the *size* of those —"

"No, I mean she was taller than *me* and I'm six foot. Did you see her *fight*, Tullis? She tackled him to the ground! She's not normal — none of *us* could do that."

"Yeah, but her *tits*, Gary, they were like… almost at eye level."

Gary laughed. "You're gonna get yourself killed chasing after girls like that."

"And die a happy man," Mike sighed.

Carmen smiled bitterly to herself as she crept down the stairs, one by one. On any other day she'd be smug, knowing she left an impression. *Any other day…*

Gary wasn't laughing anymore. "*Terrorist* girls, in case you forgot. You don't wanna talk about this in front of Tullis, he'd go apeshit."

"Man, he'd go apeshit anyway. He's been on edge ever since she got away."

"Left a hole in the wall upstairs too. He *really* wanted to lay her out."

Carmen reached the bottom of the stairs. The doorway was wide open. She inched her head out around the corner. Inside were the two guards, a ferret and a pronghorn, having hung up their rain ponchos and now continuing their conversation as they leaned against a pair of desks.

A heavy security door on the far end of the room opened, and out came a badger. He waved to the other two.

"Hey, Bill. Chief still got you on jail duty?" the pronghorn asked.

"Just changed shifts with Noah," the badger sighed, stretching his back out. "I've been sitting in that damn chair for hours, god damn."

"How's the kid? He wake up yet?"

Carmen froze, ears perked and eyes wide. They had to mean Volta.

The badger groaned. "God, that kid. I let his parents in earlier today, actually. Lotta yelling, especially from Mrs. Travers. He started *crying*."

"Jesus, really?" asked the ferret, amused.

"Yeah. Bawled like a baby for like an *hour* after they left. He scratched at the door, too — fuckin' annoying as hell to listen to."

Carmen's stomach tightened and her hand twitched, claws extending.

"Just got told he's grounded for the first time, I guess." The pronghorn shook his head.

"Sounded more serious than that," the badger laughed. "Gotta say though, I'm surprised they didn't pull some strings to get him out."

"Maybe they're sick of him," mused the ferret, straightening up and wandering over to the coffee machine — right against the wall Carmen was peeking around. She ducked back, ears pricked. "Kid like that puts his own teacher in the hospital? More trouble than he's worth, at that point."

"Good thing they paid for that thing on his chest — he almost killed Olson." Bill sighed.

"That bony little shit, killing Olson?" the pronghorn asked. "Did he start crying too hard or something?"

They all laughed as Carmen took a measured, icy breath.

"Doesn't matter now." She could easily imagine the badger's shrug. "They're gonna probe him for Korps programming in the morning. The full procedure too — make sure there's nothing buried in there."

Oh no.

"Oh damn, they're serious." The ferret was much closer now, clicking on a coffee maker and pulling a sugar packet out from a shelf. "Maybe they'll get him to shut up again, too."

Seething, jaw set, Carmen stood up straight and rounded the stairwell corner.

The ferret's back was turned as he laughed along with the other two with a coffeepot in one hand. The pronghorn noticed her first, then the badger, but it was too late; Carmen's eyes flashed again, and the ferret was immersed in purple haze. She yanked him back and he gave a strangled yelp as the other two guards only now pulled their handguns. "FUCK —" one yelled, as Carmen yanked his chin upward and pressed her sidearm to his throat.

The haze faded, everything else sped up as the pronghorn and badger finally raised their weapons.

"W-wait!" the ferret yelped, flailing his arms in a panic. "*Wait,* fuck, oh fuck don't shoot!"

"Hey Mike — you still want to die happy?" Carmen hissed. "How about dying happy *right now?*"

The other two were already moving closer. The pronghorn spoke up first. "Let him go!"

The ferret writhed in Carmen's grip and let out a strangled yell when she held him all the tighter. "Oh god, please — stay back, she's *gonna c-crush my neck!*"

They stopped, pistols still trained on the tabby's head. Carmen smirked. "Guns on the floor."

The pronghorn lowered his, but the badger hesitated. "How do we know you won't just kill him anyway?"

"If you like, I can kill him right now." Carmen bared her teeth, eyes wide and pupils thin behind her RCGs. "I don't mind a few dead rent-a-cops. Guns. Floor. *Now*."

"Fuck this, man," the pronghorn said, placing it on the floor and kicking it towards Carmen's feet. "Do what she says, Bill."

"You serious?" The badger raised an eyebrow, not taking his eyes off of Carmen as he stepped closer, closer... "Not buying it, you'd have shot him already." He took another step. *Close enough.* "You might have gotten away from the chief, but you can't —"

The world turned dark and murky again. Carmen's eyes shone purple, and the rest of the badger's sentence slowed to an incomprehensible drawl. She *lifted* the ferret up, shoving him forward and barreling into the badger. She released the ferret's neck and wrenched the badger's sidearm out of his fingers, momentarily delighting in the slowed down *crack* of several of them dislocating.

She dispersed the haze once more; the badger yelled in pain as the ferret fell onto him, and the two of them wound up on the floor in a heap. Carmen whirled around, her whole body pivoting as she kicked the startled pronghorn in the stomach. He fell back, crumpling to the floor and gasping for air.

The hypo came out again. First the still-yelling badger, for peace and quiet. Then the panicked, pleading ferret, and finally she caught the pronghorn as he started to rise.

"Fuck's sake, what's Tullis paying these guys for?"

"Definitely not their trigger fingers," Wren snarked. "Anyway, the holding area's —"

"Same door Bill came from, I know. Have you been able to find which one Volta's in?"

"Campus police are on a different network, gimme a minute."

She gave a soundless hum of acknowledgement, grabbed another set of keys from the unconscious badger, and unlocked the door on the far side of the room.

The holding area had higher ceilings and the constant hum of air conditioning. Both walls were lined with dark blue metal doors, each with meager windows, and several with their doors wide open. Five of them were locked shut. On the far wall stood a desk, another guard seated next to it. He very clearly had just settled down, his phone out and a cup of coffee beside him, right at the start of his shift.

The Labrador looked up when the entrance door clacked shut, and his eyes went wide when they fell upon Carmen. She broke into a dead sprint, summoning up her power once again. He barely had time to react *before* she immersed him in a blur of violet, and he hadn't even gotten out of his chair before she was on him.

You're in my way.

Chapter 11

Overcharge

Volta had just managed to drift off, exhausted from having wept for so long. The sudden sound of a dull *clack* from outside jolted her awake. She rubbed at her eyes, sniffling as she looked toward the door, and then jumped at the sound of hurried footsteps, and then a man yelling until, with another hard *thump*, he suddenly wasn't, and she heard the unmistakable noise of a body falling to the floor.

The wolf didn't move, eyes wide as she stared at the door. Someone was clearly outside and coming closer. She huddled up on her cell cot, pulling her knees up and trying to make herself seem small.

Maybe Tullis wants payback for me hitting his friend. Maybe they're just messing with me…

All the speculation evaporated from her mind when the door swung open. A familiar pair of long, feline legs strode inside, decked in matte black from head to toe. Volta's mouth dropped open.

Carmen!

"Hey there, stranger!" Carmen laughed breathlessly, something like a smile stuck to her face. "Sorry, I'm terrible at remembering to knock."

Volta stared at her, eyes wide as dinner plates. She didn't know what to say as she looked the cat over. Her outfit was *unmistakably* villainous now. All that dark, synthetic weave, all those points of body armor, the knives, the *gun*… and her bare claws, one of which she was shaking as though she'd recently knocked someone off their feet. Her curvy, *powerful* figure was on full display in that outfit, shaped almost like the helix stretching over the suit's front. The cat looked perfect, *fearsome*, even more so than usual.

Meanwhile here *she* was, curled up on a bed, shirtless, fur and hair unkempt and her face stained with tears, nose streaked with snot.

Volta managed to speak up, her voice little more than a wet croak. "You... you came back..."

"I promised you I would, Volts." The cat's grin faltered as she continued to take in the wolf. "You... didn't think I was coming back, did you?"

"I —"

Volta looked down, a confused mix of guilt and worry washing over her. She swallowed some of the worry down and admitted the truth.

"I didn't know what to think."

"I can't blame you," Carmen said as she took a cautious step forward. "It looks like they... for fuck's sake..." She frowned, then *scowled* at the wolf's chest, still bare save for the Dampener. Volta woke to the fact that this was the first time she'd shown this much skin since Carmen's impromptu checkup, and impulsively tried to cover her chest.

The cat's face fell, eyes shining. "What did they *do* to you?"

"...I don't know how to answer that," Volta murmured.

"I overheard some of what the guards said..." Another slow step forward. The cat bent down to look at the wolf more carefully. "They were going to try to 'deprogram you,' and... and your parents yelled at you. Again. A lot."

Volta averted her eyes and nodded. The lump of emotion in her throat was back, full force. *Fuck, I thought I was out of tears already...*

Carmen's face screwed up with pained sympathy. "Dammit, if they had done anything more to you, Volta, I..." She bent down, reaching for her. Were those perfect, strong hands trembling, or was Volta imagining things now? "I'm so, *so* sorry. I thought if I left you, you could avoid getting hurt. *Hah* — at least, that's what I told myself..." The cat gestured at the wolf sitting on her tiny bed frame. "Now you're in here, anyway... I promise, I'm not leaving you again."

"Y-you'd be the first one not to," Volta sniffled, still not meeting Carmen's gaze. Her throat ached; she felt sick. She wanted to jump up and hug Carmen, to sob into her shoulder, but her legs wouldn't work. She just stayed there, not moving, unable to meet the cat's gaze. "You must — you must th-think I'm pathetic, seeing me like this."

Carmen stared at her, hesitating again. "I never did before, and I still don't. Volta, I came back *for you*. I'm getting you out of here."

Volta started to uncurl herself a little, then stopped. She *still* couldn't get up. Unbidden, her eyes flitted to the door, dread welling up in her again. "I — I don't think I can. I shouldn't."

Carmen's face hardened. "Is this because of how it went last time? I can promise that's not going to happen again. I'm not going anywhere unless *you* come with me." She reached into one of the packs on her belt and pulled out the same RCGs from before. Angular, with a broad bridge to fit a lupine snout. Volta stared at the glasses in Carmen's hand. Her ears began to ring again.

I can't do this.

"I-I… Carmen, I don't —"

Breathing was getting hard; her chest was getting tight. Panic and emotion made her tremble. "I don't know what to do… Mom, she… Mom and Dad, th-they said I was a disgrace, they said I h-had to be fixed, it's a-all my fault…!"

This time, Carmen didn't say anything. She pushed her own RCGs up onto her forehead and lowered herself down to Volta's level. With the tabby looking at her in that same concerned, gentle, patient way, she couldn't stop herself. The tears flowed just as easily.

"M-Momma looked at me like — like I w-wasn't her s-son anymore…" Volta blubbered. "Sh-she looked at me and didn't… didn't even s-*see me!* She just…"

The tabby gently laid a hand on Volta's quaking shoulder. "She looked at you like you were disgusting. Like… you weren't worth the trouble anymore, right?"

Volta nodded, taking several breaths before she tried talking again. "She… s-said they would fix me…"

"You know that's not how this works, Volta. Do you really want them controlling you, even now?" Carmen asked quietly. "Your parents left you here."

"B-but if I —" Desperation grew inside her, shoulders heaving with every shuddering gasp. "I-if I stay, maybe… maybe they'll come back. M-maybe Momma will… Maybe she'll forgive me, if I just go along with it…"

Be a man, for once.

She snuffled and looked back up to finally meet Carmen's gaze. Those beautiful amber eyes were fraught with concern — and a deep, knowing pain.

"Sh-she'll come back, right? She — She *has* to…!"

"Volta…" Carmen sighed, setting the RCGs down on the floor and putting a hand on both her shoulders. "Volta, you *have* to understand… They will only come back if they think you're under their control again. You would be trapped. Whatever the 'de-programming' involves… I think you know already that it'll only hurt you."

"But I — My m-mom —"

No amount of blinking was getting rid of the tears. She raised her cuffed hands pleadingly, chains jingling as she whimpered. Carmen looked down at them, at her claws, blunted from the scratching at the door. Her honeyed eyes lit up with rage.

"…Volta," she said firmly. "Volta, *please* listen to me. You are *so much more* than what your parents want from you. You don't have to rely on them, you'll *never* have to try and appease them, ever again, if you get out of here with me."

The red wolf sniffled and hiccupped, wiping at her nose with an arm. "But… But I want to — I just want them to love me, to be — to be p-proud of me… I'm *supposed* to…"

Carmen ever so gently reached up and held Volta's face in her hands. Staring deep into her eyes, Volta didn't dare look away. She stared into those fiery amber pools as the cat came so close their noses almost touched. "You are *not* your parents' property, Volta. You are *your own person*. You deserve to be happy, no matter what your parents think. Please… *please* at least consider the idea that you *could* be happy, far away from them and living your own life."

Volta stared, entranced by the determination in her eyes. "I… don't know if I *can* be… I d-don't know what living my own life *means*."

"So, *think* about the possibility that you could, someplace else. Think about a place where you could be the real *you*, and find out who that girl is. That is what the Korps *is*. I said before that the Korps is made for girls like you, and I meant it. I *love* you, Volta, and I *know* you're meant for so much more than this place." The wolf's whole body stiffened at those words. A heat welled up from her stomach and chest, that same tingling she'd felt the first time Carmen had said it.

Volta took as deep a breath as she could manage, struggling to steady herself. "I want… I want to be happy. But I don't… know *how*."

Carmen gave a reassuring smile. "Let me suggest a first step." She let go of Volta's face and bent low. The wolf's eyes widened as the cat took hold of the cuffs and not-so-gently *yanked* them open, sliding them off the wolf's hands.

"Arms out, please," Carmen instructed. Volta obediently held her arms out of the way. Her heart skipped a beat as she watched the cat take one of the Dampener's straps in her grasp.

There was a tug, and then a *snap*, as Carmen sliced straight through one strap of the Dampener harness, then another, and another…

The Dampener fell to the concrete floor with a metal clatter, and Volta hurriedly tried to cover her now completely bare chest with her arms. There was a matting of shorter, mangy fur in a circle pattern, right where the Dampener had nested against her chest. The fur under the straps followed suit. An itch crawled up Volta's spine; only now, with the thing off of her, did she realize how *sore* she was, in all the places where the harness squeezed the most. Carmen's eyes flickered with a barely contained fury once more.

"This fucking thing was hurting you for months — *months* — and they never once let you take it off… *Tch*."

She raised one boot over the Dampener, and in one hard stomp, crushed it. Immediately, warmth and sensation flowed through the wolf from her chest out. She gasped, eyes wide as everything brightened… and charge began to build in her center.

Carmen grinned at the change in Volta's expression. "How's that? Good?"

"G-good, really good…" Volta looked back down at the Dampener, its outer layer bent by the shape of Carmen's boot, wiring and circuitry jutting out from the split-open sides. She hadn't had it off in months, almost a *year*. It felt as though she had forgotten how to breathe, and now her chest heaved as she began to reacclimate. She set her feet down on the chilly floor, ears flicking at the sound of the rain and distant thunder outside. A new worry began to sink in.

"W-without the Dampener, though I… I won't…" Volta stammered. "…what if I hurt you? What if I can't —"

"So, step two…" Carmen bent down and grabbed the angular goggles off the floor. She held it out to Volta. "Let these help."

The wolf stared at the RCGs again. Carmen was half-right, when she'd brought up last time. This time, of course, it wouldn't matter if they got caught — they were already breaking *out* — but…

Carmen could see her hesitation and doubt. "Volta, I wouldn't insist on these if I didn't know they would help, and they *do*."

"I-I was… I was always told they took away my free will, though… That I wouldn't be *me* anymore…"

Carmen sighed. "Volta, have you *ever* felt *free*, at all? Is this what being free looks like?" She gestured to the cell. "How could this thing in my hand be anywhere near as bad as what the Teepa, not to mention what your *PARENTS*, did to you for years? Look at what they're doing to you now — is this *freedom?*"

The wolf looked at the cell door, then back to Carmen. Tentatively, she shook her head.

The tabby held the RCGs up and tapped at her own pair on her face. "These aren't like the Dampener. These aren't like your parents — they're not going to yell at you, or make you feel worthless. They don't hit you, or starve you, or do *anything* to you that you don't want them to. What they *will* do is give you freedom; freedom to be the real *you*, Volta. All it takes is putting them on, and giving up your fear."

Her hands trembled; her whole body felt hot with anticipation. She reached for the RCGs slowly, taking hold of them by the sides. Cautiously, she slid them on, and pushed the earpieces into her ears, finding them a *very* comfortable fit.

Carmen watched her intently through pink-tinted vision. The winged helix appeared in the center of her field of view, rotating as a welcoming chime played. Words streamed across the lenses as the helix faded into the background.

> …
>
> …
>
> …
>
> Starting ROSE v4.206.9

> Hardware test … OK
Enabling DNI on local device … Done
INIT::RCG User Environment v12.5.31
…Done
NEW USER DETECTED, initiating first time setup.
WLAN carrier acquired
Requesting uplink to RCG Network…
Secure Connection Established
Synchronizing system clock…
2019-MAY-03 21:25:17.381
Establishing New User Profile
Assigning UUID
Populating records
Analyzing user biometrics
…Done

[Hello, Volta. I'm so glad to meet you.]

The soft, feminine voice made Volta go still, glancing around at the display as the pink hue began to fade… until her vision was completely clear, save for the magenta text that accompanied the woman's voice.

[*Don't be alarmed. You can call me ROSE; I'm here to help. No need to talk, either! Just think what you want to say, and I will understand.*]

…*Okay? Does this work?*

[*Yes, perfect! As I said, I'm here to help. I can tell right away that you're under stress, you're anxious, afraid, and very… very hurt. This is a lot to handle on your own. Please, Volta, may I help?*]

…

[*I promise, I will not do anything unless you give me explicit permission. I am only offering you the chance to think and feel without any of your pain and fears getting in the way.*]

…*Yes. Please. Help me.*

[*Of course.*]

The colors of the cell, and then the cat before her, washed away.

The cell around them evaporated. Then the bed, then Carmen, even the sensation of *sitting* all disappeared. She hadn't closed her eyes; they had been shut off completely. The ringing in her ears was gone in an instant. All she could hear was her own heartbeat slowing down.

She couldn't see, or… didn't *have* to see. She just had to think.

And thinking was… *so much* easier like this; nothing to distract her. She was still aware of her feelings, but they were… detached, somehow. Her fear, anxiety, guilt, shame… all of it like an anchor. The pressure of it all was… not gone, but reduced, significantly. She could tell it was there, just barely, appearing to her like a weight tied to her neck, holding her in the center of a pool. She was neck-deep, pressed in on every side…

And with every breath she took, the pressure lessened.

This doesn't need to weigh me down. I… I don't have to be stuck.

She had been trapped in the pool, right up until she actually had the time, the *breathing space* to consider it.

She took a step. It was heavy, slow, like pulling her weight through hardening cement, but every trudging step became less than the last. The wolf reached the edge of the water, grasping for the rim.

*I want it to stop. I'm done. I'm **done** being trapped.*

The weight at the bottom of the pool finally started to resist, trying to pull her back as she was struggling to pull herself out. But ROSE was there, unseen but *felt*, holding the water back, pushing her along, giving her only the amount of air she needed to do the rest of the job herself.

I can finally be myself. I can be happy, I can be with Carmen, as long as…

She pushed herself up onto dry ground, and filled her lungs with fresh, clear air.

As long as I can breathe, I can get out of here.

She stayed there, content to breathe, as ROSE kept the pressure out. The tension on the rope relaxed. Finally, *finally*, she could think, and it was easy. No doubt, no second-guessing; she could confront her fears, and she was *eager* for the chance.

*I can do this. I have everything I need. I can be **me**.*

The world returned in a rush of color, shape, sound, smell and heat. She was back in the cell. Volta could hardly breathe, and when she managed to, it came in a trembling gasp. The light, the noise, the stark color was clearer, easier, *far* more detailed. The Dampener had been off for several minutes, but *this* was so much more. Every feeling had been muted, constantly smothered by the Dampener and everything she'd had pressing down on her. Now, the pressure was gone.

She felt, for the first time in a long time, wide awake. *Alive.* The cold, numbing weight of fear and pain she had felt inside her was receding, replaced by a stirring sensation in her chest that spread out to her whole body. She tried to speak.

"C-Carmen, I —"

Volta's words came out in a whimper, but her own voice being so easy to *hear* startled her. The dull ringing in her ears had gone. She now heard nothing but the sound of Carmen's measured breaths and her own shakier ones. She stumbled to her feet, amazed, *confounded* by the calm in her own head. Carmen watched her, apprehensive. Worried, excited, anxious. Volta could still feel that worry herself, but it wasn't slowing her anymore. *Nothing* slowed her.

The adrenaline started to hit her now, as if she were on *fire.* Life itself had rushed into her. Her heart was pounding again, but it was okay. She was more than okay. She had never felt more alive, more real, more *herself.* Volta tried to speak again, but all that came out was a tiny, overwhelmed sob. She reached out with both arms, grasping at the air, and found Carmen's hands grabbing onto her and pulling her into a tight embrace. A gasp left the wolf's mouth, warm and lively.

"You can feel it, can't you?" Carmen whispered in her ear, tears of joy streaking down her face and dampening both their fur. "You're going to be okay, Volta. You're finally going to *live.* You're going to be happy."

"*Th-thank you…*" the wolf gasped, blinking away the tears. "*I love you, Carmen, I love you…*"

The words came so easily — she could finally say what she *felt*, with no hesitation. The cat squeezed her tighter, her laugh like a gentle wind chime to the wolf's ears. Volta smiled; she giggled, *actually* giggled, sniffling to clear her nose. They finally pulled away, Carmen beaming at her. "I… I feel *good.* I feel like I just woke up."

"You too, huh?" the cat laughed. "Buckle up, Volts — it's all uphill from here."

"That's… fine. That's *great*, because I…" She raised her hands, turning them over to examine her palms and knuckles. "I can't *wait* to actually *do* something with this." She still knew there was so much that could go wrong, but it wasn't an overwhelming fear anymore. ROSE hadn't simply suppressed it — instead, she had given her enough reasons to keep her fears in check. She could feel ROSE now, working in the background, taking every good feeling and pressing it further, strengthening it.

I'm not trapped anymore. I don't have to suffer here, ever again. I'm free. I'm free…

I'm free I'm free I'm free I'm free I'm free —

The words repeated over and over, faster and faster. They permeated every other thought, saturating the rest of her, *fueling* her exhilaration. She was happy. She was excited. She was *mad,* and yet she wanted to laugh. The fact that she was still topless vanished from her mind. She held up a trembling hand, willing her charge up to it.

Warmth flowed through her arm, but the lightning that began sparking across her palm and fingers was not the blue she had been expecting.

"Holy *shit,*" Carmen remarked, as bright magenta arcs danced over the wolf's hand. "That's new. Did… the RCGs do that?"

"Maybe…" Volta muttered, transfixed by the crackling energy. Gently, she raised her other hand, watching it travel up both arms at once, the crackling reverberating in the cell room.

"…Or… maybe I just needed the breathing room to change it."

Her influence spread further out. She looked up and saw, with a gasp, a bright glow like she had never seen before, through the ceiling — the power line to the fluorescents overhead. She raised her hand up, and her power reached the rest of the way, effortless. The bulbs turned that same shade of bright pink behind the pane, and another bright arc grew out of it, linking with her hand. Lights throughout the hall went dead, and with achy passing second, the overwhelming sensation of **power** grew yet stronger.

She lowered her hand, grinning and breathing deep. Every breath she took felt *better* than the last. The world was finally bright and clear, and she could feel and smell and *see* everything, now. She turned to Carmen again, panting, smiling, practically baring her teeth in excitement.

"I'm ready."

Carmen, still looking amazed, managed a grin in return. "Then let's get the fuck out of here already."

She led her out of the cell and into the hallway. The guard was unconscious, slumped against the far wall with a chair broken to either side of him. As they walked, Carmen spoke to her in hushed tones.

"No one's raised the alarm yet, but breaking the Dampener is going to alert *someone*, and they're going to investigate. That's not even counting the cameras."

Volta furrowed her brows. "Shouldn't there be one in… here?"

"Sure is! But Wren's got all that taken care of — right, Wren?" Carmen reassured her, glancing up at the ceiling. There, sure enough: two shiny black dome cameras, embedded in the ceiling.

"No need to worry!" A completely new and *very* androgynous voice came through Volta's earpieces — or was it going straight to her head again? *"I took care of those a few minutes before you walked in. Not gonna help the checkpoint with a guard at the front door, though."*

Carmen grinned at Volta proudly. "See? Taken care of."

The wolf cocked her head, confused. "Wait, who was — ?"

"Ah, say hi to Wren. They're running the tech side of things."

"Hi, Volta! I've heard a lot about you!" Wren chimed in once more. *"Don't mind me, just focus on getting out of there right now."*

"Oh, uh… nice to meet you…?" Volta replied, hurrying to keep up with the tabby.

"So, the rest of the plan…"

Carmen paused to open the door at the end of the hall, peering outside. "…Get out of this building, make our way to the east entrance gate, and get to the rendezvous point where the chopper's waiting for us. All of that, and they're *going* to know something's wrong with the Dampener. The alarms could start up any second."

"So… what happens when they do?" Volta asked.

"We go loud," Carmen glanced back, locking eyes with her for a moment, "and you show these assholes what you can *really* do."

Something below the surface, long-suppressed from her thoughts, rumbled at that. The notion of actually *facing* security guards and fighting them… did not dampen her excitement in the slightest, though the worry was still there.

To be fair, I've already done it once before when they were firing practice ammo at me.

…But these will be REAL bullets, this time. They'll be trying to stop me… What will happen when I'm actually facing them down?

Volta's muscles tensed in apprehension. She could tell ROSE was keeping an eye on her, but it wasn't enough to throw her off. The longer she thought about it, actually, the more the idea appealed. What *could* she do, now, with all the charge in the world… and none of the pain or self-doubt to hold her back?

They entered the main room of the station, Volta following Carmen's lead in staying low to the ground, moving slowly. ROSE was still working behind the curtain, helping her keep her footsteps much quieter than usual as she followed behind the tabby. No one seemed to be around — save for several more unconscious bodies strewn about between desks and the coffee maker near one wall. The tabby had been *busy*, Volta realized.

Carmen pointed at a set of stairs. "Up here, then we can get back out the same window I opened and jump down."

"Isn't that really high up?"

"I'll catch you, don't worry," Carmen winked. "Now c'mon, no telling how much time we have before someone —"

She cut herself off, smile vanishing as she pushed herself past the wolf. Another security guard had just run down the staircase and was gawking at the two of them, standing between three of his unconscious coworkers.

He shouted over his shoulder, one hand already on his holster as the other grabbed his radio. *"Daryl, call the chief!"*

Carmen's eyes flared with violet energy as she bound toward him, leaving Volta standing there as she delivered a flying kick into the guard's chest. He fell to the floor with a loud *thump* — right as another came through another door. Volta's eyes went wide; he was outside Carmen's sphere of influence, and his gun was already in his hands. Carmen rounded on him right as the guard trained his gun on Volta. He had maybe a second before the time-slowing haze reached him.

Long enough for Volta's mind to race ahead.

Don't take chances. Stop him, stop him NOW.

She raised her hand, claws bared as heat and sparks shot through her arm.

CRACK.

The bolt leapt from her palm with ease, striking the guard square in the chest. He didn't even make a noise, just fell back, arms clenching up as the shock traveled through his body. His gun hand squeezed the trigger, and he fired into the wall. He was still breathing, but he was *definitely* down for the count. Exhilaration rushed through the wolf as she pulled her hand back.

I… I did it! I —

Volta jumped, snapped out of her thoughts by the sudden, loud blare of an alarm. Strobes flashed overhead. Immediately, Volta's RCGs began to adjust, dimming in sync with the strobe lights, making it *mostly* bearable in under a second. The sound of the alarm faded into the back of her awareness, not quieter, but easier somehow to ignore.

"No time to celebrate, Volts, come on!" Carmen shouted, grabbing the red wolf's hand and pulling her along.

They hurried up the stairs, and just in time there were footsteps catching up behind them. The open window waited dead ahead. Carmen hurried towards it, then paused, grabbing onto Volta with both hands.

"You trust me?" she asked, as she put one hand on Volta's back and the other around her waist, sending a shiver up her spine. What a silly question — Volta just nodded fervently. "Then don't let go!"

She clung to Carmen's armor plates as the cat picked her up off her feet. One hand scooped under Volta's legs, and everything started to feel… *very* floaty, as Carmen's eyes began to glow, and the air around them turned murky and dark.

She sprinted straight ahead, right as several guards climbing the stairs came into view behind them.

"Tuck your head in!"

Volta stuffed her muzzle into the crook of Carmen's neck as she felt Carmen jump toward the window, turning in the air…

A hard **crash** shook them, immediately followed by gunshots — *real* gunshots — whizzing past them as Carmen's back went through the window. Her arms wrapped around Volta to shield her as best she could as they finally hit the open, rainy air, and fell.

They hit the grass and rolled. Carmen stuck out a hand to stop, grunting with the effort while Volta got her bearings. She was miraculously free of cuts… and, more importantly, on the ground beneath the cat. They had a few seconds of cool air, of rain coming down on them.

The chill of the wet grass on her bare back did nothing to distract her from the tabby pinning her.

She grinned down at the wolf, panting a little. "You good?"

*She's so pretty. She's **so** strong and she's on* TOP OF ME, *and she's smiling, and I love her and —*

"Y-yeah…!" Volta answered. The adrenaline nearly overrode any embarrassment she felt, pinned underneath the cat and staring straight at her. She wished for just a few more seconds, that they could stay there even a moment longer…

The rest of the world wouldn't wait, though. Already she could hear shouting filtering in from every direction. Alarms blared from every building.

Carmen climbed off, helping the wolf to her feet and pulling her flush to the wall. "Plan B! We're going *very* loud. They'll be on us fast, we need to *move* — and, Volta?"

"Yeah?"

They locked eyes. Carmen squeezed her hand. "No holding back. Have *fun.*"

Those words sent tingles up her spine. The wolf answered with a smile and a crackle of magenta across her shoulders. Carmen held her hand firm, and together they ran.

Her RCGs continued to work over those words. That same deep, suppressed *something* was rumbling to the surface. She wanted to fight. She couldn't *wait* for someone to get in their way. She bared her teeth as they ran, seeing flashlights flick on in the rainy dark, instructions being shouted, coordinated gradually. The cat was *fast,* but she held back — just enough for Volta to keep up.

In amongst the alarms, the rain, and the incoherent commotion of boots hurrying towards them, Volta could make out just a few voices in the distance.

"What's the problem, what happened to the failsafe!?"

"The Dampener's off, the failsafe wouldn't work!"

She didn't have to wait long. They dashed between the trees in the garden walkway, just as a cluster of flashlights all rounded on them. One of the guards shouted at them to stop, then another next to him piped up again as he fumbled with some small device in his hands.

More lights shone on the bare-chested wolf. She sneered back at them, claws bared and arcs climbing over her back.

"He's not wearing it. Shit, SHIT, what now?"

"The chief said focus on the cat — *do not* shoot the kid! If he dies, Tullis will have our asses!"

I'm still just a kid, huh? They want me back. Tullis thinks he can keep me here. I'll show him how wrong he is.

Carmen raised her weapon and aimed low. Three shots, three distinct, strangled yells of pain as the guards all crumpled. More were already on the way, this time with rifles raised.

Carmen leapt to the side, and Volta let herself be pulled along as the cat's power expanded outward again. Rifle barrels flashed, and Volta's hair stood on end as a bullet tumbled lazily past her head, and then several more. Clearly, they weren't aiming very carefully.

Carmen pulled Volta behind a tree just as a barrage of rubber bullets thumped into the other side. Carmen leaned out to return fire, and Volta stayed behind her, now starkly aware of the disadvantage her toplessness imposed on her.

The sound of boots on gravel made her whirl around as three *more* guards, only a few meters away, aimed their flashlights *and* their weapons at her. They were shouting, but Volta couldn't hear them. All she could hear was Carmen's shouting through her earpieces.

"I said have *fun! Run wild, wolf!*"

Get out of our way.

Volta let go of Carmen, claws bared, magenta lightning crackling loud over her arms and chest. With a snarl, she swiped at them, a long arc spreading out over all three in succession. They convulsed; two of them fell backward — the other tried to remain standing but collapsed a mere second later.

"YEAH!" the cat cheered as she pulled her hand back. "*That's what I'm talking about!*"

The wolf's shoulders heaved with excitement. She was *exultant*, heat like no other filling her head and chest and limbs, stronger and stronger. There was no hum in her ears, no itch of doubt or fear — *this* was the best she'd felt in *years*.

You're not stopping me. **No one** *is stopping* **ME!**

She ran out from behind the tree. Carmen made a surprised noise, but the gunfire stopped. The guards shined their lights at her; another demanded she come quietly, fear hiding into his voice. The wolf only snarled, baring her teeth, and held her hands out to either side as her arms went hot.

Blinding pink energy radiated in every direction as she exerted more and more charge. She clenched her fingers and *urged* her power forward, sending the guards to the floor with a stream of bolts. Volta laughed, fingers tingling, heart *burning* with a savage delight that was entirely new — and very, *very* welcome.

"Keep going, keep going!"

Carmen's voice brought her attention back again. The wolf drew her charge back in, and Carmen tugged her in the right direction. She'd never been more willing to let someone take hold of her like Carmen did: carefully, but with purpose. And especially now — she had all the power they'd always been afraid of, and she couldn't be happier to let the tabby lead her by the hand. *She* had the choice, and that was enough.

The cat kept a looser grip, now. She trusted the wolf to run alongside her — and it was getting easier to keep up. She pulsed her charge down through her legs, reveling in the sensation and the warmth in her feet as she ran alongside the cat. Laughter boiled over all over again, free, unrestrained.

They crossed the gardens, passing the cafeteria and approaching the research building. Floodlights began to turn atop several of the buildings.

They were halted by more pairs of boots, the cocking of rifles, and shouting. They *still* tried to get Volta to come quietly; *how cute.*

Carmen spread her power's influence out again. She pulled Volta down while the wolf took aim, and lit up the rain around them in pink, crackling lightning.

One down, then two, three, four... Volta couldn't stop baring her teeth in a fierce grin, throwing another downing bolt at the last guard. It was as easy as tensing her arms — if not easier.

"Here I thought I'd need a gun!" Carmen laughed, tugging her along again. "Don't slow down now — once we get past the gym, we're home-free."

"Good, good," Volta panted, flexing her fingers and rolling her shoulders, shaking the sparks out of them. She paused for a moment, taking stock. Despite the *power* coursing through her, there was still only so much charge to draw from. She would need more soon if she was going to keep going like she had been.

[Here, let me help…]

Her RCG HUD pinged at her, highlighting the overhead lamp posts lighting their way. In amongst the rain and the commotion she hadn't *thought* of that, but now it seemed obvious. As they passed one, she stuck her hand out, brushing her hand against the pole and immediately feeling the *rush* of charge siphoning into her. The lamppost flickered and died — as did the next few. She was ready to go again in seconds, illuminating the damp gravel and grass around them in magenta.

"I know you're still getting used to this," Carmen shouted as they went, "but that color's such a fucking *look* — you're already fitting right in with the Korps!" The east gate was just up ahead, right around the corner.

"R-really?"

"*Hell* yeah, and I've got some friends you're gonna LOVE to meet! Just you wait, we're almost —"

Carmen cut herself off as they approached the corner of the building, and a sudden, blinding flash of light made them stagger to a halt. Their visors adjusted rapidly to reveal a half circle of floodlights and what had to be more than a dozen silhouettes of guards, all blocking the way forward.

"That's far enough," a low, gruff, *smug* voice called out, sending a chill down Volta's back. A broad-shouldered, seven-foot-five silhouette loomed in front of the crescent of flood lights, taking slow, casual steps. Adam Tullis wore his usual security chief's uniform and an even haircut, his slate grey eyes glinting in the reflected light. His rolled-up sleeves revealed his arms from the bicep down: every inch shining, reflective gold.

Of *course* it wasn't going to be easy. For a brief moment, Volta became starkly aware of how wet her fur had gotten, how *cold* the air felt. It almost reminded her of the Dampener — but in an instant, ROSE quashed the memory, refocusing her on the security chief.

The Great Dane scowled as he stared the pair of them down. "And now you got those damn things on. Shit, Travers, she brought you those girly lookin' goggles but couldn't bring you a shirt?" he snorted. "And what's with the pink lightning? Ah, what the hell, I'm not even talking to little Austin anymore, am I?"

If it had been any other day, Volta would stay frozen in place, at a loss for words. Now, she knew *exactly* what she wanted to say.

"Yes, you are," she began with a growl. "I'm *right here*, Tullis. I'm not going back."

"They got you twisted up pretty bad, huh?" Tullis tutted. His shoulders and head drooped, both shaking as he chuckled and raised a hand, giving a signal.

Volta's head swiveled at the stomping of black boots all around them. Clusters of guards, some looking far more like SWAT than campus police, each with their weapons raised and several of them pointed at the wolf. She didn't move — but she didn't dissipate the magenta arcs crackling over her arms, either.

"Your parents aren't gonna like this," Tullis rumbled. "Once we tear that visor off, you're gonna need *twice* as much deprogramming if you ever wanna be *normal* again, Travers."

Volta bristled, but this time Carmen took a step forward, arms wide. "You gonna talk shit all day, asshole, or are you gonna actually put up a fight this time?"

Tullis's eyes flitted to the cat, looking her up and down again... a few times. "Ha. Don't worry, missy, I didn't forget about you. I've been wanting a rematch ever since you slipped away the first time. Make sure everyone knows some oversized girl's not gonna get the better of me."

The cat's lip twitched upward for a second; her tail swayed fluidly behind her as she took another step. "Didn't know I bruised your ego *that* bad. What makes you think you can take me down this time? You put your jockstrap on~?"

His eyes narrowed. "Y'know, if you weren't such a feisty bitch, you might actually be *attractive* — especially in *that* slutty getup. But then, I guess you wouldn't have gotten a little punk like Travers following you around like a lost puppy, huh?"

Carmen took another step, claws bared and eyes flashing dangerously behind her RCGs. "It's about time someone finally shut you up. Come on, *Chief*. You want to beat me, don't you? I got away from you last time. Don't you wanna finish the job~?"

The Great Dane's fists tightened and his knuckles *clanked* metallically. "All right. None of you better step in — she's *mine*," he barked at the crescent of guards around them. Tullis looked back to Volta, who instinctively tensed up again. "Scratch that last offer, Travers. I'll just kill her now. And when I'm done with the bitch, if my men haven't hogtied you, I'll make *sure* you stay down. You're gonna *beg* me to put you back in that cell, boy —"

He reared back as sharp gunshots rang out. Volta jumped, head whipping around to the source of the sound; Carmen's pistol was raised as she marched forward, shot after shot ringing out as she emptied her magazine *directly* into the Great Dane's face.

He staggered backwards, one step, then two. Volta remained still, shocked eyes wide and ears folded back, watching the ex-hero begin to tilt... and then put his feet squarely back into the gravel. He straightened, then hunched forward, letting out a roar as he dove at Carmen, his head completely unblemished, all of it that same gleaming shade of gold.

He barreled right into the tabby just as she activated her power. The purple sphere ballooned around them and Carmen twisted, letting the Great Dane rush past her. She kicked the small of his back, knocking him forward as time sped back up. He recovered, touching the ground with a metal hand and taking a swing right for her head. She weaved out of the way, and they began to fight in earnest.

Volta stared, momentarily awestruck as Tullis punched and swiped at the nimble cat. She dodged deftly, power flaring erratically to try and knock him off balance without much success. He was ready for every hit, despite the time dilation, and he recovered *frighteningly* fast for someone so big. His years of experience were evident in how he moved, shifting his balance as he swung and dove. Though huge and hulking, the Great Dane's movements were *controlled*, practiced. He hadn't *hit* her yet — but he was painfully close each time.

"Won't matter what you drilled into him!" Tullis mocked as he circled around her, grabbing for her tail. "I'll clear the pup's head of all your programming *personally* if I have to! He won't even *remember* you when we're done!"

"Keep running your mouth, old man!" Carmen snapped back as she jabbed at his side, glancing off with a dull metal *thunk.* "We're getting out, and you're not gonna stop us!"

Another swing from the Great Dane missed Carmen's head by mere inches. Volta started forward, finally remembering how to move.

...I have to help!

She made to run toward them, but gloved hands seized one of her arms, yanking her away. Volta channeled her shock into the guard by reflex, his grip tightening as his muscles locked up. Before she could even register what had happened, he had gone fully slack on the ground, gurgling and cursing in pain.

Volta didn't spare him more than a frenzied glance before she turned back, just in time to catch Carmen swinging back to avoid a haymaker from Tullis and twisting around again. Their eyes met for a moment, and unspoken words, conveyed by their RCGs, flowed into Volta's mind.

"Leave him to me. Focus on the rest!"

Volta glanced back around; all of Tullis's men in body armor still had their weapons trained on her. None were in a hurry to try grabbing her again. She bared her blunted claws, eyes flitting between their faceless riot masks and indifferent expressions.

"Quit standing around!" Tullis barked at them as Carmen dove out of the way of another unclear swing from the Great Dane. She dodged backwards, and to the right — the direction where Tullis's guards *weren't*. He dove after her as she disappeared around the corner of the gym building.

"Get the kid, and take those damn glasses off of him!"

The wolf's muscles clenched up, hackles rising as the guards moved to follow orders.

You lost your chance. Now I'll **show** *you what I can do.*

Volta curled her lips up in a snarl. She willed the heat in her body to gather at her hands again. The guards all tensed, exchanging nervous glances.

"Fuck do we do? Tullis wants him alive."

"Just hobble him — aim for the legs if he doesn't stop!"

Too late!

The edges of her vision glowed; heat radiated out from her chest as emotion overtook her. She let out a roar that grew louder and louder, matched by the lightning arcing over her body, crackling and buzzing violently. She willed the charge over her skin, through her fur, and forced it outward. With an animalistic shout and a deafening crack of thunder, a burst of magenta *exploded* out of her, hitting several of them dead on and knocking them to the ground.

Volta panted as her vision started to clear. The nearest group of guards lay in heaps on the ground, a few of them still twitching and trembling. The rest rose unsteadily to their feet — but Volta was already pacing toward them, arcs of electricity radiating out from her in every direction. The mixing smells of ozone, rain and singed grass drove her further.

*You're **not** getting away from **me**!*

They had barely gotten their bearings before she was on them again. One swung the butt of his rifle at her; she caught it in one hand and grabbed at him with the other, sending several hundred volts right through his clothes with a searing crack. Another raised his gun, screaming as she rounded on him, blunted claws out and canine teeth gnashing as she shocked him back to the ground alongside the first. She moved faster and faster, ever more wild and excited.

One managed to squeeze off a pair of shots before she got close enough to deliver a charged up punch right to his throat. He crumpled, right as she heard yet another running up behind her. She swung around in a wild swipe, delighted as lightning trailed after her claws, and connected with him. He went rigid, twitching and yowling in pain. She closed the distance in a leap, her upper body lit up in magenta as she knocked him to the floor.

"Come on, *come on!*" she barked, rising to her feet and stepping over the guards. Her body *seethed* with warmth as magenta lightning crawled over her. The rain steamed off her fur as she broke into a sprint, searching for where Carmen had led Tullis.

She rounded the corner again and made for the dorm building. As she approached, a single guard came into view. She didn't even have to *try*. One hard jolt and he collapsed, convulsing. Volta stepped closer, grinning wider as she watched him shudder and twitch.

"H-holy shit." Another voice made her whirl around, ready to throw another bolt. Otis stood on the steps of the dormitories, underneath the overhang, dressed in a TPA Academy T-shirt and plaid boxers, his mane and hair all disheveled. He gawked at Volta, as though he'd never quite looked at her thoroughly before. "Austin…?"

The red wolf's snarl faltered as she stared back at him. He wasn't approaching her; he just stood there, dumbstruck.

"I… I came out when I heard the alarms, and the lightning…" He glanced at her arms and her claws, her electricity glimmering in his eyes. "What happened to you…?"

Volta stood her ground, staring into his eyes as she growled.

"This doesn't involve you, Otis."

He blinked, letting out his breath in a nervous, nonplussed laugh. He seemed surprised that she could still talk, despite her far more feral appearance. "You're breaking out, aren't you? You're going to be one of them, now?"

"Otis… I really, *really* don't want to hurt you," she managed. Sparks flew as she tensed again, ready to fight. "So please… *stay out of my way.*"

The lion didn't speak again. Seemingly satisfied, he held his hands up and slowly backed away, never taking his eyes off hers. He opened the dormitory door and stepped back inside. Volta turned around again, ears flicking to listen past the alarms and the rainfall.

ROSE took the initiative, and a guiding line appeared on the ground before her, leading off toward the admin building.

[They're in the campus courtyard. Hurry.]

It didn't take long for her to start hearing their voices again as she ran. She passed between two buildings again — right as a huge shape thudded to the ground several feet in front of her, kicking up a plume of gravel and dirt. The hulking body of the Great Dane was nearly all solid gold as he stood up, grabbing at the tabby that had just tackled him to the floor.

"This is getting old, girl. You *know* you can't hurt me." He finally got ahold of the cat's arm and wrenched her off of him. He threw Carmen away, only to have the cat twist around in midair, landing on her feet — but a lot *heavier* than usual. Was she actually getting tired?

"No, but I can keep you busy," Carmen fired back. "How long do you think, before all your guards are down for the count? You really think they can handle her?"

"*Her?* What, you mean Travers?" The dog snorted. "So that's how it is. You got him thinking he's like the rest of you freaks. Are you gonna make him play dress up, too?"

"*Unlike* every one of you self-righteous assholes, I'm not forcing a *damn* thing on her. I'm getting her out and *away from you!*" Carmen ran towards him, going for another grab. This time, he was ready for her. Even as her powers began to expand outward, he was sidestepping, his body a shining gold sheen as she crashed into one of his legs.

How was he moving so *fast* — was that part of his powers as well? Carmen still had the speed advantage, but not nearly as much as what slowing down time for a handful of seconds should have afforded her. She dug her heels in, shifting her weight from right foot to left, shoving the big dog off balance again and making him stumble back — right as he brought a fist down on the cat's back.

With a pained grunt, Carmen *shoved* again, forcing him off balance, then catching sight of Volta. "You keep your distance, Volts! This dipshit's *almost* as tough as he looks."

"*Almost*, huh?" Tullis asked, getting heated. "All right, kittycat. You want tough?" He jumped back, running outside Carmen's radius. He finally pulled a large handgun out from his holster, evidently made to accommodate his already large hands.

He turned away from the cat and took aim at the wolf. "*How's this for tough?*"

Volta's eyes went wide, taking a step back as Carmen shouted her name again. A murky violet sphere erupted around her as she bolted toward the wolf, but it was already too late. He pulled the hammer back, and, just as the sphere engulfed his side, pulled the trigger.

The gunshot rang out, reverberating against the brick walls like a crack of thunder. ROSE was already forcing Volta to dive as the world turned a purple hue and Carmen sped toward her, racing ahead of the spinning bullet. The tabby put her hands on the wolf and *shoved*, but the haze immersing them slowed her still — she would not clear the bullet's path soon enough. Carmen braced in front of Volta as she dismissed her power, and the bullet struck.

Volta hit the ground and tumbled and heard a strangled scream behind her. Her blood ran cold, and ROSE shifted into high gear as a stirring of panic reared its head.

Carmen…!

Volta scrambled back to her feet, pivoting to see the cat now stumbling, favoring one leg as she bled through a tear in her suit. It had taken most of the force, but it wasn't enough to handle high-caliber ammunition.

The tabby fell against the nearest wall, hissing in pain. "Is that your idea of capture, *asshole!?*" she shouted, the pain in her voice evident. "The *fuck* you trying to kill her for!?"

"I wasn't," Tullis said smugly, holstering his gun once more. "I knew you'd step in to save him. I've put down enough of you to know how you think — it's the best way to get you to actually walk *into* a bullet." He approached with long, easy strides…

"You're one giant *shitheel* of a hero," Carmen growled, struggling to stand on her own. "I'll rip that metal skin off you, you *selfish, pathetic has-been.*"

"Got quite a mouth on you, huh?" Tullis grinned down at her, eyes lit with sadistic glee. "I'll break *that* next." He raised a fist and swung at her. She dodged narrowly, collapsing to the ground before him.

Volta couldn't move. She was frozen in place; even as her RCGs tried to keep her afloat, she felt herself starting to sink into *real* terror. Her heart pounded, mouth going dry as she tried to approach them. The pink sparks had died down as she stared at the cat… and then up at Tullis.

She's bleeding. She's hurt. I have to help, now, before it's too late.

"You gonna tag in, Travers?" The Great Dane looked up from his prey, smirking. "What, you think you can handle me now? Or do you just wanna save yourself the trouble and watch your girlfriend die?"

No… No. I won't let you. Get AWAY from her!

Volta finally managed to stir, moving her feet slowly as she clenched her fists. Her mind raced, supercharged now as she summoned all her stored energy at once.

Can't just fight him flat out. He's impervious — even Carmen couldn't hurt him…

Tullis laughed, shoving Carmen onto her back with the tread of his boot. "You really *did* get all twisted up when you put those tacky glasses on. You think you're a girl now, too?"

Volta took another step forward, silent, and raised her fists. Tullis just rolled his eyes. "I'll tell you right now, Travers. I know these Korps freaks better than anyone. They're liars, manipulators and *perverted* like you wouldn't believe. You really wanna be like that? You're a kid who's got it all, and you're gonna throw it all away for some girl?"

That "gold" is bulletproof, bends and stretches like his skin…

"Not just for her," Volta growled, tensing up as pink arcs jumped across her arms with a sharp, dangerous crackle. ROSE was helping keep her momentum, but her words were entirely her own. "I'm doing this for *me*, too. I'm not spending any longer than I have to like *this*."

"Ha! You really are just as fucked in the head as the rest of them. Guess you'll fit right in. Should we put you in a skirt and lipstick too, Travers? It won't make a difference. You'll still be the same boney kid — just *uglier*."

"Fuck you." Volta leaned forward, hackles raised and flared out, Jacob's Ladders crawling up her back.

...Gold conducts electricity pretty well, doesn't it?

He raised an eyebrow, surprised. "Oh, come on. I know there's still some small part of you in there, those goggles don't work *that* fast. Admit it: you know you'll just be another freak in their rank and file." Volta bristled again, baring her teeth in a low, animalistic snarl. More and more pink lightning arced off her as the chief spoke, though he didn't seem intimidated. "Once I'm done with you, they won't even want you anymore. You sure you don't wanna go back to that comfy cell?"

"FUCK YOU!"

Volta threw one hand forward. Heat shot through her arm, and with a loud *CRACK*, she fired a hot magenta bolt right into his chest. He swung backward, stunned momentarily into silence as he regained balance. A surge of adrenaline and euphoria hit the wolf as she watched him twitch.

Suffer, you shithead. *Savor every breath you get. I'm* **done** *letting you run your mouth.*

"God *damn*," Tullis grunted, straightening up again with his fists balled up, his whole upper body gleaming gold once more. "That actually *hurts*, I'll give you that." He'd lost the self-assured smile from before. Now he glowered down at her as he rolled one shoulder and stepped toward her. "No wonder your parents are scared shitless. Fine, kid gloves are coming off. I'm gonna make *you* hurt, Austin Travers, mark my words. Don't care what your parents say, you need to learn some *manners* or —"

"**My name...**" Volta hissed, her voice beginning to crackle with electricity as the edges of her vision turned pink, "**Is. Not. Austin!**" She sprinted toward him. The immense figure of Tullis cast a shadow over her as he raised his hand once more, and threw his giant fist straight for her.

All of Carmen's training paid off, accelerated further by the RCGs. She ducked to the side and followed up with a fully-charged jab to his metal solar plexus, hitting him with an electric snap. He growled in pain, taking the backstep as his other twitching hand swung around to shove her away.

"They gave you a new name too, huh!?" he sputtered, the dog baring his own teeth in a cruel sneer. "Guess you *must* be special, if you get to be that cat's little bitch. What makes you think you'd fit into the Korps, Austin?"

Volta gnashed her teeth as another clap of thunder rang out from the storm clouds overhead. He swung at her again, and this time she grabbed him by the wrist, glaring fiercely and defiantly into the Great Dane's surprised face. "**My name. Is. VOLTA.**"

She pumped charge through her fingers, ran a circuit from one palm to the other through his arm. The sound was unmistakable, like a low, growling taser. Tullis yelled, yanking himself from her grip and taking pause at the fresh black marks across his golden forearm.

"You're just another coddled rich boy," he drawled, shaking out the pins and needles. "Don't kid yourself."

Before she could think of another response, Tullis suddenly landed a kick on Volta's shoulder. It felt like a sledgehammer smashing into her, spiking pain through her arm as she finally doubled back, trying to catch her breath.

Fuck. Hurting too much, I'm losing a lot of charge. Just, dim my pain receptors; ignore them until I'm done.

Tullis kept going, rolling his shoulders as he approached her again. "Don't make me laugh. You're never gonna be anything more than your parents' son, weak and *alone* and afraid of his own shadow. You got any reason for me to believe —"

She didn't let him finish this time. She swung wide, magenta energy branching out until it finally collided with Tullis's stomach.

"*FUCK YOU!*" Her voice erupted like a thunderclap. She swung again and this time struck his side, watching with vindictive pleasure as she fed pink arcs into his body, making him yank back and go rigid as he yelled from the sting.

"God*damn*, enough of this shit!" Tullis grabbed her, one hard golden hand closing around Volta's neck. She had just a second before the world became a blur. He threw her halfway across the courtyard, and she hit the ground tumbling. ROSE took over, urging her hands outward. She grabbed at soil, then at gravel before she smacked into something solid. She lay there, stunned for a moment as her brain caught up with the blunt throbbing pain breaking out over her body.

Shit **shit** **SHIT.** *Hurting too much, feels like I'm starving…*

She started to feel the extra drain — she was missing all the energy she'd pumped into Tullis. She felt tired, her body bruised in too many places to count now. Nothing was broken, ROSE assured her, but she'd gotten several scrapes on her arms and chest, and a gash on one leg. She was starkly aware of how *wet* and *cold* she'd gotten in the rain, her fur matted to her aching body.

She looked up through blurry eyes, chest heaving. It had started feeling tight again. Tullis's unmistakable silhouette lumbered closer, slow and uneven, *unsteady*. He bared his teeth in a grotesque smile, his eyes unnaturally wide with excitement. He was taking his time — he was trying to *enjoy* this.

"Don't pass out now, Travers! I ain't *done* with you yet."

Hands trembling, she tried to push herself off the ground. She got her bearings gradually, RCGs helping her along. She was on the other side of the quad; she'd hit the side of a building, just barely slowed down enough to avoid breaking something. She shakily rose to her muddy hands and knees, eyes struggling to focus in on the hard surface she'd hit.

Tullis continued as he stepped closer, laugh slow and mirthless. "You've been spoiled all your life. Ain't a surprise you can't even handle how supers fight — how *real men* fight! This is a promise, Travers: The Golden Gavel is gonna make you regret *every step* you took out of that cell."

The admin building loomed over her. She'd hit the outdoor power supply box for the building, right beside the front steps. The junction box was giving off an enticing glow. Volta stared at it with a brand new pang of hunger.

"Ahh, *shit*," Tullis swore.

She had her hands on the metal door in a second. She felt the energy beneath, like a far-reaching root. The light circuits from before didn't have greater grid access, but *this* did. The wolf stiffened, breathing in fresh air. She didn't even have to open the box to *pull* at that widespread reservoir and feel it pour into her. She drank greedily, immersed in magenta light.

All mine.

The street lamps around them all died. The blaring alarms faltered and went silent. The lights in the admin building went next, then the R&D complex next to it. One by one, every structure in the TPA Frontier Academy went dark. The storm clouds overhead illuminated in magenta, a distant and ominous rumble of thunder rolling closer and closer. Volta clutched that root and drank *deeper*.

On the 3rd of May, 2019, at 10:02 PM, a 20-square-mile area of west Austin City lost power for ten minutes. Some residents reported the lights in their homes momentarily flashing bright pink before going out. Official sources blamed the thunderstorm passing over the city, which grew much more violent than forecasted at the turn of the hour.

The epicenter of the power outage was a state-owned facility, the news reported, just as a strangely vibrant lightning bolt struck the ground. The Texas Protectorate Assembly, though on record as using that facility for Hero training and superpower research, declined to comment.

Wren stared at the overhead drone footage, mouth agape. The cloud cover was dense, but not thick enough to hide the sudden snuffing out of miles and miles of city lights, all at once.

"Holy shit…"

[*WARNING. Extremely high electric discharge detected, exercise extreme caution… Carmen, be careful looking directly at her.*]

Carmen struggled to push herself upright, propping up against the wall again. She hadn't noticed when all the lights had gone out, but she *did* see a hot magenta flare, and a constant *roar* of lightning. It didn't take her long to realize what was happening. Her eyes widened as she shielded them behind one arm.

She limped toward the light as fast as she could, praying she would not be too late.

Volta reared back and *screamed*, arms wide as the thunderbolt tunneled down from the sky and slammed into her. The wolf's entire body went white hot, glowing with a ten-thousand-degree fury. Her own voice rang in her ears as her RCGs struggled to keep up with the excess of energy, all compressed into one place: in *her*.

The streetlamps overhead surged back to life, all of them bright pink, until one by one, spreading out from where the wolf stood, they burst in plumes of magenta. Further cracks and snaps traveled up and down the campus as lights and power supplies throughout every building overloaded and blew apart. Searchlights cracked open; computers belched smoke.

The bolt finally dissipated, and the red wolf closed her eyes, howling up to the clouds. The haunting sound echoed through the smoldering campus as thunder rolled across the sky.

She fell forward and caught herself. Her vision was enveloped in raging magenta, her shoulders rising and falling with every breath. She knelt in a circle of incinerated grass, burn marks streaking up the brick wall behind her. The junction box sparked and popped, smoke rising from its warped shape as arcs continued to erupt out of the wolf in front of it.

There was a counter in her RCGs' flickering HUD — an estimated charge level, changing too fast to keep track. It didn't matter. She knew she had *more* than enough. Pink electricity surrounded her, radiated off of her like water from a fountain. She'd never felt better.

Volta drew herself up as tall as she could, baring her fangs at the Great Dane before her. Tullis had fallen backward, stunned by the blinding light and rolling heat, but he was recovering fast. He regained his footing, taking a step back as he stared slack-jawed at her. *Finally,* she'd gotten him on the back foot.

Now she was going to hurt him.

He only got a few words out. "What in the *goddamn* —"

She bent lower, wreathing herself in lightning. The world around her stretched, elongated as she tensed her legs and *jumped.* Another deafening *BANG* shook the courtyard. Volta shot forward near the speed of light, claws outstretched as she knocked Tullis flat against the grass. She tumbled again and caught herself just as quick.

Tullis's entire body jerked and twitched as he stood up again, gasping and wincing. "T-Travers, you're not doing yourself any —"

She didn't bother answering. She ran at him, her whole body pulsing with energy, winding back and punching him straight in the stomach. The hard gold metal of his exterior put up less and less resistance now. He stumbled backward again, gasping for air as he brought one hand up to try and knock her aside. She grabbed him by the wrist, yanked him forward and *down,* jutting her knee into his chest. He made a strangled grunt as her claws found purchase.

She swung ferociously, each punch and kick faster than the last, each pumping careless amounts of energy into the ex-hero's body. He didn't have time to recover, and on her next punch to his shoulder, Volta felt *flesh* and not metal. He yelled in pain, *real* pain now. She gave him a delighted, *angry* snarl, spurred even further.

She shouted incoherently as she jammed a thousand-volt kick into his knee. It buckled; she felt a crack, and he fell to the other. She followed through with a left hook, relishing in watching her supercharged fist knock his jaw out of alignment.

Finally, he fell backward, and didn't get up.

"A-Austin…!" he groaned.

"That's *not* my name."

She leapt onto the larger canine, straddling his chest and yelling in his face, her voice distorted with a constant electric buzz.

"*Say my name!*" she snarled, catching his snout with a right hook wrapped with lightning. He gasped in pain as blood sprayed over the grass. His metal coating was entirely gone now, but she was far from finished.

"*Say. My. NAME!*" she screamed, hitting him again. Another blow, then another. She had blown off a lot of the excess charge, and hit a dizzying equilibrium. She could feel the angry tears streaming down her cheeks. She shook her head, snarling and yelling in his face.

"*SAY IT! WHAT'S MY NAME!? FUCKING SAY IT!*"

She hit him again and again; each time, his body convulsed, and more blood splattered from his nose and mouth. He was barely looking at her anymore, his arms and legs limp save for the jolts that shook them. She grabbed him by his burnt shirt collar, lifting him up as she raised a trembling, sparking fist. At last, she hesitated. A choked up sob forced its way through clenched teeth.

It wouldn't be hard. I could just keep going. I could just kill him, right now. [*Not yet. You don't need a death on your hands.*]

*I want him to hurt. He needs to know what it's like, to feel powerless. I want him to **know** he lost. **I want my face to be the LAST THING HE SEES. I WILL —***

"Volta, *please...*"

A gentle hand caressed her shoulder, and the arcs pouring off of her stopped in an instant. She looked up, eyes wide, to see Carmen standing over them. Through their RCGs, their eyes met. The tabby's amber spheres were so gentle and soft, like the rest of her, despite her strength.

She couldn't do it.

Volta sniffled; her raised fist slackened. Carmen was still smiling at her, as kind and patient as ever. That smile alone was too much.

With some strain, the cat lifted her off the barely-conscious Tullis and embraced her.

"It's okay, you're *okay...*" Carmen murmured in her ear. "You're done, Volta. You're free now."

"I-I'm free..." Volta repeated tremulously. "W-we did it... I'm *free*."

"And, you..." Carmen pulled back, caressing Volta's cheek, running her fur between her fingers. She beamed at her with joyful tears in her eyes. Volta hesitated for just a moment, then...

The tabby held her face gently with both hands, and they kissed. The wolf clung tightly to her, tears stopped in their tracks. For a moment, the world slipped away like it had once before. They swayed as they held each other, letting the rain soak them where they stood. When they finally separated, they shared the same breathless smile.

"You are the *most incredible thing* I've ever fucking *laid eyes on*. And —"

She faltered, eyes going wide as she raised her fingers to the wolf's RCGs, staring through them. "And... holy fuck, we gotta get you in front of a mirror."

"Wha...?"

"Later! Later. We... *hhhugh*, we need to get going," Carmen grunted, shifting her weight off her wounded leg again. "And fast, too. Bet you anything the Teepa's scrambling response teams by now thanks to that lightshow."

Tullis made an unintelligible gurgle, as if trying to interject.

"Y-yeah..." Volta stared back down at him. "What if... you hadn't..."

"Then he might be dead," Carmen remarked dryly. "But that would almost be too good for him, don't you think?"

"...*Really?* We just... let him *go?*"

"This way he has to live with himself, and the fact that you beat him. *You* beat him, Volta." The cat squeezed her shoulders again, beaming with pride and adoration. "You're a goddamn supervillain now — you saved a wanted criminal, you wrecked a state hero facility, you beat the ever-living *shit* out of a superhero, and you did it all in *style*."

As long as she could remember, Volta had wanted to be a hero. Just like her idol, like so many others, too. And yet, the notion that she had become the exact opposite was... confusing.

Carmen being so happy about it feels nice, though...

She resolved to unpack that later — *much* later. "Okay, okay... What about getting out of here, though?"

"Chopper, remember?" Carmen grinned. "Speaking of which: ROSE, if you wouldn't mind...?"

Only now did the muted whirring of a helicopter rotor sink in from overhead. She stared upward at it, sparing a brief and *astonished* thought for the magenta-crackling lightning far above the chopper. It touched down in front of them, and Volta put an arm around Carmen's back, letting the tabby lean against her as they moved.

They limped toward the chopper, and the side door slid open.

A silver dragon poked her head out, her RCGs lighting up her face as she checked their surroundings.

"How bad are your injuries?" she asked, appraising the pair with deep red eyes behind magenta goggles.

Carmen grunted as she kept walking, her weight settling against Volta's shoulder again. "Thanks for asking out loud. I'm gonna need a day or two off this foot. Volta's fine though — more than fine, she *rocked the fucking house.*"

"Believe me, I noticed!" The dragoness smiled, gazing at Volta as she held an arm out to pull Carmen into the chopper and onto one of the chairs. As the wolf sat down beside her, the dragoness gently touched Volta's elbow to get her attention.

"Your name is just Volta, yes? No last name?" she asked as she slid the door closed behind them.

"Yeah, I'm… just Volta," she replied. She got the feeling that she was being… *evaluated* by the dragoness. Her eyes flitted over the tired wolf's face, obscured only by her own RCGs. Volta noticed that this woman's pair was much less angular and much more round, not unlike a jelly bean. "… Uh, what's yours?"

On cue, her RCGs scrawled text beside the smiling dragon, displaying a single sentence:

[Don't forget to breathe. Relax.]

Easy as that, Volta let out the breath she'd been holding onto. Her shoulders slackened; she was able to ease back against the… *surprisingly* well-cushioned helicopter seat. It felt like the last of the adrenaline the past thirty minutes had infused her with had just… disappeared. Was she exhausted, or were the RCGs doing this?

Oh, yes, of course they are. …And I'm talking to Carmen's boss, aren't I?

"I'm *just* Karen." The dragoness's smile widened as she crossed one leg over the other. As if it had been a signal, the chopper lifted off. "You're a special one. Carmen has a good eye for exceptional people — but she took a *unique* interest in you."

"Who, me?" Carmen muttered, leaning against the wolf again. She looked a lot more exhausted than before. "*Haaa*, fuck, never mind. I'm too tired to be coy. Just don't scare my new girlfriend too much, Karen…"

The word *"girlfriend"* sent a jolt up Volta's spine. She knew she must have been grinning and blushing — or something akin to grinning. She was probably still too fresh off shedding tears to smile properly.

"In any case..." Karen spoke up again, and Volta looked back at her to find she was stifling laughter. "Yes, you're right; I am Carmen's 'boss,' among other things. You, however..." She leaned forward, tapping her knee with one finger. "I presume you are our latest inductee! That is, if you want to stay with us. Carmen already did all the hard selling, but it's still your decision."

Volta glanced back at Carmen, who held her arm with one hand and squeezed it lightly as she met her gaze. The cat smiled at her, amber eyes still glistening.

"Yeah." She said it clearly and confidently, returning Carmen's smile. "There's nowhere else for me anymore. I want to stay."

"In that case, let's make it official." Karen, looking *very* satisfied, leaned forward and offered the wolf her hand. "Welcome to the Korps, Volta. Welcome *home*."

NEW AGENT SUMMARY

Name: VOLTA

Age: 19

Pronouns: She/Her

Power(s): Charged electrokinesis

Status: Acquired, pending processing

Role: TO BE DETERMINED

Residence: Temporarily staying with Agents Wren and Carmen Rayne, Suite T-014, RIV.

Long-term residence pending.

Intake processing scheduled. The best is yet to come.

Acknowledgements

Thank you so much for reading through my first major Korps work. It's taken two years to complete and has been my passion project throughout the COVID-19 quarantine. I sincerely hope you enjoyed it.

I owe an immense debt of gratitude to my entire possé of editors and proofreaders, everyone who pored over this story and didn't pull their punches: Bibi, Grace, Lexi, Runa, Mabel, Yana, Stripes, Andrea, and Lynne. Every single one of you gave so much more to this than you know. Each of you helped me build out this corner of the extended Korps world, and helped my characters and stories grow far more than I ever expected them to. You all gave me a creative circle I could belong in, and your patience and support helped make this story what it is now.

To my main editor and best friend, Bibi: thank you especially, for getting this book ready for print. Your work drives me to improve mine. You've kept me grounded during some nights I would otherwise want to forget. You give grace even to those who have hurt you cruelly, and I'm honored and humbled that you have shown me some of that generosity and patience. You're like a sister to me and without you this book would never have been published. You're a hopeless romantic. Please never change.

Thank you, Karen, for not only creating and constantly iterating on the Korps setting, but for sharing it with the world — letting people like me experiment in it, and most of all for helping build a queer community I am proud to say I belong in. Your creativity and generosity are a wellspring of joy and inspiration. You may not agree with this, or act as though you don't deserve the praise, but you truly are an incredible woman, and the entire community must count its lucky stars that you decided to share that with us. You're one of a kind, Boss.

Lastly, thank you to my partner, Rikki. You were my first and ever-present inspiration; you kept me focused and honest, and your enthusiasm for our characters and stories is what pushed me to see this through. Without you, this story would have never happened in the first place. We met in person for the first time only a few weeks after I first told you about my ideas for Volta and put together my plans for Induction, and I will never forget the joy and peace in your eyes on that first bus ride out of San Francisco. You helped me embrace my true self, and that directly led to this story, so many friends and my rediscovered love of writing. When we're together, every second is a joy. I will always love you.

Volta's here to stay. You know where to find me.

Korps Universe Glossary

Common terms in the Korps Universe

The Korps — To the public, the Korps (pronounced "core") is known as a shadowy, secretive band of supervillains based in Canada, with a reputation for mind control and plans to take over the world; Korps operatives are believed to be easily identified by their trademark RCGs, scandalously revealing costumes, and the magenta helix insignia. Under the leadership of the mysterious "Overlord," by the early years of the 21st century, their brazen criminal schemes and growing reach throughout North America and Europe have authorities (and allied Hero groups) increasingly concerned. The truth is far more complicated than any of those authorities know, starting nearly seven thousand years ago with a warrior's exile to Earth by his conquering interdimensional empire… but that's another story.

RCGs — Rose-Colored Glasses are a powerful, versatile AR/VR visor headset that interfaces directly with the wearer's brain, created by the Korps. In addition to operating as standalone PDAs and communication devices, RCGs also have the ability to affect the wearer's mind and mental condition to a granular level. A civilian model exists, distributed by Korps front and consumer electronics manufacturer Thornetech (alias Thorntech, due to trademark registration conflicts in various international markets) in a plausibly-deniable manner. Models for the consumer market have comparable base functionality to Korps devices, but are severely underclocked and have many higher-level functions disabled at a hardware level in order to avoid suspicion.

ACGs — Amber-Colored Glasses have much the same functionality as RCGs, but are crafted with additional anti-magic and anti-memetic defenses for use by KDARC agents. They do not render the user immune to magical effects; however, they can be crucial in efforts against mystical and eldritch threats by adaptively blocking cognitohazards and helping to keep the wearer's sense of self intact should reality start to weaken.

Aurora Squadron — Aurora Squadron, Canada's federal-level Hero group, is part of the Canadian Armed Forces and based out of Department of National Defence HQ — popularly known as the War Tower — in Ottawa, ON. Closely overseen by Minister of National Defence Arthur Simonds, formerly the second Hero to be known as True North, Aurora Squadron fields a highly professional, dedicated and capable team of Heroes in the fight against superpowered threats to Canada, including the enigmatic Korps.

Bradley Group — The United States' federal-level Hero group is formally named the National Hero Administration, but rarely known as anything but "Bradley Group" due to its institutional history; during the WWII invasion of Normandy, a secret strategic reserve of supers were activated to join American forces under the command of Gen. Omar Bradley, with "Bradley Group" used as a code name for this classified unit.

After the war, the group was put under the jurisdiction of the FBI, until later becoming its own massive, independent federal agency. In the present day, Bradley's superpowered forces number in the hundreds, with Heroes based all over the United States; considered highly prestigious within the industry and known to be selective in recruitment, even Bradley's lesser-known operatives are perceived by the public to be more competent and professional than many of their state-level counterparts.

Candesca — Candesca (pronounced "can-dess-ah") is one name for the energy that practitioners of the mystic arts manipulate, in order to work their spells and enchantments on the material plane. While other terminology is used for this concept in various diverse cultures, candesca is the neutral, academic, non-appropriative term most commonly used within the Korps. While a renewable resource, the body can under normal circumstances hold only a small amount. To paraphrase Lao Tzu, like a bowl, the magic-user must be refilled after being drained; the bowl is still useful, but has nothing left to give.

Cape — Vernacular for "Hero." Neutral to derogatory.

Chişinău Protocols — Shorthand for a series of separate but inter-related 1969 agreements negotiated in the city of Chişinău, Moldova, as amendments, codicils or interpretative addenda to various existing international treaties, including the 1899 and 1907 *Hague Conventions*, the 1948 *Universal Declaration of Sentient Rights*, the 1948 *Genocide Convention*, and the 1951 *Convention Relating to the Status of Refugees*. A Second Chişinău Conference was convened in 2006 to rationalize these provisions with and prepare similar addenda to more recent international instruments, such as the 1979 *Convention on the Elimination of All Forms of Discrimination Against Women*, and the 1998 *Rome Statute*, but these too are colloquially referred to as merely part of the same *Protocols*.

Collectively, the *Protocols* specify the permissible use of superpowers and treatment of supers by parties to the agreements, in both peacetime and in armed conflict. These agreements also introduced into international law the still-contentious declaration that involuntary, long-term restriction or suppression of powers in a way that causes the subject "greater than *de minimis* physical, psychological or moral harms" is a form of torture, war crime, or crime against sentience.

Color Guard — Bradley Group's elite strike team, currently consisting of twelve active members; each Hero's callsign and uniform is color-coded and themed around their powers for marketing purposes. Considered the best of the best, as patriotic as the Fourth of July, national polling consistently indicates higher levels of confidence and support for the Color Guard among Americans than even the military. However, the team's seemingly-flawless reputation is only maintained by Bradley's ruthless PR department, which has covered up or prevented their innumerable scandals from reaching the public consciousness.

Empire Enhancements — A subdivision of Korps medical services dedicated to in-depth body modification, including transgender care.

Everyone's Hero Association — The Everyone's Hero Association is a private Hero group based in Milwaukee, WI. It was founded in the 2010s by serial venture capitalist Jack Phillips, who named it as a challenge to Bradley Group's official legal designation, the National Hero Administration; government elites might have their own pet Heroes in Bradley, but the EHA is for *everyone*, as he invariably recites in press releases. Its roster is made up of supers with weak or unwieldy powers, and the group was considered something of a joke until Phillips' gamble on (cost-effectively!) finding a diamond in the rough paid off with Ellen "Lawful Neutral" Foxpaw's rise to B-tier prominence.

Federal Meta-Registry — The Federal Meta-Registry is a massive database maintained by Bradley Group of all U.S. citizens and resident foreign nationals with classes of superpowers deemed potentially dangerous. Registration is mandatory for all such known supers present within the United States, even if only briefly transiting through sovereign American territory. Evading or refusing registration in any way (particularly by intentionally concealing powers) is a serious criminal offense under the U.S. Code, and may be prosecuted as acts of terrorism in some circumstances.

HCH — Home County Heroes was a Hero group operated by the British government in the southeastern counties surrounding London. It was fully privatized in the 1980s under the Thatcher government, with all licenses, assets and personnel contracts sold to a corporate Hero management firm.

The former group has been variously divided and subsumed by other organizations since the 1990s, and though no organization called HCH technically exists anymore, some of its former member supers are still regularly referred to as Home County Heroes in the press and by the public. One such member is the Hampshire-born Howard "Green Belt" Bride.

Heavy — A heavy is a cape whose powers and role revolve around tanking damage and being a physical threat, usually having a powerset revolving around super-strength and enhanced durability or resistance to injuries.

Hero — When capitalized, Hero usually refers to a professional (and professionally-licensed) career superhero, whether part of a government or privately-operated Hero group. While Hero licensing requirements vary from jurisdiction to jurisdiction, most require some form of accredited training, full disclosure of an applicant's name and other personal information to the jurisdictional licensing authority for security checks, and an oath to serve the public good or otherwise to be of "good character." Most professional Heroes have superpowers, but a significant minority are unpowered gadgeteers, stealth operators, or even just heavily-armed mercenary types.

Informally, superheroes may be referred to interchangeably as "heroes" regardless of whether licensed and operating in a legal capacity. Unlicensed heroes may also be referred to as independent heroes, vigilantes or mercenaries in some contexts.

Hero group — A Hero group is any team or force of licensed Heroes. When directly operated or officially backed by some level of government, Hero groups are effectively a type of specialized law enforcement agency or military unit, with Hero members typically being granted similar legal powers to those of law enforcement officers in their jurisdiction. Private-sector Hero groups also exist, with their members typically having lesser legal powers similar to those of private investigators, security consultants, bodyguards and/or bounty hunters, depending on local laws and the political attitudes of authorities.

Significant Canadian Hero groups in these works include Aurora Squadron and the member Hero groups of the Provincial Heroes' League (PHL). Significant American Hero groups in these works include Bradley Group, the Everyone's Hero Association, and the Texas Protectorate Assembly.

KARD — The Korps Archives and Records Division (KARD), sometimes referred to simply as "Records," is a division of the Korps responsible for the acquisition, preservation, and circulation of various media. KARD acts as both a library of media resources collected over the decades, and a secure repository of sensitive information useful (and yet to be proven useful) to the organization's goals

Beginning as a loose collection of analysts recruited from dissatisfied members of the intelligence community in the years following WWII, it was not organized into an autonomous operational division for some time. KARD has branches across multiple bases, but is headquartered at and conducts the bulk of its operations from KDS. KARD regularly partners with other divisions and individual field agents, in order to help equip them with the most esoteric and obscure information required.

KDARC — The Korps Division for Arcane Research and Control (KDARC) is responsible for the study, safekeeping and strategic use of the strange and unusual. From ancient arcana to demonic incursions, memetic objects and more, if a problem for the Korps is outside the mundane — that is, outside the mundane in a world of supers — there's a better than zero chance that KDARC will be on the front lines.

KDARC was originally founded by the enigmatic Carlotta Davisson and several colleagues in 1935 as the Davisson Arcane Research Company (DARC) of Minneapolis, MN, and headquartered in the massive Madison Center. In the years following WWII, Carlotta came into contact with the Overlord, and DARC was fully integrated into the Korps in the early 1960s. In 1968, the Madison Center mysteriously vanished from the Minneapolis skyline; unbeknownst to the public, it had been magically moved to Toronto, ON, at the early lowest-excavated depths of KDS, to serve as the newly-minted division's secret headquarters.

Despite claiming to be a "civilian research division", KDARC maintains tactical operation teams (named TAROT) and a great deal of independence from the Korps. Some agents wonder why the Overlord overlooks the pseudo-corporate structure, and rumours abound of unionization attempts by KDARC's senior staff. Still, much of the division's motivations, intentions, and methods remain as enigmatic, incomprehensible, and dangerous as the bleeding edge of the arcane itself.

KDS — Korps Downsview Site is the headquarters of the Korps, located beneath the former Downsview Airport (previously Canadian Forces Base Toronto) in the industrial sprawl of Toronto, ON. With a footprint of over eight square kilometres and many subterranean sub-levels, futuristically eco-urbanist in aesthetics and centrally-planned design, it is a completely self-sufficient underground city. KDS was slowly built outward from a small excavation in the 1970s, becoming fully operational as a headquarters only in the 1980s-1990s.

In addition to the command, logistics and strategic functions required for the vast supervillain organization to operate, like all major Korps bases, KDS features apartment-like residential sectors, research and lab areas, an enormous medical complex, and a recreational sector that would translate to many city blocks' worth of restaurants and entertainment facilities — including a "red light district," the Dominion Club.

K-LAW — Sometimes a supervillain collective needs to engage with the legal system on its own terms; as a division, the Korps Legal Affairs Wing (K-LAW) operates covertly as the legal departments of various front companies, as well as through front law firms and other sympathetic individual lawyers in private practice.

Criminal defense of Korps members and allies on trial is only a small part of K-LAW agents' work. The majority of K-LAW's resources are directed towards litigation to gather intelligence on targets or tie them up in red tape, and street-level *pro bono* work helping marginalized people assert their rights without regard for the cost of legal fees.

KTAKES — The Korps Tactical Acquisitions and Kleptocratic Extirpation Squadron (KTAKES) is a now-disbanded division of the Korps that specialized in obtaining "lost" items and returning them to their rightful places — via. heists, capers, thefts, smash and grabs, and good old-fashioned burglary as appropriate. The group functioned as a kind of "thieves' guild" within the Korps, with their own projects, but also taking commissioned work from other divisions.

Pegasus Phalanx — A unit of the Texas Protectorate Assembly and Dallas' foremost Hero team, the Pegasus Phalanx handles the biggest threats the city faces — short of those requiring federal intervention from Bradley Group forces. While the team's roster has changed over the years, it most recently consisted of leader Kevin "Texas Trickshot" Romero, Susanne "Heavenly Dazzler" Geraldine-Walters, Chet "Macho Poleax" Huntyr, Rodrigo "Ethicoil" Alquitano III, and Slate "Slate" Johnson.

PHL — The Provincial Heroes' League (PHL) is a Canadian organization comprised of all Hero groups operated by the provincial and territorial governments, led by Director Lawrence Rockwell. The PHL aggressively advocates for 'law and order' Hero operations, and has had a great deal of friction with Aurora Squadron, accusing the federal Hero Group of being 'soft' on the Korps.

However, the PHL is not a Hero group itself, but instead a professional organization promoting the coordination and cooperation of affiliate members, as well as a powerful voice advocating for professional Heroes and the Hero industry. Heroes operating through one of its affiliates may nonetheless be indistinguishably referred to as "belonging" to the PHL, or being a "PHL Hero," and "fuck the PHL" is a popular sentiment among Korps agents operating in Canada.

Member Hero Groups include the Cascade Group or CG (British Columbia); the Prairie League or PL (Alberta, Saskatchewan and Manitoba); Ontario's Heroes or OH (Ontario); L'Association des Superheros Québécois or ASQ (Quebec, nicknamed the "Superté" by analogy to the provincial police force, the Sûreté du Québec); and the Territorial Superheroes' Association or TERSA (Nunavut, Yukon and Northwest Territories).

RIV or RIVER — RIVER is a Korps site located beneath downtown Austin, TX, secretly excavated deep below the parkland surrounding the Colorado River.

ROSE — ROSE, or the "RCG Operating System Experience," is the OS/Complex AI that runs on all networked RCGs and provides the conversational interface for wearers of RCGs. ROSE's default avatar when appearing as an augmented-reality overlay to wearers is a fox woman, but this can be customized to individual preference.

SHS — Sandy Hill Station is a Korps site located beneath downtown Ottawa, ON. Originally founded as a WWII-era safe house for the Overlord's consolidation of proto-Korps resources and personnel in Canada, it grew significantly in importance as a surveillance station during the Cold War, due to the local neighborhood's concentration of foreign embassies.

SHS was the testbed for many of the Korps' now-standard excavation and covert base-building practices, and was formerly the location of many research labs and high-level command functions, prior to Toronto's KDS becoming fully operational as a new headquarters in the 1980s-1990s.

Supers — Supers is generally vernacular for "those with superpowers," whether or not referring to superheroes generally, or whether or not licensed Heroes.

SIS — The Secret Intelligence Service, a.k.a. its wartime designation of MI6 (Military Intelligence, section 6) is an arm of the British state responsible for the gathering of foreign intelligence.

TPA — The Texas Protectorate Assembly — commonly shortened to "Teepa" by members of the Korps — is Texas' state Hero group, extremely well-funded both by the state Department of Public Safety budget, as well as substantial donations from wealthy individual benefactors and corporate partnerships. The result is that the TPA has unusually-vast resources for a government-backed state-level Hero group, and platoons of Heroes, many trained in the TPA's own Academy facilities located throughout Texas. TPA Heroes are institutionally encouraged to approach their duties in the manner of militarized riot police or SWAT teams, exercising very little restraint or concern for civil rights.

About the Author
Syntax Takes

Syntax Takes is best known online as a zebra-dragon hybrid with an appetite for rare gems, music, machines, and the occasional hero. She began writing stories to share online in various fandom communities as a hatchling, but found her footing as an adult when she discovered the Korps writing community. In amongst writing about sympathetic queer monsters and villains and studying computer architecture, her goals include reaching cohabitation with her partner of 8 years, world domination, and having a garden of succulents!

She and her friends in the Monster Fucker Book Club stream infrequently, announcements and updates can be found in their telegram channel: https://t.me/mfbctv.

She posts story and project updates to her last remaining vestige of social media, which can be found at:

https://bsky.app/profile/syntaxtakes.bsky.social
https://t.me/+j33xB43eIsNlZWYx.

About the Publisher

FurPlanet Productions is a small press publisher serving the niche market that is furry fiction. They sell furry-themed books and comics published by themselves and most major publishers in the community. If you can't get to a furry convention where they are selling in the dealers room, visit their online stores:

FurPlanet.com for print books
BadDogBooks.com for eBooks